DUKE,
ACTUALLY

DUKE, ACTUALLY

A NOVEL

JENNY HOLIDAY

AVON
An Imprint of HarperCollinsPublishers

DUKE, ACTUALLY. Copyright © 2021 by Jenny Holiday. All rights reserved. Printed in the United States of America. No part of this book may be used or reproduced in any manner whatsoever without written permission except in the case of brief quotations embodied in critical articles and reviews. For information, address HarperCollins Publishers, 195 Broadway, New York, NY 10007.

HarperCollins books may be purchased for educational, business, or sales promotional use. For information, please email the Special Markets Department at SPsales@harpercollins.com.

FIRST EDITION

Designed by Diahann Sturge

Yorkshire Terrier illustration © Lorelyn Medina / Shutterstock
Gift boxes with bows illustration © AnastasiaSonne / Shutterstock

Library of Congress Cataloging-in-Publication Data has been applied for.

ISBN 978-0-06-295208-0

22 23 24 25 26 LBC 8 7 6 5 4

For Marit, a (not so) mysterious source of happiness. I'm so glad we left our problems in the same basket all those years ago.

DUKE, ACTUALLY

Chapter One

*W*hen Dani Martinez woke up on Friday the tenth of December, she thought, *It's going to be a good day.*

And then she thought, *Liar.*

But whatever, just because it was the last Friday of the semester and she was about to be inundated with forty-seven essays on *The (Not So) Great Gatsby*, it didn't necessarily follow that today was going to be *bad.*

So she hadn't done a lick of Christmas shopping, forget the fruitcake she was supposed to have started months ago. That didn't mean this particular day was *automatically* going to suck.

And just because the cherry on top of the day was going to be the English department's holiday party, at which she would "get" to see her still-not-quite ex-husband with his trade-in trollop didn't mean— Ah, forget it. This day was going to be *crap.*

Her phone dinged. It would be Leo, which would be a fortifying way to start this all-downhill-from-here day. Because of the time difference between New York and Eldovia, they often talked early in the mornings New York time. Dani missed Leo and his sister, Gabby, something fierce, missed being able to go across the hall and have coffee in the mornings. Sometimes, before she was caffeinated, she forgot he wasn't there anymore. And then it would hit her anew: her best friend lived in Eldovia, where he was *engaged to a princess*. Dani was going to be his best woman in the fall at a freaking *royal wedding*.

Eyeing the slumbering ball of fur next to her, Dani executed a slo-mo roll to grab her phone from the nightstand—she wanted the ball of fur to stay slumbering until she'd had coffee.

The text was not from Leo. Good morning. It's Max von Hansburg. Marie gave me your number. I'm in New York for a few days. Can I take you to dinner tonight?

Speaking of royal weddings. Dani blinked, surprised to hear from Max, who was Princess Marie's best friend—and her ex-fiancé. Despite having been thrown over in favor of Leo, Max was currently scheduled to serve as Marie's man of honor in the wedding.

Marie and Max's past was like a telenovela, complete with glittering balls, arranged marriages, and conniving parents. Leo had crash-landed in the middle of it, getting swept up in a gender-swapped Cinderella story that had made even Dani's stone-cold heart defrost a degree or two. Except in this version, Cinderella had left a bestie behind in the ashes. Or maybe Leo had passed the Cinderella mantle on to Dani?

Max—Dog Max, the main Max in Dani's life—did one of his signature snore-snorts. Look, she even had an animal companion like Cinderella, except hers didn't flit around helping with the tidying.

Max: The concierge at my hotel can get us into Momofuku Ko. I could send a car for you.

The thaw in Dani's heart did not extend to Human Max, who, in addition to being a member of the Eldovian aristocracy, was insufferable. *"I could send a car for you."* What, like this was *Pretty Woman*? She considered the various ways she could decline his invitation. In the end, she went with brusque efficiency.

Dani: No.

Max: Lunch?

Dani: No.

Max: A drink?

Dani: No.

Max: Coffee?

Dani: Coffee is a drink.

Max: So that's still no?

Dani: Yes.

Max: Yes that's still no, or yes you'll have coffee with me?

Dani: Listen, dude. Or should I say listen, duke?

Ha! She cracked herself up. She sat up against her headboard to allow for easier texting, eyeing Dog Max, whose breathing did not change.

Max: Baron, actually.

She knew that. She'd googled Maximillian von Hansburg when she met him in Eldovia last summer. He was, despite his personality, unnaturally good-looking. And, really, who wouldn't respond to meeting a baron by googling said baron? She had learned that he was low-level famous—or should she say infamous?—in European circles for being a globe-trotting, womanizing playboy. The European tabloids called him the Depraved Duke, which as far as she could tell was a nickname that originated when he was photographed frolicking with a mystery woman while wearing an adult onesie on the deck of a yacht during the Cannes Film Festival.

Max: My father has to shuffle off this mortal coil before I attain dukedom, and I can report that he is in fine health.

Dani: Okay, but here's my point: I am post-men. As I told you last summer.

Max: Yes, meaning you don't want to date, correct?

Dani: Correct.

Max: But what about Leo? You talk to Leo all the time. You flew across the Atlantic last summer to visit him.

Dani: Leo's my best friend.

Max: I rest my case.

Dani: What does that mean?

Max: Leo is a man.

Dani: Your powers of observation are astounding. You'll forgive me if I'm suspicious, but I seem to have read an article with a headline that referred to you as a "man-whore."

Max: Were you googling me? I'm flattered.

She didn't bother replying. She wasn't about to defend said googling. That would sound like protesting too much.

Max: My point is, I'm not asking you on a date. I merely want to spend time with you.

Not sure what to say to that and seduced by the smell emanating from her programmable coffeemaker, Dani army-crawled out of bed. Minute shifts in the mattress were enough to wake Dog Max, but once she was out of bed, she could turn on the radio and have a dance party and he'd be oblivious. She contemplated Human Max's last text as she padded to the kitchen.

Dani: Why do you want to spend time with me?

Max: I like you.

That was such a weirdly straightforward answer.

Dani: Why?

Max: Because I get the sense that you are unimpressed by the fact that I'm an almost-duke.

Dani: That is correct.

Max: I would even go so far as to say that my almost-dukeness works against me.

Dani: Still correct.

Max: I like that about you. You're normal.

Dani: Is that supposed to be a compliment or an insult?

Max: You don't like me. Therefore I like you. I'm like a kid who wants what he can't have.

That tracked with her image of him. Also, she was texting with a *baron* over her morning coffee—how surreal was that?

> **Dani:** So in this scenario, I'm a toy you want. Nice.

> **Max:** No, you're just an interesting person I would like to spend time with since I happen to be in your city.

She almost cracked as she took her coffee back to her bedroom to try to figure out what to wear that telegraphed "It's just a normal day, a day in which I continue to be unbothered by the fact that my husband is boning Undergrad Barbie, tra la la." *You're just an interesting person I would like to spend time with.* When was the last time someone had said anything like that to her? Well, never, because grown-ass adults did not speak like that, so openly and without guile. Her limited interactions with Maximillian von Hansburg suggested that he did, though. He told the truth. And even though that truth was often about his many and varied romantic and sexual conquests, there was something refreshing about his cheerfully relentless honesty. Max was a fuckboy, basically—a fuckbaron?—but he was a remarkably self-aware one.

There was also the "unnaturally good-looking" part.

> **Max:** So there's no scenario in which you'll deign to get together with me today.

She was strangely tempted, but . . .

Dani: No.

She meant it about being post-men. Vince had done a number on her, and she was *done*. Not only done dating, but done arranging her life, even one day's worth of it, to please a man. She felt so strongly about that position that she'd put it in writing. Just in case she was ever tempted.

She had never imagined that temptation coming in the form of a baron.

She set the phone on her dresser, opened the closet, and fingered the forest-green taffeta dress she'd impulse-purchased in a fit of optimistic shopping earlier this fall. She'd thought then it would be a perfect holiday dress. But in addition to being too formal for this evening's party, not to mention for her afternoon class, taffeta was a try-hard fabric. Not an "I am completely over the fact that all of you in this room knew my husband was fucking around on me but apparently didn't respect me enough to tell me" fabric. Anyway, who was she kidding? She was never going to wear that dress. A year ago, she could have worn it to the opera with Vince. But she didn't go to the opera with Vince anymore. She didn't go to the opera with anyone.

Which was *fine*, because she didn't *like* the opera. She and Vince had been scheduled, in what turned out to be the week after he left, to go see some avant-garde production about a dude who loses his nose. Dani had looked at the entry on their shared calendar and, even though she'd still been in the sobbing-hysterically stage of the breakup, thought to herself, *Well, at least I never have to go to the fucking Met again.*

She moved the dress to the back of the closet and pulled out her standard day-to-evening black dress. It was a contoured number with a pencil skirt that had a pleasingly 1950s vibe to it. She could wear a blazer over it for teaching, then lose the blazer and jazz up the dress to make it more festive for the party.

How, though? Scarf? No. If she added a scarf to the retro dress, she would come off a little too Rizzo from *Grease*—although maybe some Rizzo energy was exactly what she needed right now.

Maybe she could make a jaunty hat out of the divorce papers Vince wouldn't sign?

Because wasn't that the cherry on top of everything? Husband leaves not only her but also the *country*—to spend a year's sabbatical in Spain, where his girlfriend spends her time posting Instagram shots of herself hiking the Camino de Santiago in a bikini top—but that same husband *will not sign the divorce papers*.

Vince was back for the holidays. Maybe all that time relaxing in the sunshine with said girlfriend had inspired him to move things along? A girl could hope. Even though seven sessions of mediation before he left had not provided her with reason to do so.

Dani ran her fingers over a tangle of necklaces that hung from a stand on her dresser. She needed a statement necklace. And she needed that statement to be *Eff you very much, Vince*. No, that wasn't right. The message she wanted to send was more *Sorry, what was your name again? I have moved so far on while you were away that I can't quite remember but please sign the fucking papers.* If only she had an accessory that would communicate that.

Hang on. She grabbed the phone. Max, apparently having finally gotten the point, had stopped texting.

Dani: On second thought, there might actually be a scenario in which I want to get together with you today.

Max: I wait on bated breath.

Dani: Any chance you want to be my plus-one to my work holiday party, at which my soon-to-be-ex-husband, Vince, will be in attendance, as will his new girlfriend, who is a former student of both of ours and who is twenty years younger than he is?

Max: Is your soon-to-be-ex-husband the main character in a Philip Roth novel?

She laughed out loud.

Dani: He might as well be. He's on sabbatical this year in Spain communing with the spirit of Picasso, but he's back for the holidays.

Max: The answer is yes, but I have questions. Question the first: Is this going to be one of those elaborately complex romantic comedies where we pretend to be in love to make your ex-husband jealous?

Dani: Unfortunately, he's not technically my ex-husband. My fondest wish is to relegate him to that status, but we're not there yet legally. As to your question, let's leave it vague. No need to make out or anything.

Max: Well, that's disappointing. I do so enjoy making out at office holiday parties.

Dani: No making out at the party. Or anywhere. In addition to being post-men, I am post–making out. If pressed, I'll call you a friend. But if you wanted to do me a solid and appear to find me the pinnacle of wit, that would be appreciated.

Though, really, there was no reason Max should "do her a solid." She'd been nothing but cool to him last summer in Eldovia.

Max: Question the second: Am I myself, or am I pretending to be, say, a visiting scholar of nineteenth-century literature who is therefore extra susceptible to your pinnacle?

Dani: You're yourself.

She was impressed, though, that he knew she studied nineteenth-century literature. If she'd said anything about it last summer, it had been in passing.

Max: So what I hear you saying is that in this one very specific scenario, you find it convenient that I'm an almost-duke.

God damn him.

> **Dani:** God damn you.

> **Max:** I might even go so far as to say that you're using me for my almost-dukeness.

Dani didn't want to be this petty, but . . . Okay, yes she did.

> **Dani:** She's twenty years old. He told me she was his Lolita. That she saw the real him and that in order to take his writing to the next level he needed someone who could be a "helpmeet," and when I said we were each other's helpmeets, he said there can only be one helpmeet and one help-ee in any relationship. And then they went to Spain for a year.

> **Max:** What time am I picking you up?

> **Dani:** Five. I'll meet you there—it's a building on campus but not mine. I need to look up the address. I'll text it to you.

> **Max:** Dress code? Formal? Business casual?

> **Dani:** Dukeish casual.

> **Max:** Understood. Prepare to be the pinnacle.

Dani smiled, dived onto the bed, and prepared to be love-bombed by the other Max, the main Max, who genuinely thought she was the pinnacle, no pretending required. As he did every morning, the little Yorkie acted like waking up next to her was the greatest joy of his life, going from dead asleep to vibrating with happiness as he crawled onto her lap. He might not do dishes like Cinderella's mice and birds, but he earned his keep in other ways, filling what had been a wrenching year with seven hyper pounds of unconditional love. "Good morning, my sweet," she cooed. He yapped in greeting, and she buried her nose in his fur as she hugged him.

Maybe today wasn't going to be as crappy as she'd feared.

MAX WAS SUPPOSED to meet Dani at the faculty club on her campus, but since he arrived half an hour early, he looked her up in the school directory and had his driver drop him at the English building.

This was going to be fun. He hadn't been lying—he did like Daniela Martinez, not least because *she* didn't seem to like *him*. That wasn't something that happened. It wasn't that everyone liked him—he wasn't conceited enough to believe that. But he rarely encountered someone who didn't at least pretend to. Sparring with Dani last summer, when she'd come to Eldovia to visit Leo, had been a breath of fresh air in a remarkably stressful time. He'd only spent a day in her company, but she'd made an impression.

Dani's floor was a long hallway that had little stubby corridors off it, each marked with nameplates indicating whose offices were at the ends of the branches. He spied one with signs for "D. Martinez" and "M. Gable" and took the sharp turn, whereupon he ran into two students. Ran into one of them literally. "I beg your pardon. I didn't expect anyone to be here."

A boy wearing sweatpants and a sweatshirt with a Superman logo on it looked him up and down. "No prob, man."

The girl closer to Dani's door said, "Are you looking for Professor Martinez?"

"I am indeed."

She snapped her gum, but not in a way that seemed hostile. "Get in line."

He did. He hadn't wanted to be late and, not knowing how long it would take to get up to the Bronx from his midtown hotel, he'd budgeted too much time for the journey.

After a minute or so, a boy came out of Dani's office, and the girl went in. Superboy shuffled down the wall so he was closer to the door. Max did the same.

"Are you enjoying Professor Martinez's class?" Max inquired.

"I guess," the boy said flatly.

The girl emerged, having been in there less than two minutes, and Superboy went in. Max edged closer to the door, which was ajar, so he could eavesdrop.

"Hey, Professor M, I need you to do me a huge favor." *I need you to do me a huge favor.* Something about the way he'd phrased that rubbed Max the wrong way.

"And what would that be?" That was Dani's "I am not impressed" voice. Max smiled. He was acquainted with that voice.

The boy made a case involving a diving meet, a book forgotten on the team bus, and a thesis all worked out but not down on paper yet. Dani proceeded to systematically dismantle him but subtly enough that the kid wasn't understanding the full extent of the burns he was sustaining.

It was hot.

Dani was hot.

Interestingly, that was a fact Max could note with detachment, which was another new experience for him. All the years he'd spent assuming he was going to marry Marie had also been spent, he would freely admit, slutting around. He and Marie had agreed that their marriage would be in name only and that discreet "extracurricular" activities would be allowed—necessary, even—once they'd done their duty with the turkey baster. Still, he had viewed the past few years as his last gasp of singledom and therefore of freedom and had conducted himself accordingly.

When the world offered itself to him, he took. And when one was a wealthy duke-to-be, one had a lot of offers.

What one *didn't* have a lot of were refusals. But Dani, having made her disinterest in him clear from the moment she'd arrived on Eldovian soil, was a rare woman. Wickedly smart, deliciously witty, extremely pretty, and *not interested*. There were no hard-to-get long games being played there. Leo had told Max a bit about her ugly divorce-in-progress, and Dani herself had used the phrase *post-men* more than once. He had no doubt that she meant it.

She was a goddamn delight.

To Max's surprise, even though the boy was wilting under Dani's questioning about the thesis he supposedly had all worked out—it didn't seem he had actually read the book, which sounded like it was meant to be *The Great Gatsby*—she suddenly granted him a forty-eight-hour extension and abruptly dismissed him. "Happy holidays," she said so flatly she might as well have been saying, "Good riddance."

It was such an unexpected turnabout that Max, who had been lounging against the wall, stood up straight, startled.

"Are there any more students out there?" she asked the boy as he was on his way out.

"Students . . . no," the boy said, making brief eye contact with Max as he breezed by in possession of an extension he did not deserve.

When Max stuck his head into Dani's office, it was to find her peeling off a blue blazer to reveal a dress that looked like it belonged on Bettie Page instead of a literature professor.

"Oh!" She jumped.

"My apologies. I didn't mean to startle you. I'm merely here to ask for an extension."

She rolled her eyes in lieu of greeting him, sat at her desk, and pulled a small mirror out of a drawer. "You're early," she said to her reflection.

"My thesis is all ready to go." He sat on the guest chair and, as she started applying a deep burgundy lipstick, revised his previous assertion that he could appreciate Dani's hotness from a purely intellectual perspective. "Care to hear it?"

"I guarantee you I already have."

"None of the characters in *The Great Gatsby* have any inner life to speak of, making what is admittedly a masterfully written book into a mere melodrama."

She glanced at him with one lip painted. The contrast between the brick red of the finished lip and the pinky-beige of the natural one certainly was . . . something. "An interesting line of thought."

He thought she was going to say more, but when she merely returned to her task, he asked, "Why did you give that boy an extension? He was clearly feeding you lies. Does he know you at all?"

One eyebrow rose, though she was still looking at her reflection. "Do *you* know me at all?"

"I'm thinking the way to get an extension from Professor Martinez is to level with her. Own the fact that you erred—with time management or laziness or what have you—present a plan for ameliorating your error, and state your terms."

Ah, that cracked her. She put the mirror down and truly looked at him. *Almost* looked as though she might smile. "Did you hear the student before him?"

"No."

"She asked for a twenty-four-hour extension because she works two part-time jobs and she fell asleep at her computer last night."

"Did you grant it?"

"Yes. I told her to go home and take a nap and to take another week with the paper."

The fact that he had been correct about how to handle Professor Martinez when you were a wayward student in need of mercy was strangely, sharply satisfying. "Why?"

"Because she shows up to class prepared and has never asked for anything before. Because I see her working at the campus Starbucks all the time, and if that's only one job of two, that's a little sobering."

"Why did that boy get an extension, too? He sounded like his problem was merely laziness. I wouldn't have pegged you as a pushover."

"I have forty-seven American Lit papers to grade in the next week, so it doesn't really matter to me when they come in. And frankly, it's not worth the bad reviews on my student evaluations."

She put away her mirror and took out her phone and looked at it for a long moment. She seemed to be reading something.

He took the opportunity to contemplate the concept of Dani receiving bad reviews. It was difficult to imagine. Along with her unexpectedly blasé response to the boy's request, it created a disturbance in the mental picture Max had of her, a surprising—and intriguing—lashing of paint across an image he'd thought complete.

"You ready?" She stood and reached for her coat, and his appreciation of her dress—and her lips, and her *everything*—grew even less intellectual.

"You want to give me any background on the Picasso fanboy? Did you say his name was Vince?" he asked while he tried not to be too overt about his escalating appreciation. "Or about the new girlfriend?"

"Neither of them have any inner life to speak of, so nah." She flashed him a little smile. It was pleasingly conspiratorial. "I'm sure you—" Her speech came to an abrupt halt as he rose from her guest chair. She froze with one arm in her coat and the other out. No part of her moved except her eyes, which traveled rapidly up and down his body.

He looked down at himself. "What? Not suitably dukeish casual?" The New York trip was a short one, so he only had the one suit with him. He'd almost worn it without a tie, but in the end he hadn't been able to make himself do it. If a man was wearing a suit, he should wear a suit—all its pieces, not some haphazard, choose-your-own-adventure version of it.

"It was a pun on business casual," she said.

"I understood that. Is this not business casual? You Americans with your dress codes. You put words together that either don't mean anything or contradict each other and call it a dress code. I *could* have worn my frock coat complete with ceremonial sword."

She cracked a grin, a full, unreserved one, and he was unbecomingly thrilled to have been its source.

"You look fine," she said. "Let's go."

ALL EYES WERE on Dani as she entered the party, but for once it wasn't because of her status as the jilted wife of the inexplicably popular Professor Vincent Ricci, who had left her for a twenty-year-old named Berkeley.

Or it wasn't *only* because of that. To be fair, it probably started because of that. Vince and Berkeley coming out as a couple a hot minute after Berkeley dropped out of school was the biggest news to hit the department since the dean's office repossessed the humanities' faculty lounge and gave it to the economists for an econometrics lab. Somehow, even though Vince had undergone an ethics investigation because of concerns he'd broken the rule about, oh, *not dating students*—and had been cleared because there was no proof he and Berkeley had gotten together until after Berkeley dropped out—Dani seemed to be the subject of most of the departmental gossip. Poor, discarded Dani, replaced by a younger, tauter model.

And now Vince and Berkeley were back from their Spanish adventure for a couple of weeks. What would Dani do? What would she say? How would she act?

But it only took a second, once everyone got a load of Max, for the narrative to shift.

Because Max, in his dukeish casual, looked a lot more than

"fine," especially in contrast to the men in this crowd, who were "dressed up" in their Dockers and no-iron shirts that actually needed ironing. Max's tallness and slimness was accentuated by the tailored blue suit he was wearing like a second skin. Like it *was* casual. With his icy-blue eyes, his dirty-blond hair styled almost in a pompadour, and his angular face, he looked like that Swedish actor from that vampire show, all sharp edges and cool cobalt.

He must have noticed everyone's attention—it was hard not to, as this group was not subtle. He laid his palm on her lower back. He didn't press or push, just stood serenely while everyone gaped at them. In any other circumstance, she would have shaken him off, but she performed a quick mental cost-benefit analysis and decided that having a baron get a little handsy wasn't the worst look right now. After a few beats of silence, of posing, really, while everyone stared, he said, "Shall we go to the bar?"

Dani made eye contact with Sinéad, her closest friend in the department. Sinéad and Dani had been hired a year apart and had leaned on each other a lot in the early going, forming a kind of battlefield bond that had never gone away even as they'd found their stride and gotten busy with research and relationships.

So busy, apparently, that Dani hadn't laid eyes on Sinéad all semester outside of departmental meetings. How had that happened? Dani had been working a lot lately, but still. They used to go for drinks almost weekly. Before Vince.

Dani thought back to the list she kept on her phone, which she'd reviewed earlier, in her office, in preparation for having to see Vince. **Things I Will Never Again Do for a Man.** Not that there was any danger of falling back in with Vince. Dani was *done* with

Vince. Or would be once she finally managed to divorce his ass. But she believed in owning her mistakes, confronting her lapses in judgment. That was the only way to make sure they never happened again. Hence the list. She'd made it the day after Vince's affair with Berkeley came to light. In the beginning, she'd looked at it every day. Now it was more about future-proofing herself. It reminded her, in stark black and white, what her priorities were going to be in the post-Vince world.

As it related to Sinéad, the relevant list item was #8: **Neglect my friends.**

Sinéad raised her eyebrows in a way that was meant to communicate *Holy shit, girl.*

Dani raised hers back and hitched her head slightly to send a return message: *Meet us at the bar.* Here was the perfect opportunity to work on that number.

Max's hand stayed resting lightly on Dani's back as they made their way through the crowded room. Dani nodded and said a few hellos to colleagues as they passed but didn't stop. Better to let them wonder.

At the bar, she ordered a Diet Coke, and Max tried to order a negroni. When the bartender looked at him blankly, he shifted gears effortlessly. "On second thought, I think I'd prefer a glass of red wine."

"Hel-*lo*." Sinéad sidled up to the bar, let her gaze roam Dani, and pressed a hand to her heart. "Don't you look smashing?"

"You, too." She really did. She was wearing a blue suit—like Max, except hers was tailored to hug her curves and she wore it with an open-necked white silk blouse and red stilettos.

Dani kept the introductions brief. "Max, Sinéad. Sinéad, Max."

She was probably supposed to introduce Max as "His Honorable Lord Baron McSnootypants" or something, but she was not going to do that.

After Sinéad ordered a Guinness, she flicked Max's blue-black-and-red-checked tie. "Burberry?"

Max raised an eyebrow. He probably wasn't used to people touching his clothes. Or commenting on labels. Both were no doubt exceedingly low-class. "Indeed." He reached over and flicked the cross-body briefcase Sinéad wore. "Vuitton?"

Dani chuckled. These two dandies were perfect for each other.

"Knockoff," Sinéad said cheerfully. "I'll be paying off my student loans until I die."

"Ah, yes, the puzzling American tradition of bankrupting its young people before they even begin their careers."

"Hang on." Sinéad pointed at Max. "You're the duke. The Depraved Duke."

"Baron, actually," Max said. Dani noticed he didn't dispute the "depraved" part.

"Whatever," Sinéad said. "You're the guy who was engaged to the princess that Vince Ricci's cousin is marrying."

"I . . . might be?" Max looked genuinely confused.

"Vince Ricci being Dani's ex-husband," Sinéad added.

"Not until he signs the papers," Dani said with exaggeratedly artificial cheeriness. She turned to Max, who didn't know the whole story. "You probably didn't know that my husband is Leo's second cousin."

"I had no idea."

"Yes. I met Leo and Gabby because I married into the Ricci family."

"Vince being the cradle-robbing professor in search of a help-meet," Max said.

Sinéad cracked up. "That'd be the one. And wow, *helpmeet*. That's not a word you see much anymore."

"I thought you and Leo were neighbors?" Max asked Dani.

"We were. I'd met Leo and Gabby a few times at holidays when the whole Ricci clan was together, but I didn't know them well. When their parents died, there happened to be an opening for a superintendent in my building that I thought Leo would be perfect for. I'd heard they were looking for a place, so I reached out to let them know—despite Vince being a dickhead, his family was decent. And even though I'm in the process of marrying *out* of the Ricci family, I'm keeping Leo and Gabby."

Sinéad had been leaning against the bar, but suddenly her posture changed. "Incoming."

Dani looked over her shoulder, took stock, and whispered to Max, "The guy on his way over here is the chair of the department. We care about his inner life. His inner life needs to grant me tenure." Max made a vague noise of acknowledgment.

"Also, FYI, and don't look because *they're* looking at *you*," Sinéad whispered, "but Vince and Berkeley have arrived."

"Berkeley," Max echoed. "What an . . . unusual name for a helpmeet."

Dani ignored Max and concentrated on Vince, as much as she didn't like doing that. She was over Vince. Having moved rapidly through the shock, hurt, and anger phases of the breakup, she was currently in the midst of the questioning-one's-own-judgment phase. Hence the obsessive list-checking. But being over him didn't mean she was looking forward to seeing him. "I'm not ready for this," she muttered.

"Sure you are," Max said as the bartender set their drinks on the bar. He put a fifty-dollar bill in the tip jar—*fifty* dollars!

She really, really wasn't ready for this. Her heart started beating rapidly. Vince sitting on the sofa across from her in their mediator's office was one thing—and the last session had been months ago—but to see him here, at a work party with everyone watching to see how she was going to act, was another.

Before picking up his own drink, Max rolled his shoulders and straightened his spine as if preparing for battle. "This is going to be fun."

That was not the word Dani would have used.

Max winked and said, under his breath, "Here we go."

She braced herself and turned to face the room.

"Dani, Sinéad," her chair said as he approached, "happy holidays."

"And to you." Dani's voice was a little shaky but hopefully not so much that anyone would notice. "James, this is Maximillian von Hansburg. Max, this is James Dodge, the chair of the English department."

The men shook hands, and Sinéad piped up, "Max is a baron." She said it loudly enough that she drew the attention of a few of their colleagues clustered near the bar.

Max waved away Sinéad's declaration even as he lifted his chin. He positively oozed baron-ness.

"How do you know our Dani?" James inquired.

Our Dani. That was rich coming from the guy who had asked her to plan the retirement party for the department's longtime secretary because "you have such good taste." Spoiler alert: "You have such good taste" coming from James meant, "You are young and female." Give her tenure and maybe "our Dani" would annoy her less.

"Our best friends are getting married later this year," Max said, leaving unspoken the part where his best friend was a princess and the wedding was a royal one.

"Are they? And what brings you to New York so close to the holidays?"

"I'm doing some archival research on an Eldovian woman who spent part of World War II in New York."

He *was*? Why hadn't he led with that when he'd been texting her? Dani had been imagining Max in town for—well, she wasn't even sure. Having his own personal Christmas spectacular as he banged his way through the Rockettes?

"She was at Cambridge—also my alma mater," Max went on. "Cambridge, as you may know, was spared in the bombing campaigns because Hitler planned to use it as a second headquarters when he took over Britain. It's long been known that she welcomed German Jewish children who were part of the Kindertransport into her flat and that she went on to set up a network of students and professors who did the same. She's something of a local folk hero at home. But it seems she spent some time in New York in 1943 that wasn't previously known about. I'm here trying to get to the bottom of it."

Dani had to prop her fist under her jaw and hope she was striking a thoughtful pose instead of an "I am propping up my jaw because it keeps dropping" pose. But at least it was better than freaking out about seeing Vince.

"Fascinating," James said, and he actually seemed to mean it. "What university are you at?"

"Oh, I'm purely an amateur," Max said with a dismissive wave and a self-deprecating shake of his head. Dani was pretty sure, given the way his head stayed turned a beat too long, that the gesture was designed to let him survey the room. "Too busy with matters of state and diplomacy these days to muck about in academia," he added.

Dani had to bite back a smile. That might be true if the "diplomacy" he was talking about was happening between the sheets. She had read one tabloid account of him "romancing" the US ambassador to the Vatican, who, while single, was supposed to be a devout Catholic.

"Your Professor Martinez has been advising me," Max went on. "She's been a tremendous help, not just as a local contact, but intellectually." Max returned his hand to her back and beamed down at her. All she could do was goggle at him. "Shall we find somewhere to sit?" he inquired mildly.

"Sure."

That had the effect of dismissing James, who moved on to chat with someone else, pulling Sinéad along with him. Alone again, Max said to Dani, "May I buy you another drink before we sit? Perhaps something stronger?"

"Stronger is for *after* the party," she said quietly. She rarely drank at these things, wanting to keep her wits about her. "Stronger is for after I get tenure."

She let him lead her to an unoccupied sofa, feeling the attention of everyone in the room. He whispered in her ear as they went, "Vince and—sorry, what was her name? Sacramento?— looked like they were on their way over to the bar, so that was a little extraction. Let's let them wonder a little longer who your devastatingly handsome companion is."

Dani rolled her eyes as Max sat too close to her—he smelled like peppery pine—but she was smiling over the Sacramento joke, which was uncharitable. "Was that all *true*? I thought your degree was fake—a means of postponing your engagement to Marie."

"The degree was real. The length of time it took to complete was, perhaps, exaggerated." He took a sip of wine, unperturbed by her questioning or by the palpable sensation of everyone watching them. "And there really is an Eldovian folk heroine who spent time in Cambridge."

"What was her name?" She was suspicious, though she wasn't sure why.

"Karina Klein," he said without hesitation.

"Never heard of her."

"I don't think anyone has outside of Eldovia."

"Tell me more."

He did. For the next ten minutes, she forgot she was at a faculty party as Max launched into a tale of heroism and sacrifice. "When I was still at Cambridge 'finishing my thesis,' I found an issue of the student newspaper from Karina's college from before the end of the Michaelmas term in 1943. It was a roundup of sorts of where everyone was spending the holidays, and Karina mentioned a trip to New York. I wondered then, and I still do, why in 1943, a young, single woman—a student—would flit off to New York for her Christmas holidays."

"So you are truly here to investigate!"

"God, no. I'm here for a huge party and to avoid my family."

That was both unsurprising and oddly disappointing. "What are you—"

"Hello, Dani."

Oh, shit. She'd forgotten about Vince.

She'd forgotten about Vince. Sending a message to Vince was half the point of being here tonight. She'd been planning to pretend that she no longer gave him any real estate in her brain. But thanks to Max and his storytelling abilities, it had actually been true for a while. How remarkable.

Vince was wearing his own khaki pants and button-down, though he had a sports coat over his—he'd always been better dressed than everyone else. Berkeley, clinging to his arm, looked stunning in a white jumpsuit with a plunging neckline.

"Vince, Berkeley, meet my friend Max."

"The duke, right?" Berkeley said, eyes wide as Max stood to greet them.

"Alas, a mere baron," Max corrected. Wow, the Depraved Duke nickname must have everyone thinking Max was actually a duke.

"What brings you to New York?" Vince asked.

"Just visiting," Max said smoothly, sitting back down and sliding his arm around Dani's shoulder in such a way that implied it was *her* he was visiting. "New York at Christmastime has so much to recommend it."

Dani had the sudden notion that Max's answer to the "What brings you to New York?" question was changing based on whatever answer would paint her in the most flattering light. With her departmental chair, it had been an intellectual mystery Dani was helping him solve. With her shitty ex, it was *her*.

He was turning up his accent, too, in a way that seemed to accentuate his fanciness. Dani had had a crash course in all things Eldovian when Leo had been swept off his feet by Princess Marie and had learned that both German and French were official languages. If pressed, Dani would have said Max tended toward French over German, with perhaps a bit of British thrown in, perhaps owing to his years at Cambridge. But really, his accent sounded vaguely European-posh, like Madonna in her "putting on airs" phase.

"Speaking of visits," Max went on, "I thought I might pay one to the bar." He stood again. "Allow me to bring a round of drinks. What can I get you, Berkeley? Wine? Beer?"

While Berkeley was old enough to drink in Europe, she wasn't here. Dani glanced at Vince, though she wasn't sure why. It wasn't like he was going to jump in and say something to save Berkeley. So Dani did it, reminding herself that the girl was just that—a girl. A girl who was very likely to grow up and realize that all she had gotten in exchange for quitting college was custody of an entitled man-child who could talk a good game.

Dani pasted on a smile, held up her empty glass, and said, "I think Berkeley's a Diet Coke aficionado like I am, aren't you, Berkeley?"

"Yes!" Berkeley exclaimed.

"But I think maybe it's time for us to go?" She turned to Max and raised her eyebrows. They had accomplished more than she had dared dream this morning. Not only had she seen Vince and not died, she had come out looking good, thanks, amazingly, to Max, the perfect party accessory. This was as good a moment as any to flounce off.

Max held out a hand to help her up. "Your wish is my command." Once she was up, the hand settled on her back again. It was starting to feel normal. Dani widened her fake smile, said goodbye to Vince and Berkeley, and let herself be escorted off by a baron who looked like a movie star.

As if by silent agreement, they did not speak as Max collected their coats and held hers for her as they strolled out of the building. It was snowing big, fat, fluffy flakes, and with each step they took, Dani started to feel a little lighter. Not only was the dreaded party over, so was the semester. A week of grading—and she could do that at home in her pajamas—and she was free until January.

"Well," Max said when they were safely out on the sidewalk. "That was . . ." He quirked a brow. "Bracing."

Max. Her surprising secret weapon. He had pitched everything perfectly in there—his words, his accent, his outfit, his posture, all of it.

He wasn't wearing a hat, and the snow was accumulating in his hair, laying down an extra glazing on the cool blond. With the streetlights glinting off him, he looked like an ice prince. If she called him that, he'd probably say, "Ice *baron*, actually."

She was getting that delicious "Christmas break" feeling, that sense of another term under her belt, a pause in the grind of regular obligations. Dani loved Christmas. Or at least she used to. Last year's, her first with Vince gone, had been bleak. And Leo and Gabby had traveled to Eldovia for the holidays, leaving her alone with her sadness. Dani hadn't gotten the "Christmas break" feeling last year. She was glad it was back.

"I have a car," Max said, pulling out his phone. "Can I drop you at home?"

"No," she said, not wanting to let go of her Christmas buzz, wanting to ride this crest of joy a little longer. *Joy.* It had been a while. "Let's go for negronis."

Chapter Two

9 think negronis are supposed to be more . . ." Dani scrunched her nose as she searched for the word she wanted. "Spitting drinks. *Spitting* drinks? That's not right," She laughed, shook her head, picked up her glass, and took an exaggeratedly dainty sip.

"Sipping drinks?" Max suggested, as they seemed to be playing charades. Playing charades with Daniela Martinez at a bar in the Bronx—this was not how he'd expected this evening to end. He was going to look back on this as a bright spot in the New York trip he'd made to placate his parents.

She pointed at him. "Yes! I don't think you're supposed to chug them like I've been doing. You're supposed to sip them!" She demonstrated again, but this time she tried to get her pinky to extend, as if she were a caricature of a tea-drinking aristocrat. But her little finger wasn't cooperating. It kept springing back in line with the rest of her fingers, which were clutching her highball glass. She tried to use her other hand to hold it up, but she came close to spilling her drink.

"Allow me to assist." He was matching her pace, so they were each on drink number two, but she was smaller than he was. He set down his drink and arranged her hand so her pinky was fully extended and let go. It sprang back.

"It isn't listening!" she said with seemingly genuine dismay.

The Dani who deftly flayed the outer layer of skin off full-of-shit students was a delight, but so was, it turned out, Drunk Dani. An unexpected delight. Though he wasn't sure why he'd thought to add the "unexpected" qualifier. He knew all too well how alcohol could exaggerate people's underlying personalities.

He shook his head. No reason to go there tonight. He reached for Dani's pinky again, and this time when he got it extended, he kept hold of it lightly with his thumb and forefinger. Together, they lifted her drink, her holding the glass, him holding her pinky. It was ridiculous.

As was the gratification that followed when she successfully took a sip and they reversed course until the drink was safely returned to the bar.

"Yes!" After the glass made contact with the bar, she lifted her arms in victory, turned, and held a hand out for a high five. He laughed and slapped her hand.

The bartender showed up to check on them, and Max asked for a menu. "We should eat something."

"Pro . . . buly," she slurred, making a self-deprecating face at him, "Sorry, I'm kinda tipsy."

"No apologies necessary." He didn't think she'd want to hear that he thought she was a delightful drunk. His acquaintance with Daniela Martinez had been brief, but he somehow knew she would not want to be called delightful, at least not by him.

"I'm just so happy that party is over. I'm so happy the *semester* is over." She made a theatrical gagging noise. "I don't have to set foot in that place for almost a month."

"Not your dream job?"

"It's fine."

"Don't sound so excited."

"You know, sometimes I think I'm a professor because school has always been my default mode."

"What do you mean?"

"Well, I'm good at school. I always have been. So I kept doing more of it. And I like some of the parts of it—reading and writing, and . . ." She laughed, a touch bitterly. "Reading and writing."

Hmm. The reluctant English teacher? "Molding young minds not for you?"

"It sounds terrible. I don't mind teaching. I just . . ." She shrugged.

"What?" he pressed. He wanted to know what made Dani Martinez tick.

"I don't know. I assigned *The Great Gatsby* this semester because most of them would have read it in high school. I thought this would be an opportunity to really get into it in a more meaningful way, but it didn't work out the way I planned.

"And I hate committee service, or at least the committees I have to be on. Nobody really tells you how much of your life as an academic is going to be *committees*. But I can't say no because I'm junior, and I'm also constantly on edge that I'll be seen as not pulling my weight. You hear one too many comments about being the 'diversity hire,' you get paranoid."

"Do people actually say that?" How appalling.

"People actually say that. Maybe not in so many words, but you know what they mean." She sighed. "Do you ever sit back and look at your life . . ." As she trailed off, she leaned back as if to illustrate her words. He hovered his arm around her for fear she would lean too far on her backless stool. She must have felt the nearness of his arm even though it wasn't touching her. She looked over her shoulder in confusion.

"Do I ever sit back and look at my life and . . . ?" he prompted.

"And think, 'How did I end up here? How is this my job?'?" she finished emphatically.

He certainly did. Not in the way she meant, because he didn't have a job in that sense. But he had been thinking a great deal lately about duty and work and purpose. "What would you do if you could do anything?" Unlike him, she could.

"I wish there was a way to have my research—my writing—be of interest to a wider audience," she said thoughtfully, all traces of her previous tipsiness gone. "I don't mean that in a conceited way, like I think I'm some great intellect. Just that we publish in these obscure academic journals, and I sometimes think, *Why? What is it all* for?" She shook her head and with it shed some of her seriousness. "Anyway, no one likes all aspects of their job, right? And honestly, I'm lucky to have this one. Tenure-track gigs in English are extremely few and far between, and I managed not only to get one but to get one in New York, so blah, blah, poor me."

He was tempted to say that a person could be lucky *and* unhappy, that those two qualities were not mutually exclusive, but he wasn't sure how such a statement would be received coming from him. And he would much rather talk about her. "When do you get tenure?"

"I go up for it in about a year. And I get a teaching release this coming fall semester—my pre-tenure leave. The idea is to allow junior faculty time to really work on their tenure files, but for me it will come too late to really make a difference."

"Why didn't you take it earlier?"

"I tried, but I was informed that too many senior members of the department were already scheduled to be on sabbaticals."

Max was liking the sound of this department and its culture less and less.

Dani snorted. "Anyway, it's better this way. I already have a strong tenure file, so maybe I'll just take that semester and be a lie-about."

"What if you *could* do anything?" he asked, returning to his original question. "Hypothetically. It doesn't have to be realistic."

"I think I'd like to hole up in a garret somewhere far away and write a book that had popular appeal. A popular book about obscure nineteenth-century writers. Ha!"

"So why don't you do that?"

She looked at him for a long time, long enough that he started to get uncomfortable. "Everything is easy for you, isn't it?"

He didn't know how to answer that. Materially speaking, the answer was yes. He didn't want for anything.

"I mean, you flew to New York for a 'huge party'?" She made the air quotes with her fingers.

"Yes." That was what he'd told her. And technically, it was true.

"The Depraved Duke, right?" She laughed.

He did not. "Right."

The bartender returned, and after they ordered some pasta, she said, "Tell me about this party."

He had hoped she'd forgotten.

When he didn't answer right away, she said, "Come on. *I* told *you* all the gory details of my career ennui."

"It's an annual Christmas party held by a woman named Lucrecia von Bachenheim."

"That is a made-up name!"

"It's not, though it does have a bit of a cartoon-villain ring to it, doesn't it?" Lucrecia *was* a bit of a bully. "She helms a crowd of continental European ex-pats in New York—she's a second cousin to the Austrian archduke." And she never let anyone forget it.

"Where's the party going to be?"

"It was last night, at her apartment on Central Park West."

"And was it everything you dreamed of?"

"I had more fun at your party this evening." She laughed incredulously, but it was true. He didn't want to talk about the party, though, so in an attempt to change the subject, he asked, "What are you going to do with your first weekend of freedom? You should celebrate."

"Well, I have a ton of grading to do, but my first priority is fruitcake."

"Fruitcake?" he echoed.

"Yes. I'm on dessert duty for Christmas, and I'm supposed to be making buñuelos, from my dad's side of the family, and fruitcake from my mom's. The buñuelos are fine because I'll do those the morning of—they're a kind of fried donut–type thing, and they're best fresh. But the fruitcake is one of those ones where you soak it in boozy cheesecloth for a hundred years and I'm going to have to do a cheater's version and I'm going to be so busted."

She didn't sound overly concerned, though. "You're close to your family?"

"Yeah."

"You celebrate on Christmas Eve?"

Her eyes widened. "What's the date? It's the tenth, right?"

He looked at his watch. "It's ten past midnight, so technically, it's the eleventh."

"Then it's officially Christmas. In my world, Christmas starts on December 11. I kind of skipped Christmas last year." She stuck out her tongue and blew air over it, resulting in a kind of wind-tunnel noise that made Max smile. "I'm not doing that this year."

"Do you have a cultural or religious tradition associated with December 11?" It was an oddly specific date.

"Nope. December 11 is two weeks before Christmas. And even though I am, historically, a fan of Christmas, I am *not* one of those people who thinks we should start celebrating it in October. It's only special because it's"—she slapped the bar—"Time-limited. So I have this thing where I start 'doing' Christmas on December 11. Except for the fruitcake, which I *should* have started in October. But you were probably asking about the *official*-official celebration, like with my family."

He didn't know Dani well, but the idea of her being a secret lover of Christmas but allowing herself only a strict two-week window in which to celebrate was ridiculously charming.

"The family to-do is dinner on Christmas Eve at my parents' house, then presents in the morning. I'll stay over—they're on Long Island. Christmas Eve dinner is a huge spread, but then for Christmas morning we eat Christmas versions of kids' cereal—

Lucky Charms, that sort of thing. My sister and I weren't allowed sugary cereal as kids, except at Christmas, when my parents would buy us one box. That was all we ever wanted to eat on Christmas morning, and at some point, they started eating it, too, saying they were too tired from cooking the dinner the night before to make a proper breakfast. It evolved into a thing, and now we have a full-on buffet of trashy Christmas cereal. Then we have a reprise on January 6, which is Epiphany. That's when my dad's side of the family—they're in Mexico—celebrates. We go see my grandparents every few years, and in the off years we all FaceTime. That's part of why I'm kind of strict about when I start doing Christmas. It's a long holiday season for us!"

"That all sounds wonderful."

She looked at him quizzically, and he thought back to her saying that things came easily to him. *Not all things,* he'd been tempted to say, but he hadn't wanted to sound like a jerk.

"What do you do for Christmas?" she asked.

Nothing. He showed up at the appointed time for the family lunch and went through the motions, but that was the extent of it. "I celebrate whatever I can, whenever I can," he said by way of deflection. "I don't limit it to Christmas."

"I bet you do." She snorted. "I bet you 'celebrated'"—there were the air quotes again—"After the party last night. Who was the lucky girl?"

"I will have you know I didn't 'celebrate' after the party." It was true. He'd gone back to his hotel to brood in the sauna. "I did, however, make out with a charming partygoer in the coatroom." Not the partygoer he was meant to connect with at the party, though. Not the partygoer who had been the whole reason for his New York trip. He'd only talked to her long enough to be able to go home and tell his parents that, yes, he met her.

His duty done, he'd allowed himself to be hit on by the event's photographer. They'd had a perfectly pleasant time, hidden among the coats, but for some reason, when she'd invited him to come home with her, he'd pled exhaustion.

"Back to celebrating. If you could do anything this weekend, what would it be?"

"Get dressed up in this silly, fancy dress I bought last fall but have never worn and go see *The Nutcracker*."

He laughed, and she frowned. She must have thought he was laughing at her, which he most decidedly was not. He was merely amused by how quickly and decisively she had answered. By the answer itself, too. He had pegged her more as a Shakespeare in the Park type, not a "get dolled up for the 'Dance of the Sugar Plum Fairy'" type. Though suddenly he wanted to see this dress she spoke of. "That is a surprisingly specific answer."

"It just popped into my mind."

"You're a ballet fan?"

"Not particularly, but my mom used to take me to *The Nutcracker* every year when I was a kid. She'd pick me up on the last day of school and we'd have dinner together in the city, without my dad and my sister. I used to love it."

"Why don't you do it anymore?"

"I don't know. I went away for college and grad school, and we never picked it up when I came back." She sounded wistful. "I actually suggested it to Vince a few years ago, but he vetoed it. He said it was childish and that if I wanted to go to the ballet, I should aim higher." She curled her lip in disgust, but only for a moment before she turned thoughtful. "Hmm. Maybe I should have put that on the list. 'Not not go to the ballet'? Ha. That's a double negative."

"What list?"

"It's not important."

He wanted to press her about this list, but their food arrived. "This is delicious," he said after a few minutes of silence.

"*Max*," she said suddenly, with an urgency that made his stomach flop. She turned her body a full ninety degrees on her stool so she was facing him.

He put his fork down as his pulse kicked up. "Yes?"

"Would you think me a terrible lush if I ordered a third negroni?"

He laughed. "No, but I will not be joining you. I've hit my limit. And I will insist on taking you home."

"You are . . ." She narrowed her eyes at him. "A nice man."

He laughed some more. He got called a lot of things, but *nice* didn't tend to be one of them. "Don't tell anyone."

An hour later they were preparing to depart and she set down a credit card.

He pushed it back toward her. "Already taken care of." He'd slipped the bartender his card when she'd gone to the restroom.

"You can't just buy me dinner. And a million negronis."

"I can. I did." She was ramping up to argue. He held up a hand. "I insist. To celebrate your last day of work for a while. We have already established that I'm very undiscriminating in terms of occasions I consider worth celebrating, have we not? Indulge me."

She opened her mouth but quickly closed it. He hustled her out the door before she could change her mind. It was still snowing, and the street was lit up for the holidays. Individual shopkeepers had decorated, and there were also arches across the street itself, incorporating Christmas trees, menorahs, and crescent moons and stars. It was pretty damn charming, even for a jaded rake like him. "Shall I call the car?"

"What is the deal with this car? It just hangs around wherever you are until you summon it?"

"That is exactly what it does."

"What kind of setup is that?" she asked with exaggerated skepticism.

"I believe you call it a car service. I engage a driver to be available to me while I'm in New York."

"What kind of car is it?"

"A Mercedes, I think."

She scoffed.

He ignored her disapproval. "You want me to call it?"

"No. I want to walk."

Good. He did, too. He didn't want to go back to his dark, empty hotel room yet. He had the photographer's number from yesterday and an invitation to call her anytime, but he was still, uncharacteristically, not in the mood.

Dani stumbled. The sidewalks were slick with new snow, and she wasn't very steady on her feet to begin with. He grabbed her before she could fall, and once she was righted, he let go and offered her his arm. He was surprised when she took it.

"This is an Italian section of the city, I gather?" he asked, noting the shops with cured sausages drying in the windows as they strolled.

"Historically, but it's probably more Mexican and Albanian to-day than it is Italian. It's a hodgepodge."

"I've never been to the Bronx," he said.

She snorted. "Yeah, we're a long way from Manhattan concierges who can get you impossible reservations."

He shrugged. He wasn't going to pretend to be a man of the people. He liked his comforts. But he also liked this. "I'm a fan of New York—all of it. All of it that I've seen, anyway."

"You are?"

"Yes. It's the perfect mixture of tradition and renewal. It retains its identity even as it's constantly changing. It's resilient. Scrappy." Like he was. That sounded like self-flattery, but it was merely a fact. He'd had to be scrappy—doubly so since his brother wasn't. Perhaps he appreciated New York in a "like recognizes like" way.

"I never thought of New York like that, but you're right. Eldovia isn't scrappy?"

"Eldovia isn't scrappy," he confirmed with a chuckle. He certainly had been laughing a lot this evening. It was disconcerting to find himself, suddenly, so easily amused. "Eldovia, or at least my experience of it, which I grant is not typical, is protocol and decorum." *And, in some corners, rage and chaos.* "But it does have some things to recommend it."

"What are those things?"

"Mountains, chiefly. I live at the base of one, and I love going up it." He only said that because she was drunk. Max was not the kind of person who went around earnestly proclaiming his love for nature.

"We turn here. I think." Her brow furrowed as she tried to read a street sign. "I'm not normally this much of a drunker." She furrowed some more. "Drinker."

"No judgment here. I'm the man-whore, remember?"

"Yeah, what is that about?"

He shrugged. "I don't think it's 'about' anything."

"At some point this evening you stopped trying to get into my pants. Why?"

"Because you clearly don't want me there."

"So you're a man-whore with morals?"

"While I'm happy to take credit for being morally upstanding in my slutting around, I don't think it's actually that high-minded— or that complicated."

"What is it, then?"

"Call me crazy, but sexual assault turns me off. Coercion, all that stuff. It's what I believe you Americans would call a 'boner killer.'" He copied her signature finger-air-quotes gesture.

She turned thoughtful. "Also, why is the term *man-whore*? Why not just *whore*?"

"Marie is the only one who calls me that. Well, Marie and the tabloids."

"So what do people call you? Oh, wait, 'The Depraved Duke,' right?"

He smirked. "Not a duke, though."

"But you don't dispute the 'depraved' part?"

"Well, people used to call me a playboy, or a rake, before that unfortunate moniker stuck. It's amazing the kinds of stories people will tell about you when you're as attractive as I am." He batted his eyelashes to show he was joking. And also because he truly did not want to talk about it.

"Rich probably doesn't hurt, either."

"What can I say? I am the full package. I'm also good in bed."

"How do you know?"

"I've had good reviews."

She snorted. "How do you know your reviewers weren't blinded by your good looks and your castle full of gold? How do you know they weren't *lying*?"

Perhaps they were. Max had his faults, but he liked to think self-delusion wasn't one of them, so he contemplated the prospect. "While I understand the concept of 'faking it,' I like to think I'd be able to tell if they were *all* faking."

She burst out laughing, which was rather a blow to the ego, and he found himself in the rare position of not knowing what to say.

He didn't have to say anything, though, because she stopped abruptly and looked around. "We overshot," she declared, and steered him back the way they had come. Half a block later they came to a stop in front of a brick walk-up.

"Allow me to escort you to your apartment," he said.

"You don't have to." She was holding her keys really close to her eyes.

"And yet I do."

"And yet you don't." She tripped over her own feet.

He caught her and gently pried her keys out of her grasp. "Indulge me."

Chapter Three

When Dani awoke the next morning, it was to a headache and a note from Max.

The note was written on a business card propped up against a bottle of Advil on her nightstand. There was a large glass of water there, too, and her phone, plugged into a charger. She reached for the card, but she forgot to do her usual stealth roll, so Max woke up and started yapping happily.

"Oh, Max," she moaned, not sure if she was moaning in dismay at Dog Max's barks piercing her brain or in gratitude at Human Max for putting the Advil within arm's reach. "Good morning, my love." That was definitely directed at Dog Max. She kissed his head and tried to get her eyes to focus.

I took your dog out last night before I left, Human Max had scrawled on the card in navy ink that looked like it had come from a fountain pen. His handwriting was tall and angular—like him. He'd drawn an arrow, which prompted her to turn the card over.

Thanks for an epic evening. -M.

She turned the card back over. It was a minimalist business

card, embossed with only his name, and the nickname version at that: *Max von Hansburg*. No titles of either the occupational or hereditary variety. Then a phone number, which she supposed she already had, since he'd texted her, and an email address that, surprisingly, was a Gmail one.

She grabbed her phone, expecting there might be a text from him, but there wasn't. She wondered how much longer he was in town.

Yap yap yap!

"Yes, yes, okay, sweetie." She generally tried to get up stealthily and ingest a coffee before Max woke up, because once he was awake, he would not shut up until he got to go out for a pee.

She rolled herself out of bed. She was wearing pajamas she had no memory of changing into, which wasn't surprising because she also had no memory of Max being here and leaving her a bedside note. Oh, wait. Hang on. An image flashed into her mind.

She went out to the kitchen, and—nope. It was neat as a pin. Still, she could have sworn . . . Even though the rest of the evening after their arrival at her place was fuzzy, she had a memory of buttery bread and—

Her phone dinged.

Max: What are you doing tonight?

Dani: Making fruitcake.

That she still had to buy ingredients for. All right. Dog peeing, coffee, fruitcake-ingredient shopping. She shrugged into a coat and stuffed her feet into boots.

Max: Incorrect.

Dani: What do you mean?

A picture came through. She squinted at it as she clipped a leash onto Max. It looked like a ticket of some sort. By the time they were downstairs and he was doing his business, Human Max had sent another text.

Max: You, me, and your mother. I can send cars for you both. Or one that gets her first, then collects you, if she doesn't mind the scenic route.

What? Hang on. She zoomed in on the picture and gasped. Dog Max started yapping. It was a ticket to the New York City Ballet's *The Nutcracker*.

Dani: You're inviting me and MY MOM to The Nutcracker?!

Max: Yes. I got three tickets, and I promise not to talk.

Max: I promise to TRY not to talk.

Max: Well, I promise not to say anything untoward.

Max: I promise to TRY not to say anything untoward. Final offer.

She didn't know what to say to such an unexpectedly kind gesture.

But *was* it that unexpected? Max had gone out of his way to help her last night, both at the party and in terms of getting her settled in at home.

> **Dani:** Did we make grilled cheese sandwiches last night?

> **Max:** We did. A first for me, but you proved an excellent tutor.

Ha. She'd been right. She could have sworn she remembered bantering with Max about it. She'd had the drunken munchies, and he'd teased her about wanting cheese and carbs for dessert after her dinner of cheese and carbs.

> **Dani:** How did I get into my pajamas?

> **Max:** I ripped off your dress with my teeth and manhandled you into them. I am the Depraved Duke, after all.

> **Max:** I'll thank you to give me a little credit. You wanted to change into your pajamas. You asked me to unzip you, which I did.

> **Max:** I even averted my eyes.

Dani: You did not.

Max: Fine, I did not. But all I saw was your back. Then I waited in the living room while you changed.

Dani: And then what?

Max: And then we made mad, passionate love. I thought I could control myself, but in the end, I could not resist those plaid flannel pajamas.

She snorted. She was wearing possibly the world's least alluring sleepwear, a pair of men's-style old ratty flannel pajamas in navy and dark green.

Dani: What really happened?

Max: Nothing. You went to bed. I took your ridiculous dog out to relieve himself. You were asleep on top of your covers when I came back up. I went back to my hotel.

But not before setting her up with water, painkillers, and her phone. And she had been under her covers, not on top of them, when she woke up.

Dani: Did you tuck me in?

Max: I might have tucked you in.

Well. Damn. Dani could think of a lot of reasons to decline the ballet tickets. She didn't need charity, for one. Yes, *The Nutcracker* wasn't in the budget, which was tight now that she was floating the rent on her own. But if she'd really wanted to go, she could have made it happen. But more importantly, she'd planned to do the fruitcake tonight. She was going to watch holiday movies, too, now that it was officially Christmas according to the Dani Martinez calendar.

She had plans, was the point, and going to the Nutcracker would violate #6 on the Things I will Never Again Do for a Man list: Rearrange my schedule to indulge his whims.

Max had said, "Indulge me," several times last night, after all, and he seemed like the kind of person who was accustomed to being indulged. She didn't need to add herself to his army of indulgers.

Her resolve lasted five seconds. She zoomed in on the image of the ticket again. Those were really good seats.

Was it really Max's whims she would be indulging if she accepted? It sort of seemed more like him indulging hers. *Let's go with that, anyway.*

She smiled. She felt that same Christmas break frisson of excitement as last night.

> **Dani:** What time is the ballet? Why don't you send a car for my mom and I'll take the subway.

There. She'd accept the tickets but not the chauffeur service. Holding back something felt important.

Max: You can't take the subway in your fancy dress.

She gasped again, which set off another round of yapping from Dog Max. She had forgotten she'd told Max about the dress. She could barely remember last night, but it seemed Max had absorbed every detail. She didn't know what to say. She felt sheepish, like she was a little girl wanting to dress up and go see the pretty ladies in the tutus.

Max: Listen. I don't know how to say this without sounding like a vulgarian, but I am extremely rich. It is not a hardship for me to send a car. But if you want to take the subway, that's fine. Or if you want to forget it, I'll find someone to give the tickets to.

It boggled the mind that he could buy three tickets to *The Nutcracker*—which should be sold out this close to Christmas, so who even knew how he'd gotten them?—then just give them away like it was nothing. Not to mention send a car halfway up Long Island and back. She also thought it was interesting that he wasn't trying to hide any of this. In her limited experience with rich people—donors at the university, for example, or some of the diplomats she'd met at her dad's work parties over the years—they were always trying to pretend to be middle class. "The cost of living in New York, am I right?" they'd say, like they had something in common with her.

Not Max, though. He was who he was. A rich playboy. Not her usual type.

Not that she meant it *that* way. Not her usual type for friendship. Or anything. But somehow, with him, the extreme lack of hypocrisy sort of made up for the wealthy-playboy part. If he was the Depraved Duke, was he also the Blunt Baron?

The music from "The Dance of the Sugar Plum Fairy" started earworming its way through her mind. Well, why not let him send his fancy car? It wasn't like she was going to date him. Or sleep with him.

Or merge her bank account with his or change her research program for him or do his laundry for him—or *anything* for him.

> **Dani:** This is lovely of you. Why don't you send a car for my mom, then have it come get me? It will be nice to catch up with her, and I can lay the groundwork for my forthcoming crimes against fruitcake. Let me make sure she's free, and I'll text you to confirm times and addresses.

> **Max:** Grand. Pass my contact info on to your mother in case there are any problems. You have my card, yes?

> **Dani:** I do have your card. You have a Gmail address!

> **Max:** Yes. That's my real address.

> **Dani:** As opposed to your fake one?

> **Max:** Well, it's the one I use for my friends. The family has a domain, and I have a professional address there.

Dani: And what is your profession?

Max: Man-whore, remember?

She laughed, and Dog Max started barking again. "I'm going to the ballet, Max."

DANI WAS A younger, darker carbon copy of her mother. Max was waiting at their agreed-upon meeting spot outside Lincoln Center, and the likeness was so uncanny that he couldn't stop staring as they got out of the car. Dani had light-brown smooth skin; her mother had a pale, finely lined face. But the shape of their faces was exactly the same, down to their high cheekbones and thin, slightly upturned noses. Dani's hair was a deep mahogany and her mother's was a mixture of light brown and gray, but they had similar shoulder-length, layered styles.

He shook himself out of his paralysis and hurried to greet them. "Hello, hello."

"Max." Dani smiled. "This is my mom, Valerie Arbour. Mom, this is Max von Hansburg . . ."

The way she trailed off suggested she was unsure if she should be adding his title. He extended his hand to preempt that. "Lovely to meet you, Ms. Arbour."

"Please call me Val."

"You're a Brit!" She had an accent. "A Northerner, I think?"

"Yes! Leeds! I've lived in the States since I was eighteen, though."

He ushered them inside and to the coat check and— Oh. There was the green dress Dani had referenced. It was the color of the mountain at home in the peak of summer, but it was made of shiny taffeta, which turned the summer association into a Christmas one. The skirt was short—it came to just below her knees—but it was dramatic in the way it jutted out from her waist. It was shaped like a bell, which was an apt metaphor because the whole thing seemed exuberant and elegant all at once, like the bells at St. Stephen's in Riems pealing on Christmas morning.

He cleared his throat and, realizing he'd probably been staring a little too intensely, suggested they visit the bar. "What can I get you ladies?"

"Oh, I'd love a glass of prosecco," Val enthused.

"Prosecco for you, too?" he asked Dani, raising an eyebrow slightly. "Or perhaps a negroni?"

"Diet Coke, thanks," she said.

"Not a drinker?" he said teasingly, but he ordered a Diet Coke for her and a tea for himself. Last night had been a lot of booze for him, too. He knew better—he thought. It had just been so much fun, keeping up with Dani Martinez. And not only in terms of the negronis, but matching her wit, or trying to.

She shot him an exasperated look, but he flattered himself that it was an affectionately exasperated look, and he winked before turning his attention back to her mother. "What brought you to New York at age eighteen, Val?"

"I first visited when I was fifteen, and I met Dani's dad. I fell in love with him and the city at the same time."

"My parents met as teenagers attending Model United Nations," Dani said.

"Yes," her mom confirmed, "and we made a pact to try to return for college, and we were reunited three years later at NYU. We haven't left the city since. Well, we're on Long Island now that my husband's retired, but we still consider ourselves New Yorkers."

"Well, that's about the most charming thing I've ever heard. Model UN. I have a close friend who's a UNHCR goodwill ambassador."

"He's talking about the princess of Eldovia," Dani said drily. "That's his 'friend.'"

"I know!" Val said. "I heard all about that!"

"My dad was a translator at the UN until he retired, and my mom still teaches high school Spanish and French, so we're a very worldly family," Dani joked.

"We *are* a very worldly family," Val said with a twinkle in her eye. "After all, you're going to be the best woman at the Eldovian royal wedding."

"And I'm going to be the man of honor," Max said.

"Actually, I need to talk to you about that at some point," Dani said. "Someone from the palace has been in touch about my dress, but there must be other stuff I should be worrying about. Leo said he would tell me if I was supposed to be doing anything in particular—like, do I have to make any speeches? Are there any traditions I should know about?—but I'm not sure he's the best source for royal wedding protocol."

"I don't think you need to concern yourself overmuch, especially this far ahead of time. The wedding itself will be planned by palace staff, and it won't be that large. If your image of a royal wedding is a British one, you're off base. It won't be televised. There won't be commemorative plates. We're a small country, and though everyone loves Marie, she isn't a fixture in the headlines in the way the Brits are."

"I guess she leaves that to you."

He could not deny it. He had never really cared one way or the other before, but he found himself wishing that when Daniela Martinez—or her mother—googled him, she got something other than that horrible picture.

The bells signaling they should take their seats chimed, and he gestured for them to walk ahead of him. "We can talk more about it, but I think we merely need to show up and do what they tell us. You should probably prepare a toast for the dinner, though."

"I admit I'm a little nervous about it," she said over her shoulder as they queued up at the correct aisle.

"Don't be. I'll look out for you." The prospect was buoying. Max was not looking forward to the wedding. He was thrilled for Marie, and, ultimately, relieved to have the reprieve even though the broken engagement had thrown his plans into disarray. But his parents were still so angry. And his own conundrum aside, there was no way around the fact that Marie's marrying Leo, a cabdriver from New York, was a bit of a scandal. He'd meant what he said about the Eldovian monarchy not operating on the same celebrity plane as the Brits, but the princess's choice of groom had still made waves. Max didn't care about any of that, and he liked Leo, but that didn't change the fact that there were going to be raised eyebrows. And—back to Max and his conundrum—he frankly wasn't looking forward to all the whispers about *him*. Since everyone already thought he was a wanton playboy—the Depraved Duke—he was fairly certain the narrative was going to be that he'd only wanted to marry Marie so he could be prince and was upset to have lost his chance.

Not to mention the fact that Father plus weddings was not a winning mix.

The idea of Dani being there, though, felt like a bit of a reprieve.

The ballet was lovely, if you were into those sorts of things, and Dani and her mother clearly were. Max had always thought of the ballet—and the theater, and the opera—as formal, singular occasions. You might be sitting next to a friend or a relative or a date, but once the lights went down, the experience was, essentially, solitary. You watched the performance, and perhaps you had thoughts about it—even if they were merely "this is boring" thoughts—but you kept those thoughts to yourself.

Not Dani and Val, though. They didn't make any noise or bother anyone around them, but they kept looking at each other in delight and occasionally leaning over to whisper in each other's ears. At one point, during the iconic "Waltz of the Flowers," they clasped hands excitedly.

What must it have been like to enjoy one's parent so much?

He found himself watching them more than the performance, and when it was over and they broke into happy applause, he let himself be carried along with them. And when Dani turned to him, smiled, and mouthed, "Thank you," and he whispered, "You're welcome," he found he had never meant anything more.

Chapter Four

Dani didn't remember *The Nutcracker* being so good. She hadn't seen it since she was a girl, and she'd been wondering if her adult self would be too jaded to suspend her disbelief and enjoy a story about toys and candy and flowers come to life. But a few bars into the overture and she'd fallen right into the story, and Mom must have, too—she kept looking at Dani at the same time Dani looked over at her.

"That was lovely, Max, thank you so much," her mom said when they reached the lobby.

It really had been. Even though Dani had had to be talked into coming, she was bummed that it was over.

"May I take you ladies for a post-show drink?" Max asked as they waited in line at the coat check.

Yes. Dani didn't want to go home yet.

But her mom said, "Thank you, but no. It's a long ride home, and my husband waits up for me even though I tell him not to."

"Let me call the car," Max said, holding their coats for them one at a time.

It was just as well. Dani took her mom's arm. "I need to pick your brain in the car about gift ideas for Dad." Though maybe admitting she hadn't bought gifts yet was a dumb move—it might lead to a line of fruitcake questioning, and Dani had never been able to lie to her mother.

"Oh, no, you two go have a drink!" Mom shrugged out of her grasp. "I'll enjoy the peace of a cozy ride home."

Dani looked at Max, who had an eyebrow raised—the man had the uncanny ability to lift one eyebrow at a time—like he was daring her to do something as transgressive as have a drink with him. She wanted to, but without her mom as an excuse, she should refuse. Spontaneously going out to drinks with Max last night had been one thing. Doing it again felt like veering into list-violating territory. But really, there was nothing on it a drink with Max would be violating, except #6, and she had already violated that one by being here to begin with. And perhaps more to the point, Max wasn't a "man" in Things I Will Never Again Do for a Man sense. He was a baron who lived on another continent. There was no danger of him upending her life.

"Stay, honey," her mom said.

"It *is* the first day of the Christmas season according to the Daniela Martinez calendar," Max said.

She made the decision by not making it, by not saying anything as she let them sweep her along.

At the car, as they were saying their goodbyes, Max said something to her mom in French. Dani recognized *Joyeux Noël* in her mom's reply, but soon the two of them were conversing rapidly and animatedly—Max was *such* a flirt—and were beyond Dani's limited French.

After the car departed, Max turned to her and said, "Negroni? Three negronis?"

"What were you and my mom talking about?"

"How much I hate Christmas."

"You hate Christmas? What are you doing at *The Nutcracker*, then?"

He shrugged and said, "I'm a walking contradiction. So, negronis? Diet Coke? I admit I'm not really in the mood for a negroni myself this evening."

"Me either. I was thinking it would be nice to walk a bit."

"What's our destination?" He held out his arm.

She didn't take it. "I so rarely get to Manhattan, and unlike you, I actually *like* Christmas. I'm in the mood to stroll aimlessly and take in the holiday stuff." She gestured at the big Lincoln Center Christmas tree, aware that she sounded like a dork, but what did it matter? It wasn't like she cared what the Depraved Not-Duke thought of her.

"Let us stroll aimlessly, then." She thought he might offer his arm again, but he did not.

"This is going to sound silly, but I feel like I sort of missed Christmas last year."

"You mentioned that last night."

She should probably be embarrassed by the amount of rambling—not to mention drinking—she'd done. But again, this dude was an Eldovian baron playboy. He wasn't real. Well, he was. Obviously. He was right next to her with his cool good looks and his gray wool "fancy man" coat, but he wasn't in the sense that he had any impact on her life.

"So you missed Christmas last year?" he prompted.

"Well, I didn't *miss* it. I went to my parents' house. We did presents and dinner and sugary cereal the next morning and all that. And I remember thinking how nice it was not to have to split the holiday with Vince's family." She had added #5 to her list at that point, in fact: **Be away from my family for the holidays.** "It was the run-up to Christmas that I missed last year. Decorations, carols, that kind of stuff. You know what I mean?"

"If you had ever spent Christmas in Eldovia, you would know just how much I am acquainted with the Christmas run-up."

"Yeah, I've heard about this from Leo. There's a cocoa festival, right?" And a ball, at which Leo and Marie had made their dramatic declarations of love. She could sort of see where Max's anti-Christmas stance came from. "I'm sure it's overkill. I guess my point is that last year, I looked up and—bam!—it was Christmas."

"Why was that? Working too much?"

"In part."

"And what's the other part?"

She wasn't sure why she was talking about this with Max. Maybe because, as she'd just been thinking, he didn't have any actual stake in her life or she in his. "I was probably a little too fresh off the breakup to enjoy anything. Too raw. That's embarrassing to admit to someone who's met Vince." Now that she was out the other side, it was hard to explain what she'd seen in Vince. He was smart, she'd give him that, and she'd been flattered by his interest when she was hired into the department. But from her current vantage point, it seemed obvious that she'd let herself get too swept up in him. And not just him, but his interests, his career, his family—Leo and Gabby aside, of course. Hence the list. "I was working so hard because I had this project I'd put aside about a year previously because Vince thought we should do this *other* project together."

"What was it?"

"Cubism in literature."

"Ah, the Picasso obsession. I didn't know cubism was a movement beyond visual art."

"Yeah. Picasso and Gertrude Stein influenced each other. We were going to write a book about it. I was going to do the Stein, and he was going to do the Picasso. But then . . ." She shrugged. "He's writing it by himself now." With all her work feeding into it.

"Didn't Picasso have a teenage mistress? It sounds as though Vince is taking the Picasso cosplay a little too far."

Dani snorted, but it was so *embarrassing*. The breakup aside, knowing that you were the kind of person who would be with a man who would, in turn, date someone less than half his age was so *gross*.

Letting yourself be hurt by that kind of man was even grosser.

She looked at Max's profile, illuminated by all the New York lights, of both the regular and Christmas varieties. Max was oddly easy to tell truths to, even uncomfortable ones. "That's why I was working so hard last winter, to get back to my own stuff. To be fair, the Picasso-Stein project was a cool idea. But it wasn't something I'd been inherently interested in. I let it derail me when what I needed to be doing was working toward tenure."

She had, of course, created a list item to deal with any similar scenario in the future. It was #3: **Work with him in such a way that his interests are advanced at the expense of my own.** "I'm not sure how I let myself get so . . . seduced." She meant it in the philosophical sense, but it was probably the wrong choice of word, because now the Depraved Duke would make a joke.

He did not. He merely made a dismissive gesture. "We all make errors of judgment when it comes to matters of the heart."

"Do you, though?" Max didn't seem like the kind of person who got his heart broken. In order to get your heart broken, stuff had to stick to begin with.

He smirked. "I do not. I was trying to be magnanimous." He cocked his head as he looked into the distance. "But I do know what it's like to have someone in your life who has more power over you than you can perhaps explain."

As she was about to ask him what he meant, he pointed to a brass quintet on the edge of the plaza playing "Good King Wenceslas." They slowed down as they approached the musicians. "Is this suitably Christmasey?" he asked.

She let the warm, rich brass notes wash over her. "Yes. It's perfect." They watched in silence for a few moments, and when the song was done, she said, "I guess my point is that this year I actually feel like doing the schmoopy Christmas stuff. Street musicians! *The Nutcracker*! I was thinking I might walk over to Bergdorf's and look at the windows."

"A fine plan." He dropped a fifty-dollar bill in the open instrument case in front of the quartet.

"You don't have to come with me," she said, aware anew of the gulf between them. He was passing out fifty-dollar bills like they were quarters, and she was delighted by a ballet that was, essentially, for children. "I don't want to subject you to any more Christmas-related torture. Or any more monologues about my poor judgment when it comes to husbands."

"I'm going over there anyway. I'm at the Four Seasons."

"Of course you are." They set off, and after they crossed Broadway, she said, "You want to cut across the bottom of the park?"

"Your wish is my command."

The snow crunched beneath their feet as they entered the park. "Did you grow up on Long Island?" he asked.

"No. My parents only moved there a few years ago, after my dad retired. I grew up in Sunnyside, Queens. My mom taught at my high school, and my dad commuted to Manhattan."

"What prompted the move?"

"I don't think it was any one thing. They both love the city, but they were getting tired of the stairs—we lived on the top floor of a walk-up—and tired of fighting for parking. And my dad wanted to be near the water—he's big into clamming."

"Clamming? Is that . . . fishing but for clams?"

"Yes. You dig them up, though." She shrugged. "He kind of randomly got into it after he retired, and he was always getting up at the crack of dawn and driving out to wherever they were supposed to be good that day. My mom wasn't quite ready to retire, but she got a teaching job in Huntington, which is a town on the North Shore, and that was that."

"You're close to them?"

He had asked her that last night, and he seemed strangely interested in the answer. "Yes." He was looking at her as they walked, and he was listening so intently, it made her want to say more. "And I love the beach, so I'm always happy to visit them. My dad was always a beach person, too, though the clamming is a more recent development. We used to rent a place in Long Beach for a couple weeks every summer. And my dad grew up on the beach in Playa del Carmen, which is a bit south of Cancún. His parents owned a hotel—they still do, though they don't do the day-to-day running of it anymore. Every few years over the holidays we all go there for a visit. The beach is big in my family, is my point, so Long Island made sense for my parents. Of course they're not right on the water—that's too expensive for us commoners." She smiled to show she was kidding.

"And you have a sister, you said?"

"Yep. She's three years younger."

"And you're close to her, too?"

"Yeah, but in that weird way siblings are without there being a lot to it objectively. We love each other, but we don't have much in common. She's a corporate lawyer for a mutual fund company, and I teach and write about literature. We don't talk that much, but, you know, we're sisters."

"Funny how that happens. You can grow up with someone, spend all your time with them, and then . . ." He waved a hand in front of his face. "It's all gone once you become adults."

It occurred to Dani that in the space of two days, she'd told Max about Vince, her job dissatisfaction, and her family. He had a gift for drawing out information. He'd seemed genuinely interested, but maybe all he was doing was being polite. She, on the other hand, knew nothing about him.

"Do you have siblings?" she asked in an attempt to make the conversation more two-sided. He had sounded, when he'd talked about growing apart from a sibling, as if he'd been speaking more than theoretically.

"A brother."

Was it her imagination, or did he purse his lips a little as he spoke? "Younger, I presume? Since you're the future duke and all."

She'd been trying to lighten the mood, but he just said, "Yes. Younger." The terse, clipped tone sounded like it was coming from a different person than the carefree baron who had taken her to *The Nutcracker* on a whim. "Are you close?"

"We were until he went to boarding school in England."

She was about to ask where Max had gone to boarding school when he stepped off the path and said, "Let's make snow angels." It had snowed most of the day, though it had tapered off while they'd been at the ballet. He took big strides until he reached a patch of untrammeled snow. He stopped and turned about twenty feet from her, seeming to realize she wasn't following. "What? Is snow-angel-ing not done in America?"

"It's done if you're seven. And if you don't hate Christmas."

"Come on." He beckoned her. "You *just* said you wanted to get into the Christmas spirit this year."

"Why are you always suggesting silly, impulsive things like ballets and snow angels?"

"Why are you always resisting them?"

She almost gasped at the question, which felt like a thin, perfectly honed blade sliding effortlessly between her ribs.

The answer was that indulging in snow angels and impromptu outings to the ballet felt like exposing herself somehow. Putting on display the tender, inner part of her that was capable of taking delight in innocent pursuits, and that, in turn, felt like she was setting herself up to be mocked.

Which was sad. She had never been a frivolous person, but she used to have fun.

In one sense, the sum total of her experience with Max was him asking her to do stuff and her saying no. Do you want to go to dinner? No. Do you want to go to *The Nutcracker*? No. Can I send a car for you? I'll take the subway. Can I walk with you? You don't have to.

Vince had done this to her. Vince and his operas and his cubist literature.

No. As much as she hated to admit it, that wasn't entirely fair to Vince. The hard truth was she had done this to herself. She had let Vince turn her into this brittle, careful, suspicious person.

She had turned into a person who didn't trust her own judgment.

That was why she had her list.

But the list didn't say anything about outlawing fun. It was one thing to be post-men. But did that have to mean she was on the defensive in all human interactions? Did she have to become a misanthrope? Her parents had moved to Long Island. Leo had moved to *Eldovia*. She'd been thinking just yesterday about how she hadn't seen much of Sinéad this semester. If she saw the people she trusted rarely-to-never, what did that mean for her life? Not to be too melodramatic, but what did that mean for her soul?

Snow angels it was.

"You're not dressed for it anyway." Max started back toward her.

"No, no. Stay there. I'm coming." He grinned, and she gasped as she stepped into the snow. It wasn't a gasp that came from the shock of confronting painful truths this time, though; it was a gasp that came from the shock of confronting painful *cold* as her feet sank into the snow. She *wasn't* dressed for this, but she could hardly turn back now. Snow-angel-ing, to use Max's silly verb form, had become symbolic.

"That was false bravado a moment ago," he said when she reached him. "I haven't done this since I was a child." He eyed the snow. "I'm not sure I remember how."

She made a shooing motion to get him to move farther away. "The trick is to have a big enough patch of fresh snow." She waved her arms like she was doing jumping jacks. He did the same, positioning himself so he was next to her. "And keep your legs spread," she added, stepping wide and ignoring the stabs of pain in her pantyhose-clad ankles.

He cracked up. "Keep your legs spread. Yes. A particular motto of mine."

"Oh, shut up. No off-color jokes allowed during snow-angel-ing."

He made a show of shutting his mouth as he got himself into position. She adjusted her stance and looked over her shoulder to make sure the ground they would land on was still pristine.

"All right," she said. "Fall flat and decisively. If you slump back or are tentative, your angel will look sad."

"How do you know all this? I'm the one who grew up in the Alps. You grew up in an apartment in Queens."

"My dad used to take my sister and me to the library every Saturday, and it was across the street from a big playground. In the winter, my sister and I would make snow angels, and then we'd inch in along the top and add halos out of rocks or sticks. We had quite the technique developed."

"Your dad sounds rather wonderful, if you don't mind my saying. The library, the beach, clamming."

She smiled. "He is wonderful." Both her parents were. She felt lucky, both to have them and to be here, now, back to the pre-Christmas excitement she'd skipped last year. "Are you ready?" she asked Max, who nodded. "On three."

She counted, and they both landed with a muffled thud.

"What now?" he said through laughter.

"Oh my god, that's cold!" She was wearing a knee-length coat, so her legs were unprotected. "Flap your arms and legs." His continuing laughter was contagious, and once she started, she couldn't stop. She was making snow angels in Central Park with an Eldovian baron. How utterly ridiculous.

But also how fun.

See? She could have fun.

Max started to move like he was going to get up. "No!" she said. "Stop! The dismount is critical!"

"The *dismount*?" He cracked up again, but he went still. "What do I have to do?"

"Try to lever yourself up without making any marks outside your existing angel, then stand up at the bottom of your leg indentations and take a giant step away from the angel. The idea is to try to keep the outline pristine."

He did what she said, getting to his feet and taking not a step but a large—and graceful—leap away.

"Yes! Good job!" She, however, was having more trouble. "Ugh, my high heels aren't getting purchase on the ground. Mine is going to suck."

"Hang on." He came toward her but stopped a few feet away and peeled off his coat. He was left standing there in his suit—

the same blue one from yesterday, but today he was wearing a lavender-striped tie.

"What are you *doing*?"

He balled up the coat—the plush, expensive-looking one she'd been admiring earlier—and said, "Catch" as he unfurled it toward her.

"Oh!" She was too late to understand that he intended for her to grab it like a life preserver. "Do it again! I'm ready this time!" They both laughed as he re-threw the coat. Once they'd each got a good grip on it, he started pulling on his end. "Ahh!" she exclaimed as he levered her up. He didn't ease off soon enough, though, and she was unsteady on her feet in the snow—oh, her poor shoes—so she didn't have a chance to catch her balance. She pitched forward, stumbling until she crashed into him.

"Steady now." His arms came around her. They teetered together for a few seconds. It was as if they were dancing but doing a very bad job of it.

Once they'd righted themselves, he didn't let go. He was no doubt making sure she fully had her feet before he retreated, but it felt like a hug. Something happened to her body in that moment. It relaxed, despite the cold. It felt so *good* to have arms around her, to have someone help her bear her weight.

When was the last time she had hugged anyone she wasn't related to? Probably not since she'd been to Eldovia last summer and hugged Leo and Gabby goodbye before she got on the plane to come home.

Oh, but all of a sudden this wasn't that kind of hug. Now that they'd got their balance, she was suddenly *aware* of him. The

solidity of him. A little bit of bare skin visible on his throat between his scarf and the collar of his coat. She could see his pulse
thrumming at that spot.

She stepped away.

It felt too good. This was not something she could have. It
wasn't something she *wanted*, not beyond the weakness of the
moment. She couldn't get seduced by the momentarily buoying
sensation of a hug like that, because ultimately, she had to buoy
herself in this world. And she most *definitely* couldn't get herself
into a position where she was noticing things like hard chests and
fluttering pulses. Maybe someday, but not yet.

Max stared at her for long enough that she started to feel
awkward, but then he cleared his throat, breaking the spell, and
turned and contemplated their angels. "Well, that's not going to
win any awards. So much for a pristine outline."

"It looks like our angels got in a . . ." She shivered—a big, involuntary one. "Catfight."

"You're freezing." He moved behind her and started brushing
snow off her shoulders and upper back. As he made his way down
toward the butt zone, he pulled the coat away from her body and
brushed the snow off the fabric without touching her body. At
the hem of her coat, he crouched with his hands poised over her
calves. "May I?"

"Uh, sure. Thanks."

Another thing that felt too good? Max's hands, which were im-
probably warm, on her legs. It was only her calves, and he was
only brushing snow off them, and there was a layer of pantyhose
between his skin and hers.

He finished the snow removal, and for a moment, his big hands squeezed her calves, like he was trying to warm them up. It worked too well. There was a kind of zingy sensation on her skin beneath his fingers. She stepped away from him—again.

"This was a terrible idea." He stood. "I'm sorry."

"No, it was fun."

"Still, I think I should call the car. Do you agree?"

She could not deny that she was wet and shivering in earnest but also dealing with the echoes of those odd zings his hands had summoned. "But isn't the car on its way to Long Island with my mom in it?"

"Oh, but there are more cars where that one came from."

Of course there were. "Yeah, okay. Thanks."

He produced his phone and had a murmured conversation while he led her to the path, and by the time they'd made it back to Central Park West, another magical Mercedes was waiting.

The driver had a blanket for her. She would have rolled her eyes—it was too much, almost—except she was so cold she took it gratefully.

Once they were installed in the back, Max said, "You want to swing by Bergdorf's on the way home, or are you too cold?"

"I would love to swing by Bergdorf's."

She was still freezing as she slid out of the car at the store, but this was going to be worth it. Max appeared at her side with the blanket and settled it over her shoulders. Her first impulse was to refuse it, to protest that she would look like an idiot standing on the street with a blanket around her shoulders. But, really, who cared? They strolled, taking in the mannequins in crazy scenarios and even crazier clothing.

"This is what I mean about New York," Max said, gesturing

first at a mannequin wearing a silver ballgown riding a mythical creature of some sort over a cityscape made out of gears—and then at a person viewing the scene dressed in an Elmo costume. "New York is a goddamn delight."

Back in the car, Max gave the driver her address and raised the privacy screen between the front and back seats.

"We'll drop you at your hotel first, though, right?" she asked. It was a few blocks away.

"I'll ride along with you." He tucked the blanket around her legs and started fiddling with the heat vents so they were aiming at her.

"There's no need."

"I want to."

"Why?"

"I like you."

"You are so weird." She couldn't help but smile inwardly, though. It was still kind of painful to hear such an earnest expression of fondness, but it was turning into a good sort of pain. Anyway, here was her chance to ask him about his life.

"So you grew up with Marie?"

"Not literally. She's in a village called Witten. Well, she's actually in a palace on a hill next to the village, of course."

"Of course."

"My family is in Riems, which is on the other side of the country. Not to be confused with the island of the same name in the Baltic."

"I wouldn't dream of confusing them."

He smiled. "Eldovia is bisected by a mountain range. Marie—

and the capital—are on one side, and I'm on the other. It's not a large country, but to get from one side to the other, you have to drive over the mountains along a series of switchbacks. So while we saw Marie and her family quite a bit when I was young, it wasn't an everyday occurrence. But our fathers were friends."

"Yes, I heard. They wanted you and Marie to get married in order to 'unite the houses'?" It boggled the mind.

"Indeed. The houses of Accola and Aquilla had bad blood going back centuries. It hadn't been active bad blood, mind you, since the nineteenth."

It was such a strange thing, to be able to trace one's family so far. Dani, with her immigrant parents, knew the grandparents on each side, and her dad's mom talked a lot about her own mother, but that was as far back as she had any meaningful knowledge.

"There was a cessation of hostilities in 1898," Max went on. "After that, the animosity was limited to fighting each other in Parliament and snubbing each other at parties. But then Marie's father and mine ended up at the same French boarding school and struck up a clandestine friendship. Our family supplies some of the trace minerals used in the watches the royal family's company makes."

"So aren't the houses 'united' at that point? Why insist on marrying off their children?"

"I'm not defending it by any means, but I think they liked the idea of grandchildren in common. There's nothing to seal a newfound truce like a baby. Anyway, you're post-love, aren't you?"

Post-*men* was what Dani had been saying, but she supposed it amounted to the same thing.

"And you're a scholar of the nineteenth century," Max went on. "You of all people should understand that the idea of marrying for love—and the idea of romantic love itself—is a modern construct. In many ways, the aristocracy hasn't modernized. Political marriages are still common in our circles."

"But Marie bucked the trend."

"She did indeed." He looked so wistful all of a sudden that Dani half wondered if the Depraved Duke *was* carrying a torch for Marie. His insistence that he was happy for her and that theirs had never been a love match had seemed genuine, but she was also getting the sense that something deeper was going on with him.

But she didn't know how to ask that. "So you grew up in a castle in this place called Riems." She started to make a mental note to google it but checked herself. She had already googled Max. She wasn't going to google his *castle*, too. A person had to have standards.

"No, no. It is rather a large old house, though."

"You still live there?" As much as she loved her parents, she had no desire to live with them. But she supposed the size of the "rather large old house" might be a mitigating factor.

"I live alone in a cottage on the grounds. It used to be occupied by my grandmother, but it had been sitting empty since she died, so I moved in when I returned from university."

"How many bedrooms does this cottage have?"

"I'll have you know that it has only one. Though I suppose there is also the library. But it's small. It is rather a privileged life, though, if that's what you're getting at."

She could picture him in a cottage. As worldly as Max was, with his designer suits and his razor-sharp wit, she could also see him pottering around a library, drinking tea. "But what do you *do* all day?"

"As little as possible."

Was she imagining it, or did his snappy retort seem a little performative? "You should actually do the research into that Eldovian woman you told me about. That was a fascinating story, and that's without even knowing how it ends."

He made a dismissive gesture. "To what end, though? I'm done with school."

"You could write a book."

"Oh good god, no. That's your department."

She wasn't sure what her point was. So what if Max drifted around his posh cottage purposeless and waited upon? Just that sometimes he seemed to turn wistful—sad, almost. But then it would be gone before she could really examine it. "When do you go home?" she asked. "Any more New York bashes?"

"Tomorrow, and no. Just the one."

"I know my commonness is probably showing, but I'm still amazed that you would come all the way here for a party."

"Well, to be honest, it wasn't the party so much as it was a certain person at the party I needed to meet." He smirked. "A certain female person."

Ah. "Is that your way of saying you came to New York for a hookup?"

"Lavinia von Bachenheim is an intelligent and accomplished young lady, and I would never refer to any of my interactions with her—or anyone—with as vulgar a term as 'hookup.'" He sniffed, but in a way that telegraphed that he was teasing. "But no, Lavinia and I did not hook up. We merely chatted."

"I thought it was Lucrecia?"

"Lavinia is Lucrecia's younger sister. The party was at Lucrecia's apartment, but Lavinia is at Yale."

"Well, don't you have good taste?" she shot back—and whoa, why so snappish? What did she care what—or who—Max did while he was in town?

He speared her with a look she could not decode and didn't speak for an uncomfortably long time. When he did, he had lost his teasing tone. "My parents want me to marry Lavinia. I have no intention of doing so, but making the trip will placate them for a while."

She was embarrassed that he'd felt the need to justify himself. Time to change the subject. "Tell me the Karina Klein story again."

"Why, so you can tell me I'm wasting my life?"

"No." She thought about saying something flippant, to get them back to their usual bantering mode, but there had been an edge in his question, so she went with the truth instead. "I just like that story, and we have a long ride." She closed her eyes. She was tired, still, from her hangover, and jumping around in the snow had only made her more so. "Tell it to me like a bedtime story." When he didn't speak for a few beats, she opened her eyes. "Or not."

"No, no, close your eyes again. I'm merely getting my bearings. I don't think I've ever told anyone a bedtime story."

"None of your conquests ever asked for a bedtime story?"

"Not a one." He futzed with her blanket like he was tucking her in, and after a few more seconds of silence, he started, except this time he started with Karina's early life.

"By all accounts, Karina was a genius. She was a musical prodigy. That's what she was doing at Cambridge—violin. She was the only child of wealthy parents."

"She'd have to be, wouldn't she, to be allowed to attend university—abroad at that—in the 1940s?"

"Indeed. And to hear it told, her father was a bit eccentric. He was an inventor. He came up with an improved variation on the most common spring used in mechanically powered watches. That's where they made their money."

"Mmm." Luxury watches, she had come to learn, were a mainstay of the Eldovian economy. She was keeping her eyes closed as he talked. She hoped he wasn't offended, but she was enjoying the cocoon effect of the darkness and the warmth—she was finally defrosting.

He kept going, spinning his tale of the violin playing girl who went on to house child refugees in her student rooms at Cambridge. "The English government wouldn't use state money to support the children of the Kindertransport—they all had to have local guarantors."

"I didn't know that."

"It's well-documented, as is Karina's participation."

He kept going, his low voice wrapping itself around her and warming her as much as the blanket was.

"After the war, Karina came back to Eldovia," he said, "and started a music school. She died in the 1980s."

"She never married or had children?"

"No. She said her pupils and the children she sheltered in Cambridge were her family, and she kept in touch with many of the latter group. There are troves of letters, in archives in Cambridge and in Continental Europe."

"So the hole in the story is the trip to New York," Dani said sleepily, her eyes still closed.

"Yes, if it actually happened. I'm not sure an idle aside to the university newspaper is the most trustworthy of sources. There have been books written about her, and it's never been mentioned."

"Maybe she was a spy," Dani said. "Maybe she was working for MI6."

"Yes!" Max sounded delighted with this notion, and when she opened her eyes, he was smiling. "Perhaps she came to New York to murder a Nazi."

"Would there have been Nazis in New York—high-profile ones who would be assassination targets—in 1943?"

"I don't know. I suppose not."

Dani smiled. "Who cares? It's a good story. Karina Klein comes to New York to murder a Nazi. Tell that version."

He did, effortlessly weaving a story about Karina tracking down a German spy whose mission was to assassinate FDR. It was a great story, equal parts exciting thriller and delightfully absurd soap opera.

When Dani felt the car come to a stop, she opened her eyes, intending to thank Max for an extraordinary night, but he'd already hopped out and was opening her door. She hoped he didn't think he was going to come inside.

"Thank you for taking me to *The Nutcracker*," she said as they approached the front door.

"Thank you for teaching me how to make snow angels."

She stepped onto the stoop and turned to him. "Oh, you knew how to make snow angels."

"Well, it turns out I've been doing them wrong my entire life, so . . ." He shrugged. Because she was standing a step above him, they were eye to eye. "Live and learn." He winked.

She was tempted to thank him for coming to the party with her yesterday, too. And for the drunken dinner. And for tucking her in—both last night and in the car. And for the story, which was making her think of another story, one that had been rattling around in her head for a long time. But she didn't want to sound like she was fawning over him, so she just said, "Have a safe flight home."

"Please don't hesitate to be in touch if I can ever be of service." He stuck out his hand for her to shake. She didn't want to shake his hand, though. She wanted another hug, like in the park. But, she reminded herself sternly, that hadn't been a hug. That had been him trying to keep her from landing headfirst in the snow. Any resemblance to a hug had been purely circumstantial.

So she shook his hand. Put her mittened hand in his bare one and squeezed—maybe a little harder than she should have.

"Merry Christmas, Dani," he said.

"Merry Christmas, Max."

Chapter Five

Whyen Max landed in Zurich, he went directly to the palace in Witten. His family always spent Christmas with the royals, and it was close enough to the holiday now that he could get away with not going home in the interim. He told his parents that Marie and Leo needed him for some man of honor duties. The royal wedding was coming in handy as an excuse to be away.

"Max!" Marie was waiting for him in front of the palace when he got out of the car.

"Max!" As was Gabby, Leo's little sister. For reasons that remained mysterious to Max, Gabby was turning into his biggest fan.

"Hello," he said to Marie, and as Gabby tackled him, "Hello, poppet."

"Did you do my deliveries?" Gabby asked.

"I did indeed." He had been tasked with delivering gifts to a cousin and to her favorite former teacher. He wasn't sure why she hadn't simply mailed them, but he'd been happy to be her mule. "And," he added with a great flourish, "here's another question: Did I bring you anything?"

"Did you?" She was practically vibrating. Max had never considered himself a kid person, but twelve-year-olds, it turned out, could be rather pleasant, at least when one's approach was to swoop in and shower them with gifts while other people did the hard work.

After gifts had been opened, Marie stole him away and gave him a cup of tea. But she only let him take one sip before she said, "I heard you went to Daniela Martinez's work party."

"Well. Word travels fast."

"She and Leo talk almost every day."

He raised his eyebrows.

"How can you be judgmental about that? *We* talk a great deal. At least when you're not slutting around New York. And how is *Lavinia*, by the way?"

Max hadn't been objecting to the notion of Dani and Leo talking every day. He was merely surprised Dani had told Leo they'd been together. He'd gotten the impression that Dani was spending time with him against her better judgment, and he therefore hadn't expected her to advertise the fact.

He was also a little surprised by the censure in Marie's tone. She usually remarked on his "slutting around" with indulgent bemusement.

"Lavinia was fine." He took a sip of tea. "And now I can say I've met her." He performed a shudder that was not entirely put-on. "I enjoyed myself more with Daniela than I did with Lavinia or anyone else at the party, though."

"You have to tread with caution, Max," Marie said. "Dani can't be one of your conquests. *Especially* while you're in town considering marriage to someone else."

"I am. I did. We're just friends." Which, on the one hand, was a pity. But on the other, as he'd said, he *liked* Dani. She was going to be around, given the wedding and her friendship with Leo, so that ruled her out for anything more fleeting, even if she'd been open to the idea. "And I'm *not* considering marrying Lavinia," he added peevishly. He got this kind of needling from his parents all the time; he didn't need it from Marie, too.

"I'm not sure I believe you on either count."

He set his tea down with a flash of irritation. "Honestly, you think I'm going to hit on Dani? She's my *friend*," he reiterated. He hoped. He was looking forward to spending more time with her at the wedding. "And as for Lavinia, I merely wanted to meet her."

"That's not what you told your father."

"That's exactly what I told him. I used those precise words."

"That's not how he interpreted it."

Max was aware. "Telling him I was going to Lucrecia's Christmas party to meet Lavinia was a strategic move designed to prevent me from having to make a special-purpose trip to New Haven later to meet her. Can you imagine? *That* wouldn't be awkward."

"I'm sorry, Max," Marie said quietly. "I really have left you in the lurch, haven't I?"

"No, no. It's quite all right. One of us might as well be married to someone they actually fancy." He truly was happy for Marie and Leo. "But now that you've thrown me over"—he winked to show he was teasing—"I'm committed to my bachelorhood."

"But you have to marry someone."

"Ah, but I don't."

"What about the lineage?"

"What do I care about the lineage? If Sebastien's children are anything like him, the estate will be better off in his branch of the family. I'll do my best when my father dies, but you know I'll make a perfectly awful duke." He was trying to keep his tone light, but as always when he contemplated the prospect of inheriting, his chest started to feel heavy, which made his voice start to sound labored. "And as for my parents, all that matters is that they think I'm trying. I can string out the prospect of a match with Lavinia for at least a year or two."

In his parents' eyes, Lavinia von Bachenheim was perfect. Well, Marie, as a princess, had been perfect, but Mother and Father had rallied and were currently championing Lavinia. She was the younger sister of a wealthy and powerful Austrian family. She was studying at Yale but like her sister would no doubt make a "career" as a socialite. Everything about her met with his parents' approval.

"And how was it meeting her?"

He shrugged. "It was fine." In truth, he and Lavinia had had only a brief conversation, but it was enough to tell she had no sense of fun. She'd seemed both distracted and overly serious, which wasn't a winning combination in Max's eyes. He wasn't looking for a wife, but had he been, a sense of humor, perhaps even of adventure, would have been a requirement. Even if he were on the market in earnest, Lavinia would not make the cut.

Lavinia would never make snow angels in Central Park.

When Leo called Dani early in the morning on Christmas Eve, she got right to the point. "Hi," she said. "I think I need to get on an app."

"Merry Christmas to you, too. What kind of app?"

"Sorry—Merry Christmas. A sex app." She'd finished her grading a week ago, and in recent days she'd been experiencing . . .
urges. Dani had spent the year and a half since Vince had left
genuinely not interested in sex, or at least not sex with other people. She wasn't totally dead inside—she did sometimes turn on
old Patrick Swayze movies and, well . . . Now, though, she was
suddenly contemplating the idea of having sex with an actual human male. How did a person make that happen?

"I think you're supposed to call them *dating* apps," Leo said.

"I don't want to date, though."

"Oh, I'm aware. You should get the phrase 'post-men' tattooed
on your forehead."

She winced. Leo had been around when things were really
bad, when Vince was moving his stuff out and Dani was fighting back tears. "Right. I'm still post-men. I just want to have sex.
Without dating."

"For real?" He sounded skeptical.

"What do you mean? Of course for real."

"Last time you expressed interested in hooking up with someone, you only wanted to do it to get even with Vince."

She laughed. "Right. No, I'm not talking about revenge sex."

"Did Max do this to you?"

"What? No."

Yes. It had been almost two weeks since the Central Park hug-
with-a-side-order-of-calf-touching, and Dani was pretty sure that
was what had started this. Incidental physical contact with an
attractive man. But the origin of her newfound horniness was immaterial. Even though Max was apparently a master at the kind

of no-strings encounter she was looking for, she wasn't banging the baron. Heh. *Banging the Baron.* It sounded like a porno. "Why would you think this had anything to do with Max?"

"He's here. He's been here since he got back from New York. He told us you guys went to *The Nutcracker.*" Left unsaid was that Dani *hadn't* told him, and historically, Dani and Leo talked about everything. Though she'd told Leo about Max being her plus-one to the departmental party, she hadn't told him about their outing the next day. She wasn't sure why, just that Leo knew about her list, and to be honest, she didn't like to think of herself as the kind of person who dropped everything when a baron dangled ballet tickets. She steered Leo back to the topic at hand. "Which app do I use? Tinder? Or one of those ones where they only let girls make the first move? Stumble? What is it called?"

"You're asking me? *You* were the one who was always telling *me* to get on an app."

"That advice was theoretical. I didn't know which app." She'd wanted to tip Leo out of his grief, to get him to live a little, to do more than work and take care of his sister. And then he met a god-damn princess and moved to Europe. Talk about overachieving. "But you're right. Why *am* I asking you?" There must be someone she could ask. There was Sinéad, but—

Hang on. There was the Baron She Would Never Bang. Ha. From porno to anti-porno. He *had* invited her to be in touch if he could ever be of service. She stifled a laugh and forced herself to tune in to the rest of the conversation. After she and Leo had caught up and made a plan for a bigger chat tomorrow, including her family and Gabby and Marie, Dani hung up and considered how to broach the subject. Should she open with some kind of pleasantry? Thank Max again for *The Nutcracker*? Nah, too deferential. Wish him a merry Christmas? Why bother? He hated Christmas. Better to get right to the point.

> **Dani:** Hi. It's Dani Martinez. Which app do you use for your man-whore activities?

Max: And a good day to you, too. Merry Christmas. Christ is risen, hallelujah, et cetera.

> **Dani:** Come on. I need some advice. You invited me to let you know if you could ever be of service—don't make a dirty joke here.

Max: I wouldn't dream of it.

> **Dani:** So? Which app?

Max: I don't use apps much, but I'm on Raya.

> **Dani:** Never heard of it.

Max: It's like Tinder for horrible people.

> **Dani:** Tinder for horrible people?

Max: Tinder for rich people. Same difference.

Max: Or perhaps it's more accurately described as Tinder for famous people. You have to get approved by a committee to become a member. The idea is we all have to be discreet, I suppose? Mutually assured destruction?

Dani: That is no help to me since I am neither rich nor famous.

Max: You're also not horrible.

Max: What seems to be the problem?

Dani: I want to find someone to have sex with, and I don't know how to do it.

Max: Well, Daniela, when a man and a woman love each other very much and lie in a close embrace . . .

Dani: Oh shut up.

Max: If only you'd had this problem two weeks ago, I could have been of assistance.

Dani: I said no dirty jokes. And no you couldn't.

Max: You're overthinking this. The world is full of men who will gladly have sex with you.

Dani: I know that. I mean, if Vince can get people to have sex with him, why can't I?

Max: That's the spirit. There are probably dozens of them on your block alone.

Dani: But how do I find them? How do I find one? I only need one. But I need him to be not gross.

Max: That part might be harder. Also, it's Christmas Eve.

Dani: People can't have sex on Christmas Eve?

Max: No, but aren't you supposed to be making those Mexican dessert things and packing up your cheater fruitcake and so on?

Dani: Are you trying to talk me out of getting on Tinder?

Max: Good lord, no. I would never do that.

Dani: What are you doing right now?

Max: I'm at the palace for Christmas. I was having a late lunch with my parents and brother, but I excused myself to take a very important phone call.

Dani: Okay, well, I'll let you go.

Max: Please don't. Then I'll have to go back to tortellini and torture.

She paused. If he didn't have any advice for her regarding apps suitable for commoners, why would they keep texting? She couldn't help but be curious about his use of the term *torture*, though. It didn't sound like he had the best relationship with his family. Her fingers, poised over her phone, twitched. Damn it, she was going to do it.

Dani: Lunch with just your family?

Max: Yes. We spend Christmas at the palace, but my father always insists on a family Christmas Eve lunch, and they give us a private room. Which I very much do not want to return to.

Dani: Okay, tell me about one time you used your rich-person app successfully. Maybe I can translate your technique into a proletariat app.

Her phone rang. He was calling her. She shouldn't have gone along with the chatty texting-for-no-reason thing. "Hello?"

"I would never tell you not to get on Tinder or any other app, but please be careful."

His voice was a shock, which made no sense. She had heard a great deal of it not two weeks ago. But over the phone it felt more intimate somehow, which also made no sense. There was an ocean between them. "What do you mean?"

"Do all the things you're supposed to do. Tell someone where you are and send them the man's name and photo. Meet in public—all those precautions."

"That seems like a lot of work in order to have sex."

"Just text someone the details. Text me the details."

"Text you, halfway across the world when it's the middle of the night your time, the details about the hookup I'm about to have?"

"Yes. I don't sleep that much anyway, and I'm profoundly non-judgmental. Send me his picture and the address where you are and check in when you're done. I promise I won't be a jerk about it."

She didn't know what to say to that. She understood the logic behind what he was suggesting, but something about sending all that stuff to *Max* felt weird.

When the silence between them started to stretch out a tad too much, he said, "Or, you know there *is* another option."

She snorted. "Let me take a wild guess. You, in the spirit of charity, are prepared to fly across the ocean and help me out with this."

"Well, don't sell yourself short; I would hardly call it *charity*."

She laughed. It was actually tempting. Or it would be if he was here. And not her best friend's fiancée's best friend.

He laughed, too. Because of course he had been joking. "When are you going to your parents' house? How do you get there? How is the fruitcake?"

"That's a lot of questions. Let's see." She looked at her watch. "I'll leave in about three hours. It's not as long a journey as you might think. I take a bus to a station in Queens where I catch the Long Island Railroad, and my dad picks me up on the other end. And the fruitcake seems fine to *me*—I've been dousing it in extra booze—but my mom will be able to tell."

"I have a feeling you might be able to fool her."

"Your feeling is incorrect."

"Truly. When she and I were speaking after the ballet, we were talking about how I don't like Christmas. She wasn't having it. She was listing all the things there are to love about Christmas, and one of them was fruitcake. I said, oh yes, I'd seen yours, that you'd been so hard at work on it for weeks."

"You told my mother you'd seen my fruitcake?"

"What's wrong with that? Is that an American idiom for something untoward?"

She laughed. "No. I'm just thinking about how my mom is going to get on my case about you knowing such intimate details about my life."

"Intimate details about your fruitcake? Are you *sure* that isn't American slang of some sort?"

She couldn't help but laugh again. "You know what I mean. Vince left a year and a half ago, and she's so angry at him. She wants me to move on. Well, she'd probably prefer if I actually got divorced first, but that's taking long enough that I think she's over it."

"Why *is* that taking so long?"

"We're fighting about Max."

"Well, I *have* been called a homewrecker on more than one occasion."

"Ha-ha. Technically, Max belongs to Vince. We decided to get a dog when we moved in together. I had to talk Vince into him. He wanted a more 'masculine' breed than a Yorkie. But ultimately Vince paid, and it's his name on the adoption paperwork. In New York State, pets are treated like personal property in a divorce—

they go to the spouse who 'owns' them. But I'm the one who did everything. Every walk, every stoop-and-scoop, every vet appointment. He's *my* dog."

"Let me guess. Vince suddenly wants him."

"Yep. Never paid any attention to him, but whenever we were in with the mediator, he'd be all, 'Oh how I miss him.' We were actually supposed to have joint custody while we were in mediation—before Vince's sabbatical started, back when he was still in town—but I refused to hand him over."

"And Vince didn't make an issue of that?"

"Oddly, no. I don't think he actually cares about the dog. Well, I *know* he doesn't. But it's like Max was his wedge to hold up the divorce. And now we're supposed to be continuing with mediation while he's in Spain—we're supposed to be doing it virtually. But he's always missing the appointments or canceling them at the last minute. It doesn't make any sense. *He* left *me*. Shouldn't he *want* the divorce?"

"One would think. What must Oakland think?"

She smiled. "I feel bad for Berkeley. None of this is her fault."

"Even if that's the case, I commend you on taking such a charitable view."

"Professors are not supposed to romance students. It's a massive abuse of power."

"I wondered about that."

"There was a whole investigation. They both insist they didn't get together until after she dropped out, which may even be true. She doesn't come from money, and I gather she was having trouble financially. But even if they didn't technically break any rules, it's still gross. She's a kid. Vince can be very compelling when he wants to, making you feel like you're the center of his world. I should get the divorce done, for Berkeley's sake, if not for Vince's. If it was anything else—money, say—I would roll over."

"*Dani*. You cannot give that man your dog."

"Right?" His vehement agreement was gratifying, but she realized that here they were talking about her again. Max had a way of doing that. "What about you? Is lunch really that bad? What's the problem? Too much family togetherness?"

"Christmas seems to put my parents, my father especially, into a mode where he's taking stock. Of the family holdings, the state of the dukedom, the matrimonial future of his children. I never fare well in these accountings."

"Because Marie jilted you? How old are you, anyway?"

"Yes, among other things. And I'm twenty-eight."

"That's too young to get married! Take it from an expert. From the ripe old age of thirty-two, I can say with authority that twenty-eight is *not* old."

"It is when you're in line to inherit a dukedom and everything you do is—"

"What?"

"Nothing. I should get back."

"Tell me what you were going to say." When he still didn't speak, she added, "Come on. *I've* told *you* all the gory details of my humiliation at Vince's hands."

"I was going to say 'wrong.'" His voice had gone quiet, shed of its usual bon vivant qualities. "When everything you do is wrong."

Dani was glad, suddenly, that their texting had escalated to a phone call. While she considered what to say, she heard someone else through Max's phone. "It's Christmas Eve, darling." It was a feminine voice, so it must have been his mother. The way she said *darling* was interesting. Somehow, she made it sound like the opposite of an endearment. "What can possibly be so important?"

"I'll be right there, Mother."

"Max, I—" Dani didn't know what to say. When he'd talked about wanting to avoid his family, she'd classified that as the usual family junk. Or not even that. She'd thought of it as rich-person problems. "Have a negroni with lunch?" she finally finished weakly.

"I don't drink around my family."

"Oh, of course." Why was she saying *Of course*? As if she knew anything about his family other than the handful of vague statements he'd made about them? She was starting to wonder if Max's gentlemanly attentiveness *wasn't* attentiveness per se so much as deflection.

"You weren't humiliated at Vince's hands, Dani."

"What?"

"You said you'd been humiliated at Vince's hands."

Right. Case in point. She'd been trying to figure out the dynamic between him and his mother, and he was turning the conversation back to her.

"That is incorrect," he went on. "He's the one making a fool of himself." He was still using the quiet, restrained voice from before. Together with the odd intimacy of the transatlantic phone call, it made what he was saying sound extra true, somehow. "And everyone knows it."

She wondered if it was possible for both things about Max to be true: Could he be deflecting attention from himself *and* genuinely interested in her life? Regardless, she wasn't sure how he could say that everyone knew. Max wasn't part of her real life. He didn't know the relevant "everyone." But the quiet certainty with which he'd delivered his pronouncement was gratifying. So she just said, "Thanks."

"I have to go. Merry Christmas, Dani."

She smiled. "Merry Christmas, Max."

WHEN MAX GOT back to lunch, Father was on his fourth martini. Max wasn't sure why he was counting. He was in the habit, he supposed. It was something he'd started doing as a boy, as soon as he'd made the connection that the number of drinks consumed was directly proportional to the intensity of the anger his father would later display. Four was not a lot, in and of itself, but four before lunch was the start of a journey that wouldn't end well. The familiar stirrings of anxiety started rumbling in Max's gut, followed by the equally familiar stirrings of self-loathing. He was no longer a child. He didn't live under the same roof as his parents anymore and was fully capable of retreating to his cottage whenever he wanted. Even here at the palace, he could get up and leave and go somewhere else. They couldn't *actually* control him.

So why was he acting like they could?

Why was he sending Marie an SOS text? Why did he need Marie to rescue him when he had two perfectly good legs?

"We were just talking about Sebastien's little garden project," Father said tersely. Most people would be slurring after four martinis. But Father always did the reverse as he drank, at least up until a certain point. His speech became more precise, clipped.

"Oh?" Max glanced at his brother. He had no idea what his "little garden project" was, but Sebastien was forever brimming with outlandish ideas. He'd always been like that. Had never seen the potential problem with staging tea parties for his stuffed animals or putting on plays—like the March sisters did in *Little Women*—right out in the open where Father could wander in at any moment.

"It's more of a mining reclamation project than it is a gardening project," Seb said. "But why don't we discuss it later? It's Christmas!"

Typical Seb, avoiding conflict, smoothing things over. When would he learn that trying to please Father was a thankless task? Seb was certainly better at it than Max, but to what end? It didn't actually *change* anything. Max tried to remind himself, though, that this was his doing as much as anything. Seb hadn't been around—by design—for so many years. Perhaps he truly didn't grasp the dynamics at work.

"On the contrary," Father said. "Christmas is the ideal time to discuss it. So rarely are we all in the same place." He looked at Max as he spoke, and they all knew he was referring to how much Max traveled. But the implied criticism hardly made a dent. Max had built up tolerance, like Father and his martinis. It would take a great deal more than that to hurt him.

"How was your New York trip, darling?" Mother said. She was trying to change the subject, but she'd made a tactical error with her choice of topic. Why could no one except him seem to understand Father's triggers?

"Yes, how was New York?" his father echoed, infusing the question with a sneer. "How was the party?"

Here they went. Max wasn't sure why Father was so annoyed,

given that he'd been pleased about Max's attendance at Lucrecia's party, but they were certain to find out.

"What party?" Sebastien asked.

"I spoke to Ludwig von Bachenheim yesterday," Father said. "He tells me that Lavinia reports you and she barely spoke."

"We did speak!" Max winced internally. That had come out too indignantly. Max very much wanted not to be the kind of person whose father had conversations with other old men about what he did or did not do, but that was beyond his control. All he could control was how he reacted. "Lavinia and I had a chat about a Broadway show she'd been to see." Their conversation *had* been brief, though, and Lavinia hadn't seemed very interested. He wouldn't be surprised if he hadn't made a lasting impression.

"Who is Lavinia?" Seb asked, and Max wanted to scream. As bad as his father's heavy-handed meddling was, at this moment, Seb was almost getting to him more. His naive questioning. His naive *everything*. And in this case his innocent question was going to set off a whole chain of "discussion." It wasn't that Max expected Seb, a twenty-five-year-old younger son of a duke who had lived a sheltered life, to have street smarts. After all, Max had made sure Seb had led a sheltered life. But could he pay a little attention? Could he have the tiniest bit of instinct with regard to cause and effect?

"Lavinia is Lucrecia von Bachenheim's sister," Max said brusquely, irrationally hoping that would be the end of it.

"I didn't know she had a sister," Seb said, and Max wanted to throttle him.

"She's the younger," Mother said. "She's at Yale."

"Because you know our Max," Father drawled. "He can't be content with just any girl. She must be a genius to be worthy of him."

"What does *that* mean?" Max snapped. Lavinia had been his parents' idea. But that was Father for you. Four martinis in and he could twist anything, including reality, to suit his seemingly ever-present desire to pick on someone.

But Max didn't have to take the bait. He pushed back from the table. "If you'll excuse me."

"Sit," his father snapped.

"Max," Mother said in a tone she probably intended to be soothing but had the opposite effect. "We haven't had dessert yet."

"We have an entire afternoon of cocoa ahead of us." And martinis.

Father shoved back from the table, knocking his water glass over in the process, and one look at his face made Max wonder if he had miscounted. Father didn't usually get this degree of angry until he was well past four.

"Hello, hello!" Marie, god bless her, stuck her head into the room. She met Max's gaze briefly but didn't give anything away as she swept her attention over the rest of his family, assessing in her efficient Marie way. "I hope I'm not interrupting. I was about to take a preliminary walk around Cocoa Fest. Leo and Gabby are busy, and I was hoping to drum up some company."

She smiled brightly, and Max stifled a sigh. He was grateful for the rescue, and he'd much rather be strolling the palace grounds with Marie than lunching with his family, but he couldn't help thinking that what he really wanted was to click his heels three times and be back in New York.

Chapter Six

Max: How's the sex quest going?

Max: Any big New Year's Eve plans?

Max: How's my namesake?

*D*ani looked up from her computer, startled as a series of texts from Max arrived. She hadn't heard from him since Christmas Eve, and she had initiated that contact.

Dani: The sex quest has gone nowhere.

She had done some research on different apps, but the idea of all the getting-to-know-you chatting that would be required was turning out to be more uncomfortable than she'd expected. But that was stupid. If she couldn't make herself talk to a stranger through a phone, how well did that bode for her ability to get it on with a stranger?

Dani: No New Year's plans. I'm working, and I might watch a movie later. Living the high life here.

Dani: Dog Max—still not your namesake because as discussed, I had him long before I met you—is sick.

She was about to add that Dog Max would be fine when a voice call came in from Human Max. Were they going to be talking-on-the-phone friends now? It wasn't lost on her that this was the thing she was having trouble imagining herself doing with potential hookups. "Hello?"

"What's wrong with my namesake?"

She smiled at the lack of greeting. Unlike her imaginary app-dude conversations, things weren't awkward with Max because somehow they had skipped over the polite-pleasantries stage of most relationships. "He's not your namesake, but he has an ear infection. He started antibiotics today, and he has to wear one of those cone things so he doesn't scratch his ears."

"Aww." Human Max made a noise that was part sympathetic, part amused. "So you can't leave him alone? That's too bad."

She thought about agreeing. *Yes, I am so devoted to my dog I canceled my New Year's Eve plans to tend to him.* She looked over to where Dog Max was snort-snoring. "I could leave him alone—he's fine. Honestly, he's my excuse. The truth is, I'm committed to staying home in my pajamas and watching cheesy Christmas movies."

She almost told him the rest, which was that she was sitting and staring at her computer, thinking about writing something.

Something different from usual. And that it was his doing. His wild story about Karina Klein had ignited—reignited—the idea. But it was only a formless blob in her mind. It would probably go nowhere.

And she couldn't shake the memory of last time she'd told someone about this idea. It had not gone well.

She rose from her desk and made her way to the couch to stretch out—she'd been hunched over for too long. "Where are you?" There was background noise on his end. "Are you at a party?"

"Paris, and I am. Or I was."

"What do you mean *was*?"

"I am at a party, I suppose, but I came outside to get some air."

"So what am I hearing?"

"I'm on a terrace, and the doors to the main room are open because it's hot in there. There's a band as well as a more generalized din."

"What kind of party is it? Minor European royalty? Are you still wife-scouting?"

"Ha-ha. I wasn't wife-scouting in New York, nor am I this evening. A friend of mine was having a New Year's Eve party, and I wanted to . . . Well, frankly, I wanted to escape my family, so I jetted over."

"Ah, took the private jet to the party in Paris." She was teasing, because she didn't quite know what to make of the baron who wanted to escape his family so he "jetted over" to Paris.

"I'll have you know I flew commercial. I always fly commercial."

"You flew commercial when you came here?"

"I did."

"Huh."

"That doesn't conform to your image of me as a profligate wastrel?"

Tabloids aside, Max cultivated a certain image of a carefree-bordering-on-careless playboy. That person would charter a private jet. But as Dani had just been thinking, it didn't seem like he *was* that person. But why pretend to be a less good person than you actually were? "Why did you want to escape your family?" He had dodged that question when they'd spoken on Christmas Eve.

"Why does anyone want to escape their families?"

By which she supposed he meant it was a long story, but she wasn't sure she wanted to accept the deflection. She genuinely wanted to solve the puzzle that was Human Max. "I don't know. Why do *you*?"

He let a few beats of silence elapse, but they weren't uncomfortable beats, before saying, "Because my father is an asshole, my mother is complicit, and my brother is an idiot."

That didn't actually tell her anything, and she was gearing up to press him on the matter when the background noise on his end swelled. She pulled her phone away from her ear to check the time. "It's ten minutes to midnight there, isn't it? You have to get off the phone."

"No, I don't."

"You're going to miss New Year's!"

"I'm reasonably certain that's not true. Unless you have some kind of uncanny foreknowledge that I'm going to fall off this terrace and perish in the next ten minutes, I will, in fact, live to see the new year."

"But you should go inside and spend New Year's—"

"I'm spending New Year's exactly where I want to," he said with a quiet certainty.

She wasn't sure what to say to that pronouncement, and she was even less sure she should be as flattered by it as she was, so she just asked, "Any resolutions?" There was a long pause, so she added, "I'll tell you mine. *Get divorced.*" She'd meant to speak breezily, but her resolution had come out way too zealously. She felt a little sheepish, like she'd exposed more of herself than she'd intended to. She tried to lighten things up. "Also, related: I need to get going on one of the apps. I keep thinking about it, but I never actually do it. So I guess my resolutions are *get divorced* and *have sex*. Probably not in that order, alas."

She expected Max to have an opinion about her second resolution, to jokingly offer up his services, but he said, suddenly, quickly, in a rush of words, "I think I want to try to get a job this year."

"Pardon me?"

"Never mind."

Maybe Max had inadvertently exposed more of himself than he'd intended, too? But too bad. She wasn't letting that nugget go unexamined. "No. Tell me."

"I've been flitting around since I finished grad school. But that was eight months ago. I have no purpose."

"I thought your purpose was to be a man-whore." As soon as it was out of her mouth, she knew it was the wrong thing to say. She and Max had spent much of their limited acquaintance bantering, but he was being uncharacteristically serious now—or trying to.

"Right," he said.

"No, I'm sorry. That was uncalled for. What kind of job are you thinking of?"

He was silent for a long moment, and she feared her flippancy had shut him down, but he finally said, "My family has a mining company. My father's always after me to take a more active role."

"Why have you never told me any of this?"

Although, why should he have? Even though it felt like they were old friends, they'd only just gotten to know each other. And hadn't she noticed several times how good he was at *not* talking about himself?

"Because it's boring," he said in breezy way that made her suspect he was deflecting.

"What do you mine?"

"Copper and quartz, mostly."

"Huh."

"The one thing about marrying Marie that I was actually looking forward to was helping her with her refugee policy agenda. We'd even talked at one point about starting a foundation."

"Is there not one already?"

"There is not."

"Hmm. I always think of the royals as doing good works."

"The royal family is actually in dire financial straits. Their family company, Morneau, makes luxury watches, and the market for those has been declining for a while."

"Leo has told me some of this."

"My family, on the other hand, is obscenely rich, and when I inherit the dukedom, that will be my 'job.'" He sighed.

"You don't sound thrilled."

"I am not thrilled. I am, in fact, deeply *un*thrilled. But the point is I don't need to work. I just need to bide my time until my destiny comes crashing down on me."

"There are reasons to work besides money."

"Right," he said decisively, as if she'd answered a test question correctly. "What are those reasons?"

"You said it yourself a minute ago. To have a purpose. For some people it might be doing something they believe does some good in the world."

"But if I don't want to work for Aquilla Mining, which for the record does not do any good in the world, what do I do? I don't have any actual skills."

"I don't think that's true." She thought back to his Karina Klein story, both the real one and their silly made-up sequel. "You can tell a good story. You can talk anyone into anything."

"That's true. I'm not sure how to put that on a résumé."

"Don't you have friends who can get you some kind of rich-person job? Seats on boards?"

"Probably."

He didn't sound enthused. Maybe he wanted to do something under his own steam. "Well, you don't have to figure it all out right now." An idea popped into her head. She paused, letting it settle in her mind. Did she really want to propose this? Doing so would bind them together—if they took it seriously. It would make them into real friends, not just people who'd gone to the ballet and talked on the phone a couple of times.

It only took her a second to conclude that she liked the idea. "Let's make a pact. By this time a year from now, we'll be up one job and down one husband."

He chuckled. "How are you going to do that? What about the custody standoff regarding my namesake?"

"He's not your namesake. But I think I need a lawyer. Vince and I have been 'amicable' so far—can you hear the extreme scare quotes there?—meaning we're using a mediator. Or not using her, because Vince keeps flaking on meetings. But you know what? Mediation was Vince's idea. 'We can act like grown-ups,' he said. 'We don't need lawyers.' I went for it because at the time, a mediator sounded great. After Vince left, I realized that he never listened to me. Which is a weird thing to realize ex post facto, but it's true. He would listen, like, superficially, but whenever I said anything real—expressed a preference or tried to talk about a problem—it went in one ear and out the other."

Max gave a gratifying sniff of disapproval.

"But I've decided that mediation is bullshit," she went on. "One more way Vince is trying to control everything. I want to get divorced, and I don't want to give Vince my dog, and I don't think my waiting game is working. It's time to lawyer up."

"Good for you. Good for Dog Max. Aka my namesake."

"He's not your namesake," she said again, but laughingly, and only because that was her line.

"We need new names."

"I'm not giving my dog a new name because I happened to meet you!"

"Not new names, per se. More like nicknames. Name qualifiers."

"I do sort of think of you as Human Max and Dog Max."

"But that's so literal. There's so much else you can use to distinguish us."

"Like what? Royal Max and Common Max?"

"No! I was thinking more about physical attributes."

"I'm not sure Big Max and Little Max is any better than Human Max and Dog Max."

"Daniela," he said with performative censure in his voice. "Size isn't everything. I thought smart women such as yourself were supposed to know that."

She snorted. He was funny when he played his rake card. And his humor came with a big dose of self-deprecation. She hadn't understood that about him when they met last summer.

She wondered if a lot of people didn't understand that about him.

"I was thinking about my golden locks compared to his mangy gray, but— Oh, I have it. Max Minimus and, wait for it . . . Max Maximus! Thank you very much, ladies and gentlemen, I'm here all evening."

That was actually hilarious. "I thought size wasn't everything," she deadpanned.

"Yes, but this isn't size in a crass sense. This is a *classy* way of saying it. And you know me and Max Minimus. We are nothing if not classy."

As he spoke, the background noise swelled. She could hear the countdown starting. "Ten, nine, eight . . ."

"Are you sure you don't want to go back inside?"

"Yes."

Neither of them spoke while the rest of the countdown happened. What a year it had been. Although Vince had left the summer of the previous year, this had been the year she really *absorbed* his absence. The first full calendar year she'd spent alone.

Except not alone. She'd had Leo for some of it, and of course she had her parents. She had people she could count on. Including, it was starting to feel like, her *friend* the baron. Max Maximus.

"Three, two, one . . ." The cheers of the crowd swelled. She could hear happy mayhem getting louder.

"Happy New Year, Dani."

"Happy New Year, Max."

SIX HOURS LATER, Max was lying in bed in his hotel room not sleeping. After hanging up with Dani, he'd gone back into the party, trying to make sense of his astonishing outburst that he wanted to get a job. He *had* been thinking about the concept of meaningful employment, but in a back-burner way. When Sebastien got rolling on Aquilla Mining's latest corporate social responsibility report, or when Marie talked about her UN work—or hell, when Leo was out working on a log cabin—it made Max wish he had a calling. Max had a certain reputation as a carefree playboy. Even though the "Depraved Duke" episode that cemented it had been misconstrued, he didn't mind the reputation. Hell, he leaned into it. It wasn't untrue in a general sense. He did enjoy female company, and he didn't see the need to apologize for that. Women were fantastic.

He glanced at the figure under the duvet next to him. Carefully, so as not to wake her, he slid out of bed, grabbed his phone, and went to the bathroom.

Carefree. His slumbering companion had used that very word when she hit on him. She was an artist, and after a flirtatious exchange, she'd invited him back to her flat so she could "paint" him—and they both knew what she meant by that. She'd wanted to capture his "carefree masculine beauty," she'd said.

Max didn't consider himself carefree, but he had worked hard to become the kind of person who wasn't injured by his father's little cruelties—or by his big ones—or by the fact that he'd sacrificed so much for Sebastien apparently to no avail. He could see how that might be interpreted from the outside as carefree. And he truly didn't care what people thought of him, so in that sense perhaps he *was* carefree.

But what his reputation never seemed to account for were his two degrees from Oxford. And though he hadn't gone to boarding school like Seb, the tutor his parents had retained—the tutor Max himself had found once it became clear that he wouldn't be able to go away to school—had been a strict though not unkind taskmaster. The point was, for the vast majority of his life, Max had been a student, and a good, if rather disorganized, one at that. So the past several months, with literally nothing he had to do, had been odd. After the stress of finishing his thesis and moving home, as well as the broken engagement, it had, for a while, been pleasant enough to drift around without any responsibilities. But eventually it started to feel uncomfortable, like wearing a suit that didn't fit properly.

The problem was, he had no idea what the hell he could do. Dani was correct in that he could probably get some kind of bullshit ceremonial gig or collect a few seats on boards. But he wanted to do something real. It didn't have to be capital-I important like Marie's work. He didn't have her save-the-world personality. It merely had to mean something to someone, and to him.

But what was really puzzling him wasn't the content of his astonishing outburst so much as the fact of it. All of these thoughts had been rolling around in his head for a while, but they weren't something he'd ever imagined saying out loud.

Dani was just so easy to talk to. He *liked* her so much. She listened to what he said and said smart, clear-eyed things back, and she did not run those things through an "I am talking to a member of the aristocracy" filter. Hell, half the time he thought she listened not only to what he said but to what he *meant*.

He wanted to talk to her pretty much all the time. So, never one to deny himself something he wanted when it cost nothing to get it, he picked up the phone to check the time: 5:55. Perfect. She would still be up, wouldn't she, even if she wasn't going out?

"Max?" she said when she picked up. "Is everything all right?"

"Yes, yes; I just thought I'd wish you a happy new year your time."

"Isn't it the crack of dawn there?"

"Couldn't sleep." As per usual. "I hope I didn't wake you. I should have texted first."

"Oh, no, I was up. Why are you whispering? And what's that noise in the background? It sounds like you're on a bus."

"Ah, no. I'm in a bathroom. That's a fan. I'm . . ." *About to get caught.* Although, no. You had to be doing something wrong to get caught.

"Oh my god! Do you have a woman there?" She was exclaiming, but in a whisper, as if she, too, needed to keep her voice down.

"She wanted to paint me," he said—as if he needed an excuse? "She's an artist."

There was a long pause, and Max started to fear he'd misstepped.

"So did she paint you?" Dani finally asked. "Was it any good?"

"Well, she drew me. We're at my hotel, so she had to settle for a pen and hotel stationery."

"Does she have a studio? Why didn't you go there?"

Max hadn't thought this through. Dani was the kind of person who noticed details. Details like whispering and background noise. And now they were going to have to talk about this.

He wasn't sure why he was so reluctant. He'd called her because he'd been thinking how much he liked talking to her. This was as good a topic as any. "She suggested her studio, but I counterproposed my hotel. When I'm entertaining, I have certain guidelines for myself."

"Like a list?" she said with a degree of excitement that perplexed him. He suddenly remembered her talking, when they were out for negronis, about how she should have put something on a list.

"I suppose it is a list of sorts. A mental one. I think of them more as rules of engagement."

"So what are these 'rules'?"

"One of them is to be, the, ah, host. Rather than the guest."

"Why?"

"Because one never knows, when one departs from unfamiliar environs, what one is going to encounter."

"What is one going to encounter?"

"Paparazzi, potentially. In Europe. That wouldn't be a problem for me in America," he rushed to add, but why? It wasn't as if she was ever going to "host" him at her place.

"What other rules do you have?"

"Must we keep talking about this?"

"Yes. It's good for me to hear. Not that I need to worry about paparazzi, but I could definitely use a lesson in the ethics of hooking up."

"I wish you would stop calling it 'hooking up,' Daniela."

"What should I call it? Making love? Ha!" She laughed, as if the idea was the most absurd thing she'd ever heard.

"All right, but for the record, I don't think you should be entertaining men at your apartment."

"Double standard much?"

"Yes, and I'm sorry about it, but it's the way of the world. You don't want to end up with a creep who knows where you live."

"Point taken."

"All right, well, there are really only three other things. First, I want anyone I spend time with in that manner to be unattached. Not that I'm the morality police, but things have gotten ugly once or twice when I didn't realize that my companion was otherwise committed." He snorted. "In fact, I developed that rule at the same time I developed the one about not going to other people's houses. Or boats."

She laughed. She had a low, melodic laugh. "This is the Depraved Duke origin story, isn't it?"

"Daniela, have you been googling me again?" He was actually strangely, sharply pleased by the idea.

"Come on. If you were a commoner who suddenly found yourself friends with European nobility, you would be doing some googling, too."

He was also strangely, sharply pleased that she had called him her friend.

"You, my friend"—he said it back because it was such a satisfying word—"Are anything but common. You are also about to hear a story nobody else knows."

"Ooh. Hit me."

"The so-called Depraved Duke incident was not what everyone thinks. It started when I met a woman at the Cannes Film Festival. She invited me to her yacht, and I accepted readily. Who doesn't want to spend a day on a yacht in the French Mediterranean with a lovely, creative woman? She was a playwright."

"You have a thing for artists."

"I beg your pardon?"

"The painter in the other room?"

"Ah." He considered her theory. "It's more that I find people who make things interesting, especially things that make other people think, like plays or art or books."

"But most people who make things like that are poor. I'm surprised a playwright can afford a yacht."

"Ah, see. That is why you are going to do well when you decide to pull the trigger on your sex app. You're smarter than I am. It turned out the playwright could not afford a yacht. Her hedge-fund-manager husband, who fancied himself a film producer, *could*."

"Ah. You didn't know she was married."

"I did not. I assumed. Which I no longer do."

"So, what? You make them sign an affidavit?"

"No. I merely ascertain their status and communicate that I am only interested in a singular encounter—that's the next rule. I want to make sure they know what they're getting."

"They're getting it once?"

"Well, perhaps not strictly once. I am very good at it, remember." She snorted, and he laughed. "My point is more that I don't want anyone thinking they can catch the baron. I don't want to encourage husband-hunting fantasies."

"Which is ironic because you are a baron in need of a wife."

"Do you want to hear this story or not?"

"I do. I definitely do."

"All right. We're on the boat. I assume we are alone. Because it's a boat. At sea. Suddenly, though, we hear the sound of a motor, and it's growing louder. The playwright begins to panic. It's her husband, she says, approaching on a speedboat. No sooner has she said this than we can hear him boarding. Unfortunately for me, we are poolside, we are naked, and our clothing is below deck. There is, however, a discarded article of clothing near the pool that I only later learned was called a 'onesie.' The playwright, it turns out, has a teenage son who is accomplished at video games and plays them on some kind of online gaming platform while people spectate. He does so wearing these 'onesies.' So what do I do?"

"You put on the onesie. Oh my god."

"Indeed. And it gets worse. The playwright stops the frenzied panicking she's been doing and starts chanting, 'He's going to kill me,' over and over, such that I start to worry that perhaps she's being literal. So I jump overboard."

"No!"

"Yes! I don't want to be responsible for anyone's death." He'd been trying to make his tale entertaining, but he sobered, remembering his panic when he started to fear that the husband was going to become violent. "We weren't that far from the shore, so it wasn't as dramatic as it sounds. So, to return to the narrative, over the edge I go. I swim to the shore, and I walk to my hotel."

"In a onesie," she said through laughter.

"Just so."

"I wonder why there aren't more pictures."

"That is entirely thanks to Mr. Benz, the king's equerry. Did you meet him last summer?"

"I did. He seems very . . . thorough."

"Yes, he's ex-military. I called Marie after I made it back to the hotel, and she put him on the case. He has mob boss–style abilities to make problems go away. There *should* have been more photos. There should have been close-ups showing that the onesie was, in fact, printed with tiny unicorns."

She burst out laughing, and he was genuinely glad his pathetic story was making her laugh. It almost made it worth it.

"Why was there the one photo from the boat to begin with? Did the husband take it?"

"I have no idea. There was a staff member captaining the boat, but the playwright assured me he would be discreet."

"Well, that was a mistake."

"It certainly was." Hence the development of his rules of engagement. "The larger point of my tale of woe is that the 'Depraved Duke' sobriquet is incorrect. The . . . proceedings themselves were rather mundane, all told. The more accurate phrase would be 'Idiotic Duke.' Or 'Dumb Duke,' if we want to preserve the alliterative qualities of the moniker."

"But you're not a duke."

"Not yet, thank god."

"What's the last item on the list?"

"Hmm?"

"You said you had three other rules in addition to always wanting to hook up on your turf. You said no married women. And
no repeat performances so as not to encourage anyone to get any
ideas about marriage. But there's one more, I think?"

"Ah. Yes. No lying."

"Why would anyone be lying?"

"Well, I can't speak for anyone else, but for me it means not
telling anyone what they want to hear merely because it might be
convenient."

"Huh."

"What does that mean? Are you against honesty?"

"No! I admire it. You're very honest. Relentlessly honest, I
might even say."

He didn't know what to say to that.

"So no false declarations of love is what you're saying."

"That is what I'm saying."

"How come you can't sleep?" she asked suddenly. "Too much to
drink whilst picking up beautiful artists?"

He had not said the artist was beautiful, but he didn't correct
her. "No. I know this is probably difficult to believe given my
enthusiasm for negronis the other night, but I don't drink much."

He wanted her to ask him why.

"Why not?"

"My father is a drunk of the worst sort."

Saying that felt like a lot. He'd *wanted* to say it, but once it
was out, he found he didn't want to elaborate beyond the topic-
sentence version of the mess that was life with his parents. But

he was finding this exercise in truth-telling strangely exhilarating, so he told her another one—a different one. "I couldn't sleep because I was ruminating about my job situation."

"This may be a stupid question, but if being a duke is a job, why isn't being a baron? In historical novels, aristocrats are always, like, overseeing the manor or visiting sick tenants or something."

"My title is a courtesy title, meaning it's a meaningless title given to the sons of aristocrats."

"You people are so weird."

"You're not wrong."

"So being Baron of Aquilla can't be made into a job?"

"The title is actually Baron of Laudon. The duchy is Aquilla; the barony is Laudon." He thought about her question. "I don't think it can be made into a job. Unlike with the duchy, there are no lands or holdings associated with it."

"What does your brother do? Is he also a lie-about?"

"No, he works for the mining company."

"For real? Or is he just on the books?"

"He's legitimately employed there. We have a non-family CEO, but my brother is the executive vice-chairman and chief science officer, and he sits on the board."

"Wow, a genuine passion for mining."

"It would seem so." Though to hear Sebastien and Father over the holidays, it sounded as though Seb's passions lay more in this "garden project." Max had no idea what that meant. He probably hadn't been paying attention at some point. He couldn't give a damn about Father, but he didn't used to be the kind of person who ignored his brother.

"Okay, how about this?" Dani said. "Let's make a plan to each do one small thing toward our resolutions this week. First week of the new year—baby steps toward divorce and job."

He could get behind this. But the phrase *new year* made him remember his point in calling her. He pulled his phone from his ear momentarily to check the time. It was quarter past six. "Oh, damn it."

"What's wrong?"

"I got distracted by my 'woe is me' routine. And by telling the true story of the Depraved Duke. I was going to make you do a countdown."

"Eh, it's fine."

"All right, well, this is our year, then?"

"Yes. The year of divorces and jobs," she said through a chuckle. "Doesn't sound that glamorous when you put it like that."

"It's going to be good." For the first time in a long time, he believed it—that the future was going to be good.

She yawned. "I'm gonna go to bed."

He felt like he could probably sleep now. He wished he could get the artist out of his room, but he could hardly wake her and ask her to leave. Perhaps he would go sleep on the sofa. "Happy New Year, Dani."

"Happy New Year, Max."

Chapter Seven

$\mathscr{W}$hen he got back to Riems, Max invited Sebastien to the cottage for lunch.

"What's wrong?" Seb said after they tucked into slices of tomato-leek galette.

"Why does something have to be wrong?"

"You've never invited me here for a meal before. So either there's something wrong or you want something from me. And usually when you want something from me, you text. I'm left to conclude that something is wrong."

Well, that stung. But Max could not deny any of it. He hadn't *intended* it, but that hardly mattered. He studied his brother. They had been close as children, conspiring to run wild on the mountain any time they could escape the schoolroom—and Father. It had been easier to dodge Father in the early years. Father ascribed to the philosophy that children should be neither seen *nor* heard, so apart from dinner every evening, the boys had rarely crossed paths with him. When they weren't doing lessons, they'd been free to play "two-man up-mountain footie," which football-crazed Max had invented, and the pretend games Seb preferred without parental interference.

It wasn't until they got a little older that Father started taking an interest. And by "taking an interest," Max meant destroying toys of Seb's he deemed too feminine. Or seizing an apple strudel Seb had helped the cook make and hurling it against the wall in the dining room.

And then Max had refused to go to boarding school. What a row that had been. In addition to guaranteeing his presence at home, that blowout had taught him the efficacy of diversionary tactics. Being a bigger disappointment than Seb was a surprisingly effective strategy for drawing his father's attention—and anger.

But somehow, that early closeness between the boys, that sense of being allies, had faded away. Max studied his brother, really looked at him, for the first time in a while. Sebastien still had the close-cropped hair and too-big nose of his youth, but gone was the easy smile that used to be his signature.

"You're right," Max said, needing to clear his throat. "I don't treat you well." It was an uncomfortable thing to admit, to confront within himself, especially given that the first ten years of Seb's life, everything Max had done had been in service of Seb. It was just so frustrating that after all Max had done to get Seb out, Seb boomeranged right back. Still, they were *brothers*. "I'm sorry. It has to stop. It's *going* to stop." Max continued to study Seb, who had the same blue eyes as Max—except Seb's had gone wide with shock. "I did ask you here because I wanted something from you. I'd like your advice if you're willing to give it."

Max wouldn't have thought it possible, but Seb's eyes grew even wider.

"I want to get a job, but I have no idea how to do that."

Seb switched to blinking rapidly, and Max chuckled. "I hoped you'd give me your thoughts, seeing as you're the gainfully employed brother."

"Well . . . ," Sebastien started slowly. "I'm certain we can find you something to do at Aquilla. It's Father's fondest wish that you join the company."

Max's jaw tightened. Here he'd thought they were having a moment. But no. Seb was still Father's lapdog. If Max had been the type to allow himself to be disappointed by people, he would have felt sadness over the fact that the boy who'd suggested they try to combine their favorite childhood games and play "footie up the mountain" and *then* pretend to be wizards at the top had come home from university and fallen right into line, asking only "how high" when Father commanded he jump.

But Max wasn't that type. You start letting people disappoint you, and you're never not disappointed. "What everyone fails to understand is I don't *want* to work in the mining company." He heard but could not seem to excise the condescension in his voice.

"I don't want to work in the mining company either, Max," Seb snapped.

What? That was the last thing Max expected his brother to say.

"But someone has to do it," Seb added, and his little-brother martyrdom irritated the hell out of Max.

"I don't want any part of it," Max said, and he didn't care if he sounded self-righteous. "It's a terrible industry."

Seb looked at him for an uncomfortably long moment before saying, in a much quieter tone, "The way I see it, if I don't do it, Father will get someone else to. If I'm doing it, at least I can try to limit the environmental damage and fight for better conditions for our employees. Did you know that last year we were set to begin winding down the Rudna mine and laying off five hundred people? Did you know that I talked the board into delaying the closing for two years and committing a pile of money to a retraining fund? Do you think any of that would have happened if I hadn't pushed for it?"

Max didn't even know where the "Rudna mine" was or what was extracted there. "I had no idea. How did you get Father to agree to that?"

"Well, I got Elias on my side, so that helped." Elias was Aquilla's CEO. "I made a presentation showing that we could employ a percentage of the retrained employees in a call center I was proposing we build," Seb said, "and that since they already knew the company there would be less turnover."

"Why didn't I know about this?" Max also had no idea why a mining company needed a call center, but that wasn't his primary concern at the moment.

"You didn't have any idea because you don't pay attention," Seb said. "You cover your ears like a child when you're confronted with something unpleasant."

Not a flattering assessment.

"And when you *do* pay attention for long enough to absorb something, it's all black and white." Seb's voice was getting louder. "Mining is bad. Well, yes. But the world needs quartz, for example. What would you do without your precious iPhone? Also, we employ a great many people. Do you know how many?"

Max did not know.

"Nine thousand and change," Seb said, not waiting for Max to answer. "And forty-seven percent of them are in areas where the mine is the major, or only, employer. We're it. We close, and what will happen then?"

Another rhetorical question that made Max ashamed he didn't know how to answer.

Seb sighed, and his tone gentled. "All I'm trying to do is make our impact—on the planet, on the communities we operate in—less bad."

Max did not know what to say. After several uncomfortably long moments of silence, he went with the truth. "I'm sorry I never knew all this." He thought of Dani calling him "relentlessly honest." He was proud that someone like her saw him that way. He was not a person who refused to see the truth when it was in front of him, who declined to take responsibility for that truth. No, that was Father.

"It's all right," Seb said, and suddenly Max wondered if Seb's perpetual agreeableness wasn't about agreeing so much as it was about self-preservation. One way to not be hurt by people was to make yourself immune to their opinions, as Max had done. But perhaps another way was to simply agree with them?

"Tell me about this garden project Father spoke of at Christmas."

"It's not a garden project. It's a mining reclamation project."

"Tell me more."

"Essentially, it's an answer to the question of what happens to mines when they're not useful anymore, when they're depleted or are no longer cost-effective to keep operating. And I hasten to add that it's not as if this is an outrageous topic. It's a standard part of the planning process for mines these days. I started thinking about the Lubin mine. It probably only has five profitable years left. We don't need another call center. What are we going to do then? Abandon it?"

"Yes?"

"But what if we didn't? What if we made it into something else? Something that kept people employed and ideally also did some good environmentally?"

"Like a charity? You could do that with an old mine?"

"Not like a charity. That's what I can't seem to make anyone see. It can be a legitimate business venture. It can make money. Not right away, but as with any new business, you invest at the beginning so it can be profitable later. And yes, you can do that with an old mine. You can do lots of things with old mines if you think creatively." Seb proceeded to spin a tale of on old clay mine in Cornwall that had been transformed into an enormous domed botanical garden. "Just because this one use—mining—has run its course doesn't mean we need to walk away."

"That's astounding." Max had underestimated his brother. Probably for years. "Could we do something with a historical angle?"

"You mean a museum? Mining history? There's no reason we couldn't do that at one of our properties."

"Not mining history per se. I've been thinking about our mines in Innsbruck, actually. What do we mine there?" He should know, but he didn't.

"Quartz."

"Ah, then never mind." It had been a wild idea anyway, to think there might be a connection.

"Never mind what?"

"Well, you know Karina Klein?"

"Of course."

"I've been doing some research on her."

"You *have*?"

Perhaps Max wasn't the only one who had been underestimating his brother. "Yes. I wanted to revisit some letters of hers I knew were at Oxford. An archivist there has been digitizing them for me." He'd started looking into it after *The Nutcracker*, when the fictional tale he'd spun of Karina's New York adventure had so delighted Dani. He'd hoped to find something about a real New York trip, to what end he wasn't sure—perhaps merely to entertain Dani. But as was so often the way with historical research, looking for one thing led to another. "I ended up reading about a mine near Innsbruck that was used by the Austrian resistance toward the end of the war. I found some letters between Karina and some of its leaders."

Seb raised his eyebrows. "Look at you, turning up new information on a national hero." The praise warmed Max. "I didn't realize there was an organized Austrian resistance."

"It was small and sometimes internally at odds, but they were arming local insurgencies in the spring of 1945, and it sounds from these letters as though they were hiding supplies and arms in an abandoned mine. I idly wondered if it had been one of ours, but clearly not if they're quartz mines. You can't hide things in open-pit mines."

"We used to have tungsten mines there!" Sebastien said excitedly, and for a moment his face looked exactly like six-year-old Seb when Max agreed to take a role in a play Seb wanted to stage. "They've long since closed, but tungsten was mined underground."

"Well, then, perhaps it's worth looking into," Max said with a casualness he did not feel. He was getting excited, both about the mystery of the historical question and about the niggling feeling that perhaps *this* could be his calling. "Would those old mines still be there? Could we find them?"

"They should be. We still own the land. Actually, Oma owned the land, so it's part of the holdings of her trust."

Their father's mother had been Austrian and had come to her marriage with their grandfather with a trove of exploitable lands. This was exactly what Max had meant when he'd told Dani that marriages in their family were often made for strategic reasons.

"Finding the mines should be straightforward," Seb said, "but how would we ever discover if one of them was used by the resistance?"

"We'd look for diaries and letters. Perhaps eventually ancestors of the people involved."

"I can put you on the payroll as a historian. Or a cultural officer or something," Seb said.

"Oh that's—"

"Father will never notice."

Was it Max's imagination, or had there been a hint of a sneer on Seb's face for a second? How extraordinary. "It may end up going nowhere, so it seems ill-advised to put me on the payroll. I don't need a salary, anyway. I just . . ."

"You want to feel useful," Seb suggested, with a sudden world-weariness in his tone that made something catch in Max's chest. Max's whole mission for the first thirteen years of Seb's life had been to arrange things so Seb never *had* to sound like that. Perhaps Max's mistake had been to assume that once Seb was safely away at school, the work was done.

"Yes. That's exactly it. Why don't we work on this project to-gether and see how it turns out? You find the mines, and I'll do some historical sleuthing. If it turns out we do own a mine with some historical significance, we can discuss further."

"All right, then." Seb smiled at him and took a big bite of his galette. "This is nice," he said through a mouthful.

Max didn't know if he was talking about the food or simply the fact that they were together. Or the understanding they seemed to have arrived at, so suddenly and so easily. Perhaps all they'd needed was an afternoon alone, away from the external forces that were constantly pressing in on them. Whatever Seb meant, Max agreed, so he smiled and said, "It *is* nice."

He felt as if he had his brother back. Or, more accurately, his brother had *him* back. And he wasn't letting him go again.

Chapter Eight

 ani's first Tinder date was a bust.

On paper, it should have worked. Her pact with Max had forced her out of her paralysis, and after a lot of swiping and messaging that went nowhere, she'd finally found one Mr. Logan Bram. Logan Bram owned an apartment, loved his two-year-old nephew, and worked as a "fitness tech engineer," which Dani hadn't realized was a job, but then again, she hadn't realized "duke" was a job, either.

Also, Logan Bram was hot, in a tanned, muscly, conventional sort of way. That was the relevant point. She just needed someone who was moderately attractive and not a serial killer. The job and the apartment and the nephew didn't matter inherently; they were merely evidence that he was not a serial killer—though she supposed serial killers could have jobs and apartments and nephews.

She had done everything she was supposed to do, was the point. She'd done the swiping and the vetting and the DM-ing and the "Is he or is he not likely to be a serial killer?" risk analysis.

"This is a lot of work in order to have sex," she said as she power-walked—she was running late—down Second Avenue to the Upper East Side brunch place Logan had suggested. It sounded like something she would say to Max. It *was* something she would say to Max—and then he would remind her that he could be on an airplane within two hours. She and Max, to her continuing surprise, had settled into a real friendship. They talked on the phone every few days, reporting in on their New Year's resolution progress and shooting the breeze about life in general.

But she wasn't talking to Max now; she was talking to Leo. She hadn't taken Max up on his offer to be the person she checked in with before and after her date. For some reason, she was perfectly comfortable joking with Max about her sex problems, including him being the solution to them, but when it came to reporting in to him about *actually* having sex . . . not so much. It felt weird. Just like when she'd talked to Max on the phone on New Year's Eve and she suddenly hadn't known what to say when it became clear he'd been entertaining a guest earlier that evening.

"Maybe you need a friend with benefits," Leo said.

She pushed thoughts of Max aside. "Maybe this guy can be that. How does one broach that subject?"

"Wait until after the deed is done. No need to sign him up for the gig until you know if he has the right qualifications, if you know what I mean."

That made sense, but she hoped Logan worked out. It had taken her so long to find him. Honestly, she'd thought the whole point of Tinder was that it was easy. Apparently if you had standards, it wasn't any easier than the real world. When she'd talked to Max about New Year's resolutions, she'd expected "get divorced" to be the hard one. But here it was the end of February and she'd had a promising initial meeting with a lawyer, but she still hadn't had sex.

She thought about Max's rule about singular encounters only. That might be smarter, if less efficient, than setting up a regular thing with someone. Less risk of anyone getting too attached. Not that she was in danger of doing that. That was why she had her list. She'd perused it on the subway, in fact. Even though she had it memorized, she liked to look at it with her own eyeballs sometimes, to see it there in black and white.

She slowed as the restaurant came into view. Logan was on the patio. He looked exactly like his photos, which was something she'd been led to believe often wasn't the case. "Oh," she said to Leo, "I am going to have fun."

She did not have fun.

It started with the fact that the restaurant was a keto place.

"Brunch with no bread!" she'd joked after ordering "pancakes" made out of cream cheese and eggs. "*Life* with no bread!" She thought about the pasta she and Max had hoovered before Christmas. "Or pasta!"

"Ketosis is no joke," Logan said after ordering a breakfast "sandwich" in which the "bread" was sausage patties, as well as an assortment of meaty side dishes. "You would not believe what can happen when your body goes into ketosis."

"Right, sorry." *Note to self: no ketosis jokes.* She wasn't completely clear on what ketosis actually was, but apparently it wasn't funny. But that was fine. Once they were done with this initial meeting, they didn't need to eat together. "So, the keto diet. That must be a lot of work."

"Not really. Once you experience the amazing effects of it, you realize that it is so, so worth it. But actually, I'm transitioning to the carnivore diet."

"What's that? Like you only eat meat?" She laughed.

"Yes."

Oh, jeez, he was serious.

"Well," he added, "eggs, too. Some people allow dairy, but I haven't had dairy for four years, so obviously I'm not about to start now."

"Obviously."

"Some people do a little kale as well."

"Meat, eggs, and kale. Wow." His breath must be really bad. "And you said you're a fitness engineer? What does that mean? I'm imagining you building treadmills, but that's probably not right."

"I work on mountain bike suspension systems, mostly."

"That sounds interesting." She wondered if people in Eldovia mountain biked.

Their food came, and silence descended. She'd hoped he might ask her some questions, to keep things from getting awkward, and to keep her from having to do all the work, but he didn't. She glanced at his bulging biceps and reminded herself that after this, it didn't matter if he was a bad conversationalist who only ate rib eyes.

"Do people mountain bike in the Alps, or is that more of a North American thing?" she asked. "I have a friend who lives in the Eldovian Alps." She couldn't see Max mountain biking. The thought of suave, icy-cool Max careening down a mountain wearing all that ugly gear amused her. She had no doubt he'd be good at it if he set his mind to it. She'd never seen him not wearing a suit, so she had no idea how his biceps would measure up to the

Carnivore's, but he had a grace and an easy physicality that probably made him good at rich-people sports.

"There's a scene over there," Logan said.

He did not elaborate, so in her quest to keep the conversation going, she asked him some more questions, which he answered cordially but briefly. Eventually she gave up. She had done more than her share, and if the Carnivore wanted silence, she was okay with that.

"So what do you like to do?" Logan said through a mouthful of bacon.

At last, a question about her. Too bad she didn't have a good answer for it. *I like to read books by nineteenth-century women writers and analyze them. But maybe not as much as I should.* Okay, no. This was not the venue for a chat about her slow-moving career crisis. She thought about telling him about her secret project, but she hadn't even told Max yet. She tried to think of something this dude would not find a total turnoff. "I'm a big fan of the beach." That was true. "My parents live on Long Island, and—"

"No. I mean, what do you like to *do*?" He waved his hand between them and raised his eyebrows.

"*Oh.*" She wasn't sure why the question was so shocking. She'd been up front about the fact that she was not looking for a relationship. In a way, she appreciated the direct approach. "Uh, well . . . I guess I like to go with the flow?"

He shrugged like that was an acceptable if not optimal answer and turned to his final side dish, which was some kind of pulled pork concoction. "Yeah, okay, I was just wondering what turned you on."

Not you.

Ugh. That was terrible. Asking her that question was more than most guys would do. In her experience before Vince, which was admittedly quite a few years ago now, men usually had to be directed fairly explicitly if she wanted to have any fun herself. So she gave Logan's question serious consideration. She'd been turned on a lot lately. In fact, the sudden return of desire to her life was what had prompted this exercise to begin with. That accidental hug with Max in Central Park had started it, but then it had . . . not gone away, like a faucet left on.

Except now. It had gone away now. Someone had turned off the tap. She just kept thinking of all that meat being shoveled into the mouth that would, if all went according to plan, soon be on her. She wasn't a vegetarian, but—yuck. She tried to focus on Logan's unnaturally good looks, but she kept thinking about the meat mouth. So she transferred her attention to his biceps. Still nothing. She was back to being dead inside.

She huffed a frustrated sigh. "Logan, I am really sorry about this, but I think I'm going to have to bail."

"Really?" He looked a little disappointed, which she supposed was flattering.

"Yeah, I . . ." None of this was his fault, meat mouth aside, so she lied. "I'm coming off a breakup, and I thought I was ready, but . . ."

She *was* ready, was the thing. Or she had been, a day ago.

Logan was surprisingly good-natured about her abrupt about-face, especially when she insisted on picking up the tab—all that meat did not come cheap.

On the way to the subway, she checked her phone, which she'd silenced for brunch.

Max: I heard you're on a date.

Max: Or should I say "date"?

Max: Let me know how it goes.

Max: And also that you didn't get axe-murdered.

She pulled over to the edge of the sidewalk.

Dani: How do you know I was on a date?

Max: It's over already? Wow. Slam, bam . . .

Dani: I couldn't go through with it.

Her phone rang. "How did you know I was on a date?" she asked when she picked it up.

"I thought you were going to meet in public first," he said, ignoring her question again. He sounded peeved.

"How did you know I was on a date?" she repeated.

"I'm at the palace. Leo and Marie and I were at the pub in the village while you were talking to Leo."

She harrumphed. She'd never told Leo it was a secret, but still.

"Dani, you can't just go home with someone without—"

"I didn't. I bailed from *brunch*," she said, answering his question now that he'd finally answered hers, though his relentless focus on the logistics of her date was getting annoying.

"Oh," he said. "I misunderstood."

"All right, then." She let her irritation evaporate. He meant well.

"Why did you change your mind?"

She told him about the meat thing, spinning it into an entertaining story that had him cracking up. "I told him I was too fresh off a breakup. Anyway, if at first you don't succeed, swipe, swipe again."

"Let me know next time you're going out, okay?"

"I told Leo. Why are you being so persistent about this?"

"Because I don't want you to get axe murdered. I like you."

She flushed. That Max-style honesty continued to be such an odd mix of flattering and awkward. "You keep saying that."

"It keeps being true."

"But no one talks like that, except maybe first graders. How come you didn't get socialized out of such earnest declarations of friendship like the rest of us did?"

"Probably because I never went to school, so I didn't get socialized at all. I had a private tutor until I left for Cambridge."

"What? What about boarding school?"

"My brother went to boarding school. I didn't."

Oh. That wasn't how she'd interpreted their brief conversation in Central Park about his brother going off to boarding school. She'd assumed Max had gone, too. "Why didn't you go? Did it have something to do with you being the heir? Keeping you close to home?"

"No. My parents wanted me to go. Staying home was . . . my choice."

"But I thought you didn't like being at home? You're always trying to get away from your family."

"I had my reasons."

Max was usually such an open book. But apparently, she'd hit on one of his few off-limits topics.

"Anyway," he went on. "Indulge me. Let me be your transatlantic Tinder monitor."

"Okay, you weirdo."

"See? That's why I like you. I'm reasonably certain no one has ever called me a 'weirdo' before, at least not to my face."

"So you like me because I insult you."

"No, I like you because you tell the truth. Well, that's one of the reasons."

"What are the others?"

"Now, now, we don't want you to get a big head. Also, I need to qualify that statement. You tell the truth, except apparently when rejecting the sexual advances of men. Then you start to worry about their feelings?"

"Yeah, yeah. I take your point. Next time, I'll make sure my rejection really stings."

"Relentless honesty, right? That's what you called it?"

"I was talking about you, but yes." She could take a cue from him on that front. She slowed as she approached the entrance to the 103rd Street Station. "I'm about to get on the subway, so give me the thirty-second update on the museum project." Max and his brother, who seemed to have joined forces, had spent the last two months doing historical research and developing a proposal to convert an abandoned mine their family's company owned into an immersive museum.

"Oh my god, do I ever have news on that front. It turns out there's a local historical society, and I found a diary that is turning out to be a bit of a jackpot."

"*Really?*" The brothers had uncovered evidence of a network of Austrians working with the Soviet Union to supply a tattered resistance movement.

"It's not a literary diary—don't get your English prof self too excited. It's more like a schedule. But it does seem to confirm what I'm learning from the letters, that there were at least ten locals involved in shuttling weapons from Soviet-occupied Hungary across a network that spanned the south of Austria and into the mine for safekeeping."

"Max! This is all so amazing!"

"Hold on. That's not the most exciting part. Are you ready for this? I feel like I need a drum roll."

He sounded so thrilled. Her stomach flopped in vicarious excitement, and she obliged with a silly drum-rolling sound.

"I found a letter from Karina Klein to a man I've established as a local leader of the resistance talking about my grandmother."

"No!"

"Yes. My grandmother technically owned the land the mine was on, and I'm wondering if perhaps Karina approached her, asking if she would lend it out to the resistance."

"Holy shit, Max!"

"I know. It's why I'm at the palace. There are a few elderly people who used to work for my family who have retired to Witten. I'm going to see if they remember anything noteworthy about my grandmother in the war years."

"Is this your grandmother who lived in your cottage?"

"Yes, and I must say it is rather buoying to learn that not all my family members are terrible."

"You need to write a book!" He was being so typically blasé

about this. "You need to write several books! Not only is this a great story, but it's sort of sounding like there is more to the Karina Klein story than previously believed."

"Yes, but all I have at this point is the letter from Karina referencing my grandmother—it talks about 'asking her regarding the matter we spoke about,' so it's vague. I have no proof that Karina asked for the use of the mine, or that Oma agreed. But I take your point. Any revision to the biography of Karina will be major news, in Eldovia at least. But honestly I'd rather break the news with the museum itself than with a book—books are your department. We're starting to interview exhibition designers. I was thinking it might be too early to do that, but apparently not. Museum exhibition design. Who even knew that was a thing? Some of them have amazing ideas for making the space not just a museum underground but a community resource aboveground—having an outdoor concert venue, for example."

"That all sounds wonderful." Damn, she was proud of him. "Hey, when I'm there for the wedding, could we go check it out? How far is it?"

"There's nothing to see yet. We're at least two years from opening."

"Yeah, but the wedding is still nine months off. Anyway, I don't care if there's nothing to see. What if I want to see nothing and listen to you tell me stories about what happened there and nag you to write a book about it? What if I want to escape all the royal pomp? What if my jaded, shriveled soul can't take all the gooey happily-ever-after junk?"

"Then your wish is my command."

She smiled. "Max, it sort of sounds like you got yourself a job."

"It does, doesn't it?" He cleared his throat. "I guess you'd better hurry up and get yourself a divorce, then, so I don't trounce you on the resolution front."

"I'm working on it. It can't come soon enough."

To MAX'S AMUSEMENT, as spring turned into summer, Dani couldn't seem to pull the trigger on her sex resolution. She would arrange dates but somehow never ended up doing the deed. While he would grant that his experience wasn't representative, he was certain that with sufficient motivation, it wasn't that difficult to find a decent enough man whose breath didn't smell like hamburger with whom to do the deed.

Dani was the full package. Beautiful, funny, smart—not that smart necessarily mattered in these kinds of encounters. It did irritate him to think of her innate intelligence and wit being squandered on some Neanderthal who thought she was merely a pretty face and a nice body. But the point was, it wasn't that hard.

"Well, hello," he said, picking up her call late one August night in a hotel in Innsbruck. He and Seb were in town to meet with representatives from the museum design firm they'd hired. "What was wrong with HarlemHipster?" he asked, referencing her latest failed match.

"How do you know there was something wrong with him?"

"Because you only left an hour ago and you were supposed to have drinks first. Unless you did it in the bathroom at the bar, I am left to conclude it was a bust."

"It was a bust. HarlemHipster was allergic to dogs."

He stepped out onto his balcony. "Well you're not going to marry him."

"I can't marry him. I'm still married to someone else," she deadpanned.

"Yes, how is *that* going?"

"It was a joke."

"I got that. I just didn't laugh. I'm too focused on trying to fix your sex problems."

"My sex problems? You sound like Dr. Ruth."

"Well, my friend, here's some tough love: You are failing on the whole resolution front. HarlemHipster is the eighth man you've met up with and rejected in six months. What's the common denominator in all these encounters?"

"Are you telling me to have sex with someone I don't want to have sex with? Are you telling me I should have had sex with Mr. Meat?" He had been semi-teasing, but her voice had gone defensive and shrill.

"No! *God.* Of course not." Honestly, he was always a little relieved when she called him with a strikeout. It wasn't that he was jealous. He just didn't think any of these men were worthy of her. The one before this had been a professional *Fortnite* player, for god's sake. But at the same time, looking at the situation objectively, if she wasn't looking for Mr. Forever, but Mr. Right Now, she could stand to lower her standards.

Not that he thought she should have to.

He was overthinking this. There was one other logical explanation for her reticence. Normally, he wouldn't be so pushy as to bring it up, but he and Dani had become genuinely close over the last several months. "Is it possible your problem is that you're worried—consciously or subconsciously—about getting your heart broken again?"

"No, no," she said quickly. "I'm post-love."

"So you've said. I was just checking, but 'post-love.' I get it."

"You too?"

"Yes. Well, that's not right. 'Post' implies you've been in love."

She snorted. "So you're pre-love?"

"No. I don't think so, at least."

"Anti-love?" She laughed.

"I'm not *against* love. It's more that I'm indifferent to it. I don't think it works on me."

"Is that why you agreed to marry Marie even though you weren't in love with her?" Well. Here he'd thought they were talking about her. "Sorry," she added quickly. "None of my business."

"No, it's fine. With you, I'm an open book."

"Explain it to me, then—how you were going to marry Marie. I know the backstory. Uniting the houses and all that. But how did you square it in your mind?"

"I don't know, really. It didn't seem like such a bad scenario. I love Marie in a platonic way. She's a cross between a sister and a best friend. She's my only . . ." He'd been going to say she was his only confidant, but that wasn't true anymore, was it? Max and Marie didn't even talk that much these days, which he would have put down to her having Leo and being swept up in her new UN gig and in wedding preparations, but actually, *he* owed *her* a call. "It never felt like I was settling, because I've never found anyone I actively wanted to marry."

"Because you've never been in love."

"Correct. Marie and I had agreed we would do our duty with the old turkey baster—or with discreet medical intervention, if needed—but then we'd be free to live our lives."

"Because you need an heir."

"I don't *need* one, and now I won't have one. But that would have been the expected path, yes."

She huffed an incredulous laugh. "I swear, half the time I forget who you are. I mean, not who *you* are, but that you're a member of the aristocracy."

He felt himself flush. *That* was exactly why he liked her so much. Her declaration felt like a compliment, though she probably hadn't meant it that way. It was rare that someone saw him as a person first and a baron second.

"It sounds like a business arrangement," she said.

"It was, in a way, but remember, I *like* Marie. That's why I went along with it. There's no one I'd rather read the newspaper with every morning or gossip with every evening, or . . ."

That was another thing that wasn't true anymore. He and Dani gossiped several evenings a week. Or at random times of the day or night, such as when she was fleeing a date. They also talked about more serious matters. It was amazing—and exhilarating—how easily they could toggle between the two.

"But you were content to step aside when she met Leo," Dani said, filling in the sentence he'd trailed off.

"Well, I stepped aside."

"But not contentedly?"

"I was happy for her. I *am* happy for her." He was aware that he was prevaricating. And also that Dani, she of the sharp mind and the sharp tongue, probably would not stand for it.

"But?" she prompted, and he chuckled. He knew her too well.

"Well, I would never say this to Marie, but I'm back to square one with my parents. I refuse to marry someone under false pre-tenses, to shackle myself to a woman who will expect fidelity and devotion and all those qualities that are perfectly reasonable to expect from one's husband."

"You need another Marie—someone you like but who doesn't expect you to behave like a husband. Someone who's happy to live parallel lives." She cackled. "You should marry me. Then I can quit my job and write books full time without it mattering if they're scholarly enough and you can carry on in your usual fash-ion, blissfully free of the weight of spousal expectations."

Something in his chest both lurched and settled at the same time. Wouldn't that be lovely? He kept his response light, though. "But will you gossip with me in the evenings?"

"Of course. We already do that. The problem with this sce-nario, though, is I am thoroughly lacking in connections to the Austrian crown."

He chuckled. "There's also the part where you're post-men—I assume that rules out even sham marriages."

"Don't forget the part where I'm still married."

"Touché. Regardless of me and my problems, I truly am happy Marie found Leo."

"I think it's okay to be both."

"What do you mean?"

"Of course you're happy for Marie, but it's also okay to have feelings about the fact that your life plan has been upended. Even if you haven't had your heart broken in the conventional sense, you have lost something."

"How'd you get so smart?" he said, partly to cover the fact that her analysis, which was so generous, was hitting him surprisingly hard, but partly because he didn't want to talk about himself anymore. He vastly preferred talking about her. "And since you're so smart, you should be able to find one man in all of New York with whom to have sex."

"I don't want to talk about this anymore." Apparently, he wasn't the only one who wanted to change the subject. "The divorce, though, I *am* finally making progress on. The new papers are all done, and Vince has them—or at least Vince's lawyer has them. Honestly, it's such a relief that everything happens through lawyers now."

"And do those papers include you giving him your dog?"

"They do not. My lawyer suggested I offer him my notes on the Gertrude Stein part of the book we never finished in exchange for Max Minimus."

"Really?" Max did not like the sound of that. "All that work?"

"Well, it stings, but she said that's the point. He wants to hurt me."

But he did *hurt you,* Max wanted to say. *Why does he have to keep doing it?*

"He's likely to view it as a bigger concession than the dog, which to my mind it's not. I'm never going to do anything with those notes. The project is all tied up with him in my mind, and anyway—" She cut herself off.

"Anyway what?"

"I have an idea for a new project that is tangentially related. I won't need the notes for it, but it will broadly arise from all that thinking."

"Tell me more."

"No." He made a noise like she'd wounded him, and she laughed. "I don't even have it straight in my head yet. That's this fall's project."

"Ah." She had that semester of teaching leave coming up. "Tell me," he persisted. "I'll help you get it straight in your head."

"No," she said again. "Eyes on the prize here, dude—the prize being a divorce. If we can make Vince view this as a win for him, it might finally do the trick."

What an absolute jackass Vince was. Mean but also insecure and petty. Max wanted to hop the next plane to Spain and throttle him. He forced himself to sound calm. "That's grand. Sounds like progress."

"It is, but why does progress always have to be so painful? Get this: the lawyer wants me to be seen in public being civil and friendly in Vince's presence in case he doesn't accept the new terms. She says we need to do what we can to protect me later if he refuses to agree and forces a trial. That means acting in ways that counter the narrative he is likely to advance about me."

"Which is?"

"That I'm a jealous, vengeful hag who refuses to move on with my life. That *I'm* the one holding things up. Which I guess is technically true, but only because of Max Minimus."

"But isn't Vince on sabbatical? How are you supposed to be seen being civil and friendly to him if he's in Spain?" Vince and Berkeley were still doing Picasso cosplay and Instagram influencing in Barcelona. And yes, Max had stalked Berkeley's Instagram. Her most recent post had been of her lower body poolside, her hand balancing a glass of wine on her taut, tanned belly, captioned "Syrah with my Sweetie" and followed by literally twenty-seven—he'd counted—hashtags. It made him irate.

"He'll be back next week. We have our start-of-year departmental party in a couple weeks, so off I go to be fake friendly." She made a strangled noise.

"Do you have to be fake friendly at the party? Can you just stop by his office and have a quick, civil chat?"

"The lawyer says that unless it's going to cause me undue stress, I should go. She says it's the perfect venue to show myself as a nonthreatening, reasonable person—in case it does go to trial and colleagues have to testify." She was sounding uncharacteristically timid.

"Is that all that's bothering you?" he asked gently. Normally, Dani would be the kind of person who would embrace this sort of assignment as a necessary evil. She'd be brusquely efficient in carrying out her duties.

She sighed. "The truth is, I'm scared."

She did that sometimes. Came out with a truth deep into a conversation. It was as if she had to back herself into admitting something she didn't think accorded with the image she should be projecting. He was stupidly pleased to be the recipient of such truths.

"I'm not scared of Vince," she added in a rush. "He's not going to hurt me or anything. I'm afraid of . . . getting into it with him. It's hard to explain, but he's such a good talker. I mean, why was I in mediation for so long? Because he has this way of making you believe what he says. He has this way of making it seem like he's listening to you, when he's not actually paying any attention to you at all." She had said that before, that Vince didn't listen to her. What a monumental ass. "You didn't see it at the Christmas party because of our perfectly timed exit, but Vince has this way of talking you into a corner."

"Nobody puts Dani in a corner."

There was a long pause. Then, Dani's voice, laden with amusement and incredulity: "Did you just quote *Dirty Dancing*?"

"Did you just recognize a quote from *Dirty Dancing*?" he countered.

"I love that movie!"

"You *do*?"

"I do. But I am not an Eldovian baron."

"Marie is enamored of eighties and nineties pop culture. I've watched it with her."

"Well, it's a good movie," she said defensively. "And if you think about it, it's an oddly progressive one. Made in the 1980s but set in the 1960s, yet it's much more forward-thinking on issues of sexism and reproductive rights than pop culture is today."

He hadn't thought of it like that. "It does rather align with your interests, doesn't it?"

"Yes, but lest you think me too high-minded: oh, the dancing in that movie! That lift in the lake!" She laughed. "And honestly, I used to have a crush on Patrick Swayze when I was a kid. Or at least *Dirty Dancing*–era Patrick Swayze. My mom loved him, and I guess she passed it on to me. But as it relates to this party, since I don't have Patrick Swayze to come rescue me from my corner, I'll just have to rescue myself." There it was, the brusque efficiency that had been missing before. But he was beginning to understand that sometimes the brusque efficiency was a facade.

"Will you have backup?" It wasn't that he didn't think Dani could get herself out of any corners she found herself in, but he would prefer if she had support. "That woman I met? Sinéad?"

"She'll have my back, yeah. Honestly, when I get tenure—*if* I get tenure—I'm either not going to these parties anymore or I'm going to go wearing something outrageous, and I won't watch what I say at all—ha!"

Max bit back his impulse to issue a *"When* you get tenure" correction. As they'd grown closer, he'd come to understand that the tenure system in North America was different from in Europe. It meant job security and academic freedom for life, so it truly was a milestone. He'd creeped a bit on her web presence and those of her colleagues, and in his admittedly biased opinion, she was doing more interesting work than many of them. But he didn't want to be dismissive of her concerns, and he didn't have a handle on the departmental politics, so he bit his tongue. But privately he had confidence, and if tenure meant she could start swanning into parties wearing green taffeta dresses and telling everyone to fuck off, he couldn't wait.

Chapter Nine

*O*n the Thursday of the last week of summer break, Dani was walking on the beach near her parents' house when her phone rang. Max. It was an odd time of day for him to be calling. They talked frequently, but usually later in the day. "Hi. What's up?"

"I'm outside your building, but you're not home."

What? "I'm sorry, did you just say you're outside my *building?*"

"Yes. Surprise!"

"Max! What are you doing?"

"I'm here to be your plus-one at your party tomorrow."

"What? Why?"

"Because it was so much fun last time?"

She was speechless.

"Because nobody puts Dani in a corner?" he said into the unspooling silence.

Oh, Max. Max was such a genuinely good person underneath his breezy exterior. Underneath the European tabloid, Depraved Duke persona. He had come here purely to keep her company at the party she was so dreading. It made her throat catch. She thought of the Christmas party, how perfectly pitched all his interventions had been—the hand at her back, the stories he'd told to paint her in a flattering light. As unlikely as it was, Max von Hansburg, Baron of Laudon, had become one of her closest friends. She might even say *best* friend, except that to do so felt disloyal to Leo somehow.

"Or," he amended, when she still didn't speak, "I wanted to see you, and this seemed like as good an excuse as any?"

Her throat tightened even more as he did his signature "I like you, I really like you" thing. She couldn't figure it out. She knew her friends liked her. She didn't need them to tell her repeatedly. But then came Max, all "I think you're cool," and she got all emotional.

"Where are you?" he asked.

She ordered herself to snap out of her uncharacteristically schmoopy moment. "I'm at my parents' house on Long Island. I have a renter at my place."

"What do you mean you have a renter?"

"I rent my place out on Airbnb sometimes."

"You *do*?"

"I can't really afford the apartment on my own, but it's a great deal for what it is and I don't want to give it up. I rented it out almost every other week this summer."

"You *did*?"

She wasn't sure why he was so astonished. Except that of course he had no idea what it was like to pinch pennies.

"And now," she went on, "not only do I have the normal budget crunch, but my very effective divorce lawyer is also very expensive. I thought about getting a roommate, but, *ugh*. I ran the numbers, and I figured out if I Airbnb-ed my place periodically, I could make as much money as I would with a full-time room-mate. And this fall . . ."

She'd been going to add that since she had the teaching leave upcoming, she had more plans to rent the place out, but Max did not need a monologue about her balance sheet. As cool as Max was turning out to be, it was a little awkward that he was a literal aristocrat and she was having trouble making rent. Well, awkward on her end, anyway. He never seemed to notice, much less mind, the vast economic gulf between them.

"All right, so, I think this is the part where you invite me to Long Island?" Max said cheerfully.

"Really?" She wanted him to come to her, suddenly, so much. She'd been planning to pack up and head into the city to meet him, but it was hot and sunny, a perfect end of summer beach day.

"Well, what are you doing out there?" he asked. "Having a party I can't crash? Wait! Are you finally going to have sex?"

"No! I'm setting up for a day at the beach right now—*alone*. Though maybe I *should* get on Tinder and try to scare up some local matches. Maybe I'll have more luck here than I've had in the city."

"Grand. Send me the name of the beach, and I'll be off. I'll advise on the Tindering, too."

She laughed. Max was *here*! "You might want to buy bathing trunks." She imagined him in his sleek blue suit, striding up the beach. It was a pleasant image. But still, it was an extremely hot day.

"I have mine with me. I always stay at the Four Seasons be-cause it has a sauna I'm partial to."

"Of course you do."

"Marie likes the Plaza, but there's no opportunity to shed one's clothing and get sweaty at the Plaza."

"You can't see, but I'm rolling my eyes. Anyway, I thought you were an expert at making your own opportunities to shed clothing and get sweaty."

She was teasing him about his so-called man-whorish ways, but she'd learned he was, for lack of a better phrase, an ethical man-whore. He liked sex, and he apparently had a lot of it, but he tried to make sure that everyone had a good time and understood his "rules of engagement."

She wanted to be like that. She wasn't sure why she couldn't get her act together. She took his point that her last prospect, HarlemHipster, had been fine. So he was allergic to dogs. As Max had said, she wasn't going to marry him.

She realized that Max hadn't responded to her teasing about him making his own opportunities to get hot and sweaty. She'd expected a sharp comeback, but he'd gone uncharacteristically silent. "Anyway, definitely come on out."

And there he was, ninety minutes later, striding across the sand to the agreed-upon meeting place, where she'd set up her umbrella. Talk about dukeish casual. He wore blue gingham swim trunks, a white T-shirt, and a pair of tortoise-shell Ray-Bans. She could just *see* him on the Mediterranean yacht that had made him into the Depraved Duke. She scrambled to her feet, suddenly— weirdly—shy. She wasn't sure how to greet him, which was dumb because they talked on the phone all the time. She thought back to the couple of times on his first trip to New York when she'd surprised herself by blurting out something really personal and ended up exposing too much of herself, making herself too vulnerable. She felt that way now, except literally. Physically. She should have put a cover-up on. She should have—

He scooped her into his arms, engulfing her in a great big hug. Apparently he wasn't feeling any of the awkwardness she was. Which was good. She hugged him back, and he picked her up so that her feet rose a few inches from the sand. He still had that spicy pine smell, as he had last Christmas. She tried not to inhale too overtly.

"You are a sight for sore eyes," he declared, and with a final, extra-hard squeeze, he plopped down on her beach blanket, laid on one side facing her with his head propped on his hand, and said, "Tell me everything."

"I just talked to you yesterday."

"So?" he said, sticking his hand into the bag of potato chips she had open. "Tell me everything again."

"OKAY, GIVE THAT back now," Dani said a couple of hours later, holding her hand out for her phone, which Max had commandeered to pass judgment on her Tinder prospects. He was a little taken aback at how many messaging threads she had going. She couldn't find *anyone* decent in this large a pool? "You've done enough damage," she said laughingly as she pried the phone out of his grip.

"I'm not sure I'd call it damage," he said, but he gave the phone back. He had done some trawling on her behalf, and he was pretty sure he'd found a few diamonds in the rough, a few princes among the bad grammar and ill-advised tattoos. He still wasn't convinced that any of them were actually worthy of her, but he considered this an exercise in harm reduction. "I'm hot. I'm going back in the water."

They had spent the day cycling between swimming and sitting on the beach talking. Dani was always easy to talk to, but in person it was even easier. He told her the latest on the mine project and how it was bringing him and his brother closer than they'd been for years. She told him a highly amusing story about her current renter, who was in the city to attend an intensive miming workshop. He had mining; she had miming. The hours had flown by.

She got up with him and brushed sand off her legs. He'd tried not to be too obvious about checking her out, but he was only human. Every time he did, his previous conclusion that she was too good for the men of Tinder was ratified anew. To begin with, she was gorgeous in a sleek, black one-piece swimsuit, tall and lean and gently curved. But what grated on him was that the most gorgeous thing about her was her brain. Her brain was going to be wasted on the Mr. Carnivores and HarlemHipsters of the world.

"Ahh! It's so cold!" she said, as she had every time they'd ventured into the water.

"If you think this is cold, you should try an Alpine lake."

"Ooh, do you have a lake?" She took another step and made a face as if she were being tortured.

"I do. Well, the estate does. It's small but deep—and cold. It'll freeze your nuts off."

"I don't have nuts, Max."

"I am aware." Was he ever. "I'm trying to speak American."

She snorted.

"We also have a natural hot spring."

"Wow, I can see why you love it there." Another step, another tortured grimace. "What I would give to be in a hot spring right now."

"The trick with cold water is to plunge in and get your body moving." He came back toward her and stopped when the water was at his mid-thigh, as it was on her. Since he was taller, it put them a meter or so from each other. He pointed to a red umbrella on the beach about a hundred feet off. "I'll race you to that umbrella. Not literally, but to that spot at this depth."

He took off, leaving her shrieking and splashing behind him. He beat her and turned. She was laughing as she slogged through the water, but she slowed to a stop well before the finish line.

"That's it? You're giving up?" he teased.

"I sure am."

The idea popped into his head fully formed and fully absurd. He splashed back toward her, then out deeper, until the water was mid-chest on him. He raised his arm and beckoned her with a "bring it" gesture.

"What?"

"Come here."

"Why?" she asked, but she started coming.

"Let's do the *Dirty Dancing* lift."

Her mouth fell open as she stopped walking. "Are you insane?"

"Come on. The iconic lake lift." He gestured again. "You know you want to."

She grinned but quickly slammed her mouth shut like she was

trying not to appear delighted by his idea. Too late. And more critically, she started moving again.

When she arrived, she raised her eyebrows incredulously. "We can't do the *Dirty Dancing* lift."

"On the contrary. We can do whatever we want."

"But why? Why would we do this?"

"Why would we make snow angels in Central Park?" he countered. "Because it's fun."

"You are—"

He wanted to know what she'd been going to say before she cut herself off. "What?"

"All right," she said, ignoring his question. "Let's do it." She smiled, a bright, unreserved one, and he loved seeing it, her mouth and eyes big. Happiness looked good on her.

He forced his eyes from her face and pondered the logistics of the task. He was going to have to grab her by the hips. Well, in for a pound . . . He stepped closer, bent his knees, and hovered his hands near her body but not touching it, under the surface of the water. "Okay?"

Still grinning from ear to ear, she nodded and put her hands on his shoulders.

Not wanting to grab her ass by accident, he rested his hands on her sides and slid them down and forward until he was cradling the points of her hips in his hands. Oof. The juxtaposition of soft flesh and pointy hip bones was really . . . something.

Her smile ignited into laughter.

"What's so funny?" he teased, but he was laughing, too.

"This. You. Everything."

He resisted the urge to stick his tongue out at her. "Here we go." He bent his knees and crouched to get some momentum, then launched her up into the air above his head—or tried to. He only got her about halfway up before he lost his balance.

"Ahhh!" She was shrieking and laughing at the same time as she came down, and it was contagious. He tried to break her fall and she tried to dive, and they ended up tangled together as they went under the water. He grabbed her, feeling bad about the sudden plunge, and she wound her arms around his neck as they resurfaced. She was sputtering but still laughing.

It was the summer version of Central Park. A stumble had turned into a hug. Except instead of wearing winter coats, they were skin to skin. Goosebumps rose, though he wasn't cold. He pulled his hips away from her even as he kept hanging on to her upper body. He didn't want her to feel his embarrassing erection. He felt like a teenager.

Except not, because he had never been this carefree as a teenager.

"Sorry," he said through his laughter. "I'm no Patrick Swayze."

"It took Baby and Johnny a few tries if I recall." She said it as if issuing a dare.

He raised his eyebrows. "Again?" She nodded. "All right, let's do a countdown this time—we lift on three." She grabbed his shoulders, and he found the points of her hips. "I think I need a better grip. I'm going to hold you tighter this time." God help him. "Does this hurt?"

She shook her head no, looking at him with an uncharacteristically serious expression that caused him a moment of unexplained panic. But then they were gone—her serious face *and* his hint of panic. Her hair was plastered to her cheeks, and she wore a grin so wide it looked like it might crack her face in two.

God, he just *liked* her so much. He was so happy to be here, in the sun, in the ocean, in this moment, in what felt like grace, though grace was not a state Max had much experience with.

All right. Enough. He was being ridiculous. "Ready?" She nodded. He splayed his fingers around her hips and planted his feet in the squishy sand. "One, two, three!" He lifted, and up, up, up she went, extending and tightening her body as she lengthened her arms out in front of her.

"Eeee!" she called when his arms were fully extended and they'd reached an equilibrium. "We're doing it!"

They were, and as he tilted his head back to look at her, a sharp spike of satisfaction, of pride even, rose in his chest, as if this were an actual accomplishment. She looked like a dancer. No, like a superhero. "We're doing it," he echoed, but it came out more a whisper than the triumphant shout that would have matched the sentiment.

She looked down, and he knew they were going to fall—the slight movement had been enough to nudge them out of alignment—but their eyes locked for a moment before it happened. She'd been laughing, gleeful, but her face suddenly went serious, contemplative. There wasn't time to ponder it because the fall was underway. "Dive!" he called, and she did, bringing her arms together and tucking her head. She dragged him along with her as she moved through space, and as he fell back into the water, he started laughing again.

She popped up, the laughing, jubilant version of her pushing her hair out of her eyes. She flung her arms into the air in victory and started splashing toward him. She had one hand up, so he thought she was coming in for a high-five. He lifted a hand to meet hers, but she didn't seem to see it, just kept coming until she was *there*, winding her arms around his neck and pressing her chest against his, pressing her *breasts* against him.

He was frozen, momentarily stunned, but after a second, his brain caught up, shoving three observations into his consciousness. The first was that she was *hugging him*. She had come over here with the *express purpose* of hugging him. The second was that it was merely a friendly, triumphant hug. The third was that if he kept standing there like an idiot, he was going to miss it. So he wrapped his arms around her and lifted her up, letting himself notch his face into the crook of her neck. She smelled like salt and sunscreen, and he never wanted to smell anything else. He never wanted to *be* anywhere else.

It was only a few seconds before the world intruded in the form of . . . applause? He set her down, her face mirroring the bewilderment he felt. A group of middle-aged women stood maybe thirty meters off, smiling and clapping. "Nice job!" one of them called. "Nobody puts Baby in a corner!" another shouted.

He smiled and bowed. "Thank you!"

"Oh my god, we looked like such idiots!" Dani said.

"No, we were glorious. They're *applauding* us."

She swatted his shoulder. "Come on. Let's go home."

At that moment, he would have followed her anywhere.

"HAVE ANOTHER, MAX." Dani's mom pushed a plate of brownies toward him.

"I can't. I'm positively stuffed. But thank you." They were in the backyard of Dani's parents' house, where they had feasted on clams Dani's dad had caught—collected? Max didn't know the correct verb—and grilled, locally raised Atlantic salmon, potato and green salads, and gooey chocolate brownies. "Everything was so delicious." It might even have been the best meal he'd ever had, but that was probably as much to do with the company as with the food. He already knew Dani's mom was a delight, but her dad was great, too, regaling Max with tales of clamming adventures and life at the UN. Max even got to practice his Spanish a bit, which wasn't as good as his French, but Mr. Martinez, who had insisted on being called Carlos, was patient.

"What about Italian?" he asked. "I'm slightly better at Italian than Spanish."

Carlos answered him effortlessly in Italian, and Max whistled. "Exactly how many languages do you speak?"

"My parents bought a little hotel on the beach before I was born," he said. "They worked on it gradually over the years and eventually it became kind of fancy—almost by accident. It drew people from all over. I was always interested in the languages everyone spoke, and I turned out to be pretty good at picking up bits of them. That's why I applied to the Model UN program. And the rest"—he gestured at Val—"Is history."

"My sister and I only speak English and Spanish," Dani said, "so my parents used to speak French when they wanted to talk about us without doing us the courtesy of leaving the room." She stuck her tongue out at them. "They still do."

Everyone was so at ease with each other. It wasn't that Max

didn't understand, intellectually, that families like this existed. Marie and her mother had been this way. It was just so strange to have crash-landed in the middle of one. Unsettling at first, but then utterly relaxing. It felt as if someone had dispensed a narcotic as he listened to them talk and tease one another. Soon all the relaxation had him yawning. "I beg your pardon. I'm afraid all the food and the sun have done me in. I should be going." Darkness had begun to descend, and he couldn't stay forever, though he wanted to do exactly that. "Thank you for a wonderful evening." He looked at Dani. "And day." As lovely as Val and Carlos were, the dinner had been merely the icing on top of his beach day with Dani.

When had he last been that carefree? *Truly* carefree, not tabloid-headline carefree?

"You're not staying over?" Dani's mom said to him with seemingly genuine confusion.

It took a moment for her question to penetrate his brain, so fixated had he been on Dani. "Oh, no, I have a hotel room in Manhattan."

"Nonsense!" Valerie said. "You'll stay, and you kids can hit the beach again tomorrow. If you want to, of course. We only have a sofa bed. You probably don't want to."

He did want to. He wanted to more than anything. He looked at Dani, who said, "I don't know, man, suite at the Four Seasons or the awful sofa bed here?" She performed an exaggerated shrug but mouthed, "Stay," as she did so.

Which was how Max found himself tucked into a lumpy sofa bed in the living room of a bungalow in a town on Long Island. As tired as he'd been earlier, once he was stretched out in the dark in a pair of Carlos's sweatpants, he didn't sleep. It wasn't his usual brand of frustrating, involuntary insomnia, though.

Max had gone to bed in lots of different places. Suites in the world's most exclusive hotels. Yachts—though not the infamous one. Even, once, a hammock under the stars on Ibiza. But never had he felt the bone-deep contentment this place inspired. The windows were open, and the steady chanting of crickets outside was melding with the reassuring tick-tocking of a grandfather clock in the otherwise silent house. His body was pleasantly spent from the swimming and the ridiculous *Dirty Dancing* lifts, and the sheets were crisp and cool in the warm night. Dani was tucked into a guest bedroom down the hall that she'd tried and failed to make him take. Knowing she was near was strangely comforting.

He didn't *want* to sleep now, as tired as he was. He wanted to lie here all night, letting himself be eased, allowing the pure pleasure of being here diffuse through his veins.

Chapter Ten

*M*ax was adorable when he was asleep. He looked younger when his expressive face was at rest, when he was taking a break from dipping into his endless arsenal of wit. He looked innocent, almost, which Dani knew, objectively, was the last word anyone could use to describe Maximillian von Hansburg, the (Not So) Depraved Duke.

She hated to wake him . . . but not really. "Max," she whispered, turning on her phone flashlight but taking care not to shine it in his face. She got her face right close to his. "Max."

His eyes opened, and he let loose a slow, lethal smile. She'd been prepared for him to be confused about where he was waking up, or to be annoyed that it was so early, or to be startled such that he made a ruckus and ruined their escape. But he just looked at her like it was normal to wake up with her face a few inches from his. Like he was *happy* about it.

She placed a finger to her lips and used her other hand to beckon him. He sat up and pulled on his T-shirt—he had been sleeping shirtless. Max was not a big, beefy guy, but he was well proportioned, his long, lean muscles complementing his smooth persona. He looked like he spent a lot of time swimming in his stupid freezing Alpine lake. She felt something stirring in her. Why couldn't she feel like this with one of her Tinder dudes? Why couldn't she summon a simple, uncomplicated lust that was strong enough to overcome her fears with someone like Harlem-Hipster?

She grabbed her mom's keys and, once they were safely out in the dark driveway, whispered, "Good morning."

"Are we sneaking out like teenagers so we don't wake your parents?"

"We're sneaking out like teenagers so we don't wake my *dog*." She got in the car and turned to him as he settled himself into the passenger seat. The dim overhead light bathed his already golden features in a warm glow. His hair was disheveled and somehow all the more appealing for it. He looked ridiculous in his shoes, which she would call "fancy European man-sandals" paired with her father's sweatpants. "Are you up for a minor adventure?"

"Always," he said, vehemently and immediately. His voice was low and sleep-scratchy.

"Don't get too excited. 'Adventure' might actually be overstating it. First stop is McDonald's."

"You know, I've never had McDonald's."

"*Really?* Well, I was going to feel bad about feeding you McDonald's, but we're in a hurry and it's the only place around here that's open this early. But now I feel it's my duty to take you down a few pegs and feed you the fast food of the masses."

Fifteen minutes later, they were eating McMuffins on a beach on the eastern edge of a spit of land that extended out into Long

Island Sound, which her dad had said would give them a prime view of the sunrise. It was that time just before dawn when the sun was not yet up, but the sky had lightened enough to look more blue than black, like a harbinger of good things to come.

"Oh my god," Max said after his first bite of McMuffin. "Where has this been all my life?"

"Yeah, I know New Yorkers are supposed to be all about bodega egg-and-cheese sandwiches, but I've always found McMuffins to be a guilty pleasure."

"Whoever came up with the notion that one should feel guilty about things that bring one pleasure should be shot."

She smiled. That was a very Max-like way of looking at the world.

"Your family is great," he said.

"They really are."

"You look so happy when you talk about them."

"I'm . . . at home with them."

"What does that mean? Isn't everyone at home with their family?" He made a face. "Everyone who isn't me?"

She wondered how much to say but decided to just go for it. They'd had such a great couple of days. It was starting to feel like Max really knew her. Or, in the few ways he didn't, like he wanted to.

"You don't know what it's like to be mixed-race. Which isn't a criticism. You can't know."

He nodded. "You talked about feeling like you're the diversity hire at work."

Yes. Max listened. He just didn't get the totality of it. "Right. At work, I'm either the 'diversity hire' or else I'm 'too white.' Like, people look at my CV and then at my skin and they think, hmm, is she *actually* Mexican? That's true in the wider world, too. We spend the holidays with my dad's parents in Mexico every few years, and I feel like I'm *too* white there. It's hard to explain. I feel like I'm always navigating these two worlds but always falling short in each of them. But at home, with my family, it's not a thing. I'm just who I am."

He looked at her for a long time, like he was really seeing her, and just when she was about to outright ask him to change the subject, he said, "When are you back in your apartment?"

"Tomorrow. The mime has an eleven o'clock check-out deadline."

"So you're going in to the party, coming back here tonight, then back to your place tomorrow?"

"Yep."

"Stay with me at the hotel after the party. That will save you the back-and-forth. We can get a rollaway."

"Yeah, but Max Minimus. I'd still have to come back here for him."

"He can come. We'll drop him off before the party."

"You can't bring a dog into the Four Seasons!"

"You can if you're the Baron of Laudon."

"Of course you can." Max was too much sometimes.

And yet, was that true? She called him that, in her mind, but was it possible that he *wasn't* too much?

"Come on," he pressed. "We'll vanquish Vince, and then we'll go back to the hotel and drink champagne in the sauna." He looked down at his empty McMuffin wrapper. "And maybe get some more of these awful beautiful things. Then we can watch ghastly American TV—no offense—in our pajamas."

Dani wanted to do that, more than anything. "When was the last time you took a woman back to your hotel for a chaste sleepover?"

He pretended to think about it. "There's a first time for everything?"

She laughed. "Okay. Sounds like fun." She sighed happily and ate her greasy breakfast as they watched the sunrise. It was all immensely pleasurable, and she didn't feel guilty about it at all.

As THEY PAUSED at the threshold of the party, Max had the sensation of time folding in on itself. They were in the same place, a lounge inside the university's faculty club. There was a bar at the far end, manned by the same bartender as at Christmas.

He scanned the room. It was populated by the same types of people as before—mostly men, mostly older. He spied Dani's friend Sinéad leaning against the bar. She must have felt his attention. She looked up, took him in, and smirked—though it seemed a friendly smirk. He hitched his head to summon her—they could use an ally—and she started making her way toward them. He took note of where Vince was—standing near a window with a deep ledge that Berkeley was sitting on. Vince hadn't noticed them yet.

Max had a plan. At the Christmas party, his goal, which had only emerged as he'd gotten a bead on the situation, had been to shamelessly exploit his perceived poshness, to make Dani look good in front of both her departmental chair and her abominable ex. Max was fully aware of the power his status afforded him, and he had never been shy about using it, be it to advance his own aims or in service of others. It was bullshit, but it was reality. Today, though, he was planning to fade into the background.

"Hel-lo." Sinéad arrived and gave Dani a quick hug, assessing Max over Dani's shoulder as she did so. When she straightened, she flicked the lapel of the suit he was wearing. "Linen. *Nice.*" Yes, he'd packed seasonally appropriate dukeish casual attire.

Sinéad was wearing fitted black pants, a white button-down shirt with a skinny black tie, and a shiny green blazer with the sleeves pushed up. She looked like a Beatle dressed up for a party—in other words, fantastic. He pointed at the blazer but didn't touch her. "Silk. *Nice.*"

"You two are perfect for each other."

They both turned to Dani, who also looked fantastic in a white sheath dress and gold sandals.

"All right." He gestured to both women to come closer. "Here's the plan."

"There's a plan?" Dani said.

Max turned to Sinéad. "Her lawyer wants her to come off as friendly and not threatening in case the divorce gets ugly, so I'm thinking she should make the rounds."

Sinéad nodded. "That makes sense. Is the point widespread coverage, or are we targeting, say, the power brokers in the department?"

"Um, hello?" Dani said.

"Good question. Can we do both? Aim for maximum coverage but start with the power brokers? I don't know who they are beyond that chair I met last time—James, I believe his name was?—so you're going to have to take the lead."

"Got it. And should she talk to Vince? I'm going to say yes. A friendly conversation initiated by her and witnessed by colleagues can only be a good thing to have in the bank, right?"

"I can hear you, you know," Dani said.

Max turned to her. "Just be charming, all right? I know it will be a stretch, but think of the sauna and the McMuffin as your reward."

"Sauna?" Sinéad raised her eyebrows.

"We're going to hit the sauna in my hotel after the party," Max said.

"And dare I ask about the McMuffin? Is that a euphemism for something?"

"Oh my *god*, no," Dani said. "He means it literally. I took him to McDonald's this morning for the first time, and now he's obsessed."

"Have you tried the sausage one?" Sinéad asked. "Mmm."

"There's a *sausage* one?" Max asked.

"You guys," Dani said, "I appreciate the support, but I don't think we need a strategy for this party. It's—"

"The man who's arriving now is a senior professor in the department." Sinéad said to Max. She lifted a hand and called, "Gordon! Dani and I are talking about your seminal article on *Ulysses*. Did you know she assigned it in class this term?"

Dani huffed a defeated-sounding sigh. "Hmm, I wonder if I assigned a reading on James Joyce in my *women* writers course or my *American* lit course?"

"Chin up," Max said. "Be good, and soon it will be McMuffin time." He wagged his eyebrows to try to make her laugh. She rolled her eyes but failed to suppress a smile.

"All right." He cracked his knuckles. "Here we go."

"OH MY GOD, I'm tired," Dani said as she lowered herself onto a bench in the piping-hot sauna at the Four Seasons. It wasn't particularly sauna weather, but it was still a relief to surrender to the gloriously dry heat after what had turned out to be an exhausting, if productive, party.

She hadn't even questioned how Max had made this happen. She'd just followed the hotel employee who had let them into the spa that had closed hours ago and then into the women's locker room. It turned out that the steam rooms and sauna Max was so devoted to were inside single-gender locker rooms, and, she was pretty sure, normally only available if you booked an oxygen facial or some other treatment that would set you back a month's rent. Dani had gone into a closed stall to change into her bathing suit, listening to the woman have a murmured conversation with Max about how to let her know when they were done so she could lock up.

"She thinks we're getting it on in here, doesn't she?" Dani asked when Max, changed into his swim trunks, appeared in the sauna a minute later.

"I try not to concern myself with what other people think," he said as he unpacked their McMuffins and a bottle of Veuve from a bag he'd brought in with him.

"You are too much."

He popped the cork on the champagne. "Does that mean you don't want any of this?"

"Heck, no." She grabbed one of the plastic cups he produced and held it up to be filled. "You do know, though, that not concerning yourself with what other people think is easier when you can buy them off."

"I do know that. Wealth has its compensations." He had turned serious, almost somber. It was interesting that he used the word *compensations*, as if being wealthy was by default negative. His mood change fit with a growing sense she had of a darker undercurrent to Max's affable, pleasure-seeking exterior. There was a wistfulness to him she sometimes saw flashes of, and that, together with his tendency to deflect attention from himself, made her feel like maybe Max was actually . . . sad. "Max, I wish you would—" No. She was being weird.

"You wish I would what?"

"Nothing."

"Tell me," he insisted.

Well, hell. He'd inserted himself pretty firmly into her business earlier this evening—to good end, she had to admit. She had chatted with everyone at the party, even Vince and Berkeley. She had laughed and nodded and flattered and commiserated. It had all been a performance, and it had been *exhausting*. But Max had been there to bolster her. Unlike at Christmas, he hadn't had the aristocratic charm turned up to eleven. This time, he'd been more of a quiet, steady presence, laughing at her jokes, answering questions when asked, but otherwise keeping quiet. He had pitched everything—his own performance and the one he'd thrown her into—perfectly. They were real, true friends, friends who helped each other—which meant she could speak truthfully. "I feel like you're unhappy. Not right now but . . . elementally. I wish you would tell me why."

He blinked rapidly, his breezy facade dropping. On the surface, he was all confidence and swagger, but he would, from time to time, say something that startled her with its guilelessness. It used to be his proclamations about how much he liked her. Or his New Year's Eve declaration about wanting to get a job. Maybe she could trigger another such admission.

It worked. He took a long drink of his champagne and said, "I'm unhappy because my father is a vicious drunk. Or perhaps I should say that my father is vicious, period, since he's drunk all the time. He terrorizes all of us, but no one seems to mind except me."

The word *terrorizes* gave her pause, but she didn't want to interrupt him.

"I hate living on the estate. I have no purpose in life other than to consume resources while I wait for my father to die so I can become the Duke of Aquilla, which I very, very much do not want to do. Hell, I don't even want to be a baron." He laughed bitterly and raised his cup. "Poor Max, right?" He rolled his eyes, then closed them like he was sick of himself.

His little speech had made her want to cry. She patted the hand that wasn't holding the glass. He whipped his head up and looked at her, startled by the contact. "Yes," she said vehemently, "poor Max." She started to retract her hand—she'd only meant to deliver a quick, sympathetic touch—but he rotated his hand under hers and held on, looking at her like she was his lifeline.

Maybe she was.

She knew Marie was Max's best friend. But if he and Marie were anything like Dani and Leo, that relationship had taken second fiddle as the lovebirds embarked on their life together.

"Can I ask you some dumb questions?" she said.

"You can ask me anything," he said with a strange vehemence and still not letting go of her hand.

"Could you walk away from it? Abdicate? Is that what you'd call it in your case? Pull a Harry-and-Meghan, basically?"

"I could, but that would mean passing all the shit to my brother." He paused, pressed his lips together. "That is not something I will do." He snorted. "Well, of course when I don't produce an heir, he and his future children will be in line to inherit. But my father will be gone at that point, so I'm quite content to dump everything on him then. I just won't . . . let him shoulder everything now."

Ohhh. Something shifted in her mind as she thought about a few things he'd said over the months. "That's why you didn't go to boarding school and he did."

He blew out a breath like he'd been busted doing something untoward. "In theory, I could have gone once Seb left at thirteen. But it turned out I'd made too good a case in the first place for why I should break with tradition and not go." He wrinkled his nose, as if he were remembering something unpleasant.

"Your father wouldn't let you go when your brother did."

"It was all right. I only had two years left, and I actually liked my tutor. Well, 'liked' might be overstating it. But he was exceedingly qualified, and we rubbed along together well enough. I'd had to fight my father for him in the first place. Once Father had accepted that I wasn't going away to school, he wanted me to continue on with my boyhood teacher. It was a real battle convincing my father not to send me."

"How did you do it?"

"I feigned interest in learning about the dukedom." His upper lip curled. "I gave magnificent speeches about family and legacy and destiny and said I didn't want to be away for four years when I could be learning about the role I was born to inherit."

"And did you learn about it?"

"I certainly did." There was the lip curl again. "I learned I never wanted to be the Duke of Aquilla. But we don't always get what we want, do we?"

"Why don't you want to do it? What is 'it,' really?"

"'It' is using what we own—what our ancestors took—to make money. We had feudal land, land that tenants paid to work. Later we had—still have—mines all over Europe. Do the people who work in those mines share in the profits they generate?"

"No?"

"That is correct. So the job of the duke is to oversee the money-making, environment-destroying empire. Which my father does a half-assed job of because he's usually drunk. But he has a steward who's a decent person."

"You've spent your whole life protecting your brother," Dani said quietly.

"Well, no. I gave up when he decided to move home. But that was a mistake. Not that he needed protection anymore, but I shouldn't have . . . abandoned him like I did. I understand now that even though he made different choices than I would have in his place, he had his reasons."

"Have you ever tried to . . . talk to your father?"

"You mean an intervention?" She nodded. "We tried once. Well, mostly Seb tried, because he's the best of us, but he rallied my mother and me. It did . . ." He made a face. "Not go well. While I understand the power of addiction and would extend the benefit of the doubt to anyone else in its grip, I can't . . . let go of some of the things he's done. The damage has been too great. I can't fix him, and I don't want to try."

That seemed both reasonable and remarkably self-aware. "Understood. Can you move, at least, if Sebastien doesn't need your protection anymore? You might have years before you inherit."

"The plan was always to move to the palace with Marie."

Right. It was still hard to wrap her mind around how close Max had come to marrying Leo's fiancée.

"I wouldn't have escaped my eventual fate, of course, but when I inherited, I'd've been able to run things from afar, and . . ."

"And what?"

"I don't know. There was never anything romantic between us, but Marie and I were good partners. I felt like she would've been able to help me make the job of duke less bad. That sounds vague, I know, but she was . . ."

"A helpmeet?" Dani teased, wanting to lighten his burden, even if only momentarily, but it actually seemed like the correct word.

He chuckled. "Precisely."

"You could still move. Wait out your fate somewhere else." She had the sudden, silly notion to suggest that he move to New York. He liked New York, and they could have so much fun. But she didn't say that because it was ridiculous.

"Right, but for that I would need money—my father will cut me off if I move off the estate for anything less than marrying into a family he deems suitable. And for that, I need a job."

"And the mine project isn't paying."

"It could be. Seb offered to put me on the payroll . . ."

"But taking money from the family company isn't that different from taking money from the family?"

He shrugged. "I thought about it. I *am* working. But I . . . need to not entangle myself with my father any more than I already am."

She thought back to the word *terrorizes*, and to Max saying he no longer wanted to try to help his father. "Max, did he . . . did he hurt you?"

"He hit Sebastien once."

Max had no idea why he was doing this—"This" being sitting in a sauna holding Dani's hand and telling her stuff he'd never told *anyone*, not even Marie.

"That doesn't really answer the question," Dani said with her signature mixture of kindness and hard-assed-ness, which he supposed answered the question of why he was doing this.

He was aware that he was being evasive. It was hard, even now, even having bared so much of himself, to fully drop the impulse to deflect that had been his default mode for so long.

"Sebastien was having a tea party, which was something he liked doing," he began slowly. "He was a solitary, dreamy child with an unfettered imagination. The problem was, he was having it in the library. He was sitting there with all his stuffed animals, babbling about who knows what, when my father walked in with a minor Austrian aristocrat who was visiting. I was too young to

be attuned to matters of state, but I had the sense he was someone Father wanted to impress." Max didn't remember the man's
name, but he did remember Father had insisted that Max and Seb
wear their formal eveningwear at dinners during the visit, which
both boys hated. "I wasn't there at the start of it," he said, thinking back to that day. "But my father upended the table Seb was
using. I came running when I heard the ruckus, and when I got
there, Father was in the midst of throwing Seb's favorite stuffed
bear into the fire and telling him that only women had tea parties
and that he was an embarrassment to the family and to Eldovia."
Dani winced. "Yes, apparently a tender eight-year-old not adhering
to proper gender conditioning is a threat to king and country.
Seb had a black eye the next day." He could still see it, the gro-
tesque midnight-blue blossom against his brother's pale skin. He
could still *feel* it, too, the shame blooming in his gut when his
father's guest gasped. And the anger when Mother started trying
to smooth things over, when she looked at him like *he* was supposed to help in her twisted endeavor. "I waited for something to
happen, for there to be a reckoning of some sort—for my mother
to object or for my father to apologize."

"But nothing happened?" Dani asked quietly.

"Nothing happened," he confirmed. He remembered waiting
again, later that night in the nursery, thinking that even if Father wasn't going to apologize, surely Mother would appear with
some retroactive explanation, some words to soothe and placate.
She didn't come. And when not a word was said the next day,
Max had come to understand that he and Seb were on their own.
They couldn't rely on their parents, and since their parents were
the duke and duchess, ultimately they couldn't rely on any of the

household staff, either. "I decided then that I would use what power I had to draw my father's fire, so to speak."

"So he hit you instead?"

"Not really. A few times."

She squeezed his hand again, and suddenly he felt as though he might cry. He had always thought the times he and his father had come to physical blows were less painful memories than their other, verbal confrontations, which made a certain sort of sense. A punch was a punch. It hurt, but it ended things. Whereas a sneering examination of what Father thought Max should have learned in the schoolroom but had not yet mastered could go on and on and on. That kind of torture, Max had always thought, was more insidious than a quick slap.

Max's sympathy and concern had been reserved for Sebastien, because Seb had always been so guileless, so much more vulnerable. Max had been older and stronger. But he thought suddenly of Leo's sister, Gabby. Of someone laying hands on her in a fit of violence. He would kill anyone who did that. She was a child.

But he had been, too. A *child*. He had been a child who had deserved better.

His eyes were burning. *"Fuck."* He lifted his free hand to swipe away a rogue tear, swallowed the rock in his throat, and went back to her question. "I didn't get hit that much. I developed a well-pitched campaign of distraction. If I made bigger mistakes—more consequential ones—than Seb, what did a tea party matter?" He shrugged. "Eventually, I got taller and bigger than him."

"I'm sorry, Max." Dani spoke quietly, without the fraught expressions of outrage or shock he didn't want.

He was glad he'd told her. He was glad she was here.

And, idiot that he was, he suddenly realized he was still holding her hand. Clutching it as if it were a lifeline—perhaps it was. He let go, which was more difficult than he would have expected, and grabbed the Veuve to pour refills. "Drink up. This is getting warm."

"I have one more question."

"All right." He didn't really want to answer any more questions, but he could not deny her something that was so easy to give.

"Is it possible things will get better after your father dies? How old is he?" She winced. "I sound like I'm wishing for him to die."

"It's all right. It's a fair question. My father is fifty-three. He's in remarkably good health despite the fact that he's practically pickled in vodka. And to answer your other question, I suppose in one sense, life will be easier when he's gone. But it is difficult for me to convey how much I do *not* want to be the duke. Not to be melodramatic, but the idea of inheriting feels like . . ."

"Feels like what?"

"Locking myself up and throwing away the key." He snorted. "Listen to me. I sound like a princess trapped in a tower."

"How would a princess trapped in a tower get out?"

"Well, I think traditionally, a prince would come and rescue her."

"And you had a princess, didn't you? But instead of rescuing you, she's going to marry a cabdriver from the Bronx."

"She is indeed."

Chapter Eleven

Things were much less fraught back in the room. They ordered room service. The McMuffins had been delicious, but Max was still hungry. Apparently too much truth telling worked up an appetite. As Dani divided the steak they'd ordered to share, he perused her Netflix account on the hotel TV.

"What shall we watch? Probably *Dirty Dancing*, yes?" He squinted at the diverse array of films on her list. "First in your queue is *Love Actually*."

"Oh, yeah, that's always there. I love that movie—I've seen it dozens of times—but it's a Christmas movie, so we can't watch it."

"Incorrect. We can do whatever we want."

"Yeah, but Christmas only runs from December 11 to January 6, remember?"

"Ah, yes. I see the dilemma." He read the synopsis. "I've never seen it."

"*Really?* Oh, it's so good. And so bad. It's complicated."

"It stars Emma Thompson? Sold."

"But—"

"You don't have to watch it." He pressed play. "I'm going to, though. You can do your own thing."

He wasn't sure what was more enjoyable, the movie itself or Dani's running commentary on it. "I think the problem," she pronounced when they were about two-thirds through, "is that everyone thinks this is a romantic comedy and judges it accordingly. But it's *not* a rom-com. If anything, it's a romantic tragedy. I mean, some of the stories turn out, but even among those, there are some that are hella problematic. Like, I don't want to spoil anything, but there's one in particular that seems all sweet, but when you think about it, you're like, 'How is *that* going to work out?' You'll see."

"Is this movie actually controversial?" It was reading as benign enough to him. Charming in parts, sad in others, populated with a lot of well-liked English actors.

"In certain circles." She nodded at the TV. "Like this part coming up. Everyone I know says it's creepy and stalkerish. And I guess if you explain what's literally happening—this guy has been in love with his best friend's girlfriend all this time and now he's about to tell her when there's no way it will end well—yeah, it's creepy." Max watched as the character in question knocked on Keira Knightley's door and, when she answered, silently flipped through a series of placards proclaiming his love for her.

"But if you look at what's actually *happening*," Dani went on, shaking her finger at the TV, "if you look at the way they look at each other, it's not that creepy. He knows it's never happening. He knows he's been a dick about it. He knows she knows he knows.

It's his way of closing the door on it, saying he's going to be less of a dick going forward. I think it's actually rather lovely. I like that line, 'At Christmas you tell the truth.'"

"Being less of a dick," Max said. "Something to aspire to."

She threw a pillow at him. He caught it and watched her watch the rest of the scene.

"I don't know," she said, sighing as the man walked away from Keira Knightley's house. "It's a memorable scene. I guess there's just something about an unrequited crush."

Yes. "There is, isn't there?"

WHEN DANI WOKE the next morning in Max's giant, posh bed at the Four Seasons—Max himself was on a shrimpy rollaway—it was to the sound of an incoming text.

She read it through bleary eyes. She and Max had stayed up until four talking. Not even about anything of consequence, unless you considered bickering about *Love Actually* of consequence. She suspected he'd been leaning into the meaningless banter because he had exhausted his well of revelations. And what revelations they had been. Surprising, but only in the way that stories of cruelty always were. In another, deeper sense, they were the missing piece to the mystery that was Max. The explanation for why he was always deflecting attention from himself and embracing his bad reputation.

But actually, there was still a bit of a mystery, and that was how he had retained his guileless ability to express emotion. To say, *I like you and I want to hang out with you*, when he had grown up with such unkindness.

She was suffused with tenderness toward him. Not pity, because she knew he wouldn't want that, but her heart broke to think of the little boy trying to protect his brother. And of the man that boy had become. Her wonderful, strong friend.

She'd have thought they'd run out of things to say last night, given that they'd now spent almost forty-eight continuous hours together, but they hadn't. In fact, they'd fallen asleep talking in the dark, like teenagers at a slumber party.

"Oh my god!" she exclaimed as she read the text.

Max sat bolt upright in bed, his hair sticking up like he'd stuck a finger into an electrical socket. "What? What's wrong?" Max Minimus started barking. He was in Max's bed, the traitor.

"A text from Vince." She read it aloud as she tried and failed to get her dog to come back to her bed. "'I've signed the papers. I'm on my way to your place to drop them off. I'd like to see you in person.'"

"Well, I'll be damned," Max said, scratching Max Minimus's head. "Perhaps that party was more effective than we knew."

"I have to get there." She threw back her covers and hopped out of bed.

"I don't know why he can't courier them." Max sounded peeved.

"Or give them to his lawyer, which is what he was supposed to do, but probably he has to have the last word or make me jump through one last hoop." Dani dug in her overnight bag as Max Minimus finally left Max Maximus's side and yipped around her heels. "Which is fine. I don't care anymore. I'm getting my divorce and my dog, so he can make whatever little speech he wants if it makes him feel better."

Max got out of bed. "I'm coming with you."

"Do you have enough time before your flight?"

"Yes. I don't fly private, but I'm not above playing the baron card in order to cut the security and customs lines."

"Okay," she agreed, pausing to smile at his bewildered expression. He had probably expected her to object. Historically, that was what she had done whenever he'd offered her something. Not today. If he could bare his soul to her, she could accept his help without arguing. In fact . . . "Any chance you can order up your magical Mercedes?"

"I can indeed."

She clapped her hands. "Okay, come on, Maxes. I'm getting divorced!"

"THE AWKWARD PART is that the mime is still in my apartment," Dani said laughingly as they got out of the car at her building. "I'm going to have to receive my divorce papers out here." A waist-high ledge separated the sidewalk from the building's property, and she boosted herself up and sat on it.

Max peered up at where he thought Dani's windows were. It bothered him, the idea of her having to clear out of her place to make room for strangers. While he understood intellectually that rents were high in New York, it still rankled.

But not as much as the sight of Vince strolling up did. He wanted to fucking punch the man, an impulse he checked both because he was not the kind of person who went around punching people, even people who deserved it, but also because the rational part of his brain knew that punching Vince was not the way to get Dani the divorce he wanted.

She wanted. The divorce *she* wanted.

So he swallowed his rage and said, "Why don't I go around the corner with my namesake?" He assumed that if Vince had signed the papers, he had given up on the canine custody battle, but there was no reason to remind him what he was missing out on.

Dani's eyes flickered to Vince and then back to him. She seemed uneasy. He wasn't accustomed to that. The Dani he knew tore the outer layer of skin off idiot students and charmed her way through parties as the situation called for. He thought back to her telling him that Vince was a "good talker." And she'd said on more than one occasion that Vince didn't listen to her.

"Unless you'd prefer I stay?" He forced himself to issue the question mildly, as if it didn't make any difference to him one way or the other. But suddenly, he wanted nothing more than to be her backup. For her to *want* him as her backup.

"Would you?" she asked quietly.

"Of course." He reached for Max's leash. "May I?"

"Yes. Thanks." He could sense her bracing herself. He knew the feeling. Wondering what was about to happen, even though experience should have taught you exactly what to expect. Perhaps it wasn't bracing so much as hoping. Which he should know better than to do by now.

But this wasn't him. This was Dani.

"Dani," Vince said. He glanced at Max but did not acknowledge him.

"Hi, Vince," she said with no intonation at all. Despite her nerves, she was pitching her voice and her posture perfectly. "I—we—were about to take the dog for a walk." She gestured back toward Max. Maxes.

Vince glanced over again, his expression hard to read. "Can we go upstairs for a bit?"

"I don't think there's any need to," Dani said, and Max swore he heard the second, unarticulated part of her sentence. *Because there's a mime up there already.* He pressed his lips together so as not to smile.

"You have the papers?" Dani asked.

"I wanted to talk to you."

"All right." She was deploying the same tone she'd used to wish "Happy holidays" to that boy pleading for an extension last Christmas.

"Could we . . . do that alone?" Vince asked.

"I don't think there's any need to," she said again. Max was fairly certain Vince was wondering whether he and Dani were an item. He was happy to let that question go unanswered. Or, hell, if it would move matters along, he was happy to fan the flames a little. He took a step toward her.

"Berkeley and I broke up," Vince blurted. "Last night. After the party."

There was a beat while Dani absorbed that bit of news before she said, "Oh, that's too bad."

Vince seemed to be waiting for her to ask for details. Instead, she merely gazed evenly at him.

"Mistakes have been made," Vince said as he took a step toward Dani. Max took another one, too, from the other direction, though he was cognizant of not wanting to turn this into some kind of duel. "I'm willing to admit that mistakes have been made."

"Vince, you remember when you taught freshman comp?" Dani said suddenly. "That first year I arrived, you were stuck with two sections of it?" She looked over her shoulder at Max, as if including him in the conversation, and added, "He hated it."

She turned back to Vince. "Remember the thing about avoiding passive language where possible? 'Mistakes have been made' is some top-notch passive language. You want to talk? Let's talk about those mistakes. Let's do me first. What mistakes have I made?"

"You really don't think we have anything worth saving here, Dani?" Vince said, sidestepping her question entirely. "All our time together, just down the toilet?"

Oh, for fuck's sake. As if it wasn't Vince himself who had done the flushing. Max clenched his jaw and exhaled, but the air through his teeth came out as a sort of whistle-growl, which drew both Vince's and Dani's attention—Dani looked over her shoulder briefly at Max before turning back to Vince.

"You know what?" Dani said. "I'm sorry I said that. There's no point in talking about it. Why don't you give me the papers, and   "

"Oh, you're fucking a duke now, so you're too good for me?"

"Baron, actually," Dani said, and Max chuckled as he waited for her to correct the actual substance of the allegation.

She did not.

Max found he enjoyed being thought of as the kind of man Dani would choose as . . . what? Someone to sleep with? Someone to *be* with? Well, either or both. He would take whatever fake status she was conferring. He puffed up his chest, aware that while he might have avoided a duel, he was now acting as if he were in a nature documentary. He wouldn't be surprised to suddenly hear David Attenborough's voice narrating. *Notice how the European male stakes his claim by straightening his spine and throwing his shoulders back.*

Dani, back to being preternaturally calm, was staring at Vince with her eyebrows raised. Vince looked at Max, who smiled and pulled Max Minimus's leash in a little. *Yeah, asshole, I got the girl* and *the dog.*

Of course, he actually had neither, but again, he was enjoying the fiction a great deal.

Vince slumped forward with a sigh. It was subtle, but David Attenborough noticed. *The American male is signaling defeat. The documents required for the dissolution of his union with the American female are in the satchel he carries. Will he hand them over? It is not uncommon for an American male in this position to retreat in the hopes he will live to fight another day. See how he pauses with his hand in the satchel? But . . . there are the papers. He hands them over. He tries to catch the American female's hand as he does so, but she's too quick for him. The papers in hand, she retreats, moving to stand near to the European male and the small canine.*

"Thanks, Vince," Dani said, and suddenly her voice had more emotion in it.

"So this is it?" Vince said, holding out his palms as if she were robbing him. She was, in a way, Max supposed. She was taking herself from him. Her presence, her attention. Her all-around amazingness. Max had been gloating earlier, reveling in Dani's obvious preference for him over Vince, but this *was* it. The end of a marriage. The culmination of a lot of struggle. And even though Dani was getting her wish, it was bound to be caught up in some mixed emotions.

"This is it," Dani said quietly. "Goodbye, Vince."

Max had the momentary fear that Vince wasn't going to leave. He and Dani had nowhere to retreat, what with the mime upstairs. But Vince gave a little nod, said, "I'll see you at work," and turned to go.

They watched him in silence for what felt like an eternity. When he disappeared around a corner, Max turned to Dani.

She burst into tears.

Oh, shit. He closed the space between them and took her in his arms. He thought about saying something meant to comfort but decided not to. He simply held her.

After a few seconds, she pulled back and started trying to apologize.

"None of that." He led her back to the ledge she'd been sitting on before, settled them both on it, and slung one arm around her shoulder.

"But why am I crying? I'm glad." She shook the papers she was still holding. "I'm relieved. This is what I *want*."

"Well, it's still the end of an era, isn't it?"

She blew out a breath and swiped at her eyes. "I guess it is. I'm mostly still so mad at myself. I wasted so much time with him. What was the matter with me? Where was my judgment?"

"People don't change overnight, I don't think," Max said, thinking about how he and his brother were finding their way back to each other. Or hell, how they had fallen away from each other to begin with. Neither had been a smooth, linear process. "I don't think it's that useful to look at who he is now and ask what you saw in him. He must have had his redeeming qualities. You must have had some fun, once?"

She nodded. "Yeah."

"Eventually, the bitterness will fade, and you'll be able to look back with equanimity. He'll be a colleague for whom you have some fondness, or at least a colleague for whom you hold no rancor. It will just take a little time."

"Why are you so good at giving breakup advice? Have you ever actually had a girlfriend?"

"I have not." He smirked. "I'm just smart." He pulled a handkerchief out of his pocket and handed it to her.

"A handkerchief! How old-world of you." She blew her nose. "In the movies, you always see the guy giving the girl the hankie, but you never see what happens to it after it's all snotty."

"What happens is the girl keeps it." A car pulled up in front of the building. "Ah, that's my ride." The driver emerged, and Max held up a finger to indicate that he was coming.

The door to the building opened, and a man with a suitcase came out.

"Oh!" Dani exclaimed. "Hi! Was everything okay with your stay?"

The man—the mime—rushed over and grinned and nodded.

"You don't have to be out for another hour," Dani said. "I had to meet someone here, but you don't have to go yet."

The man gestured to an imaginary watch, and then flung his arms out like a bird, or . . .

"You have a flight to catch?" Dani guessed. "Are you flying out of JFK?"

The man nodded yes with a degree of enthusiasm that seemed better suited for having been told he'd won the lottery.

Dani grinned and pointed at Max. "He can drive you."

The mime became disproportionately excited, gestured his thanks to Max, and pointed at Dani and mimed counting stars in the sky—he counted to five and pointed at her again.

"I think I just got a five-star Airbnb rating," she said laughingly.

Max waved at his driver. "We have a passenger." He turned to the mime. "Could you give us a minute?" The mime performed an elaborate farewell routine, and Dani and Max were alone again.

"Max." She turned to him. "I don't want you to go!" She made a silly, self-deprecating face and grinned at him.

Well. He wasn't sure anyone had ever said something that made him feel this good. And normally he would change his ticket in a heartbeat. "I wish I could stay, but I'm flying to Innsbruck to meet Seb for a series of meetings regarding construction permits."

She smiled, her tears gone. "That sounds like something a person with a job would say."

"Well, remember, I'm not getting paid."

"An almost-job. To go with my almost-divorce." She shook the papers. "If I understand the process correctly, we file these, and then at some point there's a judgment, and eventually a certified copy arrives in the mail."

"I beat you, though. We'll be breaking ground next month." And of course, there was her other resolution—the sex resolution. Typically, he would make a joke about that here, but he found he didn't want to. He didn't want to talk about it at all.

"Overachiever." She swatted him on the chest, and before she could retract her hand, he grabbed it, pulled her into a hug. He felt that was allowed, that after all the revelations of the past two days, this was a thing they did now.

She must have agreed, because she came easily. They stood embracing silently for a long moment.

"I'll see you at the wedding in November," she said with what seemed like artificial cheerfulness when they finally parted.

"How long will you be in Eldovia? You should stay a while. You have the teaching leave this fall. You're planning to be a lie-about anyway, yes? So come lie about with me."

"I'd love to, but I don't want to leave Max Minimus for that long. After a few days without me at my parents' place, he starts to get weird and mopey. I haven't booked my ticket yet, but I'm thinking four, five days at most."

"I assumed you'd be bringing my namesake with you? Like last time?"

"No. Not doing that again. He freaked out being confined to a tiny crate under the seat on the plane.

"Well, that's too bad," he said, understating the matter entirely. Just because he had somehow developed an emotional dependence on Dani didn't mean he could expect her to arrange her life to accommodate him.

He made himself get into the car. He had a mime to take to the airport. He rolled down the window, and she came to stand beside it. "Until November," she said.

"Until November," he echoed. It was too long to be without her, but what choice did he have?

ON HER WAY out of what looked like it was going be her last meeting with her lawyer, Dani checked her phone to find texts from Max.

Max: How do you feel about private jets?

Max: We know how I feel about private jets, but what about you? Environmental disasters that are never worth it, full stop? Or are there situations in which you could justify it?

> **Dani:** Like what kind of situation?

> **Max:** The kind where I send one for you so you can bring my namesake to Eldovia and he can roam around the cabin as much as his heart desires while the flight attendant dotes on him, thus enabling both of you to pay a long visit to Eldovia. You can stay with me, and I'll leave you alone to work on the mystery project.

> **Max:** Mostly.

> **Max:** As long as you agree to gossip with me in the evenings.

Oh, Max. Dani's heart squeezed at the generous offer.

> **Dani:** I think that's going to be hard to justify. If you, an almost-duke, can fly commercial, I'm pretty sure that I, a certified normal person, should too.

> **Max:** Yes, but I don't have a tiny neurotic dog to think about.

The phone rang, and he started talking before she greeted him. "How about this? My parents fly private all the time. Most people in my circles fly private. I never do. I have a reputation as being environmentally minded."

"I thought you had a reputation as being depraved."

"Publicly. I have a reputation among people who actually know me as being environmentally minded. In fact, it's one of my father's favorite things to fight about. Namely, he does not care about it and likes to mock the fact that I do."

"You should hire a PR company to start marketing you as the Green Baron. You could dress in a World War I uniform, like the Red Baron. Except, you know, green."

He chuckled. "Right. So let's say I had flown private one time in my past. One time out of the hundreds of flights I've taken. Would that make my Green Baron reputation any less meaningful?"

"No?" Dani ventured. She was a bit confused, but that seemed like the answer he was looking for.

"Right. So now, *you* can take one of those private flights that *I* never did."

"Is this like buying a carbon offset?"

"Yes! Exactly!"

"A baron offset?"

"Call it what you like. And you can rent your apartment out while you're gone, so you'll actually turn a profit."

She paused, imagining a couple of weeks—or more—spent in Eldovia. She'd get to see Leo and Gabby beyond the whirlwind of the wedding. Max Minimus could cavort in actual nature—there would be mountains and the hot spring. She also couldn't turn her nose up at the cash she'd make doing an Airbnb rental over Thanksgiving.

And there was Max. She'd get to spend time with Max. Nature and money were cool, but the prospect of getting to hang out with Max for an extended period was too good to pass up. "Would you think I was a terrible person if I took you up on this offer?"

"Yes," he said, totally deadpan. But then he added, "No. You walk to work every day, so that's as good as buying a carbon offset.

"Maybe I *can* buy a carbon offset!" She wondered how much it would cost to offset a private flight to Eldovia.

"You can't, but I will."

She was flooded with affection for her friend. "Max, you're all right."

"I'll try not to let it go to my head."

"Thank you," she said, turning serious.

"You're welcome," he said, doing the same. "Send me your preferred travel dates—but please come for a nice long stretch if you can; I promise you'll have lots of time to work—and I'll take care of it."

Chapter Twelve

Oh!" Max was startled as he exited his cottage and almost bumped into Sebastien, who was standing there in the November sunshine with his knuckles raised, poised to knock. "Hello."

"I was hoping to speak to you."

"I can't right now. I'm off to meet Daniela Martinez's plane. She's coming for the wedding. She's Leo's friend," he added, though he had no idea why, as characterizing Dani as "Leo's friend" didn't begin to cover it.

"I know who she is," Seb said.

Of course. Everyone knew all the details about the royal wedding. The wedding that was supposed to be Max's. And chief among those details were the salacious ones—the fact that not only was the groom a nobody from the Bronx, his only attendant was also going to be a nobody from the Bronx. A *female* nobody. Mother had been talking about it nonstop.

"Can't you just send a car?" Seb asked.

Max studied his brother's face. His forehead was deeply furrowed. "Is everything all right? Has something gone wrong in Innsbruck?"

"No, no. Everything's fine. I was merely going to . . . Never mind. We can talk later."

"You want to ride to the airfield with me?" The plane was landing on a private airfield an hour's drive from the estate.

"May I?"

"Of course. I'll appreciate the company." Not really, because Max was a selfish bastard and he wanted Dani to himself. But he and Dani had three weeks to talk. Three glorious weeks. He had convinced her to make such a long visit by assuring her she could spend the first half of it working on the estate. Then they'd go to the palace for the wedding, then to Innsbruck to see the mine and have a holiday.

"So you're having an affair with Leo's friend," Sebastien said as their journey got underway. "Is that wise?"

Ah, here they went. "I am not having an affair with her. We're friends."

"I thought she was Leo's friend."

"She's not allowed to have more than one friend?" Even with his eyes on the road, Max could feel Seb's wince, and yes, that had come out a little snippier than Max had intended, but honestly. "I invited her to spend some time here before the wedding, since Mother and Father are away." Their parents were holidaying on Sardinia and would be back a few days before the wedding, by which point Max and Dani would already have left for the palace—ostensibly because their man of honor and best woman duties required them to be there early but really because there was no way he was going to subject Dani to his parents. She would meet them at the wedding, of course; it was unavoidable. But their impact would be diluted there—he hoped. "And after the wedding, we're going to Austria with Leo and Marie."

"Isn't that a little odd? You're tagging along on the honeymoon?"

"Really, it's them tagging along with us." He'd mentioned he was taking Dani to see the mine, and suddenly they had extra hangers-on. Marie insisted that they wanted to spend some time with Dani—he knew the feeling—and see the mine project in progress. After a couple of days in Innsbruck, Marie and Leo were going to continue on to a posh Indonesian resort, alone.

"What's going on with you?" Max asked his brother. The point of him being along for the ride was so he could talk, not so he could interrogate Max about Dani.

"Oh, nothing."

"So you're spending two hours round-trip with me in this car because you love me so much."

Seb rolled his eyes. "I think you love yourself enough for both of us."

Max grinned. One of the unexpectedly delightful dividends of his repaired relationship with his brother was that they could needle each other again. They'd lost that for a long while, but one thing Max had never lost was the ability to tell when something was bothering Seb. He had a certain way of picking at his fingernails when he was anxious, and he was doing it now. "What's wrong? Out with it."

"Nothing's wrong. I just . . . have something I need to tell you."

"All right."

He glanced over. Seb lowered his hands to his lap and looked

Max in the eye in a way that made Max fear something might be seriously wrong, but Max had to return his attention to the road. "The thing is," Seb said, "I'm . . ."

As he trailed off, Max's mind got to work filling in the blanks. Seb was in trouble of some sort? Angrier than he'd expressed for all the years Max had been mentally checked out? Deathly ill? "What? You're what?"

"Don't run us off the road, but I'm gay."

Of course he was. Max didn't know why he hadn't seen it earlier. He huffed a laugh.

Seb sucked in a breath and turned toward the window, hurt.

"*Seb.*" Max let go of the steering wheel with his right hand and grabbed his brother's left. "I'm sorry. I'm laughing at *myself*. At how obvious it was—or should have been. I'm sorry I didn't see it." Another glance over showed that Seb's eyes had gone wide, and Max rushed to add what he should have led with. "It doesn't make a whit of difference to me. In fact, it makes me *happy*. It makes me happy to think of you being more authentically yourself. I'm glad for you and glad you told me. I'm sorry if you felt you couldn't previously."

"Really? That's it?"

"Well, excuse me for forgetting to pack my rainbow confetti."

Seb laughed and took his hand back. "I was expecting more of the opposite reaction, to be honest."

"From me? Really?" That stung.

"No, not really. I'm sorry. That's not fair. You're just so . . . heterosexual."

"I am not!" Max protested reflexively.

"You're not?" Seb's jaw dropped.

It was Max's turn to laugh. "No, I am. But I like to think I'm a modern sort of heterosexual. I'm very live-and-let-live."

Seb smiled. "I meant that you're such a playboy."

Right. He used to be, anyway.

"You've been chasing girls since you were a teenager."

"Whatever reputation I have doesn't mean anything about my character," Max said, not telling Seb that he was in the middle of the longest dry spell of his life. "Expect a negative reaction from Father, not me." His stomach grew heavy wondering if perhaps Father *had* known somehow. If that was what had been behind the tea-party tantrum all those years ago. "You *haven't* told Father, have you?"

"God, no. No. I can never do that."

"You could, though. If you wanted to. I'd have your back."

"He'd disown me."

"Probably," Max agreed. And when Max inherited, he would re-own him. It was a pleasant thought, the idea of undoing some of his father's damage. One good thing about becoming the duke. "It would definitely mean a change of career, though, as he'd probably have you fired in addition to disowning you."

"I know. I just feel like . . ."

"Someone has to be the do-gooder at the company," Max supplied. It was interesting how heavy a yoke duty was for Sebastien, the younger son, who should by rights be fucking off to have orgies in the Mediterranean—or perhaps cavorting around a library, which was more Seb's style.

"Anyway," Seb said, "I didn't mean all that about you being a playboy. Well, I *did*. But I knew you weren't going to turn your back on me. I was just . . . worked up to tell you. To tell anyone."

"Am I the first person you've told?" That was flattering.

"Well, technically, you're the second."

Max tried to think who Seb would have told. His brother had always been a bit of a loner. He had some friends who— Hang on. "Oh my god! You're seeing someone!"

"I am not," Seb said, but he was blushing furiously.

"Who is it?" Max started shoving Seb's shoulder, because apparently, he had regressed to age twelve. Seb shook his head. "So you're going to drop this bomb on me, but you're not going to tell me who."

Seb smirked. "That is correct."

Max's mind started sifting through the possibilities, but the sobering truth was that he didn't really know that much about his brother's life. "Is it someone I know?"

Seb smiled all at once, as if it was a reflex, but then schooled his face.

"It is!" Max exclaimed.

"Well, you don't *know him* know him. You know *of* him, I think."

There went the smile again. Damn. His brother was smitten. Max was dying to know who it was, but he refrained from pushing. He would mount an investigation later.

They talked about the mine project until they arrived at the airfield. As Max cut the engine and turned to Seb, Seb said, "So we're . . . okay?"

"Yes," Max said emphatically. "We are *grand.*" He unbuckled himself, leaned over, and planted a purposefully slobbery kiss on Seb's temple. "We are grand, and you are grand, and I love you." He was so damn glad he had his brother back.

Perhaps Seb's confession had primed Max to be extra emotional. Or perhaps he was that excited to see Dani. Either way, he found himself practically buzzing with anticipation when a small plane appeared in the distance.

They watched as the plane landed and taxied. A stairway dropped, and a few minutes later there she was, paused at the top of the stairs, one hand wrapping a bright-red scarf around her neck, the other arm tucking Max Minimus into her side. Something inside Max settled into place. She caught sight of him and smiled as she set the dog down. He bounded down the steps and headed straight for Max, yapping all the way.

"Hello, my little friend," Max cooed, stooping to pick him up and chuckling when Max Minimus started licking his face. "Lovely to see you, too, my good boy."

"What is *happening*?" Seb asked with wonder in his voice. "Who *are* you?"

Max, suddenly aware that he was not the type of person who got all mushy with tiny dogs, cleared his throat and straightened, trying to recapture some dignity. Normally, he would have swept Dani up in a hug, but he settled for a quick, formal kiss on the cheek on account of Seb's scrutiny, though it did occur to him that his brother had told him a huge secret and here Max was being conservative in greeting his platonic friend. It was just that Seb would misinterpret. Max performed introductions while Max Minimus relieved himself. It was strange seeing Seb and Dani together. Between the two of them, Max felt so . . . tethered. In a good way—as if he owed these people something, but that owing was not unwelcome.

A steward arrived with Dani's bag and Max Minimus's crate

and loaded them into the car. Max held the door for Dani. "Your holiday awaits, milady."

RIEMS WAS CHARMING. As they drove to Max and Sebastien's family estate through the darkening night, they had to pass through the city itself, and Dani couldn't help but exclaim over the narrow cobblestone streets and the half-timbered architecture that looked like something out of a storybook. It was November, so lots of the shops had twinkly Christmas lights up.

The von Hansburg brothers were pretty darn charming, too. She already knew that about Max, of course, but his younger brother was friendly and warm, if a bit shy. The fact that he'd come along to pick her up was such a nice gesture.

"We're not that far out of town," Max said as the stone buildings started to thin and eventually disappeared in favor of countryside. "It's a thirty-minute walk if you're ever inclined to make a prison break."

"If you're ever inclined to make a prison break, you merely have to call on me, Daniela," Sebastien said with exaggerated courtliness.

"I meant if she needs a break from *us*," Max said.

"Ah, yes." Sebastien sobered. "Well, at least Mother and Father are absent."

Dani had been relieved by the news that Max's parents would be away. She was morbidly curious about them, these people who had raised Max, and tormented him, too, but glad she didn't have to meet them until the wedding.

The estate was beautiful. Riems was in a valley—you could see mountains on all sides in the distance, the tallest of them capped with snow. One was smaller and closer than the others, and the estate was nestled at its foot in a landscape of gardens—mostly barren for the season, but she imagined they were lovely in the summer—surrounded by forest.

"We'll drop you at the main house," Max said to his brother.

"Daniela is staying with you at the cottage?" Sebastien asked, and if Dani wasn't mistaken, he was surprised, though there hadn't been censure in his tone.

"She is," Max said mildly. "We'll come up to the house and have dinner with you, though. I've already made arrangements with Frau Bittner."

They said goodbye to Sebastien, and Max turned the car down a gravel-lined road that led away from the house, which was an enormous, multi-winged, imposing stone thing with red tiled roofs. "Max, does your brother think we . . ." She waved her hand back and forth between them.

"Oh, probably. I would have corrected him, but I didn't want to give away the surprise."

"What surprise?"

"He'll come over later and see it and be assured that nothing is happening between us," Max said, ignoring her question. He waggled his eyebrows. "Your fruitcake is safe under my roof."

"Why is it *my* fruitcake that's safe from *you*? I thought you and I were about equal-opportunity slutting around."

He threw his head back and laughed. "Touché." He looked at her for a beat too long—she was about to tell him to keep his eyes on the road—and said, "I'm so glad you're here."

She was, too.

Max's cottage was perfect. There was no other word for it. It was small and made of the same stone as the main house, and it was crisscrossed with vines. Max led her to a big, weathered wooden door with an oxidized knocker shaped like a lion's head and unlocked it with a long, skinny key that looked like a prop from a haunted house more than an actual functional key.

"Here we are," he said with obvious pleasure as he took her coat. "This was originally what I think English speakers would call a dower house, but it hasn't been occupied by a dowager since my father's mother died—before I was born."

"Your grandmother the Nazi-resister!"

"Mm," Max said in a way that struck Dani as evasive, but she didn't have time to parse his response, because she was too busy looking at everything. She was in Max's home! In Eldovia!

The place looked like Max—it had an air of old money ease but not of the stuffy variety. There were Persian rugs everywhere that were probably priceless heirlooms, but they were worn and mismatched. His living room looked like the genuine version of the aesthetic that "shabby-chic" Instagrammers spent their lives chasing. He led her through a small kitchen outfitted with modern appliances but that also contained an actual fireplace with a pot hanging next to it and a deep sink with both a modern faucet and an ancient pump handle on it.

In the back corner there was a trapdoor in the ceiling with a rope handle dangling down. He pulled it, and a narrow, steep staircase fell, startling Dani. He gestured for her to go ahead of him, and she climbed the rickety staircase, which was really more like a ladder.

And emerged into the garret of her dreams.

"Are you *kidding* me?"

"I am not. Remember that first night in New York? I asked you what you would do if you could do anything, and you said hole up in in a garret and write. You won't tell me about the mystery project, but I assume it's something that needs to be written."

Oh, Max. Max who listened and remembered. Max who coaxed her to make snow angels and do *Dirty Dancing* lifts. Max who conjured ballet tickets and garrets.

"Perhaps you don't remember." He grinned. "That was two negronis in."

"I remember," she said, her voice a little squeaky as she took it all in. The open space spanned the top of the cottage and featured slanting walls that created cozy nooks. The ceiling was crisscrossed by wooden support beams, the unfinished nature of which contributed to the same worn-luxury look of the rooms downstairs. There were more timeworn Persian rugs on top of rustic, sightly uneven whitewashed wooden floors. There was a queen-size bed in the middle of the space piled high with white bedding of the sort you saw in rich-people advertisements, expensive but wrinkly because it was one-million-thread-count linen. On one side of the bed was an armoire and a full-length mirror on a stand. On the other, nestled against a large stone chimney, was a little sitting area with a love seat and coffee table.

And of course on the far end of the space was a desk perfectly sized to nestle in a dormer with a window that overlooked the mountain.

"There are a few drawbacks," Max said, "namely no bathroom. You'll have to come downstairs and share with me." He crossed to the desk and picked up the end of an extension cord draped over it. Dani followed it with her gaze to see that it lined the edge of the floor until it disappeared under the bed. "The only outlet is on the other side of the bed," he said. "And it's going to be dark in here at night. And cold. It's suboptimal, but—"

"*Max*." She hated to interrupt him, but honestly. "This is *amazing*." She spun in a slow circle to take it all in once more. "*Amazing*." And she wasn't just talking about the room.

"There's more," he said with a grin as he beckoned her over to the desk. "This attic used to be storage. I was under the impression that it was all my mother's old equestrian things—she used to be quite the rider, and all her old saddles and trophies and the like were stored up here. And indeed, when I started clearing the place out, that's mostly what I found. But . . ." He pointed to a stack of wrinkled, yellowed papers.

"Oh my god!" She knew, without him saying anything. "Oh my god!"

He produced a pair of white cotton gloves from his pocket, the kind you'd use to handle fragile artifacts, and handed them to her. "These are going to the exhibition design firm tomorrow, but I wanted to show them to you first."

She pulled the gloves on, her hands shaking with vicarious excitement. "I don't read German."

"Look at the names, the opening and closing salutations."

"'Liebe Karlotta,'" she read.

"Karlotta was my grandmother's name."

Dani's excitement notched even higher as she flipped the paper over and read the name of the writer. "Karina." She gasped, even though she'd known that was what she'd find. "Max! And they were on a first-name basis, it seems!"

"There are half a dozen letters there. It looks as though my grandmother did give over the mine to the resistance, and she funneled money to them as well. She didn't want her husband—my grandfather—to know. The letters were hidden under a floorboard that had been covered with boxes for who knows how many years."

She set the letter down carefully. "This is going to be huge, isn't it?"

"It is." He smiled like the cat that ate the canary. "I wish I could find Oma's letters to Karina. I'm following a few leads on that front, but even without them, yes, this will be major news."

She was so thrilled for him. She peeled the glove off her right hand and held it up for a high-five. He slapped her hand but then grabbed it. Used it to reel her in. "I'm so glad you're here," he said into her hair as he hugged her tight.

She was, too. It felt so good to leave all her Vince junk behind, to be off the teaching treadmill for a while.

But that wasn't all. This feeling of relief and rightness wasn't just about what she had left behind. It was about Max. Smart, kind Max. They were going to have so much fun, and she was so happy to be here with him.

Chapter Thirteen

The next morning, Dani awoke in bed alone. There was no Max.

Minimus, she mentally added. There was no Max *Minimus*. She threw a sweatshirt over her flannel pajamas—Max had warned her that the cottage was cold, and he had been right—and made her way down the ladder. The kitchen and sitting rooms were empty, but she found the Maxes in bed together.

"Good morning." She made a kissy face at the dog, who lifted his head from where he was snuggled into Max's side and let loose a happy bark of greeting, but instead of bounding over to her as he normally would have, he merely turned, licked Max's cheek, and tucked himself back in.

Max Maximus lowered the newspaper he was reading and made a kissy-face back at her.

She rolled her eyes. "Are you trying to steal my dog?"

"Yes, Daniela. Our friendship has all been an elaborate long con aimed at stealing your mongrel." He mock scowled at Max Minimus. "Who, I hasten to add, snores like a dog of significantly larger stature."

"Did he sleep with you?"

"He arrived around three A.M." Max Maximus shrugged. "I can't help how irresistible I am."

"You better watch yourself, or I'll sic my lawyer on you. I can have custody papers sent over while you're lazing about."

He hopped out of bed, and Max Minimus followed. "I may appear to be lazing about, but I've actually been plotting. I have a proposal."

She followed him into the kitchen and watched as he measured coffee into a French press. He paused and looked at her over his shoulder. "Do you drink coffee? Tea? I find it odd that I don't know that about you."

"Coffee. Gallons of it. But why should you know?" When they'd woken up together at the Four Seasons, they'd rushed off to intercept Vince, so there had been no morning beverages.

"I can name all eight of the men you've rejected since New Year's, so it seems odd that I don't know how you take your coffee."

"I take it black."

"Like your heart."

"Exactly. And I will have you know that I've rejected *nine* men since New Year's."

He pointed to a chair, and she sat while he filled the kettle. "Nine? I thought you were letting me know when you were going out. I thought we were up to eight."

Crap. She'd been teasing him, but she'd blown it. She purposefully hadn't told him about that one—there hadn't been any need to, and he got so worked up about the safety aspect of her dates.

He had stopped puttering around the kitchen and was staring at her with an eyebrow raised in a way that communicated that she wasn't getting any coffee until she talked.

She sighed. "It wasn't a Tinder thing. It was . . . a reality thing. A barista who works at a coffee shop I sometimes go to."

"So, what? He just propositioned you?"

"No, he was taking a break and the shop was full, so he couldn't find anywhere to sit. I invited him to join me. I've gotten to know him pretty well in a small-talk-at-the-cash way—he knows which roast I prefer, and I know he's a stand-up comic."

"No wonder you rejected him."

"He's actually really funny," Dani said, aware that she was digging her own grave. "I've googled him—some of his gigs are on YouTube. It's really smart humor."

"Is he ugly? Is he an assault to the senses?"

She shook her head. "No. He's pretty cute. Young." There was her excuse. "Too young."

"What does that mean?"

"Twenty-four."

She thought he was going to rebut, but he asked, "So how do you get from sitting in the coffee shop together to potentially getting it on?"

Her face heated. "I don't know. He kind of . . . strongly implied that there was a standing offer." When Max started to object, she added, "Not in a gross way. In a flirty way that gave me an out." She shrugged. "Which I took."

Max looked at her for a long time. "Why? Here we would seem to have the perfect man. You know him—well enough, anyway. He's funny and smart. He has a job. He is *not* too young, at least for your stated purpose. As far as we know he sometimes eats plants."

Dani smirked. "He's a vegetarian, actually."

"See! He's perfect!"

She hated talking about this, even with Max, who was the easiest person in the world to talk to. It made her feel cornered, afraid, even. Just like she'd felt in that coffee shop.

Max set a mug of coffee in front of her, sat down, and beamed his cobalt eyes at her—into her soul, it felt like. "Tell me what's really happening here."

He wasn't going to let her off the hook—of course he wasn't. "I don't know. I think I want to have sex. I mean, I *do* want to. I have the . . ." She waved her hand around in the air. He copied her gesture with his eyebrows raised questioningly. "Sex feelings," she finished lamely.

A corner of his mouth quirked upward. "You have the 'sex feelings'?"

God. This was mortifying. "You know what I mean."

He smirked and made a "continue" gesture.

"But when I get into a situation where the idea of having sex is no longer theoretical, the sex feelings . . ." She wiggled her fingers and let her hand float up above her head.

He mimicked her again, taking the hand he'd been using to gesture for her to keep talking and letting it float up, too.

"They disappear," she said. "Okay? Are you happy?" He actually looked pretty happy, probably because he enjoyed mocking her. "The sex feelings get replaced by panicky ones."

His face sobered. "Perhaps you're not ready."

"Oh, I'm ready. I am so ready, you don't even know."

"So what is the problem, then?"

Was she going to tell him the truth? Well, why not? Relentless honesty, right? "I think I'm afraid I'll get my heart broken again." She winced as soon as it was out.

He wasn't as surprised as she would have expected. "I thought you were post-love."

"I am! But what if I have sex with one of these guys, especially one of the decent ones, and . . ."

She didn't realize she was making yet another gesture until he mirrored it. "Is this the 'I had sex with this relative stranger one time and his moves blew my mind so much I accidentally fell in love with him' gesture?" he asked.

"Uh, I guess so?"

"I'm sorry. I'm not trying to make fun. I'm trying to understand. When you rejected HarlemHipster, you said it *wasn't* about the risk of heartbreak."

"I know! It doesn't make sense! I just . . . ." She pulled out her phone and opened the Notes app. She had never imagined showing anyone besides Leo the list. But it was as good a way as anything to explain since she couldn't seem to do it. And this was Max. He knew everything anyway. She handed it over.

"'Things I Will Never Again Do for a Man,'" Max said, because of course he was going to read it out loud. He paused a long moment before saying, "Ah, yes," as if he recognized the list.

"Number one: 'Be financially dependent.' Good. Number two: 'Pretend to like things I don't or pretend not to like things I do.' Ah, that's the ballet bit, isn't it?" He looked up, and she nodded.

"Number three: 'Work with him in such a way that his interests are advanced at the expense of my own.'" He snorted. "Fucking Picasso."

See? Max *did* know everything. Nothing on this list was going to surprise him.

'Number four: 'Move.'" He looked up at her questioningly. "I don't understand that one. I thought you liked your apartment."

"I do. I do now. But I had a great rent-controlled apartment before. It was closer to campus, too. I wanted Vince to move in with me, but he wasn't into it. He said we needed to have a new place for our new life together." She rolled her eyes. "I mean, I don't regret it. I wouldn't have ended up being neighbors with Leo otherwise, but the larger point stands."

"Right." He went back to the list. "Number five: 'Be away from my family for the holidays.' That makes sense. You have a great family. Number six: 'Rearrange my schedule to indulge his whims.' Number seven: 'Clean up after him.' Number eight: 'Neglect my friends.' And, finally, number nine: 'Fake an orgasm.'" He chuckled. "Good for you." He set the phone down and regarded her thoughtfully. "I can't argue with any of this. I also don't think it will do any good for me to suggest that having sex one time with one man isn't going to magically make any of these things happen, because I think you know that in your mind."

"I do."

"But you don't know it in your heart. You are afraid. Vince hurt you more than you like to admit, perhaps even to yourself."

She nodded, still painfully embarrassed, but also relieved that Max had gotten to the truth without her having to say it.

"I feel as though this is the part where I'm supposed to make a speech about not closing your heart off to love, and yet I'm not the right person to make that speech."

She smiled. "That is exactly why I like you."

He smiled, too, but was there a touch of wistfulness in it? A hint of the sadness they'd talked about at the Four Seasons?

"It would seem you are at an impasse."

Something was happening inside her body as he stared at her in that super-intense way that was becoming more common as of late.

It was the sex feelings. For Max.

Which was never going to happen. Max had a list of sorts, too, his so-called rules of engagement. And although she was on his turf and *definitely* wasn't trying to entrap him into marriage, she was, technically, still married. Ha. As if that was the only reason it would be a bad idea to follow her loins in this case. She could make another list of those as long as the one he was perusing.

She shook her head and forced herself to smile. Deflection time.

MAX WAS TRYING to play it cool, but what Dani had said shocked him. It shouldn't have. It was obvious now that *of course* she had been finding fault with all these men, Mr. Carnivore aside, because she was afraid of being hurt again.

It just didn't match up with his image of her as fearless, take-no-prisoners Professor Martinez.

But it was also making him question his own judgment. Finding out he hadn't been seeing, really *seeing*, his favorite person in the world properly was unsettling.

"It *would* seem that I'm at an impasse," she said, her eyes twinkling. She was back to her usual self. Or to who he used to think of as her usual self. "But I have another theory. Maybe it's *not* so much that I'm afraid of getting hurt."

It was. He knew it as surely as he knew his own name. Now that he saw it, he couldn't unsee it.

"What if it's not that complicated?" she went on. "What if I'm having some kind of subconscious block about still being married?"

That wasn't it. She'd shared something uncomfortable and she was backpedaling, trying to find another, easier explanation for her behavior. She might not even be doing it consciously.

"Do you think that's possible?" she asked when he was silent too long.

No. "You're asking me?"

"You know me better than anyone."

Well, damn, that was flattering. "Even Leo?"

"Don't tell him, but yeah."

Extremely flattering. It felt like an accomplishment, being the person who knew Dani Martinez best.

He didn't want to abuse that position, and he wasn't about to tell her how she felt, but he was certain her take was incorrect. He supposed she could be protecting her heart *and* have a subconscious block about still being married, but he truly didn't think so. He settled for saying, "I suppose the only way to test your theory is to wait for your divorce judgment and see how you feel. If you find yourself spontaneously wanting to jump comedic baristas, you'll know you *were* hung up on the legalities of still being married."

She smiled. "I think that's it."

It wasn't, but all right.

"I swear to god, the moment the divorce is final, I'm going to do it with the first moderately attractive man I lay eyes on."

He laughed. "So you're just going to grab the nearest man and proposition him?"

"Watch me. I will."

He knew she was jesting, but he very much did not want to watch her do that. "Perhaps a more considered approach would be better."

"Oh, shut up. You don't know what this kind of dry spell is like."

"I do actually. I'm in a bit of one myself. Since New Year's Eve, in fact."

"*What?* Why?"

"I'm not sure. I think perhaps I'm a tad thrown off by my own marriage problem. I'd been slutting around in anticipation of my own impending nuptials. One would think, once they were canceled, that I would have accelerated my slutting around rather than tapered it off." He shrugged, unable to explain his own behavior. Or lack of behavior.

"Well aren't we a pair?"

He was tempted to suggest that they join forces, so to speak that was the logical, bantery comeback—but for some reason he could no longer joke with her about that. "I have a plan for today that will distract us from our mysteriously enduring celibacy. How do you feel about a hike up the mountain? It's my favorite place in the world, and I'd very much like to show it to you. I've spoken to the kitchen, and they can pull together food for us, and there's the hot spring as an inducement. We can practice our *Dirty Dancing* lift.

"If you want to," he added, studying her face, which suddenly seemed to contain a great deal of emotion he could not identify. "We can also just stay here so you can work."

"No," she croaked. Something strange was happening. Her voice sounded almost pained. "I want to."

"Max Minimus can accompany us, if you like." He patted the little imp, who responded by licking him, which should have been off-putting but somehow was not. "It is a fairly steep hike, though, so we could leave him with the gardener, who's a lovely old chap and a bit of a pied piper for the animals on the estate. He has his own dog, and there are some resident stray cats that hiss at everyone else but follow him around like he hung the moon. It's up to you."

"Let's leave him. He's not really an athlete." She sounded herself again.

"Grand." He got back up and refilled her coffee. "Drink up."

An hour later, caffeinated and breakfasted, they strolled off the manicured part of the property and Dani said, "Well, clearly my dog is going to hold a grudge against me for the rest of my life once he's back in New York." They had left Max Minimus rapturously cavorting in the snow with Lorena, the gardener's Sennenhund, who was four times his size. "Playing all day after slinking off to sleep with a baron last night." She shook her head and mock-scowled. "The traitor."

Max had been in bed last night doing his usual insomnia thing when something vaguely wet nudged his shoulder. "Something vaguely wet" had turned out to be Max Minimus's nose, so he'd lifted the covers, and after a moment of shuffling to get comfortable, his namesake had fallen asleep nestled in his armpit.

Oddly, Max had fallen asleep, too, and wakened refreshed several hours later. That was unusual.

"Like, seriously," Dani said. "I haven't woken up without Max Minimus for years. Even when Vince was still in the bed, Max slept on *my* side."

Max wanted to tell her to come sleep in his bed with them, that they could have a big slumber party, but of course he didn't. But damn. He wanted to . . . cuddle her. Her dog, too, fine, but mostly her. It wasn't a sexual thing. Well, that wasn't true. But it wasn't *only* a sexual thing. He couldn't turn off the constant simmering *awareness* of her. She was gorgeous. Her face and her brain and her *everything*. But he accepted that the feeling wasn't mutual. He accepted that the feeling was profoundly ill-advised. So, in the spirit of taking what he could get, he was happy to carve out the garret of her dreams and just . . . be near her.

They spent the walk up the mountain talking, as was their way, about nothing and everything. It was snowing, but the trail was shaded so they didn't have to tromp through much accumulation. Usually when Max went up the mountain, he could feel himself relaxing. It was probably a combination of the objectively calming effect of being in nature and a conditioned response from the days when he and Seb would literally escape up the slope, leaving the tension and dysfunction of the house behind for a while.

But add in the presence of Dani, and he was extra relaxed. Though perhaps *relaxed* was not the right word. All the banter and crackling of wits that occurred in Dani's presence required him to be on his toes, necessitated a degree of concentration that should have been the opposite of relaxation but somehow was not. He felt as if he were in "the zone" that athletes sometimes talked about, that there was a flow and order to the universe he was tapped into, that perhaps his destiny wasn't going to be as oppressive as he'd always thought.

An hour into their hike, Dani dropped a little bomb he hadn't seen coming.

"Okay, I'm going to tell you something a little shocking."

"I am bracing myself even as we speak," he said to her butt. In his defense, they were walking up an incline, and she was ahead of him.

"It's about the mystery project. I think I want to try to write a novel. That's what I've been working on this fall—the research for it."

"Yes." Of course she should write a novel.

"Yes?" She laughed, stopped, and turned. "That's all you have to say?"

"Well, obviously you're going to be brilliant at it." He tilted his head to look up at her—the slope was such that she was taller than he was. "What's it going to be about?" He pointed up the path, signaling that they should keep going.

"Remember I told you about that Gertrude Stein–Pablo Picasso project I worked on with Vince?"

The notes for which she'd handed over as part of the divorce settlement. "I do indeed." He refrained from growling, but it was difficult.

"While we were working on that project, I started thinking about Alice B. Toklas, who was Stein's longtime partner. Stein willed her all this priceless art—she owned Picassos and Matisses and all that since she palled around with all those guys. But because her relationship with Toklas had no legal standing—it couldn't have in that time, obviously—Stein's relatives claimed the paintings. They stole them, basically, and Toklas struggled to make ends meet and later died in poverty. What must that have been like? To lose this great love but also these beautiful images she left you." She shrugged. "I don't know where I'm going with this. It's just this idea that won't let go of me. A lot of the themes of Toklas's life overlap with what I've done academically. And she was a writer, too. So I could write a critical thing about her, but this feels like . . ."

"A novel," Max finished.

"It really does. Actually, I owe you for getting me started thinking about fiction again. I'd idly thought, before, about doing something, but when you told me that wild Karina Klein story in the car on the way home from *The Nutcracker*, it was like something opened up in my brain."

Well. Max very much hoped he was not blushing.

"When my lawyer floated giving up the Stein notes in exchange for Max Minimus, I thought well, I don't have to give up what I *learned* doing that research. Sure, my name isn't going to be on the book Vince writes, but no one can stop me from making up a story."

"This is sounding better and better." Not only did Max like the idea of all her work not being for naught, he really liked the notion of her writing a cooler, better, more popular book than Vince. He would cheerfully admit to being petty that way.

"You really think so? I admit I was feeling kind of weirdly embarrassed about telling you—which is why I haven't. Vince thought it was a weak idea."

"Well, Vince is a weak man," he said dismissively.

"The problem is I have no idea how to write a novel. I write *about* literature; I don't write literature."

"Well, does anyone know how to do something until they do it?"

"No?"

"Don't sound so confident."

"I'm *not* confident."

"Well, you should be."

She stopped and turned again to look down at him. "I already wrote the first chapter. Will you read it?"

"I would love to." He was flattered to be asked.

"Tonight?"

"Yes."

She smiled almost shyly, which was unlike her. "Okay. And then I want you to read me your grandmother's letters so I can nag you about writing a book, too."

"It's a date." He couldn't think when he had looked forward to something more.

NEARLY TWO HOURS later, Max led Dani into a clearing that took her breath away. It had stopped snowing and the sun had come out, bringing low light to a blue sky. Towering, dark-green coniferous trees iced with a thin layer of the morning's snow surrounded a small spring lined with dark-gray stones. Wisps of steam floated up from the water's surface. It was like a postcard that had been run through an "Alps" filter.

As they stood and contemplated the vista, something in Dani's chest lurched and loosened. At the same time, which should have been impossible. But the idea of running away with Max—up a mountain, for heaven's sake, and then to arrive here, in this impossible tableau felt like . . . Well, it felt like healing, as melo-dramatic as that sounded. "Are you *kidding* me with this place?"

Max chuckled. "It is lovely, isn't it?" He smiled a little wistfully. "A nice reward for the strenuous hike up. Seb and I used to come up here all the time. This mountain continues to be one of the great compensations of life as the heir to the Duke of Aquilla."

There was that word again: *compensations*. He'd used it at the Four Seasons, when she'd teased him about being rich enough to talk his way into the closed spa.

He dropped his backpack near the edge of the pool, shrugged out of his coat, and leaned down and unlaced his hiking boots. He straightened and peeled off his shirt. God. He looked like a model, the angles of his face complementing the mountains be-hind him and his eyes almost the same color as the sky. He looked like he should be in one of those expensive watch ads you saw in *The New Yorker*. Except maybe not, because he wasn't wearing a watch. Or a shirt.

And here came the sex feelings. She felt a bit shaky, like a damsel in distress in need of a fainting couch, even as a kind of steady warmth bloomed inside her.

She took a deep breath to try to right herself. The air smelled piney. Like Max had the few times she'd gotten close enough to pick up his cologne. He smelled like his favorite place.

He had been wearing swim trunks under the pants he was shedding, and Dani was wearing her swimsuit under her clothes, so she took off her boots and struggled out of her clothing. "Oh, oh, it's cold!" She hopped up and down on the freezing rock. At least the shock of cold jarred her out of her swoony weakness of a moment ago.

"Careful," he warned. "The dusting of snow will have made it slippery." He held out a hand, and before she could overthink it, she took it.

The hike had been challenging, and she'd worked up a bit of a sweat under her parka, and the sudden addition of the cold air was making her shiver violently.

"Big step down, then there's a ledge under the surface," he said, holding her hand like he was an old-fashioned gentleman helping her down from a carriage.

Stepping into the hot water was nothing short of glorious. The heat after such an extreme blast of cold made her tingle all over, and as he led her to the far side to sit on a deeper ledge, she heaved a deep, slow sigh. It felt like the cold, piney air was cleaning her lungs from the inside as her muscles surrendered to the blissful warmth.

"Wooow," she breathed, and he smiled. "What's with all these stones? It's like a fancy outdoor spa."

"This is a natural spring, but my father's mother had it reinforced with these stones to make it a more comfortable—and less mucky—experience. To hear it told, she was quite the devotee."

"This grandmother of yours just gets better and better."

"I wish I'd known her."

"But you do now, a little bit, don't you? From the letters?"

They talked for a while about the magnitude of Max's find, and when their conversation came to a natural lull, he asked, "Are you all toasty now?"

"Yep." She held up a wrinkly finger. "Turning into a prune. I'm actually getting a bit overheated."

He pushed off the ledge he'd been sitting on, moved to the

middle of the spring—it was the size of two or three hot tubs—and said, "*Dirty Dancing* lift."

"You were serious about that?"

"Would I joke about *Dirty Dancing* lifts?" When she didn't answer, merely cracked up, he said, "Come on. It will cool you off."

"All right, you weirdo." She moved toward him, lifted her arms over her head as she got close. He came in smooth as anything. As his hands splayed her hips, they were totally in sync. He lifted, and she jumped like this was a choreographed routine they'd done a thousand times.

"Eee!" she said as she reached the top of the lift. The cold mountain air was making steam rise off her hot skin. It was exhilarating. It was silly.

It was perfect.

"Don't dive," he said from below her. "There's probably enough clearance, but let's not test it. I don't want you to hit your head on the rock."

"Okay."

She expected him to sink down in the water, to lower her like an elevator, but instead he executed a move Patrick Swayze would envy, rolling her down into his arms. As they grinned at each other, both of them panting, she could almost believe they'd completed a triumphant, end-of-the-movie dance that had turned all their critics into applauding fans.

He held her there for a moment, their smiles fading in unison. She could see her breath. It was mingling with his. It felt like they were looking not just at each other but *inside* each other. It wasn't uncomfortable—he already knew everything anyway—but it felt . . . weighty somehow.

As quickly as it had arrived, the moment of seriousness evaporated, like the steam rising from the surface of the water. He winked and set her down.

And when he hopped out of the spring and produced a towel from his bag, came to the edge, and held it out for her, she let herself be wrapped in it. Let both the silly exhilaration from the top of the lift and sudden intimacy that had come afterward wrap around her, too. It was a good feeling, to be cocooned in protection and warmth and rightness.

She told herself not to get used to it.

AFTER THEY GOT back to the cottage, Dani took a shower and didn't even bother getting dressed again. Max had ordered a late dinner from the kitchen at the main house, which seemed to function as his personal room service, and she joined him in her pajamas. He'd laid their dinner out in the library, on a coffee table next to a crackling fire.

"Well, don't you look cozy?" he said.

"Was I supposed to dress for dinner?" He clearly had, having swapped his hiking attire for jeans and a button-down shirt.

"No," he said, flashing a grin. "Not at all. Hang on." A minute later, he reappeared in his own pajamas.

After dinner, she read him the opening pages of her novel. *Her novel.* Such a strange thing to think. It wasn't that unusual for professors of English to detour into fiction-writing, but she had honestly never thought she would join their ranks.

"I love it," he pronounced when she was done, and relief overtook her.

"I don't know what happens beyond this. Maybe I should stare at that Matisse painting for a while." The painting in question played a central role in her first chapter. "I've googled it, of course, but maybe I'll go see it in person. It's in the Museum of Modern Art in San Francisco."

"Oh, hang on." He popped up and started scanning bookshelves that lined two walls. Not finding what he was looking for, he gestured her to follow him.

She trailed him to his bedroom, which like the rest of the cottage, managed to be both posh and modest at the same time, the walls covered with oil paintings, but unlike the stuffy portraits of ancient von Hansburgs she'd seen in the main house when they had dinner there last night, these were exuberant landscapes and colorful still lifes, a few of them in need of straightening.

There was a bookshelf next to the bed. He bent next to it and scanned the titles on the tall lower shelf. "Aha!" He produced a book of paintings by Matisse and flipped to the index. "Maybe it's in this. What's the name of the painting?"

"*Woman with a Hat*," she said.

He squinted at the index. "Yes! Here it is." He shuffled through the pages until he found it and turned the book toward her. "Not as good as the real thing, but better than on a screen."

He plopped onto his bed, which was unmade but piled with the same posh-looking linens and duvets as upstairs, extended his legs, and patted the mattress next to them. She snorted—slumber party with the baron—but stretched out next to him. Max Minimus jumped on the bed, too, and Max shifted to accommodate him as if this was a thing the two Maxes did.

Wait. Had Max been patting the bed to signal her or her dog?

Well, whatever. She wasn't letting her dog get ahead of her in the pecking order.

They looked at the painting together and talked a bit more about the book. Then, as promised, he translated his grandmother's letters for her, and they talked some more about what their discovery meant—for the mine project but also for the historical record. Eventually, she started getting sleepy. Ugh. She had to heave herself out of bed and up the stairs to the attic. "I should go." She didn't want to. She didn't want to go anywhere—upstairs or to the wedding or back to New York and the job she was lucky to have. But life wasn't a fairy tale. "Come on, Max."

Max Minimus lifted his head, looked at her, and tunneled back into Max Maximus's armpit. Max Maximus smirked.

"*Max.* Come. Time for bed."

She spoke sharply enough that he did, but she could tell he wasn't happy about it.

She wasn't, either.

Chapter Fourteen

Max was aware that when he looked back on Dani's visit to Riems, he was going to think of it like a movie montage. She usually got up early and worked on her book. When he and Max Minimus got up an hour or so later—yes, Max Minimus continued to appear in Max's bed in the middle of the night—they took coffee and breakfast up to her. Then they'd spend the morning working.

After lunch, they'd hike or visit Riems. After dinner, which they generally had in front of the fire in the library, though once they ate with Sebastien in the main house, she might work some more, but there was usually a point at which she climbed down the ladder and they ended up talking late into the night.

Early on the fifth day of Dani's stay, he woke to the sound of her coming down the ladder. It was dark, and a glance at his phone told him it was five A.M. She appeared in silhouette in his doorway. "Max," she whispered.

"Hello," he'd said back, at full volume.

"Oh!" He'd startled her. "Sorry. I'm just trying to get my dog. Lately when I wake up and he's not there, I get up and write, but I can't keep it up. I'm too tired." He wasn't surprised. They had been staying up late and she'd been getting up early. "But then, stupidly, I couldn't fall back asleep because apparently even though I'm exhausted, I'm emotionally dependent on a seven-pound Yorkshire terrier to actually fall asleep."

He tried to make Max Minimus go with her. He really did.

All right, he didn't try that hard.

When the mutt responded to her summons by yawning and burrowing deeper into Max's armpit, he could have removed him. Picked him up, handed him to Dani, and shut his door behind them.

Instead, he scooched himself, his armpit, and the dog it contained to one side of the bed and threw back the covers. When she hesitated, he started to get up, aiming to hand over Max Minimus, but she shocked him by getting into the bed. They didn't touch. They didn't talk. She just rolled over and went to sleep.

And so did Max.

A few hours later, he opened his eyes to find her staring at him. They were on their sides facing each other. She smiled. He did, too.

"I thought you were an insomniac," she said.

"It must be the soothing snores of Max Minimus." She probably thought he was in jest, but he had slept remarkably well these recent nights after the arrival of his canine bedmate. He pushed back the covers. "Do you want to take a writing break or—"

"Max?"

His blood went cold. It couldn't be. They were in Sardinia.

"Darling?"

"*Shit.*"

"What's wrong?" Dani asked.

"Get—" He was about to exhort her to get up, but to what end? Where was she going to go? Was she going to climb out a fucking window because he wouldn't stand by her? No. Instead he said, "I am sorry in advance. Just remember that."

The door burst open. His mother rarely came to the cottage, but when she did, she didn't let little things like respect for privacy, or closed doors, stand in her way.

"Max, darling, didn't you get my texts?"

Dumbly, he picked up his phone, which he'd taken to silencing because the only person he generally texted in the middle of the night was currently in his house—and in this case, his bed. The notification screen contained two messages from Sebastien that were short enough to read in their entirety.

> **Sebastien:** Parents back!

> **Sebastien:** Mother on her way to you!

Well, damn.

Mother's eyes widened. She was struck dumb, which normally would have amused Max, given how rarely that happened. She knew about his reputation, of course. It was a frequent topic of "discussion." But he'd never brought a woman to the estate.

Not that Dani was "a woman" in that sense. But to argue that, given how this looked, would be ridiculous.

He cleared his throat. "Mother, this is Daniela Martinez. Daniela, this is my mother."

Neither woman said anything immediately—they were both like deer caught in headlights. Max Minimus barked as if annoyed to be left out.

"Right," Max said. "And this is . . ." Oh lord.

"McMuffin," said Dani quickly, and god bless her.

His mother raised her eyebrows. "How . . . charming."

Max Minimus started growling, and Max had to stifle a laugh.

Dani rose from the bed, shot the dog a look that silenced him, and extended her hand as if she weren't wearing pajamas. "It's a pleasure to meet you. Your estate is lovely."

Mother's "good" breeding kicked in, and she fake smiled. "How nice to meet you, Ms. Martinez. If I'm not mistaken, you're one of Leonardo Ricci's . . . people."

"Was there something you wanted, Mother?" Max said loudly.

"There are many things I want, darling, but we can't always get what we want, can we?" she said, still looking at Dani. After a beat of silence, she transferred her attention to Max. "I came to tell you that we're back early from our holiday."

"I can see that."

"I came to discuss dinner plans, too, but perhaps another time is better."

"I think so."

Max remained still while Mother made her way out of the room, waiting until he heard the front door close before he turned to Dani. How was he going to apologize?

She burst out laughing. She laughed so hard, she started waving her hand in front of her face as if she were apologizing for laughing.

It was contagious. How extraordinary. Laughter was *not* Max's customary reaction to encounters with his parents. Even Max Minimus joined in, barking happily alongside them.

"I'm sorry," Dani said when she got control of herself. "What a . . ." She was still shaking with aftershocks. "What a disaster. What do we do now?"

"I suggest we make ourselves as scarce as possible for the rest of the day."

"So basically you're saying we should hide."

"No 'basically' about it. That's exactly what I'm saying."

OVER LUNCH IN a café in Riems, Max received a curious text from his mother.

> **Mother:** Please bring your friend to dine at the main house. Drinks at seven. I'd like to meet her properly and apologize for intruding this morning.

"Hmm." That was unexpectedly civilized.

"What?" Dani asked. He turned the phone to her. "Should we go?" she asked. "We should go, right?"

"I don't know," he said, trying to reason through the situation as he spoke. "I suppose, if she's feeling magnanimous, it might be a good idea, but that doesn't account for my father. You're going to meet them at the wedding, of course, but now that they probably think . . ." He copied the same waving-between them motion she'd done earlier. "It might be better to get it over with here. And I can explain that we're not . . ." She made the same gesture, and he laughed. "Mind you, it will probably still be, if not horrible, an unpleasant evening."

"Well, my evenings here so far have been extremely pleasant. I could do with a little unpleasantness, or else you'll never be rid of me."

He could only wish. Having Dani here was a balm for his soul, as corny as that sounded. When she was around, the circumstances of his life, the ones that usually chafed, faded in importance. She made him feel like he existed as a person, an interesting and worthy person, independent of those circumstances.

Plus, she was just so damn fun.

And he feared he was falling for her dog, who was proving the cure for the insomnia that had plagued Max his whole life.

That evening, walking with Dani toward the main house, he said, "Listen. I have no idea how this is going to go. My parents are huge snobs."

"I can take it. Leo told me about some of his first encounters with the king. If he can survive it, so can I."

He wasn't going to let them be horrible to her, though. "I'm not sure Leo's experience is that instructive. My father is, elementally, much worse than King Emil." Max was confident, though, that even if dinner was a disaster, it wouldn't change anything about his relationship with Dani. She *knew* him. She wasn't going to judge him by his parents. The thought was exceedingly buoying. It felt like . . . insurance. A buffer that made his parents' machinations matter a little less than usual.

At the house, Frau Bittner greeted them in the foyer. She normally only did that if they were having a formal dinner with guests. But perhaps Dani was that guest. His parents did know how to roll out the protocol when it suited them.

"Max." As they approached the dining room, Seb slipped out

the door, leaving it ajar. Chatter flowed from the room, which sounded like it was full of more people than Mother and Father. "Did you get my text?"

"Oh." Max patted his empty pocket. "I didn't." He'd left his phone charging at the cottage. He had to stop ignoring his phone. Just because he was with his favorite texting partner in person didn't mean there weren't other people trying to reach him.

"Max," Seb said urgently. "Father has—"

"Max, darling, is that you?"

Seb shot him a vaguely ominous look as Mother came to the door and beckoned them inside.

And there were the von Bachenheims. Lavinia and her parents.

"Let me introduce everyone," Mother said gaily.

Goddammit.

WELL. IT WASN'T like Dani had thought Max was lying about his father. She'd wondered, though, if Max's experience of his present-day family dynamic was overly influenced by his child-hood. Sometimes patterns endured in one's mind in a more en-trenched way than in reality. She'd seen a little of that with Leo and Gabby after their parents died.

But no. Max's dad, aka the Duke of Aquilla, was a complete dick.

It didn't start so badly. Max's mother introduced Dani as Max's "American friend," in a way that felt snotty even though you couldn't actually pinpoint anything wrong with it.

As they were seated, things started to unravel. During the first course, everyone conversed separately, and she continued to speak mostly to Sebastien, who was on one side of her, and if she suspected he was monopolizing her attention so she didn't have to deal with Mr. von Bachenheim on her other side, she appreciated it. But when the plates were cleared and the next course laid down, the conversation shifted to encompass the whole group.

"Miss Martinez," the duke said, drawing everyone's attention but then making them wait while he took a slow sip of his wine, the ruby liquid made sparkling by the enormous chandelier overhead glinting off the crystal goblet. "Where are you from in New York?"

"It's *Dr.* Martinez," Max interjected from across the table where he was seated next to Lavinia.

Bless Max and his relentless championing of her, but now was not the time. She appreciated the intervention in theory, but this was only going to fan the flames of his father's . . . what? He wasn't angry, at least not outwardly. But there was something going on, and it wasn't good.

"Oh, it is, is it?" the duke said in a way that suggested he was humoring someone—either Max or Dani herself, she wasn't sure which.

"I grew up in Queens, but I live in the Bronx now," Dani said, returning to the duke's initial question.

"Mmmmm." He drew out the single syllable, almost as if he didn't believe her, which was maddening, and Max's mother and Mrs. von Bachenheim said something to each other in murmured German.

"What kind of medicine do you practice?" the duke asked after another drawn-out sip of wine.

"Dr. Martinez is a professor of literature," Max said before Dani could answer.

"Ahhhh," said the duke. It was hard to put her finger on it, because nothing about the words he was saying were inappropriate or rude, but the way he delivered them, in a smug tone and punctuated with long, drawn-out syllables, made it seem as if some private conclusion he'd previously had about her had been ratified.

"She's a scholar of nineteenth-century American literature," Max went on, and oh god, he needed to stop. Max, Mr. Emotional Intelligence, the guy who handled her fraught work parties like he had a degree in psychology and cheerfully called her out on her Tindering bullshit, apparently had no sense of how to handle his father. It was almost like he was baiting him.

Oh. That was exactly what he was doing. He'd told her he used to do this, to draw the fire from his brother. And now he was doing it for her.

"How exciting," said Lavinia of all people, and she genuinely sounded interested. "Do you have any particular specialty?"

"Well," Dani said carefully, "mostly nineteenth-century literature by women."

"Oh!" Lavinia exclaimed, with such force that the whispers between the mothers stopped. "Have you read any Edith Wharton?"

"I have."

"Oh!" Lavinia said again, and in another circumstance, Dani would have laughed at her wide-eyed enthusiasm, which was both delightful and out of sync with the context. "I am studying in the United States at the moment, and last summer I decided to read some American literature. When one is educated in Europe, one's exposure to American writers tends to be limited to Twain and Hemingway and Hawthorne. Men, all."

"That can happen," Dani said sympathetically, not wanting to get into a big conversation while everyone else spectated.

"Well, I read *The Age of Innocence,* and, oh!" She looked around. "Has anyone else read it?" The assembled aristocrats looked at her blankly. Taking that for a no, she turned back to Dani. "I was devastated. And yet I could not seem to stop, and in short order made my way through the rest of Wharton's oeuvre."

Dani smiled. "Wharton will do that to you."

"Dr. Martinez's PhD dissertation was on Wharton," Max said. Dani hadn't realized he knew that.

Lavinia excitedly transferred her attention to Seb, who was seated next to Dani. "Sebastien, will you trade places with me so I may converse some more with Dr. Martinez when the next course comes?" She turned to Max next to her. "You won't mind, will you, Max?"

"Not at all," said Max, though Dani could tell he was as befuddled by Lavinia's outburst as she was.

Over chicken schnitzel, Lavinia proved charming. Astonishingly, she seemed genuinely interested in talking about Edith Wharton. In a different setting, Dani would have enjoyed chatting with her, but she could tell that even though the others were, superficially, involved in their own conversations, they were simultaneously eavesdropping. Dani felt like a specimen under a microscope. Still, she managed to make it through to the end of the meal, thanks in large part to Lavinia's kindness.

Until over coffee—or, in the case of the duke, kirsch—the duchess suddenly said, "I've had Frau Bittner make up a room for you, Daniela. She can show you to it whenever you're ready."

"Daniela is staying with me at the cottage," Max said quickly, saving Dani from having to answer.

"Nonsense," Max's mother said. "She's a guest at the estate. She'll stay in a proper guest room, not in the drafty old dower house. And I've asked Frau Bittner to arrange a tour for her tomorrow since you'll be busy with our other guests."

"I've made the cottage attic into a bedroom," Max said to his mother, before turning to the von Bachenheims. "And I'm terribly sorry, but I'm afraid I'm otherwise engaged tomorrow."

"You're housing your guest in an *attic*," the duchess said sharply. Interesting how they could be rude to Dani, but when it was convenient they were suddenly worried about etiquette.

"I am, and I assure you it's been quite overhauled. She's writing a book, and she needs solitude and quiet. And I'm swamped with my own work and have a meeting I can't reschedule."

The duchess pursed her lips, and the duke outright laughed. What an absolute bastard. "Are you now? What kind of 'work' might that be?" The duke caught Mr. von Bachenheim's eye and smiled as if the two old men were in cahoots.

"Actually—" Sebastien said, but he stopped talking when Max shot him a quelling look.

"I think it's best discussed later," Max said with what looked superficially like calm, though Dani knew it belied roiling emotions.

The duke sneered and looked like he was about to say more, but the duchess turned to him and seemed to silently communicate something that made him sniff and look away as if in surrender. Dani wondered if the duke and duchess were on "good behavior" because of the von Bachenheims. It was hard to fathom this icy snootiness as "good" behavior, but given some of the stories Max had told, it seemed possible.

Apparently satisfied that she had her husband under control, the duchess expelled a dainty sigh and turned her attention to Dani. "Daniela, I am sure you can understand that my husband and I have high hopes for our children, yes?"

Dani knew this was a trap, but what could she do but nod?

"Therefore I am sure you will understand that sometimes we as parents have to steer our children away from certain . . . projects that aren't a good use of their particular . . . talents."

"*Mother*," Sebastien scolded his mother. And, oh, he pushed back his chair and stood. "*Please.*"

Dani was surprised. She expected Max to defend her, as he seemed to be spoiling for a fight, but to hear it told, Sebastien's usual approach to family strife was to try to keep the peace. She looked at Max, who, judging by his raised eyebrows, was also taken off guard by Sebastien's outburst.

"Please, what?" the duke asked, sneering at Sebastien, who now seemed unsure how to proceed. "Is your mother offending your tender sensibilities, boy?"

"I . . ." It seemed like Sebastien's outburst had been impulsive and uncharacteristic enough that he had backed himself into a corner. He didn't know what to say next.

Max did, though. "Sebastien," he said, drawing everyone's attention along with his brother's, and *oh*. Max was *angry*. Not that she'd really ever seen him angry, but it was easy to tell. His normally relaxed posture had grown hard. His face was hard, too, like someone had battened down a pair of shutters that usually stood open to let the sun in. Ironically, he was going to make a good duke someday, with his ability to express extreme emotions with small, restrained adjustments to his body and face. "Sebastien," he said again. "Daniela and I are finished dining, but I need to have a word with Frau Bittner on my way out." He sounded a little like his father, oddly, each word carefully enunciated and gilded with ice. "Perhaps you would be so kind as to escort Daniela back to the cottage."

Chapter Fifteen

"Max!"

Max groaned as he stopped walking. He was almost free. But of course it was not to be.

It was Lavinia, which was an unexpected turn of events, emerging from around the corner after Max finished informing Frau Bittner that Dani was *his* guest and that as such, *he* would apprise the staff of any arrangements that were required. He disliked putting her in an awkward position, but he wasn't letting his mother's vile little domestic coup go unchecked.

"Max." Lavinia was breathless as she hurried to his side. She had to have been lying in wait to intercept him like this. God. He just wanted to get out of there.

"I'm sorry about all that," he said, gesturing vaguely back toward the dining room.

"No, *I'm* sorry," Lavinia said. "I had no idea you didn't know we were coming. I'm mortified."

He softened. "It's not your fault." Lavinia might not be the woman for him, but she didn't seem the conniving sort. He'd expected her to be more like her social-climbing sister, Lucrecia, but she'd done them a good turn back at dinner, expressing enthusiastic interest in Dani's work. He didn't know if it'd been a calculated good turn or if she'd been genuinely interested in talking to Dani about literature. Either way, she'd defused the situation. For a while.

"I must speak with you." She hitched her head back toward the dining room. "They're still in there. Can we go somewhere else?"

He stifled a sigh. He wanted to get back to Dani, not talk to Lavinia. But none of this was Lavinia's fault. "Of course." He led her to a small parlor he deemed sufficiently far from the dining room and closed the door. "They won't miss you at dinner?"

"I pled a headache after you left." She winced. "Which probably isn't helping your cause. Now they're going to think I had my tender feelings hurt."

"My cause?"

She didn't answer his question, just stared at him long enough to make him uncomfortable. "Would you like to sit?" he asked, for lack of knowing what to say.

Again, she ignored his question, but she did start talking. "My father told me you were . . . interested in me," she went on. "I'm embarrassed that I barely gave you the time of day in New York. I was distracted, and I'll be honest, given what I'd heard, you didn't seem . . ."

"Like the kind of person you'd be interested in shackling yourself to for life?"

She smiled a sad little smile. "Something like that. But then when my father started pushing this visit, I googled you and found your master's thesis. I read it."

"You did?" He had not been impressed by Lavinia in New York, but he supposed he'd been distracted, too. He'd been thinking about Dani, wondering how she would react if he texted her.

"I did. I thought it was so interesting. And then I started thinking about how you used to be engaged to Marie, and I like Marie so much and think so highly of her. So I thought . . ." She sighed. "I thought it couldn't hurt to meet you. It's so difficult, you see, when one is . . ."

He didn't know how she had intended to finish that sentence, but he supposed if you were the younger daughter of Harald and Larissa von Bachenheim and you had an intellectual bent, life could be difficult. "When one is expected to 'marry well'?" Max finished.

"Yes," she said vehemently. "You know."

"I do indeed."

"I thought, well, perhaps you wouldn't be the worst option, given my circumstances." She winced. "That sounds terrible. I'm sorry. I'm not good at this. I'm socially awkward."

"On the contrary, you were very kind at dinner. There's no need to apologize. I know exactly what you mean."

"I had no idea you were attached. The last thing I'd ever want to do is come between you and your girlfriend."

"Daniela is not my girlfriend," he said reflexively.

She looked at him for a long time. "But you wish she was, yes?"

He was all geared up to deny. Deflect. *I am not the girlfriend type.*

But it wasn't true. It used to be. It used to be so true, it had felt like an immutable part of him.

If the past week, with all its talking and cavorting, felt like a movie montage, he knew what kind of movie it was. A romance. Or, worse, one of those dreadful Hallmark movies Americans seemed to love where they just made up a fake European country so they could have a fairy tale free from the inconvenient constraints of reality.

Given his aversion to self-deception, Max had to face the truth. He might not be the girlfriend type, but he was, it seemed the Daniela Martinez type.

He had a full-on crush on Dani. He eyed Lavinia. How had he ever thought she was naive?

She flashed him another of her sad smiles. "It's complicated for people like us, isn't it?"

"It is," he agreed.

The smile turned warmer. "But Daniela is rather wonderful, isn't she?"

What could he do but agree again? "She is."

"Max," Lavinia said, "I have an idea. For how we could help each other."

DANI WAS SITTING at her desk in the attic when Max arrived back at the cottage. "Knock, knock," he said from the bottom of the stairs.

"Come on up."

She turned in her chair as he appeared through the trapdoor, illuminated from below by light from the kitchen. He paused, and they looked at each other for a long moment. He was so dear to her, this man who saw her like no one else ever had.

"I'm sorry," they said in unison, and it had the effect of breaking the aura of heaviness surrounding them.

"Why on earth are *you* sorry?" He crossed to the bed and flopped on it backward, his head at the bottom and his stockinged feet up by the headboard, like he was too tired to lay down the right way, forget walking the extra ten steps to the sitting area.

She got up and joined him, but she sat with her back to the headboard. "Because your parents are horrible." She winced. "I'm sorry." She winced again. "I already said that. I'm sorry your parents are horrible, but I'm also sorry I *said* they were horrible."

"They *are* horrible." He shrugged like that was the normal way of things, which she supposed it was. "It's just that their horribleness is usually aimed at me, not at innocent bystanders," he said to the ceiling. "And believe it or not, it's usually much worse. That was them tempering themselves because they had an audience."

"I guess they didn't want to make a bad impression on the people they hope will be future in-laws."

"Mmm."

She'd expected a more dramatic reaction, for him to shudder and fall back on his usual refrain about how he was never going to marry. "Lavinia doesn't seem so bad?" she ventured, though she had no idea why.

He looked up sharply—he had still been staring at the ceiling. "Not bad as in I should marry her or not bad as in she's a decent human being?"

"I don't know," she said, though in her mind she was strongly going for option B. "She seems too young for you."

"She's only four years younger than I am."

"Right."

"You're four years older than I am," he said.

"Well, *I'm* not going to marry you."

"I *know* that. I merely meant that four years is not that big a gap when you click with someone."

When you click with someone. Did that mean he thought *they* clicked? That was flattering. And true. Obviously. She wouldn't be here in his attic in the freaking Eldovian Alps otherwise, stretched out on a bed with him. *Platonically* stretched out, but still. Or, wait, did that mean he thought he and *Lavinia* clicked?

"What if you *did* marry Lavinia von Bachenheim?" She had an illogical impulse to keep questioning him on the topic, like being unable to stop probing a toothache with her tongue.

"I'm not going to marry Lavinia von Bachenheim. She has no sense of fun."

"Yeah, but if you *did*? And what if she wanted to hyphenate her name? Would she be Lavinia von Bachenheim-von Hansburg? Or Lavinia von Bachenheim-Hansburg? Or maybe, since you're such a progressive dude, you could combine your names and be Max and Lavinia von von Bachenheim-Hansburg. Or—"

"I'm *not* going to marry Lavinia," he snapped.

She blinked, not at all accustomed to such a harsh tone from Max. "Sheesh. Okay."

He rolled onto his side and propped his head on one hand. "I'm sorry. I'm being a beast."

"Is Sebastien single? I know you said you won't walk away and leave him to shoulder the burden of being heir, but maybe if he was happily coupled, it *wouldn't* be such a burden." She knew she was grasping at straws, but now that she'd seen what kind of pressure Max was under, she wished there was a way for him to get out from under his duty.

Max chuckled. "Sebastien is apparently *not* single, but Sebastian, it turns out, is *also* not straight."

"*Really?*" She was surprised Max hadn't told her. Also a little hurt. She'd thought they told each other everything.

"Yeah. He told me he was gay the day you arrived. I would have told you," he said, addressing her unarticulated wound, "but I wasn't sure if it was my place. He didn't specifically ask me not to, but I thought I should keep his confidence. I was the first person he told—other than the mystery man he is apparently seeing."

"Wow! Of course I won't tell anyone. You can trust me."

"I know. I do." He was giving her a strangely intense look. She'd been getting more of those lately, but this one was on steroids. His brow was furrowed, and if she didn't know better, she would have said he was angry over the fact that he trusted her. But then his face relaxed. "As it relates to Sebastien, I must now double down on my original stance that I can't leave him to shoulder the burden of being heir. Can you imagine? My god, my parents would probably make him marry a woman, and he'd probably go along with it to keep the peace."

"What if your brother walked away, too?" she asked. "Is there a dreadful, social-climbing cousin in line like in Jane Austen novels?"

He chuckled. "There is a cousin. He's seven. I can't quite see my way through to dumping this all on a seven-year-old." He sat up and spun himself so he was right way round on the bed, next to her. "Listen. I appreciate that you're trying to solve my problems, but they're fundamentally unsolvable. We need to talk about what we do now."

"What do you mean?"

"I think we should leave at dawn. Head to the palace a bit early."

"Leave at dawn! Like a Western!"

"I would suggest leaving now, but driving over the mountain in the dark is a bad idea."

"What would you tell your parents? I suppose our man of honor and best woman duties could kick in early."

"I could tell them that, but that would require me to talk to them. I did more than enough of that this evening, and honestly, I'm inclined to just leave. Get up before the sun and run away."

Dani smiled. "All right, Clint Eastwood. We leave at dawn."

Chapter Sixteen

*W*hen they got to the palace, Max was surprised to find Sebastien already there.

"He arrived in the middle of the night, and he's in the yellow bedroom," said Marie, who greeted them outside. "You know, the one we all used to play Narnia in because the armoire was so huge? I don't know if he's there at the moment, but you could try."

Sebastien had arrived in the middle of the night? Max had been in earnest about the drive over the mountains being ill-advised. And oddly, when he'd texted his brother and said he and Dani were leaving first thing this morning and asked him if he wanted to join them, Seb had merely said he would see them there. Max had assumed he'd meant later. He feared there had been an incident at the palace, something bad enough to drive Seb away in the wee hours. Still, though, why hadn't he come to Max?

"Dani!"

It was Gabby, who appeared from around a corner and broke into a run at the sight of Dani. They embraced as Leo approached at a more sedate pace.

Gabby was talking a mile a minute next to the now-embracing Leo and Dani. "God, I'm glad you're here," Leo said. He kept hugging her, like he couldn't get enough of her. Max perfectly understood.

"Come see the ballroom!" Gabby said, pulling on Dani's arm. "They're already starting to decorate it for the reception, and it's so pretty! Or, oh! Maybe we should go down to the village. You haven't been here in the cold weather. The tree is up, they've flooded the square for skating, and—"

"Why don't we show Dani to her room, and then we can make a plan?" Leo said to Gabby.

"Good morning." Mr. Benz, the king's equerry and all-around palace fixer, appeared, and Max stifled a groan. Whatever plans any of them had—ballroom inspections or stealing Dani away and heading down to the village—would now go up in smoke. "Dr. Martinez, welcome back to the palace. We met last summer. I am Matteo Benz."

"Yes, of course. It's nice to see you again."

"Lord Laudon." Mr. Benz nodded at Max.

"Mr. Benz." Max nodded back. He could feel Dani's attention. She was no doubt internally rolling her eyes over the formal title. That was Benz for you. He was a stickler for protocol and was probably the only person currently resident in the palace who would use Max's title. And since he was also the only person resident in the palace who could make embarrassing photos disappear like magic, he had Max's respect.

"I'm glad you arrived a little earlier than planned," Mr. Benz said to Dani. "We have much to do."

As if he had invisibly summoned her—for all Max knew, he

had—a woman arrived from around a corner. "This is Verene, the princess's dresser. I believe the two of you have been corresponding about your dress?"

"Oh. Yes."

"Daniela!" Verene rushed forward and took both of Dani's hands. "You are even more lovely in person."

"Verene tells me she needs you for an urgent fitting," Mr. Benz said. "It's my hope that after that, you and I could discuss the protocol associated with the wedding."

"But then I get her!" Gabby said to Mr. Benz. "I haven't seen her for months!"

"Well," said Mr. Benz, with a twinkle in his eye that only Gabby seemed to be able to inspire, "I have taken the liberty of having some lunch delivered to the wardrobe room, and I thought you might show Dr. Martinez your dress, too, Miss Ricci, if that suits."

"Yes!" Gabby said.

"And when do I 'get her,' Mr. Benz?" Leo asked with a wink at Dani. "She is, after all, here to be *my* wedding attendant."

Mr. Benz sniffed, but there wasn't any real rancor in it. The stuffy Mr. Benz and the freewheeling Leo had come to a détente last year, and it seemed now that they were genuinely friendly. "You, Mr. Ricci," said Mr. Benz, doing a poor job stifling a smile, "will have to fend for yourself. I have a royal wedding to put on. That it is yours is immaterial."

Dani met Max's gaze as she let herself be swept away. He wondered if she was thinking what he was. No more late-night tête-à-têtes, no more ridiculous 1980s choreography.

It was just as well. He had to nip this infatuation in the bud. Dani wasn't looking for a relationship. And even if she was, he had seen that list. *Things I Will Never Again Do for a Man.* While he was fairly confident he could pass muster on a few of the items— she would never have to pretend to like something she didn't around him, and he flattered himself that in the extremely hypothetical situation in which orgasms were relevant, they would be real—most of her list items ruled Max out entirely.

And it wasn't as if her list was the only thing keeping them apart. She didn't think of him that way. He didn't think of her that way. Mostly. Or at least he hadn't until . . . Well, damn it. He didn't even know when he'd started thinking of her that way. When Lavinia had prodded him on the matter? Perhaps it dated from when Dani had held his hand and listened to his fears in the sauna. Or even all the way back to when they'd made snow angels in Central Park.

"I believe you will find your brother in his room, Lord Laudon," Mr. Benz said, rousing Max from his thoughts, "if you would like to say hello."

After making plans to meet up with Leo and Marie later, Max went in search of his brother. As he climbed the stairs to the third floor, a rogue thought popped into his head. Was *Mr. Benz* Sebastien's boyfriend? Was that why he knew where Seb was right now, or was that merely more of Benz's usual omniscience? Seb *had* said Max didn't know but "knew of" the person in question.

Is Mr. Benz why Sebastien had arrived early?

Mr. Benz came from a noble but impoverished family. Ironically, his "bloodlines," as Mother would call them, were impeccable.

Which made Max wonder if Mother and Father would approve of the match—if they could be made to approve of Sebastien's homosexuality to begin with.

Max couldn't really see Seb with the equerry. Seb was introverted and sensitive, but he wasn't humorless like Benz. Perhaps Mr. Benz had a hidden wild side. Max thought about Lavinia's proposal from last night. Sometimes, people surprised you.

Then he thought about the fact that *he*, the Depraved Duke, had a *crush*. Sometimes you surprised *yourself*.

Reaching the Yellow Room, Max rapped on the door and called out as he pushed it open. "Seb! You sly bastard! I think I've figured out your—"

Seb was standing at the window in his room next to a giant man Max recognized as the head of palace security. They both turned as Max paused in the doorway.

"Max!" Seb seemed surprised, though Max couldn't think why—he knew Max and Dani were arriving today.

"Everything appears to be in order, Mr. von Hansburg," said the security officer. He nodded at Max. "Lord Laudon."

"Max, you remember Torkel Renner, the royal family's head of security? He was—"

"Having a look at this window," Torkel said. "There will be wedding banners hanging from the windows, and a preliminary inspection turned up the fact that the latch on this one is broken, which is a security concern."

"A broken window latch on the third floor is a security concern?" Max asked. Though he supposed he shouldn't be questioning the palace's longtime head of security. One probably attained that position by being attuned to details like window latches.

"We can't be too careful," he said in a monotone. "There will be lots of guests on site." He had that flat affect that FBI agents always did in American movies—his face seemed made of stone. Max half expected him to whip out a pair of sunglasses and an earpiece. "Everything seems in order here." He nodded to both brothers and departed.

Max moved farther into Seb's suite and sat on a sofa. "I didn't expect to find you'd arrived ahead of me."

"I left rather abruptly last night. I suppose I should have texted you."

"Why didn't you?"

"Because you would have told me to wait until morning, and I . . . did not want to do that."

"Did something happen with Father?"

"No, no. I simply decided to leave. I'm sorry if I worried you."

"I worry about your driving over the mountain in the dark, that's all."

"Oh, that was . . . not a problem."

Hmm. Max's Mr. Benz theory was looking more and more plausible. Benz had a way of making things happen. Pictures of unicorn onesies disappeared; people were spirited away over mountain ridges in the dead of night. "What do you think of Mr. Benz?"

"The equerry?"

"Yes. He seems even more uptight than usual, with all this wedding to-do." Max tamped down a smile.

Seb *did* smile—ha. "Well, he and Leo seem to have struck up an unlikely friendship, and Leo tells me Benz is a secret aficionado of American jazz." Seb looked at the door. "You might expect that with someone like Torkel, but Benz?"

Max lost his battle with the stifled smile. "I'm on to you, you know."

Seb heaved a big, annoyed sigh of the sort he used to when they were boys and sank onto the sofa next to Max. "Really?"

"Don't worry. My lips are sealed."

"Nothing can ever come of it, anyway."

"Perhaps. Perhaps not."

"He's a member of the palace staff!"

Yes, but not really. Benz was from an old, distinguished family, as the men behind the throne generally were. "You'd have to come out for this to be more than a theoretical discussion. Which, for the record, if you want to do, I am wholeheartedly and unreservedly behind you."

Seb sighed again, but this one was more defeated-sounding. "I'm afraid of him, Max."

They were talking about Father now. "I know."

"I don't want to be. I don't want to be the kind of man who's afraid of his father."

"Well, you have reason to be."

"So do you. But you're not afraid of him. You're not afraid of anything."

That wasn't true. Max was afraid of lots of things. The future foremost among them. A future in which he was alone. A future in which Dani Martinez didn't live in his attic.

"Thank you for standing by me," Seb said.

"Marie and Leo and I are walking down to the village to go skating. I'm here to ask if you want to join us."

"What about Dani?"

"I hope she can come. She's been spirited away for dress fittings and wedding nonsense." He smiled. "Perhaps you can have some influence there and help me extract her." Sebastien's brow furrowed, and Max held back from telling him to invite Benz skating. One von Hansburg brother's unlikely and ill-fated infatuation at a time.

THE NEXT FEW days were such a whirlwind of dress fittings, rehearsals, and royal protocol lessons, Dani hardly got to see Max.

Well, no. Dani hardly got to see *Leo*. She had to remind herself that Leo was the reason she was there. So when he popped his head in to yet another dress fitting and invited her to have a pint with him, she had to say yes.

Again, she had to remind herself that "had" to say yes was the wrong way to think about it.

"And here I thought having you in the wedding was going to mean I would actually get to *see* you," Leo said after they'd ordered at the pub in the village.

"Yeah, sorry, who knew going to royal wedding finishing school would be so time-consuming?"

"If I'd known you could be gone from New York for so long, I would have tried to lure you *here* earlier."

She didn't know what to say to that. She'd felt weird telling Leo she was spending a week in Riems with Max before she came to the palace. So weird that she *hadn't* told him until a few days before her departure.

"Did you have fun with Max?"

"Why are you saying it like that?"

"I'm not saying it like anything."

"Okay, sorry."

"I thought you were post-men."

"See! You *are* saying it like something." She paused, told herself to rein in the defensiveness, and started over. "I am post-men. Max is a friend." She poked him in the shoulder. "Like you." Then, feeling like she should say more, added, "I'm sorry we haven't talked as much lately. That's on me." *Because I've been too wrapped up in Max.*

"No, it's my fault." He made a face. "This wedding is going to be the end of me. I knew Marie wasn't going to be a bridezilla, but I wasn't counting on Mr. Benz."

"He's very . . . thorough, isn't he?"

"I owe him a lot, and we've actually become friends—sort of— but damn, sometimes I want to throttle him."

Leo and Marie's happiness was due to Mr. Benz, as hard as that was to fathom. He'd set things up so they were able to overcome the king's objection to their union. Dani wanted to ask about that. How *did* one overcome such objections?

But why did she want to ask that?

"How was Riems?" Leo asked.

"It was great for a while. Max made me a writing space, and I got a ton of work done."

"But only for a while?"

"His parents came home unexpectedly early from a trip."

"Ah."

"Have you met them?"

"I have." He curled his lip.

"Honestly, I felt like I'd been transported into a soap opera.

They were horrible." She didn't know if Leo knew about Max's childhood. The only reason he would was if Max had told Marie, and Marie had told Leo. It was strange, having a topic she had to tread carefully around with Leo. She used to tell Leo everything.

"It really is a whole different world," Leo said, "and not just in the obvious ways. The trappings of extreme wealth, you expect. What trips you up are the subtle machinations."

She laughed, but only because the phrase *subtle machinations* was so spot on and so not something she'd expect Leo to say. "I'm not sure they were so subtle in this case, but I know what you mean. They're trying to marry him off to someone, and I think they viewed my presence as a threat."

"Was it?"

"No," she said quickly. "Of course not."

Why, then, did that feel like a lie?

But that was ridiculous. In what universe was Dani's presence in Max's life a threat to his future? Honestly, she needed to get over herself.

"Unlike Max's parents, the king doesn't seem so bad anymore," she said in an attempt to shift the subject. Leo had told her stories of his first visit to Eldovia, and when she'd met the king herself on her first visit, he had definitely been snooty. But he seemed to have mellowed.

"It's Gabby, I think. He's crazy about Gabby."

"Don't you think you should take some of the credit? You know, for raising the kid he's crazy about? Not to mention making his daughter happy?"

"Nope. We coexist. As long as he's decent to Marie, which he is, we're all good."

"So he's fond of Gabby?"

"He treats her like a granddaughter. Spoils her rotten. She cracked his stone-cold heart. They write each other letters about books even though they live under the same—giant—roof. Benz loves her, too. I think that's half the reason he and I have become friendly." He snorted and rolled his eyes.

"Gabby lost her parents, and now she has all these new people who love her. I think it's great."

He grumbled. "Yeah, okay, it's great."

"You know what else is great?" She bumped her shoulder against his. "You're getting married! I hope you don't lose sight of that elemental fact among all this pomp."

He was trying—and failing—not to grin.

"What are we talking about?" Imogen, the owner of the pub and a friend of Leo's, asked as she came over to check on them.

"We're talking about how Leo's in looove." Dani drew out the syllable and made a face at Leo.

"Oh my god, don't we all know it." Imogen rolled her eyes, but she was smiling. "God help us all until this wedding is over."

"Are there lots of people in town for it?"

"They're expecting a few hundred guests. And I'm full up." Imogen pointed at the ceiling—she had guest rooms above the pub. "But if you mean tourism, or media, I don't think there will be a lot of attention. Eldovia doesn't really do tourism, other than of the skiing variety, and that's not based out of here."

"And there won't be tabloids trying to get information?" Dani asked.

"No. The royal family doesn't command that much attention.

It's not like the Brits, or even Monaco. The only one the tabloids seem to care about is Max von Hansburg."

Right. "Leave it to you to choose the lowest-key monarchy to marry into," Dani teased Leo.

"And thank god for it," he said, raising his glass.

Imogen produced menus. "Are you staying for dinner?"

They did, and they lured Max and Marie down to join them. Marie wasn't a celebrity in the way that Meghan Markle appearing at the local pub would be, but she did cause murmurs when she showed up. Imogen relocated them to what she called a snug, which seemed to be a huge wooden booth that had a door that closed.

The food was great, and the conversation was easy. After their plates were cleared, Leo scooted closer to Marie, and they started whispering, their heads together looking at something on a phone.

Which left Max, who was sitting across from Dani. They didn't speak, just looked at each other and smiled. Like they had an inside joke. Like they both had a few screws loose. She didn't even know, except that it felt impossible to stop smiling.

She'd missed Max these recent days. They'd seen each other only in passing, and though they'd been texting up a storm, it wasn't the same. She had gotten used to the rhythms of him. Of banter and silence, of attention and retreat. In fact, *attention and retreat* pretty much summed up their entire relationship. Max could talk her ear off and make her never want to stop talking, but he could also create attic garrets and give her long stretches of time alone so she could work. She tried to tell herself that when she went back to New York, it would merely be a longer episode of

retreat. She would see him again. Probably when he next decided
to pop into town for a party—be it one of hers or one of his.

She didn't like thinking about his parties, the places he picked
up artists or met potential brides.

He tilted his head, and his smile changed. It didn't go away, not
entirely, but it grew kind of . . . wistful?

Damn, she was going to miss him.

"So how's the online 'dating' going?" Leo asked, startling her.
Dani withdrew her attention from Max—it was harder than it
should have been—and turned to Leo. Apparently, the lovebirds
were done with whatever it was they'd been whispering about.

"It's on hold. I've decided to wait until I'm officially divorced."

Leo frowned. "Why?"

She sighed. She didn't really want to get into it.

"It's okay if you aren't ready," Leo said.

Dani tamped down a flash of annoyance. Now they were going
to have to talk about her too-high standards, or her uncharacteristic prudishness, or whatever spin Leo was going to put on it. She
was going to have to trot out her line about how she was planning
to jump the first man she laid eyes on after the divorce was final,
ha ha ha.

"Honestly," Max said brightly, "I have to endorse Daniela's
method—from experience, alas. Did I ever tell you about the time
when I was at Cambridge and I developed a bit of rapport with
one of the librarians there? Well. She was not quite divorced, and
let me tell you, that was a mistake."

Off he went with his story. He knew she didn't want to talk
about her dating life, or lack thereof, so he was distracting every-

one. Drawing their attention with tales of his own misdeeds, just as he had done for his brother throughout their childhood.

It struck her as funny that Max knew the real reason she was hesitating on the online-dating front—fear of getting her heart broken again—and Leo, her supposed best friend, did not.

Chapter Seventeen

The morning of the wedding dawned clear and sunny. Dani had breakfast with Leo and Gabby, and they went on a long hike in the woods surrounding the castle. She had to hand it to Mr. Benz: he had everything planned and running so smoothly, there wasn't anything to do besides show up for hair and makeup at one o'clock.

"I can't believe you're getting married," Gabby exclaimed, stopping as they emerged from the woods and the palace came into view. It was an impressive structure to begin with, made of pale stone, studded with fairy-tale turrets, and perched on the snow-covered hill next to the village. But decked out as it was for the wedding, with gold banners flowing from nearly every window, it was breathtaking. "I can't believe I *live* here."

"You and me both, kiddo," Leo said.

"Don't call me kiddo," Gabby said, and something twisted in Dani's chest. Gabby always used to say that, but unlike before, the admonishment didn't seem to have any real heat behind it. Gabby had settled in well. She was working with a tutor until her

German was good enough for her to attend the village school, but she seemed integrated into the social life of the village and was a particular friend of Imogen's nieces.

Leo and Gabby had a whole new life, and it suited them. Dani was going to miss them when she went home. She thought she'd gotten used to being without them, but seeing them now, here, was like reopening a wound that hadn't quite healed.

She had to get off this schmoopy line of thinking about how she was going to miss everyone when she was back in New York.

Back at the palace, the wedding preparations were rolling out as planned, thanks to the presence of a small army being commanded by Mr. Benz.

The only snag in the proceedings was that Dani managed to break the heel off one of her shoes. Mr. Benz whisked away both the shoe and Dani's apologies, and Verene got to work making some last-minute adjustments on Dani's dress.

"Knock, knock." Max stuck his head into the dressing room. "Is everyone decent?"

"Yes, come in, Max," Marie called from the chair where she was having her makeup done.

Dani smiled. She'd been wondering when Max would turn up. And wow, was he ever . . . something. She had told him once that she tended to forget that he was a baron. That had been true in New York. And even on the estate in Riems, when they'd been tucked away in his cottage or tromping around on the mountain. But here, now, he was every inch the baron. His outfit made him look like a freaking Disney prince. He had once threatened to wear a "frock coat complete with ceremonial sword" to her departmental party, and this must be that. He wore plain black pants, but the top was a deep blue jacket that made his eyes pop, but it was longer than a normal jacket and was covered with pins and bobbles and topped with a yellow sash.

"Well," he said, making eye contact with Dani first as he came farther into the room, "doesn't everyone look . . ." His eyes traveled down her body in a way that made her heart kick up, but oddly he looked almost angry. "Amazing," he finished in a deadpan tone, although he had yet to lay eyes on anyone else.

He held her gaze for too long, and she had the sudden notion that she might burst into flame. Damn Max. How did he do this to her? And he wasn't even touching her, like the other times he had inspired the sex feelings, with the snow angels or in the ocean. He was just *looking* at her.

Leo cleared his throat. Crap. Whatever had been happening hadn't escaped Leo's notice.

"I wasn't expecting a crowd," Max said, seemingly unaffected by their stare-off. He looked between Marie and Leo. "I thought you weren't supposed to see each other before the wedding."

"We do what we want," said Leo, who was wearing a plain, formal black suit over the objections of Mr. Benz and the king. In another display of "I do what I want," he had refused the ceremonial titles that would normally be bestowed upon him as the husband of the monarch-to-be.

"Grand," Max said. "I've brought the bride a treat, but if you groom's-side people are nice, perhaps we'll share." He caught Dani's eye again and winked as he produced a bottle of Dom Pérignon.

"I'll put yours here," he said to Dani, setting a flute on a dressing table after he'd distributed glasses to everyone else—Verene was still futzing with Dani's dress. "And for the flower girl," Max said, turning his attention to Gabby, and then to the door, through which appeared a palace worker holding a sparkling pink drink. The drink-bearer was followed by several more people, one pushing a cart and others bringing covered dishes and tableware, which they set up into a mini buffet.

"Max," Marie said with fondness. "You think of everything. I didn't realize how hungry I was."

Mr. Benz appeared holding Dani's repaired shoe, and Max said, "All I did was the drinks. Credit to Mr. Benz for the food."

"Everything should be bite-size and free of sauce or anything that might ruin gowns," Mr. Benz said.

"So thoughtful of you," Max said, beaming at Mr. Benz in a way that made the equerry frown. "It's so nice to know that one's loved ones are being so well looked after."

"Daniela, my dear," Verene said, "this hidden zipper at the side of your gown isn't hiding well enough. May I ask you to raise your right arm and turn away from me?"

The resulting pose twisted Dani away from everyone and had her effectively hiding behind her arm. So when she heard a phone buzz from near where she'd left hers, she said, "Is that mine? If so, can you grab it, Leo?" Leo knew her code from back when they were neighbors, and he used to read Vince's texts to her when she couldn't bear to do it herself. "Actually, silence it. It won't be anything important."

After a moment, she heard Leo chuckle.

"What?"

"It's actually pretty important. It's from someone named Caroline, who I'm gathering is your divorce lawyer. She says, 'I know you're out of town. Wanted to let you know that the judgment is in. As of today, you are officially divorced. Congrats.'"

Dani's stomach dropped, and without thinking about poor Verene, she whipped around and made eye contact with Max, who was already looking at her.

It was funny that her eyes found him in a room full of people. There was Leo and Mr. Benz and the servers still buzzing about setting up the snacks. So many people between them. But he was the only one she wanted to see.

I swear to god, the moment the divorce is final, I'm going to do it with the first moderately attractive man I lay eyes on.

Her joking vow crash-landed in her mind. She wondered if he remembered it.

His eyes were burning as he stared at her. They contained blue fire, like in the center of a flame—the searing, powerful part.

He remembered.

She started to sweat, which was not good for her delicate crepe dress. She tried not to fidget, but she had butterflies all of a sudden. But they weren't just in her stomach; they were all over. She kept looking at Max, though, and he kept looking at her.

"Is it bad luck that you're getting divorced the same day I'm getting married?" Leo asked, breaking their spell. She could tell from Leo's tone that he was joking and maybe also that he was trying to save her from herself.

Because if she held Max's gaze any longer, she was going to make good on her pledge from so long ago.

"The cars will be arriving in forty-five minutes for the drive to the chapel." Mr. Benz looked up from his phone. He made a slight gesture with his head, and the servers scurried out of the room. "I'll leave you now, but please don't hesitate to summon me if you need anything."

"Oh, Mr. Benz," Max said breezily, apparently having shaken off the intensity of a moment ago. It was disconcerting how easily he could make the shift given that Dani was still internally reeling. "Might I trouble you to check in on my brother?"

"Of course. Is everything all right?"

Max beamed at Mr. Benz. "Yes, but I believe there is one small matter with which you could assist."

"Certainly. Unless I'm summoned, and again, please don't hesitate to do so, I'll be back before the cars are scheduled to arrive." Mr. Benz left, Max smiling after him.

Verene patted Dani's arm. "All done, dear."

Dani hitched up her skirt so she wouldn't trip as she stepped off the pedestal she'd been standing on for alterations. Without her even seeing him arrive—last she knew, Max had been on the other side of the room making strange faces at Mr. Benz's back—Max was there with a hand.

He helped her down, which wasn't unusual, but the fact that he did so without looking at her was. Max was solicitous. She'd gotten used to it and no longer even felt, much less indulged, the impulse to shut him down when he offered help. But usually a hand extended in a situation like this would come with a wink or a smile, or at least eye contact.

The other part that was unusual? She was shaking like a leaf. Not because of wedding nerves, but because of *him*. And it wasn't just the generic "sex feelings." It was a visceral *wanting* that was startling in both its intensity and suddenness. He was only touching her lightly with his hand, but it felt like he was touching her all over.

As soon as she was down, he let go.

Maybe he did remember her vow. Maybe it had popped into his head as suddenly as it had into hers, and now that he had it in mind he was actively not looking at her.

And if that was the case, why was she disappointed?

When the cars came to collect them, Dani went in one with Leo and Gabby, and Max got in another with Marie.

Thank god. Max couldn't even look at Dani, which was an unsettling turn of events. Normally looking at Dani was one of life's little pleasures.

But, oh, god, he was so screwed.

Something had happened to him when he'd walked into the room earlier and laid eyes on her. She'd been wearing a simple, white, body-hugging dress with a drapey neckline.

Max was not the kind of person who believed in visions, or fate, or any of that. But looking at Dani standing there in that white dress, her hair done up in an elaborate braided updo, he underwent some sort of . . . moment, a record skip in his chest, where he saw himself at a different wedding.

He had a moment when he thought, *Mine*.

And then the text from the lawyer, as if fate were a real thing, as if it had decided to favor him for once.

After the record in his chest stopped skipping, he'd ordered himself to calm down. It wasn't as if he actually believed any of the stuff they'd joked about. She wasn't going to jump the first

man she saw. It wasn't as if her marital status had truly been holding her back. It had merely been an excuse.

But, oh, how he wanted her to jump the first man she saw, and
oh, how he wanted to be that man.

Which was one thing. That part wasn't surprising. That part
wasn't new.

But the part that had to do with the real reason she'd been
holding back: she was worried about her heart getting involved
once she finally did the deed. She was worried about her heart
getting broken.

Max wanted to be that man, too. To be the one to whom she
gave her heart.

If Dani gave him her heart, he wouldn't break it. He would actively do everything in his power to not break it. No matter what
it cost him. If he could have that vision, her in a white dress, her
eyes finding him automatically in a room full of people, he would
do *anything*.

Dear god.

"Well, this is it," Marie said.

He wrenched his thoughts from the fact that his entire world,
the foundation on which he'd built his self-image, had crumbled.

"Is everything all right?" Marie laid her hand on his arm as the
car pulled up in front of the small chapel on the palace grounds
where the ceremony was taking place.

Marie deserved his attention. His problem with Dani—and it
was a problem, because there was no way she would ever let
herself be with him, not in the way he wanted—wasn't going anywhere. He could tell Marie about it, but not today. Today was
hers.

"Everything is grand." He patted her hand that was on his arm. "You're getting married, and not to me! I couldn't be happier for you."

"I'm getting married, and not to you!" she echoed incredulously. "I'm getting married to Leo!" She grinned as if she could not believe her good fortune. They held hands and looked at each other for a long moment, neither of them needing to say more than that.

"Max. Good to see you." King Emil was waiting outside the chapel, and Max dipped his head. Max reached back into the car to help Marie out, but Verene, who had arrived ahead of them, pushed him aside and began consulting with Marie regarding dress extraction strategy. "I had a lovely luncheon with your parents and brother today," the king added.

Max made a noncommittal noise. His parents had arrived this morning, but he'd managed to avoid them thanks to his man of honor duties. He was hoping to lean on those duties, and on the plan he and Lavinia had cooked up, to continue avoiding them all day. Especially once his father started officially hitting the bar. He only had to get through a few more hours. He was leaving for Innsbruck in the morning. With Dani. Who he currently could not look at for fear of combusting. Or crying. Or both. But that was another problem to be dealt with later.

Another car pulled up. It would be Leo and Gabby and Dani, which was Max's cue to leave. He stuck his head into Marie's car and whispered, "Break a leg, my friend." She made a kissing gesture at him, and he hightailed it into the church. They had decided that despite the gender-swapped best woman and man of honor designations, they would hew to more traditional roles for the ceremony, which meant Max would join Leo at the front of the chapel and Dani, along with flower girl Gabby, would process behind Marie.

He still didn't want to see Dani. Well, he *wanted* to. But he couldn't.

Not that he could avoid it. After a few moments, a string quartet began playing, and Marie and her father appeared at the head of the aisle. Marie's dress didn't have a train, but Dani smoothed the back of her knee-length veil as she set off. Dani smiled at Gabby, and the two of them started walking.

Oh dear god. The record skipping in his chest had been replaced by an anvil. It was hard to breathe.

Dani spent the first few steps of her procession looking at the back of Marie's dress, probably to make sure everything was in order. When she started to lift her gaze, he knew somehow that her eyes would find his first.

He looked away before they did, forced himself to keep his eyes on Marie, who was looking very princessey in a dress with a huge, poufy tulle skirt.

He tracked Marie's progress down the aisle, staying with his strategy of not looking at Dani. He needed to not miss his best friend's wedding.

And he needed to stop staring at what he could never have.

Chapter Eighteen

Where the hell was Max?

Dani looked around the ballroom. She was seated at a head table on a raised dais, so she had a bird's-eye view with which to confirm that the answer was *nowhere*. She had survived the wedding—it had been lovely, but she'd been nervous—and now all that remained of wedding-party duties were the toasts. Which, as she eyed the dwindling receiving line Marie and Leo were helming, were supposed to happen soon.

She was getting annoyed. Every time she and Max talked about this wedding, going all the way back to their first conversation about it at *The Nutcracker*, he had assured her he would look out for her. Not that she needed him. Mr. Benz was hovering and could be hailed. But Mr. Benz could not buoy her the way Max could. She brooded as she reviewed her notes. When the royals and Leo—did Leo count as a royal now, even though he'd declined the formal title?—entered to a great big cheer, there was still no Max. After the new couple was seated, Marie leaned over Leo and Gabby to speak to Dani. "Do you know where Max is?"

"I'm sorry, I don't."

Marie frowned, and once more, Dani surveyed the ballroom. He was nowhere. But his parents were here, which both relieved and annoyed Dani. If they were here, it meant they weren't somewhere else being beastly to him. But that also meant he was AWOL for no reason.

She felt a hand on her shoulder. It was Mr. Benz, handing her a microphone.

"I thought the baron was going first?" she whispered. Her protocol lessons had taken—she'd been instructed to address Max as Lord Laudon and refer to him as "the baron" when in public.

Which was fine. Because that was what he was. It was good to remember that.

"There's been a slight change of plans," Mr. Benz whispered. "Lord Laudon is delayed, so I think it's best if you go first, which means you need to welcome everyone and thank them for coming before you start."

Great. Winging it at the royal wedding.

"I have the utmost confidence in you," Mr. Benz added, and when she turned to look at him, he smiled sincerely. He seemed to mean it.

She wondered what the delay was if it wasn't Max's parents. It wasn't like him to—

Oh, but there he was. Slinking in a side door.

With Lavinia.

Which was fine.

Lavinia was a nice person.

She was also quite the sight to behold, dressed in a long, jade-green column of a gown with matching emerald earrings. Her hair was done in an elaborate updo.

Max had his head bent as they walked so she could speak into his ear, and whatever she was saying was making him smile.

Well, crap.

Dani had been thinking it wasn't like him to go missing from a responsibility, but that wasn't right, was it? It wasn't like the Max she knew. But it *was* like the Depraved Duke to be late to the royal wedding reception because he was busy chasing after a goddamn cousin to the Austrian archduke who also happened to be an *extremely nice person.*

"Unless you feel you can't?" Mr. Benz prodded.

"No. I can." She accepted the microphone, took a fortifying breath, stood, and said, "Good evening, ladies and gentlemen. If you would indulge me in a few words?" She glanced at Max, who had taken his seat, hoping for an encouraging nod or a wink of solidarity, but he wasn't looking at her. All right. She was on her own.

She did everything she was supposed to do. Welcomed the guests. Introduced herself. She was confident with a dash of self-deprecating humor thrown in. She told funny stories about Leo and segued into a less humorous and more heartfelt ending. She actually made a few people get misty.

She did a damn fine job. Take that, Your Royal Highnesses.

She sat to an enthusiastic round of applause, and as Max started talking, she picked up her drink and took a big, relieved gulp.

"Welcome to my wedding. Ah, no! I jest. It's not my wedding

anymore, is it?" He smiled at Marie and Leo with a mix of affection and impishness as the crowd laughed. She supposed he wanted to address the elephant in the room. He made sure, though, to telegraph his love for the couple and his genuine excitement over their union. He did a bang-up job, handling what could have been a fraught situation with his signature breezy humor and emotional intelligence. Dani cast a glance at the crowd. Lavinia, seated next to Max's mother, was rapt.

When Max was done, he sat on the other side of Marie, which meant Dani no longer had to look at him—and that she was done with her official duties. She was relieved on both counts.

She understood that she couldn't simply disappear for the rest of the evening, and really, she didn't want to. She wanted to celebrate Leo's wedding. She just needed a break. So as the servers started bringing the first course, she got up and headed toward the exit. There was a parlor outside the ballroom set up for the wedding party to use as a green room. It had comfy chairs, beverages, and, most critically, a door that closed. She would sit for a few minutes, get her shit together, and shake off this mix of Max-inspired attraction and annoyance. Then she would go back into the ballroom, and hopefully whatever weirdness was going on between Max and her would be gone. Because, honestly, they were supposed to go to Austria tomorrow.

Maybe he wanted to take Lavinia instead.

Well, whatever. Dani was going to Austria with Leo and Marie. Max could do what he wanted with whomever he wanted. It was no concern of—

Just as she escaped the ballroom, a hand came down on her shoulder. Oh, shit. She knew who it was. She could *feel* who it was.

"Wait." His voice confirmed it.

Damn it. "I just need to step out for a moment." Her own voice was less familiar. It was too high. It sounded like it belonged to someone playing her in a movie. It felt like that, too, like she was reciting a line. *I just need to step out for a moment.* It *was* a line. It was a *lie.* What she needed to step away from was *him.* And she'd almost made it.

"You looked at me first."

"What?" What was he— Oh. *Oh.* She gasped as goosebumps rose on her skin.

He remembered.

She was frozen in place, shivering with his hand on her bare shoulder, his skin on her skin. She was his prey, and she could no sooner move than if he'd literally caught her in a trap.

"Don't pretend you don't know what I'm talking about."

He sounded angry, which was such an uncharacteristic emotion from Max, at least when it came to her.

She needed to turn around and face him. She'd pulled up her big-girl pants and gotten through that toast, and she could do this, too.

She pivoted in place. He didn't take his hand off her shoulder, just let it rest lightly against her skin as she turned and settled it more heavily on the ball of her shoulder when she finished her rotation.

She had compared Max's eyes before to the cool blue center of a flame, but now, despite the fact that his body was calm, that his palm on her shoulder was still and dry, his eyes were a wildfire raging out of control. She had always thought of Max as funny and breezy and easygoing with a hidden center of deeply felt emotion. But now he looked like he'd been turned inside out, like all the tender, emotional stuff was on the outside, plainly visible for anyone to see.

"I did look at you," she said slowly, relieved that her voice came out sounding like her again. "But then *you* stopped looking at *me*." And for some reason she couldn't articulate, that loss of his attention had hurt.

"Because I *couldn't* look at you anymore."

"Why not?"

"Because then you would see everything." He moved his hand from her shoulder across her suddenly tender skin until the heel of his palm rested lightly over the notch in her collarbone and his fingers radiated up her throat. She had the sudden, absurd notion that maybe he *was* on fire, inside. His hand, though it was barely touching her, hovering almost, brought heat as it traced a path through her cold-pebbled skin.

"Which isn't, in itself, a bad thing," he added, "but we had a wedding to get through." He smiled, a little half smile, and he looked more like his usual self, even if it was a *sad* half smile. "That's done now."

"So now it's okay for me to see everything?" she whispered.

"You already saw almost everything. So what's another inch? What's the last little bit?" The sad smile turned almost unbearably fond, and even though it was him saying he was showing her everything, *she* felt almost painfully vulnerable, like she was made of new skin forming under a bandage that someone had ripped off too soon.

She knew what they were talking about. Even though they were speaking in strangely cryptic terms, she knew what "everything" meant. But she wanted explicit, verbal confirmation. "'Everything' being that you want to have sex. With me."

He did not hesitate before saying, simply, "Yes."

Yes. She wanted that, too. Hadn't she always? Or at least for a long time? Hadn't she wanted him to the exclusion of others—hence her Tinder problem?

"Yes," he said again, taking his palm from her and laying it on his chest. He sounded . . . devastated.

Yes. The word rose through her consciousness every time he said it.

"I guess now that I'm not married, I'm eligible under your rules of engagement."

There was a pause before he said, "That's true."

"And I'm certainly not trying to entrap you." She tried to laugh but found she couldn't get the sound around a lump rising in her throat. What was the matter with her? Max had propositioned her a bunch of times, early in their acquaintance. This wasn't new. What was new was that she was going to say yes.

There was another pause. "Right."

"And there will be no lying on either of our parts," she said. "We both know what this is—and isn't. So that leaves the rule about doing it on your turf. How do we handle that one? Is your room here sufficient? It's like a hotel room, right?"

He blinked about a thousand times. "I don't think that rule matters in this case."

"Why not?"

"Because I've never had sex with someone I—"

"What?"

"With someone I . . . already trust. With a friend." He scrunched up his face like he'd tasted something bad.

She smiled. He was so himself, and so dear to her. "And we'd still be friends, right? After?"

"*Yes*," he said, so vehemently that it made his voice crack.

"So . . . when do we do this?"

The sour face was replaced by a more familiar grin. "No time like the present?"

And just like that, all the seriousness and intensity of the day, of the moment, was gone, shed like an old skin, and *Max* was back. She laughed. "We can't bail on the wedding to go have sex."

"I'm fairly certain we can do whatever we want, but all right." He took a step back. "Meet me outside my room when this bloody evening is over. It's in the northwest wing on the third floor. Do you know where that is?"

"Yes." He took another step. She so very much didn't want him to go. "Do you want to dance later?"

"No."

"No?" she echoed laughingly.

"I can't *dance* with you," he scoffed.

"Why not?"

"I can't touch you. God. I can't even look at you."

"But you're going to do a lot more than—"

He held up a hand. "Later. That's later. I'll see you later."

"Are you going to go back to ignoring me until then?"

"Yes. Yes, I am."

Chapter Nineteen

At *least I have Lavinia,* Max thought to himself as he twirled his unexpected ally around the ballroom. *At least I have Lavinia* was not a sentence he had ever imagined himself thinking.

As was typical for Eldovian weddings, the regular dancing was interspersed with formal waltzes and traditional folk dances. "If you dance the ländler with me later, our parents will die of happiness," she said, breathless and pink-cheeked from the fast-paced waltz.

"Grand idea," he said.

"But perhaps that is too much." She frowned as she looked over his shoulder.

"No, no. This was a brilliant idea."

That night in Riems, after the disastrous dinner, Lavinia had shocked Max by proposing they join forces at the wedding to keep their parents at bay. "What if we give them what they want?" she'd asked. "Or I should say, what if we *appear* to give them what they want? That way we can actually enjoy ourselves without feeling that we need to be constantly looking over our shoulders. And also, your father won't . . ."

"Ruin Marie's wedding by throwing a tantrum?" Max had supplied, marveling over how thoroughly he had misjudged Lavinia at that first meeting in New York.

He had happily signed on to her diabolical plan. She had been correct in that their ploy had effectively neutered their parents. As for her other argument, he couldn't really say he was having fun without having to look over his shoulder. But that wasn't a flaw in her plan so much as it was about the fact that Dani would not sit still. He'd meant what he said earlier. He didn't want to be near her until this interminable evening was over. He couldn't look at her. If he had to, he was at risk of throwing her over his shoulder caveman-style and carrying her out of here regardless of the fallout it would create.

He felt trapped in his own skin. As if he were on fire, and not in a good way.

But what could he do but focus on Lavinia and try to act normal? Even if he wasn't sure what that meant anymore.

A few hours later, he had danced the ländler, eaten cake, and endured a long conversation about the king's decision to make some changes to Morneau, the royal family's watch company, when his mother appeared at his side.

"Max, darling, I'd like to take your father upstairs."

Other than a brief conversation in the receiving line after the ceremony, he'd succeeded in his mission to avoid his parents. But he couldn't avoid this. "Max, darling, I'd like to take your father upstairs" was code for "Your father is drunker than usual and about to embarrass us." Max and his mother had an unspoken agreement to put aside their differences and join forces to extract his father in these sorts of situations.

Max sighed. "Where is he?"

"He's talking politics with Lucille Müller."

Lucille Müller was the leader of the far-left opposition party in Parliament. She was not a good person for Father to be talking to, especially if he'd been keeping up his usual pace at the bar. Remarkably, Max hadn't been counting this evening. He looked around for Sebastien, who apparently hadn't been counting either, because he was nowhere to be seen. "All right. Let's go." He steeled himself.

In some ways, even with all the chaos and unkindness that characterized his family interactions, these rare moments when his mother asked for his help managing his father were the worst. They didn't happen very often. Only when they were in public and there wasn't household staff on hand.

It was in these moments that Max was reminded how elementally alone he was. One would think, given that his mother was asking him to help, that there would be a sort of solidarity in the act of trying to manage Father. There was certainly a common understanding of what needed to happen. But somehow that didn't translate into actual understanding. Understanding of the emotional variety, the sort that was supposed to travel, unconditionally, from parent to child.

"You and Lavinia looked like you had a lovely evening," Mother said.

"Yes," he said flatly.

"Your father was very happy."

"Grand. That is the most important thing, after all."

"Max." She huffed a martyred sigh. "Don't start."

He eyed Father. He was right in Lucille's face, jawing about something and shaking his finger. The crowd had thinned considerably, and their heated argument was beginning to draw the attention of people near them.

"Don't you ever get tired of it, Mother?"

She looked at him for a long time, and for an instant, he thought he saw something different in her eyes—a flash of uncertainty, perhaps? It was gone before he could puzzle it out. "I'm sure I don't know what you mean."

As they approached Father, Max ran through what would happen. Mother would apologize for interrupting and make some case for why they needed to leave, and Max would engage Lucille in conversation. That was their first strategy, and it might work. If they needed to escalate, Max and Mother would switch places, and Max would hiss in his father's ear that he was embarrassing himself and the family and strong-arm him out of the room.

That would work, but there would be a cost. Father, humiliated, would turn his rage on Max. He wouldn't hit him. It would just be words. Words, Max reminded himself, slid right off him. He was a well-seasoned pan, impervious.

Max stopped walking and looked around.

No, he looked for *her*. Even though he'd had an ever-humming awareness of her, of her presence in this ballroom haunting him like a ghost breathing down his neck, he'd been trying to avoid *looking* at her. Out of self-preservation. But now, though it defied logic, looking at her felt like an *act* of self-preservation.

There she was, at a small table with Leo, deep in conversation.

Some wisps had come out of her hairdo. They had their heads together, and their faces were lit by the flames of a candle on the table, making her skin glow.

She looked up and right at him, as she had earlier that day, during the dress fitting. As if she felt him. As if they felt each other.

"I'm not doing this."

Mother, who'd proceeded a few steps ahead of him before noticing his absence, turned. "I beg your pardon?"

"I've been helping you extract Father from potentially embarrassing situations since I was a child, and I'm not doing it anymore. I've spent my whole life listening to you two tell me what's wrong with me. Seb and I have spent our whole lives being abused by Father while you stood by and let him. Why would I *help* you? Why have I been helping you for so long?"

He huffed a laugh. He couldn't believe he'd said that, but he also couldn't believe how easy it had been, in the end. "I'm going to leave now. Good night, Mother."

"You can't just *leave*."

"I can, though." It was a revelation, an overdue one. He laughed again. Wait until Mother found out he and Lavinia had been faking all evening.

They thought he was such a loose cannon, and he supposed in some ways he was, if you looked at the external shape of his behavior and judged it against an arbitrary standard. He didn't act the way they thought the firstborn son of a duke should act. But when it came to this, when it came to shame and complicity and pretense, he toed the line every time. Why? Seb didn't need his protection anymore. And Max didn't give a flying fuck what anyone else thought.

Except *her*. And she *knew* him. He found Dani in the crowd again. She was still looking at him. She had probably been keeping him in her sights this whole time. He nodded at her and pointed at his watch. A slow smile blossomed on her face. Her smile was knowing, seductive. The one that broke out on his face in answer was dopey. He could feel it. But he couldn't do anything about it, so he hitched his head toward the exit. *I'm leaving now.* She held up a finger. *I'll follow in a bit.*

And then he left. He just left.

Mother had left him alone that night in the nursery, but he saw now that he hadn't actually *let* himself be left. He had spent his whole life proclaiming that he didn't care about his parents' indifference, that he was immune to their little cruelties. But part of him had held on.

Max had always thought that abandonment felt terrible. But it actually didn't, not if you were really, truly abandoned. If you were no longer in anyone's debt.

It felt like freedom.

There was a lightness in his step as he strode out of the ballroom. He jogged up the steps to the third floor. He wasn't sure what the hurry was, only that little bursts of energy were propelling him, compelling him to move.

He paused after opening his door. It sounded like Seb was in his room across the hall—it sounded like he was doing jumping jacks in there.

He crossed the hall and rapped on Seb's door, wanting to try to put into words his big revelation, to tell him about how he'd left Mother to deal with Father and how doing so had felt like a sort of liberation. He pushed the door open.

Ohhh.

Seb was not alone.

Seb was also not dressed.

Neither was the man who dived in front of Seb and covered him with his body.

And that man was not Mr. Benz. He was much bigger. His giant torso blocked Seb entirely from Max's view. It was Torkel Renner, the head of palace security.

"Well. I got that wrong, didn't I?" Max said as there was some scrambling on the bed. The men had been on top of the covers, and now it looked like Torkel was trying to get Seb underneath them. "Really, really wrong." He chuckled.

He started to leave, but Seb's face popped up over Torkel's shoulder. "Max?"

"Yes. My apologies." Torkel looked over his shoulder and glowered at Max. "I'll be—"

Seb patted Torkel's bulging biceps and whispered, "It's all right, love."

It's all right, love? Well.

Torkel moved off the bed, apparently unembarrassed about the fact that he was flashing Max his ass, pulled on a pair of pants, and turned and stood next to the bed with his tree-trunk arms folded over his chest. He looked like the bodyguard he was. If bodyguards went shoeless. And shirtless.

"I don't want to hide anymore, Max," Seb said quietly.

Something caught in Max's chest. That sounded like a version of what Max had come here to tell Seb. Max wasn't the only one who had had enough of the old ways. He cleared his throat. "I know. I'll help you."

"Will you?"

"Always."

Seb glanced at Torkel, who was still standing there like a statue. "But maybe you could help me tomorrow?"

"Yes, of course. Well, I'm leaving early tomorrow morning, but I can—"

Seb shook his head and laughed. "I meant it more metaphorically. We can talk when you're back. I'm taking a little trip myself." He glanced at Torkel and tried and failed to stifle a smile. Sebastien had never had a poker face. That had been half his problem as a child. That had been what Max had always been trying to protect—Seb's openhearted warmth.

Max generally *did* have a poker face, but he couldn't stop the grin he felt emerging. "Are you, now? Where are you going?" Seb started to try to answer, but Max raised his voice and talked over him. "Are you sure it's wise to travel alone? You *are* the son of a duke. Perhaps you'd better ask Marie if she can spare someone from her security team to accompany you." He laughed. He was still Seb's brother, after all.

A cushion from the bed came sailing at his head, because Seb was still his brother.

Suddenly Torkel was at his side, his hand on the doorknob. Max wasn't sure how it was possible for such a large man to move so quickly and gracefully. "I think you'd better go now, Lord Laudon."

"And I think you'd better start calling me—"

The door shut in his face.

"Max."

He turned.

The feeling he'd had all night, of not fitting properly in his skin, went away, completely and all at once. It was as if he'd dropped back into his body, like he *belonged* in his body in some elemental way, like the whole *point* of his body was that it was the vehicle he used to interact with Daniela Martinez.

She was standing at the far end of the dimly lit corridor.

He found himself at a loss for words, which was unprecedented when it came to her. There were always words between them, so many words, whispered into phones late at night or, when he was very lucky, into the space between them as they sat side by side on a beach or in a car queued up at the McDonald's drive-through.

She looked at him with a small smile that was half-fond, half-mystified. Perhaps she was facing a word shortage of her own.

They didn't need words, it turned out. They could just stand there and stare at each other, smile like idiots and not ask a single question or consult a single list. That feeling from earlier, that the foundation on which he'd built his life was shifting, went away. He was sturdy and new and strong, standing on solid ground. He held out a hand.

She started toward him, and when she reached him and put her hand in his, he picked her up and twirled her around like they were in a goddamn movie. As the twirl wound down, she hiked her dress up and out of the way and wrapped her legs around his waist. He used a foot to kick open the door he'd left ajar. Someone had come in and turned down the bed and switched on the small bedside lamp. He walked straight to the bed and lowered her onto her back.

She pulled him down with her. For a moment, they stared at each other, their faces mere inches apart.

"Hi," she whispered, startling the hell out of him.

"Hi," he rasped back.

She smiled, and he thought his heart might break in two. But in a good way. For once.

And then, finally, finally, after all these hours, after all these months, they kissed each other.

Chapter Twenty

*I*t had been a long time since Dani had had a first time with someone, but she remembered that it was usually a bit awkward. Intentions were muddy, heads tilted the wrong way, nerves impeded.

With guys before Vince, and with Vince, too, in the early days, she used to fret about what it all meant. Are we a couple now? What happens next?

There was none of that with Max. And although she'd been momentarily freaked out when he'd cornered her with his "You looked at me first" possessive growling, it had only taken her a moment to understand that yes, she had looked at him first, and yes, she was going to sleep with him, and maybe even, yes, she had discarded all those Tinder guys because they *weren't* him. He knew about all her junk, and she knew about all of his. They were best friends. Nothing was going to change.

Except they were going to have some really hot sex.

They were completely in sync. So in sync that by the time she told herself to lift her head to kiss him, he was already kissing her. They were kissing each other.

His lips were soft but merciless as they moved over hers, and she met him. They were kissing each other like they knew how, like they'd been doing this for years. They did know how, she supposed. The way to kiss Maximillian von Hansburg was to hold nothing back, to extract the maximum amount of pleasure from the experience. She let her jaw slacken even as she continued to kiss him. He groaned, and she felt the slow, sensual incursion of his tongue in her mouth. Nothing had ever made her feel this way, languorous and frantic at the same time. He'd been holding himself on his forearms above her, but he shifted his weight to one arm and clamped a hand on her jaw, as if he wanted to make sure she wasn't going anywhere. It made her laugh. She was never going anywhere. She was going to die here, kissing Max, and die happily.

Her laugh came out like a moan, though, and he swallowed it.

She wrapped her legs around his waist, as she had outside in the corridor, but this time they were horizonal. She wanted him on her, the full weight of him. So she pulled, hard, and he groaned again and let his lower body fall even as he kept working her mouth without interruption, stroking his tongue against hers. Her dress was already bunched up, so the maneuver had the effect of shoving his pelvis against her mound. She was wearing only the smallest, sheerest pair of panties beneath her dress because she was morally opposed to Spanx and anything else would have shown through, and his baron-pants had buttons in front. She whimpered involuntarily. The contact had been a bit painful, but mostly because she'd been unprepared for it. She could tell, though, that underneath the shock of contact, there was something else, something liquid and warm and wonderful.

He must have heard only pain. He was off her in an instant, sitting back on his heels and frowning down at her underwear. He frowned some more, more deeply, as if they offended him. Before she could puzzle it out, his hand was on her. Not in a sexual way necessarily, more like he was putting pressure on a wound. He rested his entire palm, warm and large, on the front of her panties, obscuring them from view entirely. She liked the look of his hand on her like that, the presumption of it.

She wanted to do the same to him, but all she could reach, given that he was, unintentionally or not, pinning her to the bed, was his torso. So she did it with her voice. Issued an order. "Take them off."

He smiled and pulled them down as she lifted her hips. He returned his hand to the same spot. "I'm sorry I hurt you."

"You didn't hurt me."

"Are you sure?" He slid his hand down so the meaty part of his palm rested over the thatch of curls between her legs. He made little circles, as if soothing her, watching her like a hawk the whole time.

He was putting pressure on her clit, but indirectly, by dint of the weight of his palm. It felt good. She wanted more. She let her legs fall open, and he sucked in a breath as his gaze whipped down from her face.

She had done some overdue grooming in advance of her failed Tinder dates, she supposed because each time, she'd deluded herself into thinking she was going to actually do the deed. And she had fretted every time. She had been out of the dating pool for so long. Should she take off more? What was normal? What was expected? What was alluring?

She had no worries about that now. None.

Max had shifted his hand a little but hadn't changed its angle. It was perfect—or almost perfect. Opening her legs had exposed her clit, and she wiggled her hips around until—oh. The perfect amount of pressure. He started to move his hand, and she shot hers out and clamped it down on his even as she rolled her hips, rocking against the base of his palm.

He got the message and pressed a little harder, causing a sharp, involuntary inhalation. She'd had hand jobs in her life, but they had always involved fingers. But there was something about the firm yet diffuse pressure of the edge of his palm that was working for her.

Well, come on, there was something about *Max* that was working for her. Her beautiful friend she trusted absolutely.

It didn't hurt that, as he used to joke, he was very good at this. He kept up the pressure, moving his hand in tiny circles as he stared at her, the blue flames burning high.

"Are you going to be able to come like this?" he whispered.

"Yes," she whispered.

"Can I kiss you again?"

"Yes. Kiss me again." *And never stop.*

THERE WAS SOMETHING almost unbearably erotic about being dressed in a suit while Dani lay on the bed in front of him with her dress bunched around her middle. The juxtaposition between her dishevelment and the fact that Max was fully and formally attired was hot as hell. And when she started shaking and moaning as she came beneath his palm, he wondered if he would ever get over it.

He also wondered if she was all right. As she rode the aftershocks, he kept his hand on her, hoping now that he'd used it to get her off, he could also use it to anchor her. If this was her first time being with anyone since Vince, since the divorce that had come through *today*, she might be unexpectedly emotional.

"Take off that suit."

Or perhaps not.

He took off the suit—so quickly he ran into trouble as he tripped over his own feet trying to get out of the pants—and pitched forward onto the bed.

She rolled out of the way, laughing, and twisted herself into a pretzel trying to get her dress over her head and unhook a complicated bra with crisscross straps in back. He helped her with the latter, and eventually, they ended up in a tangle of limbs and laughter.

You are beautiful, he wanted to say, because she was. Her pinned-up braids were half undone, and she had small, perfect breasts shaped like teardrops.

You are beautiful. It was the only sentiment in his head. He wanted to say it so badly, but he knew she wouldn't want to hear that from him, at least not in the intense, reverent tone it was sure to be delivered in. So he kissed her to make himself shut up.

She kissed him back with abandon, but not for very long. Probably because she was aware that she'd come and he hadn't. She was probably more aware than he was, given how he'd been living in his head, mooning over her, but when she touched him for the first time, he was, suddenly, *aware*.

"Dear god," he bit out as her hand closed around him.

"Is this okay?" she whispered.

He laughed.

"I'm going to take that as a yes."

"Yes," he gasped, as she tightened her grip and moved her hand up and down his shaft.

Max had fancied himself, before Dani, a skilled lover. He could last a long time, usually. It had been so long, though. In order for this not to be over two seconds after it started, he needed to—"Oh, no."

She laughed, but not *at* him, he didn't think. She sounded delighted.

As his body shuddered, he watched her laugh, and he was pretty damn delighted, too.

"Do you have any condoms?" Dani said a few minutes later, while they were lying side by side panting.

"My god, woman. You may be ready to go again, but I need a moment."

She laughed. "No! I meant for next time."

Next time. Had Max ever heard two better words?

She rolled over. "Oh, wait. Is there not going to be a next time? Was this"—she waved her hand between them—"It? Do I have to follow the same rules as everyone else?"

He captured the hand, cognizant that getting too cuddly was not advised for a variety of reasons but unable to help himself. "There is going to be a next time." He grinned. "And I don't have any condoms. But I'll get some."

"Not from Leo and Marie, though, right?" she said quickly.

"Because we're not going to tell them about this?" he asked carefully.

"Are you kidding? No. They wouldn't understand."

He was fairly certain he didn't understand, either. "What wouldn't they understand?"

"Us. Our thing. I would say friends with benefits, but it's more than that."

His heart, which had only recently returned to normal, picked back up. "It is?" The ground beneath him had shifted today, but he wasn't flattering himself that Dani was going to see this as anything they could actually *have*. Things hadn't shifted that much.

"Yeah. I mean, it's perfect, right?"

Yes.

"Like, I'm here," she went on. "We can do this without violating your rules. And whatever my deal was with the potential Tinder dudes is a nonissue. And we *know* we're not going to ruin our friendship." She looked alarmed suddenly as she jerked her head up. "Right?"

"Right. Of course not." He played with her hand a bit. "But how is what you're describing not friends with benefits?" He was trying to understand. He wanted to know what she expected from him. He wanted to know what he could have.

"I guess it is." She shrugged. "I just feel like . . . we're us. We don't need labels. I mean, you're my favorite person." He jokingly preened, but inside, it wasn't a joke. She took her hand back and used it to swat his chest. "This feels like an extension of that. Also, at the risk of inflaming your already healthy ego, I gotta say . . ." She fanned herself with her hand. "You weren't lying when you said you'd had good reviews." He grinned and did some more mock-preening. "Like, what was that?" she exclaimed. "I usually can't come unless I'm on top, but you do some weird mojo with your palm, and bam!"

"I was merely following your lead," he said, though he noted her preference for being on top. As pleased as he was to have been proclaimed her favorite person, not to mention a sex god, he remained dissatisfied with her explanation about the nature of their relationship. Were they friends with benefits, or were they, as she'd said, "more"? But he wasn't going to press her. He didn't want her to overthink things and end up calling it—whatever "it" was—off. So, with more difficulty than he would have expected, he changed the subject. "I could go across the hall to my brother's room. He'll have condoms." He would, right? Max frowned. Hopefully Seb was using condoms.

"It's hard to imagine your brother having sex. He's so buttoned up."

"It's even harder to imagine him having sex with Torkel Renner." Max still had not fully recovered from his shock.

"Who's Torkel Renner?"

"The head of palace security."

"The big beefy guy with the mirrored sunglasses?"

"That's him."

She whistled. "Well, he seems like he's very good at his job. I'm sure he's extremely competent in . . . other areas as well."

"The thing is, I'm fairly certain they're in love." It was still so astonishing. But he supposed sometimes these things happened with no warning. He glanced over at Dani.

"Do you think Sebastien will come out?"

He thought back to Seb's statement about not wanting to hide anymore. "I think he will."

"How is that going to go over?"

"I don't know." He cast his mind back to his confrontation with his mother, which, remarkably, had been only an hour ago. "But I do know that things are changing around here."

"What does that mean?"

"Have you ever thought about how in English, the word *abandon* has two vastly different meanings? To abandon someone is to leave them, but to do something with abandon is to really throw yourself into it?"

"Are they really all that different? If you're doing something with abandon, it means you don't care about the consequences. You're leaving behind the consequences, in a way."

"Hmm." It was odd. If Max thought objectively about everything that was swirling around in his mind—the fact that he'd had sex with Dani, first and foremost, but also Seb and Torkel, Seb's potential coming out, the idea of changing how he related to his parents, it should have made him uncomfortable. Hell, it should have made him panic.

But somehow, lying next to Dani, he was calm. As settled as he'd ever felt in his life. It was that same feeling of embodiment from earlier, but this time he also felt like his spirit, for lack of a better word, was involved. Everything felt profoundly right, so right he wasn't worried about any of the upheaval that was to come. He welcomed it, in a way, if it would allow for more of this settled feeling.

"Do you really not have a condom?" Dani sounded incredulous.

"I really do not have a condom."

"Why not?"

"I didn't expect to be having sex here." He would have thought that was obvious.

"You didn't expect to be having sex at a wedding? Aren't weddings a major place where people hook up? Weren't you trying to break your dry spell?"

He didn't know what to say to that. He distinctly remembered going through his travel toiletries case to come here and dispassionately thinking, *Toothbrush, check; toothpaste, check; deodorant, check; condoms, don't need those.*

"What about Lavinia?"

"What about her?"

"You were laughing with her when you came into the reception. You were late because of her. I had to start the toasts."

Oh. He hadn't made the mental leap from "hooking up at a wedding" to Lavinia the way Dani apparently had. "All right. You got me," he said, trying for humor. "Lavinia and I were doing it in the coatroom. That's why I was late."

It didn't work. She didn't even smile.

Was she *jealous*? Was he a monster for wanting her to be? "I was laughing with Lavinia because, to my great surprise, she suggested a little subterfuge to get both sets of parents off our backs. We decided to be seen looking cozy, to make people fill in the blanks." He wagged his eyebrows, trying again to amuse Dani. "Apparently it worked."

She still didn't laugh. "So Lavinia does have a sense of fun?"

"Pardon me?"

"You said you weren't going to marry her because she didn't have a sense of fun. She seems to have one after all."

"I suppose she does." He had indeed misjudged Lavinia based on that first meeting.

Dani raised her eyebrows as if she was coming to some conclusion that was supposed to be obvious.

Again, he had to wonder if she was jealous. Was that even possible? And again, why did that give him a little thrill?

He thought back to that night at the cottage, when she'd quizzed him about Lavinia, making jokes about them hyphenating their names. He'd snapped at her and felt bad about it immediately. Now, like then, he wished he could rewind. He was not the sort of person who played games, so he set out to explain, to ease her mind if it needed easing.

"I'm not going to marry Lavinia," he said carefully, trying to sound as though he meant it, because he did, but trying not to be so vehement that he sounded angry. "I was never going to marry Lavinia." He found himself in uncharted territory, wanting to reassure a woman that he only wanted her. But leave it to him to find the only woman in the world for whom such a declaration would be a death knell. Even though she apparently didn't want him to want Lavinia? He was confused. He didn't like being confused.

"I should go," Dani said suddenly.

Ah. He had not said the right thing. He should have continued to laugh off her questions about Lavinia.

"It's late," she said, "and we have to leave early."

"All right," Max said, and it was all he could do not to grab her hand, to say, *Stay.* But he knew enough not to do that.

When she left, he lay back down. That feeling of being perfectly balanced in his own body and mind was gone.

Chapter Twenty-One

$\mathcal{W}$hen Dani saw Max the next morning, the weirdness that had characterized the end of their time together last night had, thankfully, evaporated. He winked at her as she strode across the foyer to join him where he was standing with Marie and Leo. "Sorry I'm late," she said, trying to inject into her words a breeziness she did not feel.

"Overslept?" Max inquired mildly, but with a twinkle in his eye that told her everything was fine between them.

She sent him a private eye roll, but she was hugely relieved, so she couldn't help sending mixed messages by pairing the eye roll with a smile. She was embarrassed by how she'd overreacted to his having a laugh with Lavinia. But it was okay. Max understood her. He had seen her fears and witnessed her less flattering moments, and it hadn't changed anything between them.

Well, it *had* changed the fact that her ever-simmering attraction to him could now be acted on. That wasn't "normal," but it was pretty awesome. Unfortunately, it couldn't be acted on *now*, but a person couldn't have everything.

"Last night was rather exhausting, wasn't it?" Marie said.

Max cleared his throat obnoxiously.

"I was trying to find my dog to say goodbye," Dani said, shooting Max a look. Max Minimus was staying at the palace while Dani and Max toured Austria. "Gabby came to get him earlier this morning and spirited him off. This place is so big, it took me a while to find them."

A few hours later, they checked into their hotel rooms in Innsbruck. Marie and Leo had a honeymoon suite on the top floor and Dani and Max had adjoining rooms the next floor down.

She wondered how things were going to go. Were they going to have sex again? She hoped so, and they'd joked about needing more condoms, but that was before things had gotten a little awkward. As Dani and Max opened the doors to their rooms, he winked at her, and, okay, yes, they were going to have sex again. She dropped her suitcase inside her door and without turning on any lights went straight to the adjoining door and yanked it open.

He had done the same with his door but was slightly ahead of her so he was already waiting for her.

"Hi," she said.

"Hi," he echoed, as he had done last night. Max never used the word *hi* in real life. He was too posh for that. He always said the full *hello*.

She launched herself at him, and without missing a beat he picked her up. She wrapped her legs around his waist in a way that had become familiar. They did it almost of their own accord, simply because it was the next phase of the move.

Look at them. They had "moves." All those *Dirty Dancing* lifts had actually been practice.

"Marie and Leo are going to be here any minute," she mumbled against his mouth as she kissed him. "Marie is all hyper."

"I know." He moved his lips along the edge of her jaw and spoke against her skin. "I told her to take a rest, but she's got a whole agenda for the afternoon."

"Why isn't her agenda going at it with her new husband?" She tilted her head back. She wanted him to pay some attention to her throat.

He did, letting his face slide down the side of her neck. Because he knew, somehow, what she wanted. "Damned if I know. If—"

A rap on his door startled them both. He grunted his displeasure and held onto her for a beat too long. She had to pull herself out of his grasp—which was actually flattering, but her heart kicked up several notches at the delay it caused. They could not be caught like this.

She fled to her room, and a few seconds later, she heard his door opening and him saying, "You don't waste any time, do you?"

"I'm full of energy," Marie said. "I'm giddy to be done with the wedding!" There was a pause. "No offense, Leo."

"None taken," came Leo's voice. "You can't be giddier than I am on that front."

Dani stared at herself in the mirror. Her cheeks were rosy. She looked rested—which she most decidedly was not. Maybe it was actually . . . happiness? She wasn't sure she'd recognize that at first glance. It had been so long.

"Shall we go see the mine?" Marie asked.

"Are you sure you want to spend the first several hours of your honeymoon underground with me?" Max asked teasingly.

Leo snorted, but Marie said, "I'm sure. I'm so excited to see what you've been doing."

Dani steeled herself, pasted on a smile, and went through the adjoining door. "I am, too." It was true. She was proud of Max and couldn't wait to see his project coming to life.

An hour later, clad in hard hats and steel-toed boots, they were listening to Max talk as he waved his arms around. "This will be a counter where people can get headphones for self-guided tours," he explained. As he took them around what would become the aboveground part of the museum, he was animated in a way Dani hadn't seen before. Previously, when they'd talked on the phone about this project, he'd used the phrase *history come to life*. She could see it, but she could also see *Max* come to life. This was exactly the kind of thing he would get excited about—historical and meaty. A great story that had meaning for how people lived today. The museum was going to be stylish and bold, but once you went underground, revelatory and maybe even transformative. Hmm. That sounded like someone she knew.

They took a work elevator down, and as Max narrated during the journey, explaining what the descent would be like, she could picture it perfectly.

Once down, he launched into a story about a local woman who organized meals for the men who shuttled weapons here. "We found all these plans she'd written down. She had a garden herself and had sources for some of the ingredients she lacked. A neighbor, for example, had a yard full of turnips. She would concoct meals from whatever people had."

"But what is *this*?" Marie asked, veering over to a corner that looked like it was meant to display letters—she assumed including those from Karina Klein to Max's grandmother. Marie was standing and reading, and she probably knew Max's grandmother's name, because it didn't take her long to catch on.

"Oh my god! Max!"

He smiled and went to stand beside her but didn't speak.

She kept reading. "Where did you find these?"

"Those are replicas, but the originals were under the floorboards in the attic at the cottage."

She turned to him, her hands in front of her face with her fingers spread wide. "This was already amazing, but you know this is going to be a revolutionary piece of news, yes?"

"Indeed."

"And your parents are going to act like they knew all along."

"I can't control what my parents do."

"Marie is right," Dani said to Max later when they'd broken off into pairs to explore the cavernous space. Leo and Marie were poking around at the far end, out of earshot. "This is amazing. And not just because of the family connection."

"It's mostly Seb," Max said glibly.

Annoyance sparked in her chest. "Don't do that."

"Do what?"

"Was this Seb's idea? Is Seb a historian? Did Seb find the documents you're using to bring this place to life?" She snorted. "You are so full of shit."

He blinked, startled by her outburst, and, after a beat, laughed incredulously.

"What? Has no one ever told you you're full of shit?"

"Certainly not someone who is going to—I hope—sleep with me later today."

"Well, this place is *yours*. It's just like you."

"What does that mean?"

"It's stylish and—"

"It's not stylish. At the moment, it's merely a bunch of rock."

"But you can tell it's going to *be* stylish."

He shot her a self-satisfied smile. "Ah, yes. Do go on."

"I was going to say it's stylish and slyly smart—the smart part sneaks up on you, which is a pretty good way to organize a museum, it seems to me. But I don't know. I might have to take it back. I don't want you to get a big head."

"Would this be an inopportune time for me to mention that I have procured some condoms? Two of them, to be precise."

"Two of them?"

"You wanted more?"

"That seems like an oddly specific number. Do they usually come in twos in Europe?"

"They do when you're begging for a handout from your younger brother, who is so busy banging the head of palace security, he isn't sure how many he can spare."

Good for Sebastien. "In this scenario, how does the head of palace security find time to, I don't know, actually secure the palace?"

"Apparently even heads of palace security get holidays. They're going to Athens for a week and then on to some remote Greek island I've never heard of for another."

"So *everyone* is on a sex holiday."

He burst out laughing. "I do intend to go to a store, mind you, and procure a proper box. I just haven't had a moment yet, so I prevailed upon my brother before we left this morning."

It was true. They'd left the palace at the crack of dawn and aside from their thirty-second make-out at the hotel, they hadn't been alone since.

"What are we doing after this?" She looked around for Leo and Marie.

"Marie is suggesting lunch, then there's this tower from the Middle Ages she wants to climb."

"Is there any way we can . . . not do that?"

He raised his eyebrows. "Apparently the views are phenomenal."

Dani grinned, thinking back to her early meetings with Max, when he would jokingly try to get in her pants. Time to turn the tables—except this time they both knew it wasn't actually a joke. She attempted her best leer and said, "I can think of a view I'd rather see."

He clapped his hands and shouted, "Marie! Leo! Time to go!"

MAX HAD HAD a lot of sex in his life. He'd had sex with a lot of people he liked. In fact, he made a point to have sex *only* with people he liked. So he was accustomed to the way a mood could shift during sex, from serious and heated, say, to lighthearted and silly. There were lots of flavors of sex.

What he hadn't experienced was the almost painful tenderness that nearly doubled him over as Dani came through the adjoining door and dropped her bathrobe—they had showered in their respective rooms after emerging from the mine covered

with dust—and said, "All right. Time for some things that require condoms."

She made a "bring it" motion with her fingers. She was trying
to be funny. He should try to tip himself out of this uncharacteristically emotional state, to match her playful mood. He should
laugh. Pick her up and drop her on the bed and tickle her.

He could not do those things. He couldn't get over the fact
that she was *here*. Naked and trusting and confident and glorious.
She was so familiar to him, yet as the afternoon sun slanting in
through the window painted stripes on her bare shoulders, she
was also a complete and utter shock.

He couldn't breathe properly. His hands came to his stomach,
as though he needed to clutch his belly to keep his insides from
spilling out. He had been standing when she came in, and somehow he'd ended up sitting on the edge of the bed. Perhaps his legs
had given out without him noticing.

"Come here," he said, and she did, unhesitatingly. She must
have picked up on his mood. All traces of laughter disappeared
from her face as she strode toward him. He was wearing a bathrobe, too, and he opened it just before she straddled his lap.

"Oh, god." He was learning that with Dani, his body responded in two ways. There was the usual way, led by his dick,
which had gotten so hard at the sight of her that it was almost
painful. And when she settled herself on him, there was a sense
of both relief and torment. But there was another pain, too, the
tenderness from before, alchemized into something keen-edged
and powerful. The first pain—sexual desire—was familiar. He
knew how that worked. They would have sex, and he would find
relief. The second pain, though, that bone-deep ache, made him a

little frantic if he thought about it too hard. What if it never went away? What if he never caught his breath? What would happen when she went back to New York?

She slipped her hands under the lapels of his robe as she ground down on him, and he shoved away his spiraling thoughts. He cupped her face with both hands and brought her mouth down on his. Her hair was wet and cold as it hung like curtains on either side of his head. He lowered his head and began lavishing attention on her breasts, letting his hands slide down over her throat and collarbones, noting the hissing sound the stroke summoned from her. He let loose a shaky sigh when he reached her breasts. They were two perfect handfuls, and he kneaded them, reveling in the feel of those gorgeous brown peaks stiffening under his touch. When he lowered his mouth to one tight nipple, she moaned.

"Oh my god, Max," she panted.

"Does this feel good?" he asked, switching to the other nipple.

"Yes," she breathed, and she shifted on his lap. She was wet and warm, and his hips bucked up against her without the involvement of his conscious mind.

When he could no longer take it, when he felt he was in danger of coming without getting to use one of those condoms— without getting to be inside her, the prospect of which blew his goddamned mind—he fell backward. He pulled her with him, thinking of her saying yesterday that she found pleasure more easily when she was on top. Also thinking, as she fell with him, how very much he enjoyed looking up at her.

They kissed like that for a long while, sipping and nipping, their tongues tangling. The moans she was making were driving him wild; it sounded like she was drunk on pleasure, and he loved it. But when they started to shade into frustration, he tore his mouth from hers and said, "Condoms are on the nightstand."

She looked down at him, blinking dumbly, then in the direction of the nightstand, then back at him. Her pupils were blown and her lips were red and puffy, and he never wanted to look at anyone or anything else again. He had done that. *They* had done that. Emotion was cresting inside him again, but he forced it down and made himself adopt a teasing tone when he said, "You know, should you find yourself wanting them."

She wanted them. She slid off him, and he sent a silent, soothing assurance to his poor beleaguered dick. *She's coming back.*

She did come back, but she was fumbling with the condom wrapper, so he took it from her and sheathed himself. He stayed on his back, and she looked at him inquisitively. He raised an eyebrow. She was in charge at this moment. She was always in charge when it came to him, whether or not she realized it.

She climbed on. And oh, had he ever felt something so good as Dani Martinez inching down his dick? She blew out a careful breath, and he joined her. She was tight and hot and . . . her. When she was fully seated, she went still, so still that the room was utterly, preternaturally silent. She was back in the path of those rays of light. One of them hit the side of her face and made a Rorschach blot of sunshine. She did not move. She did not breathe.

That twisting, tender feeling started in his chest again, coiling up like a snake rising, and he feared that if she didn't stop staring at him like she could see inside him, the prickling sensation moving up through his throat might lead to tears. He opened his mouth and whispered a command. "Breathe."

She did, and she moved, too. "Thank god," he said, apparently out loud, but it didn't seem to matter. She stayed upright, her hands planted on his chest and her hips rocking back and forth as she huffed out short breaths. She was still staring at him, but somehow the addition of movement and sound beat back the tidal wave of emotion threatening to overtake him. He clamped his hands onto her waist and tried to move in rhythm with her.

Her hair dripped on his chest.

"Oh my god, Max," she said again. "Oh!" He let one of the hands that was on her waist slide around and down, and he burrowed his thumb between her folds.

Her eyes went even wider, and she looked for a moment as if she, too, was having trouble holding back tears. But it must have been a trick of the sunlight, because suddenly she smiled, although to say "she smiled" did not begin to capture what was happening on her face as she grinned in what looked like a mixture of disbelief and joy. As she started coming, she started laughing. He went back to gripping her waist with both hands—tighter this time—said, "Hold on," and allowed himself to buck his hips up, big, almost violent pumps that had her gasping through her continuing laughter and what looked like her continuing orgasm. One, two, three, and with a groan, he was joining her.

Afterward, they stared at each other. He was stunned. Dazed. But when she started to pull away, he snapped out of it and held onto the condom so she could peel herself away.

She flopped down on him, panting, and he was as stupidly pleased as a child being passed a note by a girl he had a crush on. Last time, at the palace, she'd lain down next to him but not touching him. This time, she was draped over him as if this was a thing they did.

Well. That had been fucking glorious. He threaded his fingers through her still-damp hair and said, "We should have started doing this a long time ago."

"No we shouldn't have. This is perfect."

"You mean you wouldn't have been ready before?" Maybe she truly *had* been hung up on the fact that she'd still been legally married.

He regretted the question because it made her pull away. She laid on her back next to him, staring at the ceiling. "It's more that being here feels like being on holiday from real life, you know?"

He wasn't sure he liked that idea.

"But even though I don't think we should have done this any sooner than we did, I *do* think we should figure out when we can do it again." She turned her head and blinded him with a smile.

He glanced at the clock on the nightstand over her shoulder. "I don't see a way out of dinner with Leo and Marie. We can't avoid them any more than we already have."

"Yeah, I know. And really, I don't want to."

"Speak for yourself."

"Well, they're leaving in the morning."

"Mmm. I'm counting the hours. We'll see them off, and then you're *mine* for four solid days." Something flared in her eyes. She liked that notion. "We can lose the second room." And there went the heat in her gaze. She *didn't* like that notion. "Or not."

"I like to have my own space."

"Of course." He should have remembered her list. She didn't

want to feel like she was giving up things for a relationship. Not that this was a relationship. Unfortunately.

"I can pay for it, though."

"No, no." Somehow, he had talked her into this whole trip being his treat. After the private jet, it had been easier to convince her to accept gifts, but just because he would love nothing more than to spend the next four days in a room with her didn't mean he should presume she felt the same. He would need to distract her, though, or the argument about who was paying for the room would ramp up.

He pounced on her and started kissing her neck. "How do you feel about doing it in restaurant bathrooms?"

"I am against it."

"Really?"

"Yes! Gross!"

He performed a theatrical sigh. "Well, I shall simply have to hold out, then."

Chapter Twenty-Two

The next day flew by in a haze of sightseeing and sex. After they got up and saw the royal couple off, they went right back to bed and stayed there for a good long time, followed by an afternoon spent exploring the city. They climbed the tower they'd skipped before, poked around in shops lining the pretty cobblestoned streets, and ate and drank until Dani was full to bursting. After a nap, they ordered an array of munchies from room service for dinner and dined outside on Max's balcony, watching the sun set.

And now they were rolling around making out like teenagers on Max's bed.

Damn, Max could kiss. Kissing Max made Dani realize how much she loved kissing for its own sake. They kissed for what felt like an hour, gradually losing their clothing but in unspoken agreement that they were in no hurry to move things along.

Dani wasn't sure when she'd had so much fun. Well, that wasn't true. She'd had this much fun in Riems, before Max's parents got home.

Okay, no. This was more fun. Because of the sex. With Max.

Honestly. She was like a starving woman being ushered into an all-you-can-eat buffet. And Max was a feast. He was a generous lover, always attentive to her pleasure. It felt like they were in sync, like, as cheesy as it sounded, they were moving and thinking and breathing as one when they came together. It had never been like that for her. Not that she'd never had good sex, but this kind of immersion, this total attunement with another person, was new. She figured it was because she and Max were such close friends, because he knew her better than anyone.

Getting it on with the Depraved Duke had a lot to recommend it.

Once, watching him sleep, she entertained a little flash of fear that something about this, something she couldn't quite name, was going to come back to bite her. Was it *because* they were such close friends? *Because* he knew her better than anyone? No. Life wasn't a rom-com. People didn't lose friends in real life, at least not friends like Max, because they slept with them. She dismissed the fear as quickly as it had arisen, aided by the fact that he suddenly woke up and grinned at her.

"Come here," he said, pulling on her arm. She had been sitting up in bed, reading while he napped.

"Ahh!" She laughed as she lost her balance and tumbled forward, but quickly sobered as she landed against his chest. She had forgotten how good it felt to touch someone. To exhaust yourself with someone.

She tried to lay herself out on him, mashing her breasts against his chest both because it felt good and because he seemed to really like her breasts, which was nice because they were definitely not Hollywood breasts. If she had been the kind of person who was insecure about her body, the smallness of her breasts might have gotten to her. And if she had been that kind of person, Max and his focus on them, on her pleasure as if it were his single abiding imperative, would have cured her of that.

He wasn't letting her stretch out on him, though. He resisted, pushing her so she was upright again, but straddling him. "Get up here," he said, almost peevishly, pointing to his mouth.

"What do you . . . oh." *Oh.* She wasn't the type to embarrass easily, but she could feel her cheeks heating. She could feel her core heating, too.

"Now you're getting it." He swatted her butt. "Scoot this pretty bottom up here and sit on my face."

"Oh my god." She almost came from those words alone.

She was learning that in the bedroom, Max was direct, guileless, and generous. She wasn't sure why that should be surprising. He was like that in life, too. But he had a way of stating things so directly. It wasn't dirty talk in the traditional sense. His point wasn't to get her off—at least she didn't think it was. And he was bossy, but not in the dominant sense. He would never push her to do anything she didn't want to. She couldn't imagine anything he would suggest that would fall into that category, anyway. It was like he knew, always, what would feel good, what was optimal in any scenario, and announced his intention to do that thing.

It sounded so simple when she thought about it like that.

"Or don't," he said with a smile, and started to sit up. Here was a case in point—he thought she wasn't into what he'd suggested, and he was regrouping.

"Hang on." She pressed her palm against his chest and pushed him back down. "Give me a second."

"What? You have to think about it?"

"No. I just have never done it . . . quite like this before."

"Well, listen," he said with mock sternness. "I'm being resourceful. You've told me, and I have observed, that you like being on top." He held up his thumb and pointed to it with the opposite index finger, like he was making a visual list. "Happily, I also like you being on top."

"You like everything," she said, trying to swat the thumb he was still holding up.

He pulled it out of her way and added an index finger to his list. "I have also observed that you enjoy it when I go down on you—and again, our interests are perfectly in alignment." He took the two fingers he'd used to make his list and tapped his forehead. "So I took my big brain and put those two things together. My god. It's almost like you're sleeping with Elon Musk."

"Elon Musk? Gross!"

"Hmm. Elon Musk is a mood killer. Noted. Mark Zuckerberg?"

"Ugh!" She couldn't help but laugh, though.

"Perhaps it's the tech-sector angle you're objecting to in these analogies. Who else is known for their intelligence? Hmm. Angela Merkel?"

"Oh shut up."

"You know what would be an extremely efficient way of getting me to shut up right at the moment?" He wagged his eyebrows and licked his lips.

Well. Who was she to pass up this opportunity? She scooched

herself up until she was kneeling over his face. "What if I smother you?"

"Ah, what a good way to go."

"But then Sebastien will have to be duke."

He lightly swatted her butt. "This is not a good time to talk about my brother. Or my dreaded fate."

"Yeah, yeah, point taken. I—" And, wow. He looped his arms around her thighs like he was anchoring her to him—or him to her, she wasn't sure which—pulled her down, and . . . went to town.

Historically, Dani had enjoyed oral sex, but honestly, she'd never totally gotten the hype. It had never been at the top of her list. But there was something about the combination of Max's mouth moving against her and the pressure from being on top. There was *also* something about the noises he was making. He was clearly enjoying himself.

She couldn't keep herself from moving, and she couldn't hold back the obscene-sounding moans that were slipping out, because dear god, she was writhing around on his face and she had never felt anything so good. She never wanted it to end, but it was going to, and soon.

"Oh my god, Max!" she cried as an orgasm started to overtake her. Absurdly, it felt like it started in her toes and moved up her legs in a wave, coming to a head at the juncture between her thighs, where his mouth met her, and just kept . . . exploding. She, not historically a screamer, screamed.

He chuckled, and the vibrations joined the aftershocks zinging through her core.

She lifted herself up onto her knees and looked down at him.

His face was wet—and nearly split in two from the widest grin she'd ever seen on him.

She was struck by the astonishing thought that she had never felt this good before, and she didn't mean just physically.

MAX COULDN'T SLEEP that night, which normally would be nothing new but *was* sort of new given that since he had been sharing a bed with Dani—or her dog—he'd been sleeping like a baby. Tonight, he had too many thoughts zipping through his brain. Around midnight, overwhelmed by them, he sneaked out of his room and went into the bathroom of Dani's and called his brother. It was not lost on him that last time he'd made a covert phone call from a hotel bathroom, it had been *to* Dani.

"Remember how you said you didn't want to hide anymore?" he said when his brother picked up.

"Hello to you, too. No, you didn't wake me. How's the honeymoon going?"

Seb was joking, but the time with Dani here—and in Riems—*had* felt like a honeymoon. Max had been free from the oversight of the wider world and completely wrapped up in Dani. Emotionally, before, but now physically, too. "You said you didn't want to hide anymore," Max pressed on. "And I said I'd help you. Which I meant," he rushed to add.

"Yes. That came out a little melodramatically," Seb said, "but the sentiment was genuine."

"So you want to come out. To Mother and Father."

"To everyone, I suppose. I don't want to . . . live this way anymore."

"Good," Max said, perhaps a tad too urgently.

"Max? Are you all right?"

"I'm in love with Daniela Martinez," he blurted, "and I don't know what to do about it."

There was a slight pause before Seb started laughing.

"I beg your pardon?" He was a sorry specimen, he realized, but he wasn't sure he deserved mockery.

"I'm sorry," Seb said. "I'm not laughing at you, or her. She's amazing. Of course you're in love with her. It's the idea of you being in love with *anyone*. It's so . . . not you."

"Well, that's my point," Max plowed on. "I don't think the me everyone knows really *is* me. Not anymore, anyway."

"Ah." Seb had shed all teasing from his tone. "So you don't want to hide anymore, either. Is that what I'm hearing?"

Yes. That was exactly right. "What do I do, Seb?"

His brother didn't answer right away. Max wondered if Seb, like him, was thinking about how profoundly the tables were turned with that question. It used to always be Max leading Seb. Clearing the way for him.

"Does she know how you feel?" Seb asked. "Does she feel the same?"

"No on both counts."

"How do you know she doesn't return your feelings?"

"Even if she does, she won't let herself. It's . . . complicated."

"Ah. Too bad. You *are* in need of a wife."

Max chuckled. "Can you imagine if I went home and told Mother and Father that I was done with Lavinia and was marrying Dani?" He thought back to his grand exit from the wedding.

Seb turned serious. "You know, Max, you can marry whomever you want. They can't prevent it. They can make life unpleasant for a while, but ultimately, they can't do anything about it."

"Actually, I have to tell you something." He filled Seb in on how he'd refused to help Mother round up Father at the wedding and about how it had felt like a decisive shift in how he related to them. "Of course, I have no idea how things are going to be when I get home. They'll probably try to pretend that nothing is different. As far as Father is concerned, there *won't* be anything different. It won't be as if Mother will have said, 'Maximillian refused to assist me with wrangling you in your embarrassingly inebriated state.'"

"And you want him to know," Seb said.

"Yes. I realize that it probably sounds hollow, given all the other times that I've behaved in ways that have displeased them, but—"

"This time it's different," Seb said vehemently, finishing the sentence the way Max had been planning to. "You're done playing by their rules."

"Indeed. But I don't know how to make them see that."

"We'll cross that bridge when we come to it."

The *we* in that sentence felt like a tonic.

"Anyway," Seb said with a chuckle, "I'll come out when I get home. They'll lose their minds, then your not behaving the way they want won't seem so bad."

Seb was in jest, but it was another example of how much the tables had turned. Regardless, Max didn't want to lose track of the fact that his brother was planning to do something momentous. "I wonder if the world has changed enough that they won't care that you're gay."

"I've wondered that, too. But it doesn't really matter because they *will* care that it's Torkel who's my . . . person. They'll see him as a servant."

"It is very *Upstairs, Downstairs* of you." Max couldn't help but find his brother's use of the phrase *my person* adorable.

"Joking aside," Seb said, "I think all you can do is try to keep the truth in front of you. Try not to hide it or hide from it. That's what I'm attempting to do."

Hmm. That was both well put and profound in its simplicity. "How'd you get so smart?"

"This is the part where I'm tempted to make a crack about how I went to a vastly superior school while you stayed home and worked with a tutor, but I think this is *actually* the part where I tell you that I know why you did that."

Max made a dismissive noise.

Seb wasn't having it. "I know. I know why you stayed home. What I *haven't* known is how to say thank you. But it's overdue. So thank you."

Max's instinct was to deflect, to minimize, but he thought about what Seb had said about trying not to hide the truth or to hide from the truth, so as uncomfortable as it was, he said, "You're welcome."

Seb cleared his throat. Perhaps he was discomfited by the uncharacteristically honest exchange, too. "I haven't given you the advice you wanted as it relates to Dani."

"It's all right." There wasn't a solution, really. There wasn't a *problem*, even, except that now that he'd acknowledged how utterly, wildly in love with her he was, it was hard not to have that be front of mind at all times.

"All I can say," Seb said, "is if I were you, I would do whatever I could to hold on to her."

MAX DIDN'T FALL back asleep. He was consumed with thoughts of his brother. He had learned, these past months, that Seb didn't need his protection anymore. That he was more strategic, and braver, than Max had given him credit for.

Max thought about his desire, his need, to signal somehow to his parents that he was going to live life on his own terms. He glanced at Dani, asleep next to him under the duvet. An idea was taking shape in his head. Perhaps there was a way he could get a version of what he wanted. A facsimile. It would be better than nothing. He would have to tread carefully, though. When the sun started to filter through the cracks in the curtains, Dani woke up and smiled at him. He smiled back and said, "What if we got married?"

"Ha-ha. Good morning to you, too." She was on her back, and she reached her hands over her head and stretched in such a way that her head turned away from him.

"I am entirely in earnest."

"All right," she said, still stretching, still not looking at him. "I'll marry you, but I have conditions." She rolled back over, her eyes twinkling. She pulled her hands together under her chin in a way that made his heart twist. "I want everyone to address me at all times as Baroness Daniela von Martinez. Hmm. What else? Oh! I want Max Minimus to get a gold-plated collar. No, wait. Solid gold." She laughed but cut it off quickly and turned genuinely contemplative. "But would a solid gold collar even work? Would it be flexible? I'll have to get back to you on that one." She shook her head, and the twinkle returned. "But certainly he can have a solid gold tag. Ha! I demand a solid gold dog tag! Okay, what else? I'm sure I can do better than this with my list of conditions. Give me a sec."

"You can have all those things. Marry me, and you can have whatever you want."

Her smile faded, replaced by a confused scrunch of her brow. "Oh, come on, Max. I was kidding."

"I know you were, but I'm not." He grabbed her hand and laced his fingers through hers. "Think about it. You're tired of your job. I'm tired of toeing the line with my parents. I . . ." *I love you.* But he couldn't say that. It was too soon—for her, not for him. She herself had said that the fastest way to get her to run for the hills was with a declaration of love. "Everyone would benefit. It wouldn't be that different from what Marie and I had planned on, except . . ." He waved his free hand between them, not knowing how to say *Except we get to have mind-blowing sex.*

And I will secretly love you.

She took her hand back. She looked aghast. He was spooking her, which was fair enough. He tried to get them back into a joking mode. "There are family jewels, if you want them."

"I don't want them." She sat up and moved to the edge of the bed, covering herself with a sheet. "Why would you think that? Why would you think I would *marry* you?"

He was making a hash of this. "Will you let me start again?"

She made a sarcastic, exaggerated "hurry-up" gesture.

"Forget the marriage part. That part was a fleeting idea, but the impulse behind it wasn't. I was lying here earlier thinking about how much I would miss you when you go back to New York, so what if you just don't? You don't have to marry me. Shack up with me, as I believe the Americans say. You can hole up in the garret and write, or we could move to—"

"You think I'm going to just quit my job and come here and be your fucking *ducal mistress*?" She got off the bed, grabbed her discarded robe, and turned away from him as she put it on. When she turned back, her expression was no longer incredulous. It was angry. "Is that what this has all been about?" She waved her hand at the bed. "I'm divorced for a day and you swoop in, ply me with orgasms, then try to get me to . . . what? Be your piece on the side? Or have a fake marriage? I get to choose between column A and column B? How generous of you."

"No!" He tried to control a growing panic. "You're misunderstanding. That's not—"

"What is *wrong* with you? Have you been listening to *anything* I've been saying?"

"I'm not explaining this properly, but this"—he mimicked her hand wave—"Has . . ."

Made me realize how in love with you I am. How in love with you I've been all this time.

He couldn't explain that she was different. That she was the one who had changed him. That she was The One, period. He had calculated that she would not want to hear that. But it *was* the missing piece in everything he was proposing. Perhaps he should have led with that, damn the consequences.

"And what?" She started up again when he couldn't find the

words to make this right. "In either of these scenarios I'm sup-posed to just up and move to Eldovia?"

He looked away so he wouldn't cry. He'd been going to say, earlier, that they could move to Witten to pass the years until he inherited, and then she'd be close to Leo and Gabby. But he didn't think more talking was going to help at this point.

"*You* just found *your* feet on the whole meaningful-employment front," she went on. "So, really, how *dare* you suggest I quit my goddamn job, Max?"

He had done this entirely wrong. Or perhaps he was naive and it *was* wrong. Perhaps he couldn't have *any* version of what he wanted. He should have left well enough alone, dropped her off at the airport for her flight home in a few days, and said goodbye until the next time she was in need of a plus one at a work party.

She shook her head and started backing away. "I thought you were my *friend*." Her voice had cracked on that last sentence.

"I am your friend." Oh, god. He hoped that was still true. "I—"

She held up her hands, gesturing for him to stop talking, and she kept backing away. She backed herself all the way to the ad-joining door. "If you're my friend, you will stop talking right now. If you're my friend, you will leave me alone for a while."

He nodded. What choice did he have?

"I'm going to go now."

"Will you let me know when you're ready to talk?" he asked quietly, his mind whirring as he tried to think how, when she was ready, he could repair the damage he had done.

What he *didn't* realize until after spending the morning "leav-ing her alone," as she had asked, was that not only had she backed out of his room, she had backed her way out of the hotel, out of the continent, and out of his life.

DANI CALLED LEO on the way to the airport. She hated to interrupt his honeymoon, but it couldn't be avoided. "Can you do me a favor and get a message to Mr. Benz?"

"What? Where are you? Are you okay?"

No. She was not okay. Her whole world had been upended, and she had lost her best friend. But she couldn't say that to Leo, who was *supposed* to be her best friend.

She never should have allowed Max to displace him. The only way she could think to explain it was the lobster-in-a-pot analogy. Max was always there, and he was so warm. He'd kept her so safe and cozy that she didn't notice the temperature rising to lethal levels until it was too late.

She considered lying, making up some reason she needed to talk to Mr. Benz, but Leo would find out soon enough. "I'm going home. I'm on my way to the airport. I'm taking a puddle jumper to Zurich and a taxi from there to the palace to pick up Max, then back to Zurich for a flight home. Could you ask Mr. Benz to round up Max? I should be there in about four hours." She didn't have a lot of time to spare, given the flights she'd hastily booked, and she wanted to make sure her dog wasn't being taken on a mountain jaunt or something when she arrived to collect him.

"Hang on." There was some murmuring, and Dani tried not to lose her cool. She would have preferred to make her exit with only Leo knowing about it, but there was no way that was happening. And it wasn't like Max himself wouldn't tell Marie. For all she knew, he already had. He had respected her desire for privacy this morning, but had it lasted? Eventually he would have knocked on the adjoining door and found her gone.

Leo came back on the line. "Marie says she'll ask Mr. Benz to have someone drive Max to Zurich to meet you."

She waited for more, but miraculously, that was it. "Thank you."

"Do you want to talk about it?"

"I really don't." Though she knew she wasn't going to get away with that forever. "Not yet. I need some time alone. Call me when you get back?" He hesitated. "Leo. I'm *fine*. I'll be fine." It was, she was pretty sure, a lie. But no need to ruin his honeymoon.

"All right. But you call me if you need me, okay?"

"Yes."

Less than an hour later, Dani was on a plane. As it taxied along the runway, which was surrounded by mountains silhouetted against a setting sun, she realized that her worst fear, the one she had told herself was utterly irrational, the one that had stopped her from sleeping with any of the Tinder guys, had come true.

She'd had sex with someone and gotten her heart broken in the process.

The worst part was she had slept with Max *because* he wasn't one of the Tinder dudes, because he was supposed to be safe.

No, the *worst* part, the part that made a pit of shame open up in her stomach when she thought about it, was that she had wanted to say yes. She had wanted to say, Yes, I will *upend my entire life and stay here with you.*

She had fallen in love with Max. That was the terrible truth.

But at least she had her list. And it had saved her in the end, hadn't it? The list was supposed to keep her from making a mistake, from gradually subsuming her life into that of a man—a man who didn't love her. And Max didn't love her. Not like that. *No lying*, he had said. Relentless honesty. Max would never tell her something that wasn't true.

And he hadn't. He hadn't said, "Marry me because I love you. Move in with me because I love you." No, it had just been another business arrangement with a friend, like he'd had with Marie.

But it wasn't his fault. He had never misrepresented himself to her. He had *told* her, time and again, that he wasn't capable of love.

It wasn't his fault she'd fallen in love with him. So really, she had only herself to blame.

Chapter Twenty-Three

Two weeks went by without a word from Dani, and Max was as gutted as ever.

He'd thought about calling, had written and deleted a thousand texts. But what would he say? She had specifically asked him to leave her alone, had said she would let him know when he was ready to talk.

After Vince left, I realized that he never listened to me.

That was what she'd said about Vince. The topic had come up several times. Max would let himself die of heartbreak before he'd be like Vince fucking Ricci. Clearly, he had already misstepped by cornering Dani with an unwelcome proposal. He wasn't about to do it again.

But Max didn't know what to do with radio silence from Dani. It was turning him into a captive animal pacing a too-small cage. He had told her about his fears and his secret ambitions. He had told her about the pain he had never thought to try to put into words. He had looked at her and allowed a blade made of ruthlessness and tenderness in equal measures to pierce him.

And now she was gone, and he was still bleeding.

What had he been thinking? He hadn't been, clearly. He'd just been so swept off his feet.

His phone rang, and as it did every time, he jumped. Every call, every text notification, had him falling over himself to see if it was her. And if not her, he hoped for his brother.

It was Marie, and he didn't answer it. She was due back, so it made sense that she was calling, but he didn't want to talk to her. She would have some version of tough love to lay on him, which ordinarily would have been fine—ordinally he might even have signed himself up for it—but Max really didn't want to start up some kind of childish "Don't tell Leo I said this, because he might tell Dani" chain.

He wanted his brother.

The phone rang again, startling a small smile out of him. Finally. He fumbled to answer it. "Are you back?" Max was still in the hotel in Innsbruck. Every day he woke up and told himself today was the day he'd go home. And every afternoon before checkout, he called the front desk and extended his reservation. Going home to Riems felt like too much. That last disastrous dinner aside, he and Dani had had such a wonderful time there. He didn't know how to go up to the attic and find her not there.

"I'm on the way home," Seb said. "We just landed in Zurich."

"Is Torkel driving you?" His own situation aside, Max wanted to meet Torkel outside the context of the palace.

"No. We landed with no leeway before he had to go back to work, so I ordered a car."

"Did you have a good time?"

Max could practically hear Seb smile in response to his question. Good. At least someone was happy.

"I'm sorry I wasn't in touch. We were . . . off the grid this past week."

"I wager you were."

"How did it go with Daniela?"

"I asked her to marry me and she said no and ran away and now she's not talking to me."

"What? Max! Why would you do that?"

"Because I love her." *Because I'm not sure how to be in the world without her.* He didn't say that part, though. He was already stepping out of character here. "But then when it became clear it wasn't a welcome proposal, I downshifted and tried to get her to move in with me."

"That was ill-advised. If anything, you should move to New York."

"*What?*" Max almost dropped the phone, he was so shocked.

"New York suits you—a lot more than holing up in your cottage twisting yourself into knots to avoid the main house and its occupants docs, anyway."

"Well, that's fine, but it doesn't do me any good in actuality."

"It does, though. Just go there."

"I can't move to New York," he said reflexively.

"Why not?"

Could he move to New York? He'd been going to suggest to Dani that they could live in Witten. He'd been thinking of that as an option if his parents made living on the estate impossible. If Witten was a possibility, why not New York?

"You remember when Marie was going to abdicate?" Seb asked.

It took Max a moment to adjust to the abrupt change of subject. "Of course I do. How do you?" Max and Marie had talked about the prospect, but she hadn't had to pull the trigger since her father had come around at the last minute.

"She told me about it," Seb said.

"She *did*?"

"Well, I asked her about it."

Sebastien and Marie knew each other well, of course, given how close the two families were, but Marie was a little older than Max, even, and although she'd always been kind to Seb, Max had never known them to communicate independently. Why was Sebastien asking Marie about abdication? He wasn't inheriting anything.

"She told me you helped her," Seb went on, "that she was about to burn it all down and you were with her every step of the way."

"Well, it turned out not to be necessary."

"My point is you seem to be willing to go to great lengths to ensure the happiness of the people you love. Why aren't you willing to do that for yourself?"

"Because then all the shit that's coming my way would become your problem!"

"Ah," said Sebastien. "There it is."

Max tried to backtrack. "I didn't mean—"

"You protected me all those years," Seb went on. "If you want to walk away now, that's all right with me. It's my turn to shoulder some of the burden. But honestly, I don't know that that's necessary. As with Marie, I think it can be avoided."

"So, what . . . If I . . ." Max was still so gobsmacked, he was having trouble forming sentences. "What do I do? What do we do?"

"Well, first we stop hiding, which for me means coming out. Then—"

"Don't say anything to them until I get home, all right? I can be there this evening."

"Where are you?"

"Still in Innsbruck."

"Ah." He didn't ask any more questions, probably because Max still being in Innsbruck perfectly illustrated Seb's assertion that he was hiding.

"So you come out, and then what?" Max prompted. "You said, *first* we stop hiding. What's next?"

"Next we live our lives the way we want to. If Mother and Father don't like it, if they make it too miserable, we live our lives somewhere else. And Mother and Father aside, if we need to go somewhere else—New York, for example—to live our lives the way we want to, then we do that."

"What about the company? What about your job? If it doesn't go well, you know Father will have you sacked."

Seb made a noncommittal noise. "I became one of the world's foremost experts on mining remediation while no one was paying attention. I'll get another job."

"But—"

"You, though, I don't know." Seb snorted. "You don't have any actual skills. You can come live with me if you can't fix things with Dani."

"*Sebastien.*" Max forced some older-brother gravitas into his tone. "Where is all this coming from?"

"It's coming from spending two weeks not looking over my shoulder. It's coming from spending two weeks being happy."

The idea that Seb was so suddenly, and so utterly, happy buoyed Max. "You're just going to tell them you're gay?" He already knew the answer. "But later, after I get home," he added quickly.

"I'm just going to tell them," Seb confirmed. "And yes, I'll wait until you get home." Max could hear the smile in Seb's voice again.

"Aren't you afraid?"

"Of course I'm afraid. I'd be an idiot not to be. But ultimately, you have to ask yourself—and I'm talking about *you*, not the proverbial you—is that fear worth more to you than what's potentially on the other side of it?"

Well. Max allowed himself, for a moment, to imagine that— the other side of the fear. "But if I . . . went to New York." It was hard to say it. "I would have to come back when he dies." Despite what Seb said, Max would never walk away and leave him to deal with the dukedom.

"Perhaps. But perhaps there's more than one way to be a duke. And you know who gets to decide about that?"

Max chuckled. "The duke?"

"Exactly. But don't think that far ahead. Get a place in New York. Come and go. You travel so much anyway. Will it really be all that different? When Father dies, we'll make a plan. *We'll* make a plan. Even if you're the one inheriting, it's not your burden alone."

Max heaved a shaky breath. It sounded pathetic to his own ears, but he was so bowled over. By Dani, and now by this. This allyship that should not be a surprise but somehow was.

"Max." Seb's tone was fond but a touch exasperated. "I love you, but you're making this harder than it has to be."

"I don't even know if she'll have me. Forget that, I don't even know if she'll ever speak to me again." That was the crux of the matter. He could go to New York, yes, but what was he going to say to Dani when he got there? Double down, except this time lead with "I love you" and hope it turned out better? Or just try to get everything back to what it had been?

Although . . . perhaps whether Dani would have him or not *wasn't* the crux of the matter. It felt like the most important thing in the world, but perhaps what Seb was suggesting had its own logic.

Was Max ready to do everything Seb was talking about—was he ready to remake his life and his reputation—without Dani? He had been thinking about how she was worth it. But for him to upend his life so utterly, *he* had to be worth it, too, didn't he?

"UH, HELLO?"

Dani shook her head. She was talking to Sinéad. Theoretically. She hadn't been listening, and Sinéad was holding her beer aloft in what looked like a paused toast. Dani lifted her glass and clinked it against Sinéad's, but after setting it down and realizing she'd forgotten to take a sip, she had to reverse course.

"That is the most pathetic toast I've ever seen."

"Yeah, yeah." She took a sip. It had been just over two weeks since she'd gotten home from Eldovia, and she was trying to do the things that a person did when she was not heartbroken.

One of those things was go to the holiday party, even though going to a work party without Max felt *wrong*. Another one of those things was reconnect with local friends. She'd been emotionally absent all summer and fall. So she'd invited Sinéad out for an early dinner before the party and now they were standing at the bar in the faculty club waiting for the shindig to begin.

"What's the matter with you?" Sinéad asked.

Dani lowered her voice. "What if I don't want to be a professor anymore?" She couldn't believe she was saying this out loud. "What if I want to do something else?"

Sinéad, ever-unflappable, didn't freak out. "And what would that be?"

"Write books."

"You've done that."

"But what if I wanted to write a novel?" She hadn't touched the Gertrude Stein book since Riems. It hurt too much. It was so tied up with Max. Max, who, when she'd said, "I think I want to try to write a novel," had said, simply, "Yes."

"Then you write a novel?" Sinéad said. "Which, for the record, is an entirely unremarkable thing for an English professor to do." When Dani only nodded, Sinéad said, "Any more questions?"

"What do you call it when you go on vacation and have a lot of sex and then you come home and you don't know how to feel?"

Aww, crap. That had just come out.

"I think you call that a fling," Sinéad said.

Right. "And what do you call it when you have a fling with a friend?"

"I think you call that a mistake."

Yep.

"Unless . . ." Sinéad raised her eyebrows.

"What?" Dani asked, sorry she'd started this conversation.

"Unless you're mischaracterizing your relationship with that person."

"No, we're definitely friends. Or we were."

"But is that all you are?"

And there it was.

"We're talking about the duke, aren't we?" Sinéad pressed.

"Baron, actually." Sinéad raised her eyebrows even higher, and Dani sighed and said, "Yes."

"Do you love him?"

"Does it matter?" It didn't matter if she loved Max. *He* didn't love *her*. Max didn't lie. And Dani would die before she would repeat her past mistakes for another man who didn't love her. She was never going to quit her job and move to Eldovia. Well, she was never going to move to Eldovia. She was, however, thinking about quitting her job. But not really. Just idly. Because quitting a tenure-track job was *insane*.

Sinéad shrugged. "I personally can't think of anything that matters more, but okay. You do you."

Maybe this "hang out more with local friends" plan had been a bad idea. Dani needed Leo. Her friendship with Leo had always been refreshingly free of analysis. They were the same that way. They didn't have to—or want to—talk about everything.

She missed him. He had been trying to reach her since he got home from his honeymoon yesterday, but she'd been dodging his calls. It had been shitty of her, and she resolved to call him when she got home.

"Well, hello," Leo said when he picked up the phone. "How great of you to finally make time in your busy schedule to call me back, no matter that it is in fact one A.M. here. Allow me to get straight to the point: Max is devastated."

She winced at the one A.M. part. She'd gotten so used to calling Max whenever. "I'm sorry. I'll call you tomorrow."

"No. No. Hang on a sec." Some rustling followed, and some low whispering that was probably him talking to Marie. "Okay, hi, Max is devastated."

"I don't want to talk about Max."

"I'm sure you don't. I just wanted to state for the record that Max is devastated."

"How is that my problem?" She winced hearing those words coming out of her mouth. They were a defense mechanism. Because she was so confused. How could Max—*Max*—be devastated? How had he have gone from glibly asking her to move to Eldovia to "devastated"? Something was getting lost in translation.

"So it's one in the morning, and you've called me to talk about something other than Max," Leo said, with a hardness in his tone that was unusual. "Go ahead."

"How was your honeymoon?" she asked weakly.

"I'm going back to bed. Call me later if you want to chat."

"No! Wait."

He waited, but she didn't know what to say. She didn't know if she *could* say anything without crying.

He sighed, too, and when he spoke, he sounded softer, more like the Leo she knew. "If I had asked you, say, a year ago, when you were pretty much over Vince but he was dragging out the divorce, if you would ever consider another relationship, what would you have said?"

"A relationship that didn't violate any of my list items?"

"Yes. A relationship that didn't violate any of your list items."

"I would have said maybe under very specific circumstances."

"And what would those be?" he said with exaggerated patience, like he was talking to Gabby when she was getting hyper.

"They would be the circumstances dictated by the list, Leo." She, by contrast, was sounding decidedly snippy. But honestly, Leo knew about the list. Why did he need this explained to him? "He would have to integrate into my life. Do things on my terms. I finally have everything arranged the way I want it. Career is good. I'm on track to get tenure. I can legit afford my apartment now that I'm renting it out every once in a while. Why would I give up any of that?"

"I know I'm supposed to issue a vaguely 'You go, girl' cheer, but maybe the answer is you would give that stuff up for something bigger."

"Like what?"

"Love? Love that is not quantifiable in list format? Love for someone who doesn't have the same flexibility in life that you do?"

"But I'm post-love. And Max is . . ." Devastated?

"Right." Leo's voice had lost its edge but had taken on a totally blank tone, which was somehow more upsetting than the exaggerated patience of a moment ago. "I gotta go. It's one A.M. I'll talk to you later."

He hung up on her.

Chapter Twenty-Four

"I'm going to get a place in New York," Max said. "A pied-á-terre." He glanced at his father, who was sipping a digestif of kirsch. He didn't react at all to the news, surprisingly.

"That's a good idea," his mother said absently as she picked at her torte—Max and Seb had decided Max should wait until dessert to make his big pronouncement, even though that meant Father would be deep in his cups. "What is that? An hour or two to New Haven?"

New Haven, Connecticut. Where Yale was.

Where Lavinia was.

Amusingly, his parents had bought their act at Marie's wedding, which meant Max was in their good graces in a way he hadn't been for years. Perhaps ever.

He could have jetted off to New York and they'd have been none the wiser. For now. But that would require pretending that everything was the same, that his confrontation with his mother the night of the wedding hadn't meant anything. And everything his brother had said about not hiding, about freedom and happiness, was still rattling around inside him.

It was truth time. He huffed a quick, fortifying sigh. "There's nothing between Lavinia and me. We were merely pretending to be enamored of each other so we could enjoy ourselves at the wedding free from your oversight. I'm getting a place in New York to be closer to Daniela Martinez." *If she'll have me.* But one thing at a time. And he was moving regardless.

"I forbid it," Father said tersely.

All right, then. Max hadn't really thought he would get away with simply stating his intention. Part of him didn't want to. Time for a paternal reckoning. He turned to Mother. "Did you manage to get Father out of the wedding without my help—and without embarrassing the family name?"

"Max!" his mother exclaimed while his father rumbled with anger.

Ignoring her, he turned to his father. "I know how much you care about how everyone in this family behaves. The ironic part is that you're the embarrassment. And I'm not just talking about your drunken scenes. You are a monster. You've spent my entire life hurting me. You've spent *our* entire lives"—he gestured to Seb—"Hurting us."

"You will never see another cent from me, boy." Father spoke quietly, which was a bit surprising, but his eyes were bulging and his face was red.

"I assumed. I've been helping Sebastien with a mining reclamation project. It's an immersive museum of sorts, and the design firm we've employed has offices in New York. I'm going to do some consulting work for them." He left unspoken the implication: *I don't need your money.*

He also skipped over Oma's ties to the project. He wanted to protect that knowledge, to make sure his parents didn't find a way to twist it or to profit from it. They could find out about it when everyone else did.

"Oh, darling," Mother said, "they're using you because they think you'll get them clients. It's like when Liesel Schrodinger fancied herself an interior designer." She laughed cruelly.

She might have been correct, but Max didn't care. It was a start. An actual job that wasn't tied to his family. Max and one of the firm's partners had been working so well together on the Innsbruck project that he didn't think the offer was only about his wealth and connections. Regardless, he intended to prove himself worthy.

Everyone looked at Father. Father was sweating heavily. Perhaps he was just getting warmed up. Perhaps they were in for the biggest eruption they'd ever seen. "Is that all?" he finally bit out.

It was.

Well, it wasn't. There was still the little—massive—issue of Daniela Martinez. But Max had declared his independence in matters financial and geographical, and that was what was relevant here. "Yes."

Father spoke with an aura of eerie calm. "Then you are no son of mine." He then turned to Sebastien, as if anointing him heir right then and there.

Max and Sebastien had spent yesterday planning, and had agreed that Max would drop his bomb this evening and that they'd let it settle and see what the outcome was before regrouping and making a plan for Seb to drop his. It was a coordinated, two-stage campaign.

Seb must have decided a change in strategy was in order. With all three of them looking at him, Max's quiet, unassuming, *brave* younger brother smiled cheerily and said, "Mother. Father. I'm gay. And I'm in love with Torkel Renner. He's my boyfriend."

Max had his eyes on his father, whose affect remained strangely flat, but his mother's sharp intake of breath drew his attention. "Torkel Renner?" Her brow knit, as if she knew but could not quite place the name and wasn't sure how she wanted to react until she did.

"He's the head of palace security." Seb, cool as a cucumber, picked up his heretofore untouched kirsch, took a sip, set it down, and added with the merest hint of a shrug, "I thought you should know, before you decide to disown the heir, what you're getting from the spare."

A loud *thunk* from the head of the table drew everyone's attention. That was more like it. Father was having a delayed reaction, but his fist pounding the table was merely the open volley of all he would want to communicate. It was a gavel presaging his judgment. They would hear from him now.

But, it turned out, they wouldn't. That noise had not come from his fist. It had come from his head hitting the table.

THE NEXT AFTERNOON, Dani cued up *Love Actually*. She hadn't seen it since last summer when Max had talked her into an out-of-season viewing. It was still technically out of season, today being only December 9 but close enough. Sometimes, when your life was falling apart, you needed a Christmas movie.

As she watched the opening sequence from the kitchen, where she was making a grilled-cheese sandwich, just like she and Max had done last year after the holiday party, something lurched inside her. She stumbled into the living room and sat down next to Max Minimus on the couch.

The opening scene was a series of people greeting each other at an airport—couples and family and friends embracing and crying and reuniting while Hugh Grant, in a voiceover, talked about love. She looked at it with new eyes as she thought about when she'd come off the plane before the wedding and her heart had leapt to see Max. Or when he'd surprised her on the beach, dispensing what remained the most satisfying hug of her life and saying, "Tell me everything."

Dani had told Sinéad it didn't matter if she loved Max, but that wasn't true. It did matter. Hugh Grant was right. Love always mattered, even if it hurt. And it *did* hurt.

She loved Max, and he didn't love her back. But Max wasn't Vince. Max had never lied to her. And he did love her in some fashion, of that she was sure. He was her friend. He had made a mistake in asking her to move in with him—or to marry him, for god's sake. He had hurt her deeply when it seemed like he was disregarding everything he *knew* was important to her.

That stupid list. She had to face the fact that her list had not protected her like it was supposed to. "So much for my list, Max." Max Minimus barked as if in agreement.

The ironic part was that when she examined her heart, Dani *was* willing to sacrifice what she'd thought she wanted for "something bigger," to use Leo's phrase. But as much fun as she and

Max had, as much as he got her in a way no one else did, she couldn't be with someone who didn't love her.

What had she told Max about this movie? It seemed like a rom-com, but really it was a romantic tragedy. But as Hugh Grant said, love was still all around.

All right, then. She was sad—gutted, really—but it was a relief to have thought things through.

The question was: What happened next? She was still angry at Max for thinking she would upend her life to indulge his whims. But was she going to throw out their entire relationship because he had made an error of judgment? No, she was going to tell him he'd hurt her feelings, apologize for running away, and make things right with her friend. She would keep her true feelings to herself. She would live through her own personal romantic tragedy. She had done it before, and she could do it again. The heartbreak would fade—eventually—and she'd still have Max.

Assuming she got off her ass and called him.

Her phone rang before she could pick it up. She harbored a momentary hope that it would be him, but she knew even before the call display showed Leo's name that it wouldn't. She had told him not to contact her, and Max *listened*.

Well, Leo would do. She needed to apologize to him, too. She hadn't been very reasonable last night.

"Leo. I'm—"

"Max's father died this evening."

She gasped. Max Minimus started whining, as if he knew somehow. "What happened?"

"Keeled over at the dinner table. Heart attack. There's going to be an autopsy, but the leading theory is that all the drinking did a number on his cardiovascular system." Leo paused. "Though I'm not convinced it wasn't shock. But I'm not supposed to say that, as apparently Sebastien is racked with guilt."

"Sebastien? Why?"

"This all went down at a dinner in which Sebastien came out to his parents and Max told them he was moving off the estate."

"Moving? Where was he going?"

"New York."

"*What?*"

"He got a job with the design firm that's working on the mine project. He was going to get a place in New York."

"Why?"

"Hmm. I wonder."

Maybe Dani wasn't the only one who hadn't told the entire truth that morning in Innsbruck?

"He was going to take a red-eye that landed in New York on the eleventh. He was strangely adamant about the timing. I think it had something to do with a movie you watched with him once? He said there was a line in it about telling the truth on Christmas?"

At Christmas you tell the truth.

Oh god. Did she dare hope that his truth was the same as hers?

Did it matter? If it was truth-telling season?

All right. New plan: She was going to tell him everything. She was going to tell him she'd fallen in love with him. If he didn't return her feelings, they'd deal with it together. But she let herself hope that maybe this wasn't going to be a tragedy after all.

"You said *was*, past tense. Max *was* coming here, but now he's not?"

"Well, that was before his father keeled over. He can't leave now. He's the duke."

Max was actually the duke.

She got up, yanked open her closet to grab her suitcase, and said, "I'll be on a plane tomorrow."

Chapter Twenty-Five

I've got to call Dani," Max said to Sebastien close to midnight at the end of a whirlwind day, his first full day as the duke. "First thing tomorrow." It was a pity his apartment-in-New-York plan had been derailed by Father's death. And that his perfectly timed trip couldn't be made. But Dani still had to know how he felt, so a phone call would have to do. "In fact, I should do it now." He wasn't sure what was stopping him. Well, he did know: abject fear.

"Mmm," Sebastien said noncommittally, looking at his phone, which wasn't like him—Seb always gave him his full attention. They were sitting in Father's library, but Seb's mind was elsewhere.

No, they were sitting in *Max's* library.

No, they were sitting in *their* library. As Max had told Laurent, the estate's steward, he was committed to a new way of doing things. And even if he didn't know exactly what that was yet, he knew that it involved collaboration with his brother.

"I'm thinking we should hire a new head of security for the estate," Max said loudly, which still didn't get Seb's attention. "Perhaps Torkel. How much do you think we'd have to pay him to lure him away from the palace? It would be a bit of a comedown, I suppose, in professional terms, to go from being the head of security for the king to being the head of security for a mere duke. I may have to think of some other perks I can offer him."

By the time Max was done that little speech, Seb had tuned back in and was shaking his head with an exasperated smile. "You've got to call Dani," he said. "I heard you. I think you should go to New York now."

"I beg your pardon?"

"You were planning to go there tomorrow, yes?"

"Yes, but that was before Father died. That's when I thought I was going to be moving there."

"You can still get an apartment there. If you leave now, you can still make it in time for your ridiculously romantic December 11 gesture."

"But there's so much to do here."

"It can wait. Laurent said as much."

"Mother is—"

"Mother is what? She's shut up in her rooms, and I doubt we'll see her for days."

It was true. Max had accepted, the night of Marie's wedding, that Mother was never going to be who he wanted her to be. But somehow, he still hadn't expected her to sink into abject and total sorrow at Father's passing the way she had. He'd thought her more cunning than that. But she seemed genuinely felled by grief and had been barricaded in the ducal apartment, refusing visitors.

"I can deal with her if she needs dealing with." Seb grinned and typed something into his phone.

Honestly. "If I'm getting in the way of you texting your boyf—"

"Max." Seb set down his phone. "What have we learned in the last year?"

"What do you mean?"

Seb rolled his eyes. "We've learned that love is more important than duty, you numbskull."

Could Max really do this? Could he just get up and fly to New York and leave the mountain of bureaucracy that needed his attention? Decide to scale it later? "Do you really think I can—"

"Excuse me, Your Grace."

It took Max a moment to realize that he was the *Your Grace* in question. He turned to the door to find *Mr. Benz?* "What are you doing here?" Although perhaps this was something that happened when one was a duke—the king's equerry showed up unannounced.

"I understand you will be traveling to New York," Mr. Benz said.

Sebastien smirked and set down his phone.

"What did you do?" Max said to his brother.

"I've taken the liberty of booking you a flight," Mr. Benz went on, "but we need to leave now."

Max shook his head at his grinning brother. "All right. Let me pack a few things."

"No time," Mr. Benz said brusquely, handing him a leather envelope. "Here are the necessary documents. You can get anything else you need in New York. I have a car waiting."

Well. Apparently he was going to New York.

DANI TURNED ON her phone when the plane touched down in Zurich, expecting a text from Leo, who was picking her up. There was none, so she typed one to him, telling him she'd arrived, as she made her way off the plane.

The passengers were disgorged into a glassed-off area in the terminal and directed by signage toward customs. Dani stretched and yawned as she shuffled along. She hadn't really thought through what was going to happen once she arrived. It was close to one A.M., December 11. The first day of Christmas. Too bad it was too late to go to Max.

Though, maybe it wasn't? When one was planning a wild, dramatic declaration of love, did it matter if one arrived at a socially acceptable hour? Besides, even if he didn't love her back, Max would need her. His father was dead, and he had ascended to the role he had never wanted. It was settled; she was going to ask Leo to take her directly to—

A sharp rapping on the glass wall next to her startled her. She turned and— "Oh my god!"

It was Max. Here, in the airport. In the waiting area to board the plane she'd just gotten off, which was scheduled to return to New York.

She was stunned into immobility, frozen in place even as he started gesturing frantically. His hair was wild, and so were his eyes. He had one arm in his coat and one arm out.

"What are you doing here?" she finally said dumbly. He couldn't hear her, of course. But she couldn't make any sense of his waving of arms, nor could she read his rapidly moving lips.

He stopped all of a sudden, went quiet, and held up his index finger. He was asking her to wait. She nodded. He turned away for what felt like ages, doing something she couldn't see on one of the chairs in the waiting area.

Her heart started thundering in her ears as she watched the people around him start lining up to get on the plane she'd come off. Oh god, she was going to pass out right here in the arrivals area of the Zurich airport.

When Max finished with whatever he'd been doing, he came back to the glass, and he was smiling. Flashing her one of his cat-that-ate-the-canary Max grins. She felt a little more grounded. Whatever was going to happen, that smile told her that she hadn't lost her friend.

He slapped a ripped piece of paper against the glass. It looked like part of a printed boarding pass that had been ripped off. He'd written in the margin, in his heavy, angular handwriting.

I'm sorry.

Before she could react, he replaced it with another scrap of boarding pass.

I love you.

She gasped. Tears appeared from nowhere, and she had to wipe them away to make sure she didn't miss anything he'd written on a series of scraps he was holding up to the glass in quick succession.

I was coming to New York to tell you that.

Because at Christmas you tell the truth, and the truth is that I'm in love with you.

I'm sorry I proposed to you.

Well, I'm not sorry, but you know what I mean.

I hope you don't think this is creepy like in the movie.

She burst out crying.

His face fell. *Shit.* She was crying because she was so overwhelmed. So relieved. She dropped her bag and dug in her purse for something she could use to write on. Nothing. Well, screw it. She opened the book she'd been too anxious to read on the plane.

When she was done, she held the title page up to the glass. *I'm sorry, too.*

She flipped to page one, where she'd written in the margin. *I love you, too.*

And on page two: *I'm going to stop now because writing in this book is killing me and I think if I don't go through customs, eventually someone will object.*

He was standing there with his jaw hanging open, looking as stunned as she'd felt a moment ago. She pointed urgently down the hallway she was supposed to be traversing. He nodded, shaking himself out of his stupor, and walked in parallel with her for as long as he could. They walked and looked at each other and grinned like fools. When she had to leave him to enter the customs hall, he pressed his hands over his heart and pointed, she thought to indicate that he would be waiting for her on the other end.

When the customs agent asked her the purpose of her visit she said, "I'm visiting . . . my boyfriend." Then she laughed. And when she burst out the other end, there he was. Max. She had no idea how everything was going to play out. Where they were going to live, if they were even going to live together, what she was going to do about work.

But none of it mattered when he stopped walking about twenty feet from her and made a "come here" gesture with his fingers. He moved his hands around so that he was ready to catch her *Dirty Dancing* style.

She burst out laughing and called across the space between them, "Are you kidding?"

"Would I kid about something like this?"

"I suppose not."

"We *have* practiced it in the water twice."

"We're going to look like fools."

"That's true," he said cheerfully.

Oh how she loved him. Her funny, kind, beautiful Max. "Well, all right, then," she said, and she took off running.

AFTER A TEARFUL—AND heated—reunion at the cottage in Riems, Max tried to propose again.

"Look," he said, as they lolled around in the bed in the attic. "I want it noted for the record that I mucked it all up in Innsbruck. I got my argument mixed up."

"What do you mean, 'your argument'?"

"You're the English professor. You know. You're supposed to open your essay with a topic sentence that's your argument." He grabbed her palm, opened it, and pretended to write on it. "*Then* give supporting statements." He mimed writing lower on her palm. "I skipped the topic sentence. I confused you."

She laughed. "So what was the topic sentence supposed to be?"

He closed his hand over hers and squeezed. "I love you, and therefore I want to marry you."

"And *then* you get into the crown jewels and the solid gold dog tags and all that."

"*Exactly.*"

"What about your rules?"

"Oh, fuck my rules."

Dani was a little startled. Max had an endearingly formal way of speaking, and though he let loose the occasional *damn*, she rarely heard anything stronger than that. She leaned down and kissed him. Grabbed his cheeks and planted one on him, both of them grinning.

"So what about it?" he said when she pulled back. "Will you marry me?"

"Not yet."

He clutched his heart and fell back onto the bed.

"Max. It's too soon. Think of all the upheaval we've both experienced. Think of all the upheaval that's to come."

"Yes, yes," he said, rolling his eyes like he knew she was right but didn't care. "We should wait a bit." He turned serious as he stared at her for several moments. "What about now? Will you marry me now?"

"Still no."

"I'm not going to stop asking, you know. I'm going to ask you every single day."

She smiled. "I look forward to it."

THE NEXT WEEK and a half was a whirlwind. Dani tried to help Max and Sebastien as much as she could, but mostly that meant staying out of the way as they worked through stuff with the guy who was in charge of the estate and with the CEO of the mining company. She had one fraught encounter with their mother when they randomly encountered each other in a corridor and Dani tried to express her condolences, but other than that, the widowed duchess—was she still even a duchess? Dani didn't know—kept to herself.

Mostly Dani wrote. Suddenly, she was able to work on the novel again. Max installed her in the cottage, and the hours and pages flew by. When she grew stiff from sitting at her desk for long stretches, she walked the grounds and up the mountain and immersed herself in the hot spring. She was starting to get familiar with the rhythms of Riems.

Max came to her at night. She held him and listened to him as he muddled through a swirl of mixed emotions regarding his father and the advent of his tenure in a job he had never wanted.

On the evening of December 22, when he climbed the stairs to the garret, he said, "I booked us a flight for New York tomorrow."

"What? Why?"

"So we can spend Christmas with your family." His brow furrowed. "I am invited, yes?"

"I told them we weren't coming!"

"Why would you do that?'

"Because we're here! Because your father just died! Because you're the duke now!"

"Well, if you recall, dukes get to do whatever they want." He smirked. "And this duke wants to go to New York for Christmas. See your family. Perhaps ingest a million negronis for old time's sake. Eat some Christmas morning cereal. I've got *Nutcracker* tickets, too, for us and your mother. Anyway, you can't be without your dog any longer." He tilted his head and turned thoughtful. "I'm not sure *I* can be without your dog any longer. Isn't that odd?"

"Is this about my list?" she asked. "Because—"

"No. This is about Christmas and where we want to spend it. I for one vote for New York."

She'd been about to say, "Fuck my list," and she really meant it. She had learned from Max that sometimes you had to let yourself feel what you felt, even if what you felt went against all reason. Sometimes you had to let yourself change course. Sometimes you had to let yourself love people, even if they had the power to hurt you.

"But what about your mother? Can you leave her for Christmas?"

He sighed and sat on the edge of the bed. "My mother isn't going anywhere. Perhaps by next year, things will look different. But right now, yes, I can leave her. Right now, I choose to leave her."

Well.

"And Sebastien is in agreement," he said, anticipating her next objection. "He's going to the palace for Christmas." Max wagged his eyebrows. "Marie invited Mother to join them, but she has declined." He smiled. "So . . ."

"I guess we're going to New York tomorrow." She grinned and hugged him.

"Probably now you'll agree to marry me, yes?"

She pulled him down onto the bed. "Not yet."

"Okay."

"You know I can't just move to Eldovia. I'm not doing a Meghan Markle. I can't move somewhere ninety percent of the populace is white."

"I know," he said. "I get it." And she thought he actually did.

Chapter Twenty-Six

$\mathcal{M}$ax spent the happiest Christmas of his life in New York. Which was amusing because it was also his first Christmas as the Duke of Aquilla, a fate he had been dreading for so long.

Though he had witnessed it last summer, he continued to be amazed by what it felt like to be among a happy family. There was mockery, but it was gentle. Gifts and hugs were exchanged easily. The fruitcake, which, speaking of gentle mockery, Val repeatedly informed them she had started in October, was delicious. They FaceTimed with the group at the palace. And Max had his namesake back—Max Minimus spent every second he could curled up next to Max, which was stupidly gratifying.

After *The Nutcracker*, Max and Dani moved to her apartment and worked. She wrote, and he turned his attention to the estate and the transition.

Best of all had been his meetings with Sebastien, Laurent, and Elias, the CEO of Aquilla. Max had been forthright with everyone, telling them that while of course he wanted the estate to make money, he also wanted it to mean something. "I don't even know what that means," he'd said. "I don't know anything." The four of them had decided to write a mission statement that would govern the running of the estate and the company, and they'd each come to the table with a draft, which had launched them into a lengthy and useful discussion they agreed to continue in person when Max was back after Dani's family's January 6 celebration.

He hung up the phone early one morning to Dani setting a cup of coffee in front of him. He nodded his thanks, but she only let him take one sip before she took the cup away from him, straddled his lap, kissed him, and said, "I only caught the tail end of that conversation, but I have to say you sounded remarkably like a person with a job."

"I did, didn't I?" He grinned against her lips. "You know what people with jobs make?"

"No. What do they make?"

"They make excellent husbands. Will you marry me?"

She laughed and kissed him again. "Not yet."

BY NEW YEAR'S EVE, Dani had quit her job.

"So that's it, I guess," she said when she'd finished reading the latest email on the matter from her now-former boss out loud to Max, who was puttering around in her tiny kitchen. "You have a job now and I don't." She had quit her job just before her tenure review was meant to start. It kind of took her breath away. She was being either epically stupid or audaciously bold. She was going to write her novel and see what happened. If it worked out, it worked out. If it didn't, she'd have to figure out something else. Regardless, she was moving to Eldovia. Sort of. They were keeping the New York apartment, though. According to Max, they were going to come and go, "whenever the hell we want to, separately or together." She had to admit, it sounded like a pretty good life.

Max appeared from the kitchen holding a bottle of champagne and two flutes and regarded her. "How do you feel?"

"I feel . . . a lot of things."

"And what are those things?"

"Excited. Scared. A little bit stunned."

He handed her a glass, filled it, and sat next to her.

"This is really going to be okay?" she asked.

"What is 'this'?"

"Us. This thing we're doing. I don't even know what to call it. Coming and going between here and Eldovia. Dating, I guess. Can a duke date? And you were the one who was supposed to make changes on the job front, not me, remember?"

"Of course a duke can date. A duke can do whatever he wants, remember? And as for the New Year's resolutions, yes, we got them a bit jumbled, but why not embrace that fact and, I don't know . . . marry me? Instead of dating me?" He winked. "Then you can one-up yourself—you can lose one husband and gain another."

True to his word, and true to his tendency to guilelessly declare his feelings, Max asked her to marry him at least once a day. But at the same time, he kept arranging things so she would be more comfortable with reality as his wife. As a duchess.

Dani smiled and said, "Not yet." She always made sure to say, "Not yet," instead of no, because she *would* marry him one day. She just needed to . . . slow down a bit. To let herself grow into the idea of it.

He rolled his eyes. "Would you like some champagne with that refusal?"

"Why yes I would, thanks."

The buzzer rang before he could pour. "That'll be the food. I'll get it."

Back inside, Max stooped to plug in the lights on the little tree they'd gotten and turned off the overhead light. Whistling for Max Minimus, he stooped and fed him something from his hand.

"Did you order my *dog* a McMuffin?"

"I'm only giving him the sausage patty," Max said defensively. He sat next to her and patted the space next to him on the other side. Max Minimus hopped right up, and Dani rolled her eyes. Max opened his McMuffin. "Mm. I think the real reason I like you so much is that you introduced me to these."

She started to swat him, but he intercepted her hand and pressed it to his chest, which left her holding a glass of champagne in one hand and feeling the steady thrum of his heartbeat beneath her other. They looked at each other, and a lump rose in her throat. His eyes did that blue-burning thing as a wave of emotion passed over them. After a moment, the look softened, and he smiled. He set down his sandwich and raised his glass without breaking eye contact with her. "Happy New Year, Dani."

"Happy New Year, Max."

Epilogue

When Dani Martinez woke up on December 11 the next year, she thought, *It's going to be a good day.*

On the surface, it was like any other winter morning in Eldovia. She eased herself slowly out of bed so as not to wake either of the still-sleeping Maxes.

She did not succeed when it came to Max Maximus, who opened his eyes and smiled sleepily at her. He didn't move, though, as he knew how important her coffee was to her—and he knew that if he dozed and kept the dog asleep, he'd be rewarded in a few minutes with a cup of his own, delivered to him in bed.

And since it was Sunday, the only day her boyfriend, who, in an interesting twist, was turning out to be a bit of a workaholic, took off, they were planning to walk up the mountain.

It was also the day after she'd gotten the news that her novel was going to be published. It was just a small publisher. It wasn't—probably—going to be a bestseller. It wasn't going to make her rich. But she had done it. She had officially left one career and started another.

She didn't bother treading lightly as she climbed the stairs back up to the garret. The noise she made was enough to wake Max Minimus, who popped his head up from his preferred spot in Max Maximus's armpit and began yapping happily.

"I'm so proud of you." Max smiled as she handed him his coffee.

"So you said last night, about a thousand times," she said, but she was secretly thrilled by his praise. "I'm proud of you, too."

"Me?" He yawned. They had flown in from New York two days ago, and he was still jet-lagged. "I haven't done anything."

"Oh, my mistake. I would have thought keeping an estate and a company running while you refocus the priorities of said estate and company and maintain a side gig consulting on museum design was something." The Innsbruck mine museum was going to open this coming spring, and the firm he was working with had called upon his expertise for a few other projects. "Not to mention beginning drafting a book that will rewrite the postwar history of Eldovia with new information about Karina Klein." As predicted, the news about Karina had made quite a splash among the few historians Max had told, and he had a contract with a university press for a book that was part national history, part family history. He even had some leads on Karina's mysterious New York trip. So now there were two writers toiling away in the garret. And two reasons to keep up their two-countries lifestyle. "But, right, you haven't done anything." She grinned and shrugged playfully. "I guess I was wrong."

He sat up and grabbed her. Max Minimus yipped while they made out.

"I should take him outside," she said against his lips, waiting for the question.

He merely grunted and kept kissing her. Leave it to him to deviate from the script on today of all days.

The yapping escalated, and he relented, letting go of her and mock-glaring at the dog. "All right, all right."

She clambered off him and went in search of her robe—they slept up here but kept their clothing in Max's old bedroom, which had been converted into a closet.

"Will you marry me?"

There it was. She turned. He was sitting on the edge of the bed, bending over as he pulled his underwear on.

She smiled. "Yes."

He fell off the bed.

"Did you just say yes?" He popped up to standing.

"I just said yes."

"Shit!" He started scrambling for his pants, even though he only had one leg through his underwear. "I'm not ready!"

"You're not ready? You've only asked me a million times."

"I know, but you've lulled me into complacency with your relentless rejection," he said as he dug around in the pocket of his pants. He shuffled over to her, his underwear down around one ankle, fell to one knee, and held out his closed palm.

"Oh my god, have you been carrying a *ring* around in your pocket all this time?"

He shot her a signature Max smirk. "I have not been carrying a ring around all this time. I have been carrying this around." He opened his palm to reveal a golden object. She picked it up. It was a dog tag. It was heavy and shiny and had MAX engraved on it in a fancy script font.

"Dani," Max said, his voice all scratchy, "I love you. I love your dog. Will you *finally* marry me?"

She smiled down at Max, her Max, her blue-eyed, dukeish casual best friend, protector, and lover, and said, "Yes."

Acknowledgments

$\mathcal{M}$y thanks to:

My friend Sandra Owens, who not only provided feedback on an early draft but is my daily dose of sanity.

Patricia Ruiz-Rivera, who helped me think about what Dani's experience, and that of her family, would be like.

My friends Emma Barry and Erika Olbricht, who read with an eye toward Dani's job and straightened me out on several things. Any irregularities that remain do so because this is a fairy tale. (Only in fairy tales do people get tenure-track jobs in the cities of their choice right after grad school, and only in fairy tales does everyone attend departmental parties and do those parties have open bars!)

My friend and favorite historian, Amy Bell, for help with the World War II stuff. In fact, we pulled up next to each other at a drive-in movie in the COVID-upended summer of 2020, rolled down our windows, and talked at a distance about mines and bombs and the resistance while we waited for the show to start— and that show was *Dirty Dancing*!

My friend Marit Grunstra for advising on dogs and such and for being the best surf-and-turf, I-heart-not-camping friend a girl could ask for.

Carina Guevara for the stunning cover art.

My agent, Courtney Miller-Callihan, for her unwavering support and steadfast good counsel.

My editor, Elle Keck, for embracing the "Hallmark, but make it spicy" vibe of this series from the get-go, and for helping make this book shine. Everyone at HarperCollins, especially Andrea Monagle and Rachel Weinick for careful polishing and shepherding of the manuscript.

The citizens of Romancelandia, for your lively debates on *Love Actually*. I hope you don't excommunicate me.

Keep reading for a sneak peek at
Jenny Holiday's next wonderfully
romantic story of Christmas
in Eldovia, where Mr. Benz
finally meets his match.

Coming Fall 2022

$\mathcal{A}$s usual, the last thing that went in the suitcase was the Post-It. *change, or die.*

Cara plucked it off the mirror in her bedroom and set it on top of her final packing cube. She wasn't sure why she always just laid it on top of everything when the rest of her stuff was so meticulously packed, clothing and shoes and notebooks nestled together as snugly as a game of Tetris. She supposed it was because she liked opening her suitcase at the other end of her trip, at a hotel room in Miami or Madrid or Milwaukee, and having it be the first thing she saw. But one of these days, an overly aggressive TSA agent was going to select her for a random screening and the Post-It would get lost in the shuffle.

Which would be fine. It was just a thing. A visual representation of a sentiment that existed independently of its depiction. She could write those words on a new Post-It any time. It wasn't even sticky anymore—it had to be inserted into the mirror's frame to stay up—and the ink was faded. She'd thought, over the years, about going over it with a Sharpie, but she kind of liked the way the emerald-green ink she'd used as an eighteen-year-old had faded to a dental-office mint. It reminded her how far she had come. How much she *had* changed, and therefore by definition that she was still here, not only not dead but thriving. Doing better every year than the last, getting closer and closer to her goals.

A glance at her phone informed her that her Uber was five

minutes away. Time to get the big goodbye over with. She checked her last-minute essentials list against the contents of her shoulder bag: passport, phone, computer, chargers, briefing binder, sudoku book, Mr. Spock.

"You haven't had to travel over Thanksgiving for years," her mom said as Cara clattered down the rickety stairs from her attic bedroom to the kitchen. Cara had half hoped her parents would not be up. It was four in the morning.

But no, they were up to see her off. They did that. Her mother was wearing her sad face. Because her mother loved her, Cara reminded herself, and was disappointed that she'd be away for Thanksgiving. It grated on Cara, though, the cognitive dissonance required to be upset that Cara was traveling over the holiday and to simultaneously be looking forward to a big Thanksgiving dinner in the house Cara paid for. Not that she begrudged them the house or the dinner—or anything. Never that. Just that for someone who had struggled a lot in life, her mother sure had selective memory. What about all those years her mom had encouraged her dad to pick up shifts on Thanksgiving, or even Christmas, because he got time-and-a-half for them?

"The person who was supposed to go has shingles," Cara said for the tenth time.

"I know. I just don't understand why *you* have to be the one who takes his place. You've given so much to that company for so many years."

"And 'that company' has given so much to me." *To us.* She tried to say it without any censure in her tone, in a way that wouldn't offend her mother's robust sense of pride.

It didn't work. "I know. I know," her mom said quickly, turning away and aggressively stirring the pot of oats she cooked every morning, though not usually at four A.M., and Cara felt like shit. As usual, her mother could read her mind. Being so close to one's parents was a double-edged sword.

Cara started over. "I have to go because this is a big, important project, and I'm the one who knows it best, after the guy who's sick." She was his boss, and that's what you did when you were the boss. At least that's what you did when you were a senior associate who was someone's boss. She reminded herself that she loved her job. She loved the travel that came with it, too. At least historically, she had. But she'd been on the road so much lately; she'd only just gotten back two days ago from a monthlong stint in San Diego. She was tired—like, in-her-bones tired.

"Honestly, I'd never even heard of Eldovia before last week," her dad said, setting down his copy of the *Daily News*. As was his endearing way, he was oblivious to the undercurrents swirling around Cara and her mother.

"I don't think a lot of people have." And that included the partners at CZT, aka "that company," before they'd been invited to bid on the job. Cara had heard of Eldovia, but only because she had memorized every country and its capital when she was in eighth grade, back when she was in a particularly aggressive education-is-the-way-out-of-poverty phase. "It's tiny. It doesn't do much." Except make luxury watches, and her parents were not luxury-watch people. The Alpine micronation didn't even make that many watches anymore. Hence the big, lucrative contract. And the Thanksgiving trip.

Her mom turned back from her oatmeal, her eyes shiny. Dammit. Cara was being bitchy because being bitchy was easier than being disappointed. She had a tendency to lash out when she was feeling vulnerable. She didn't want to miss Thanksgiving with her family any more than her mother wanted her to. She didn't want to spend her red-eye flight awake and cramming—though she knew this file, she hadn't been heavily involved in the day-to-day details of the project.

At least her parents would have each other. She was going to be alone on the other side of the ocean. Ugh. She resolved to try to get at least some sleep on the plane. Being so tired was making her uncharacteristically emotional.

She steeled herself. She'd missed holidays before. She could do it again. And even though she didn't get paid for working over a holiday like her dad used to, her annual performance reviews always made mention of her reliability. She was a team player. A respected leader. Those adjectives accreted. She had worked hard for those adjectives.

"I'm gonna miss you, lassie," her dad said, and as he stood and wrapped her in his arms, which had always been her safe place, she said her daily prayer of thanks that Patrick Delaney had chosen to claim her as his own.

She let him hug her for longer than she normally would have because she needed time to get her shit together, to make sure the lump in her throat was well and fully swallowed.

"We'll light a candle for you in church on Thanksgiving," her mom said, her voice back to its usual lilting warmth.

"I'll be back in time for Christmas," she said into her dad's shoulder. Barely, but she would make it. She was scheduled to land the morning of Christmas Eve day. "And we'll FaceTime constantly." She broke the hug with her dad and avoided eye contact with both parents. "And I'll make partner soon." The brass ring. The goal she'd had since her first day of work at CZT as a twenty-one-year-old intern. Once that happened, she would stop having to do Thanksgiving duty when Brad from Manufacturing Operations came down with shingles. She would be able to be more selective about which projects she got personally involved in, and choose where, when, and how much she traveled. You paid enough dues, you stopped having to prove yourself.

She assumed.

That was the plan anyway, and she'd come too far not to stick to the plan.

* * *

As much as he didn't want to, Matteo decided at the last minute to go to the airport himself. He could have sent a car. There was no reason he personally had to make the trek to Zurich, much less physically go inside and hold up a sign that said "Ms. Cara Delaney" in order to welcome the woman who would be his undoing. He did it anyway.

Matteo would freely admit that he was the sort of person for whom duty mattered. Well, perhaps that wasn't entirely fair. That made him sound like a protocol droid. It was more that *tradition* mattered.

So when the king charged you with personally making sure that the hotshot American management consultant was welcomed properly, when he asked you to be her interpreter and tour guide, you went to the airport yourself. Once you started deciding how, or god forbid, whether, to do certain parts of your job, you might as well give up and throw open the doors to the forces of chaos.

Speaking of the forces of chaos, a woman burst into his field of vision, suddenly there when she had not been before. He had been keeping a close eye on the doors that disgorged passengers from the customs hall—he'd thought. But there she was.

She was wearing a black pantsuit and the highest heels he had ever seen on a woman in Eldovia in the winter. She approached at an impressive speed, given those shoes, pulling a small rolling suitcase behind her. The staccato clacking of her heels joined the steady buzzing sound made by the bag's wheels to create an ominous, crescendoing symphony. Her dark, almost black hair was pulled into a severe chignon and, along with the black suit, provided a stark contrast to her skin, which was almost as pale as the snow falling outside. Her eyes were a deep, dark blue, like the sky over the mountains after a storm. She looked like an angel.

He huffed a self-disgusted exhalation. Honestly. He needed to take the hyperbole down a notch or several. Cara Delaney was not bringing good tidings of great joy. If she was an angel, she wasn't a good one. He arranged his mouth into the shape of a smile but took care that his eyes did not convey any warmth. "Ms. Delaney?"

"Yes." She stuck out her hand in that aggressive way Americans had. Her nails were varnished in a red so dark it was almost black. "A pleasure to meet you," she said in a tone that suggested there was in fact nothing whatsoever pleasurable about making his acquaintance as she attempted to break his fingers.

"Likewise," he murmured, squeezing her hand as hard as she

was squeezing his. It was ridiculous, these displays of dominance, when everyone, except perhaps American management consultants, knew that when it came to getting what you wanted, soft power was a great deal more effective than brute force. Bone-crushing handshakes and shoes that should be subject to EU weapons regulations were not only empty signifiers, they suggested an underlying lack of confidence that could be exploited.

He made a mental note.

"I know you'd been working closely with Bradley Wiener to prepare for his arrival," she said. "I hope getting me instead isn't too much of a disappointment."

He was supposed to rush to assure her that she could never be a disappointment. Instead, he kept his face expressionless. "I do hope Mr. Wiener's health is improving?" To think of all the effort Matteo had invested—speaking of soft power—in . . . well, frankly, in manipulating the Wiener gentleman.

It wasn't that he thought he could have any real impact on the economic policy of Eldovia. At least not given that the king had made up his mind about the job Ms. Delaney was here to do. But that didn't mean he couldn't play a role in shaping *how* that job was done. In minimizing the chaos and injury she was surely here to visit upon them.

He'd done so much work already on this front with Mr. Wiener, worked to convey the rich culture that was Eldovia, to explain the importance of tradition and continuity. And now he had . . . her. He would have to start all over, just as he was headed into his busiest time of year, too.

Well, there was nothing for it. The only way out was through, onward and upward, etcetera, etcetera.

Ms. Delaney did not address Matteo's inquiry about her colleague's health. "I can assure you that Brad has oriented me to the file."

The file. As if an entire nation, its well-being and prosperity, could be reduced to something so pedestrian as a *file*. But he needed to remember that in her mind, it could. It already had been.

"I didn't realize you would be meeting me," she said.

He did not know if she was remarking on the fact that he hadn't merely sent a driver—as he should have—or if she was complaining that the king himself was not on hand to roll out the red carpet. "I am equerry to His Majesty, King Emil. Are you familiar with the role?" He asked because many people weren't. Americans often thought he was a butler. Not that there was anything wrong with being a butler. It was an honorable way to make a living performing an important service.

"Yes. I've seen *The Crown.*"

God preserve him. His impassive façade almost slipped.

"As far as I can tell," she went on, "being an equerry is like being an executive assistant. Everyone thinks you're a secretary, but really, you make the entire ship go."

"The ship? I beg your pardon?"

"It's a *Star Trek* metaphor. The captain can talk a good talk, but the person who actually makes the ship go is the engineer. If he—or she, but let's face it; on TV it's usually a he—doesn't want the ship to go, it's is not going, no matter what the captain says."

Hmm. What a curious, and unexpected, analogy.

"But choose your metaphor," she went on. "The wind beneath your boss's wings. The man behind the throne." She cracked a smile, which she held for a beat, clearly trying not to laugh. She lost the battle and let loose a low, throaty, delighted chuckle that seemed at odds with her corporate-goth persona. "Which I guess is not a metaphor in this case, because you literally are that."

"Well, not literally."

"What?"

"I don't literally stand behind the throne." There wasn't even a literal throne, at least not in the way she imagined.

She rolled her eyes ever so slightly, which surprised him. He would have expected "Don't roll one's eyes at the client" to be a first principle.

Of course, he wasn't the client. He was the concierge. He tried not to bristle overtly.

"Are you aware," she said, "that the dictionary recently revised the definition of 'literally' to include 'in effect,' or 'virtually'?"

"I am, but that doesn't mean I approve. A word cannot also mean the opposite of itself simply because enough people agree." He was aware that he shouldn't be speaking to her like this. King Emil hadn't charged him with being a concierge in quite those words, but that's what his request had amounted to. And concierges didn't get high in the instep with their guests.

She stared at him for a beat too long before saying, "I see how this is going to be."

"Do you?" He was still doing it. He couldn't seem to stop.

"I do." She was getting impertinent, too.

All right. Enough. He had one task here, one simple task, and that was to welcome Ms. Delaney. Not one minute into his acquaintance with her, he was already faltering. But honestly, he'd had encounters with irate diplomats that had riled him less. He took a fortifying breath. "Shall we go collect your bags?"

She nodded at the small suitcase of doom she'd been pulling behind her. "This is it."

"That is all you have for such a long stay?"

"I travel a lot. I have packing down to a science."

"Mm." She probably had everything reduced to "a science," including how she planned to strip Eldovia of its identity and traditions. She was likely a card-carrying member of some efficiency cult or other that had a lot of Greek letters and/or acronyms in its name but really did nothing more than teach you how to write a to-do list and drill into you the discipline to carry it out. "Well then, shall we?"

"Sure."

Here they went.

About the Author

JENNY HOLIDAY is a *USA Today* bestselling and RITA Award–nominated author whose work has been featured in the *New York Times*, *Entertainment Weekly*, the *Washington Post*, and BuzzFeed. A member of the House of Slytherin, Jenny lives in London, Ontario, Canada.